IN LOVE AND FRIENDSHIP

Newcastle, 1890. A school outing to Cullercoats Bay almost ends in tragedy when two girls are cut off by the incoming tide, but from the panic and confusion something wonderful emerges – a lifelong friendship between three girls, each a world away from the other two. Intelligent and ambitious Ruth, Lucy, with a terrible secret hanging over her, and Esther, protector of her little brother Davy, forge a strong and unbreakable bond that will see them through the years ahead from childhood to the heartbreak and responsibilities of courtship and marriage.

IN LOVE AND FRIENDSHIP

IN LOVE AND FRIENDSHIP

by

Benita Brown

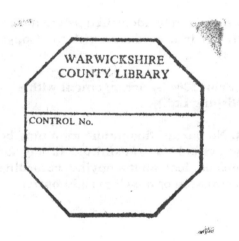
Magna Large Print Books
Long Preston, North Yorkshire,
BD23 4ND, England.

British Library Cataloguing in Publication Data.

Brown, Benita
  In love and friendship.

    A catalogue record of this book is
    available from the British Library

    ISBN   0-7505-2116-3

First published in Great Britain 2003 by Headline Book Publishing

Copyright © 2003 Benita Brown

Cover illustration © Gordon Crabb by arrangement with
Alison Eldred

The right of Benita Brown to be identified as the author of this work
has been asserted by her in accordance with the Copyright, Designs
and Patents Act, 1988

Published in Large Print 2004 by arrangement with
Headline Book Publishing Ltd.

Magna Large Print is an imprint of Library Magna Books Ltd.

Printed and bound in Great Britain by
T.J. (International) Ltd., Cornwall, PL28 8RW

To my family

Some of this novel takes place in Whitley-by-the-Sea, sometimes called Whitley. After years of being confused with Whitby in Yorkshire, Whitley-by-the-Sea became Whitley Bay in 1902, and is still known by that name. The story goes that a local man died while visiting Scotland. The mourners waited at St Paul's church for the funeral to begin, but his body had been sent in error to Whitby. This sad incident finally prompted the change of name.

Chapter One

Tyneside, July 1890

'Go away! You can't sit with us!' Jane McKenzie squinted up at Esther through the bright sunlight. Jane's carroty curls framed her freckled face and her small features were sharp with fury.

As Esther backed away she caught her foot on a stone, stumbled and lost her balance. Instinctively she stretched out her arms to break her fall, and the brown paper bag she was carrying fell from her grasp. The contents spilled out on to the sand. She heard Jane laugh.

Esther stared at her sandwiches in dismay. They were covered with sand. She leaned forward and gathered them up. She shook each one separately but most of the sand stayed in place. She tried to brush it off with her fingers and then took a cautious bite from the corner of one of them. Salty grit crunched between her teeth. The sandwiches were ruined.

Nevertheless she put them back into the bag. She was hungry. She would find somewhere to sit where no one could see what she was doing and she would open them up and try to lick off the filling of meat paste. She began to get to her feet. The knee she had fallen on was hurting.

Not one of the girls in the group offered to help her; they all remained seated as they ate the packed lunches that the school had provided for the end-of-term summer picnic on the beach at Cullercoats. One or two of the girls had brought extra treats from home. Lucy Shaw had a batch of home-baked fairy cakes; they were packed in a biscuit tin lined with greaseproof paper.

A few moments before Lucy had taken the tin out of her school bag, opened it, and offered it round. Seeing Esther standing uncertainly nearby, she had smiled up and held the tin towards her. That was why Esther had walked towards the favoured group of girls; perhaps Lucy had been inviting her to join them. But whether Lucy had simply meant to offer her a cake or whether she had meant Esther to sit down beside her, Esther would never know. And now, as a result of Jane McKenzie's spiteful outburst, Esther would have very little to eat at all.

And Jane hadn't finished with her. 'Pooh!' she exclaimed suddenly. 'Can anyone smell something?'

The others stopped talking. Jane held her nose with a finger and thumb of one hand and pointed in Esther's direction with the other. The others began to laugh.

'Yes,' someone said, 'I can smell something ... something horrid!'

'Is it rotting seaweed?' one girl asked.

'Or a dead fish?' another suggested.

'Let me see.' Jane pretended to study Esther. 'No, it's not a fish,' she said. 'It's only Esther Robinson.' Then she added menacingly, 'Are you still here? I told you to go away.'

Esther turned and fled. Her face was hot with

shame and she could feel the tears starting. She was angry with herself because she should be used to it by now. Then she heard Lucy say, 'Stop it, Jane. The poor girl can't help it.'

'Why not? My mother says that just because you're poor you don't have to be dirty – and smelly!'

Lucy didn't reply to Jane's remark but Esther heard a flurry of movement behind her. 'Wait!' a voice called. 'Esther, come back.'

She felt a hand on her shoulder and turned to see Lucy smiling at her. 'Don't take any notice of Jane,' she said. 'Come and sit down.'

Esther shook her head. 'It's not just Jane. The others wouldn't like it either.'

Lucy's wide blue eyes looked troubled. She didn't try to contradict her. 'Well, shall I sit with you?' she suggested. 'We can find a place against those rocks over there and watch the fishing boats come in to the harbour when the tide turns. Look, they're waiting just beyond the piers.'

Esther shook her head. 'No, you should stay with your friends.' She thought she saw a look of relief pass across Lucy's pretty face.

'All right then,' the other girl said. 'But, here, take this.'

She held out her hand. 'I've brought you a cake. Oh dear, it's a little squashed but it will taste just as good.'

Esther looked at the cake sitting in a little fluted cup of wax paper. The top had been sliced off, cut in two, and arranged like wings set in a dab of butter icing. One of the wings was broken.

'Go on, take it.'

Suddenly Esther reached out, snatched the cake from Lucy's hand and hurled it away from her. 'I divven't want it,' she said. 'You're just giving that one to me because it's broken!'

'No, that's not true! It happened when I was running after you. Esther, come back.'

But this time Esther didn't heed her. She ran up the beach towards the curve of the cliffs that jutted out, almost dividing the bay into two. There were caves there; she would find one and hide in it until it was time to go home.

As she ran towards the shadowy area under the rough cliff face, Esther did not know that the whole episode had been observed from high above her. On a ledge about halfway up, Ruth Lorrimer sat by herself. Ruth was small and dark; good-looking without being truly beautiful. She was clever, and although the other girls liked her well enough she did not always choose to mix with the crowd. Especially not today.

When they had first arrived at the beach there had been a nature talk by the shoreline.

'Turn the stones over gently,' Miss Foster had told them. 'Like this.'

The teacher had stooped to raise a stone that lay half submerged in a rock pool, and the class had 'oohed' with delight at the tiny crabs that scurried away sideways.

'The creatures that live there need the stones for shelter,' Miss Foster had continued as she replaced the stone gently. 'Seaweed provides shelter too, so leave it lying. Always put things you have found back in the rock pools. If you take living creatures away from their homes they will quickly die.'

After the talk Miss Foster, and Miss Williams, the pupil teacher, had organized beach games and then, at last, the girls had been allowed to find their own places to sit and enjoy the picnic. The sandwiches had been given out when they had assembled at school that morning. They had been told to bring their own drinks – bottles of lemonade or water – and a towel, for after they had eaten they would be allowed to make their own amusement for a while and paddle if they wished to do so.

Ruth's stepmother had pursed her lips when she was told about the towel and, after a great deal of grumbling, had taken one from the box where she kept old household linens which were to start a new life as washing-up cloths and dusters. As for providing an extra treat for the picnic lunch, that was out of the question.

Ruth's father had remained silent while his wife complained but, that morning when Ruth opened her schoolbag to put in the bottle of water, she'd found a twist of paper containing two sugar mice with string tails. The kind they kept in a big glass jar in the window of the corner shop.

Ruth had no one particular friend at school but she would have been welcome to join any of the groups of girls. Instead, she had chosen to sling her schoolbag across her shoulder and climb up to this eyrie. The other girls' laughter and carefree gossip would only have made her more miserable than she already was. She needed to be alone.

Miss Foster had forbidden them to climb up the cliffs so Ruth had waited until the teacher and her assistant were seated on their tartan rug in the shelter of the ramp of the lifeboat station. Miss Williams, not much older than her charges, had perhaps forgotten for the moment that she was anything but a girl enjoying a day by the sea. But Miss Foster, shading her spectacles with one hand, scanned the beach occasionally to see if the girls were behaving themselves and not being a nuisance or causing annoyance to the handful of other visitors. It did not occur to her to turn and look at the cliff face. Climbing the cliffs had been forbidden and it was unheard of for any of her pupils, especially Ruth Lorrimer, ever to disobey an order.

Even if Miss Foster did look round she probably wouldn't notice her, Ruth thought. Her dark grey school dress blended in with the craggy shadows. School uniform had not been obligatory today. As a special favour on the last day of term Miss Foster had told the girls that they could wear their own choice of clothes; something pretty, if they wished. But, again, Ruth's stepmother had objected.

'You'll have to keep your good clothes decent for when you start work,' Ada Lorrimer had told her. 'You'll not get owt new until you can pay for it yerself.'

Ruth wasn't the only one wearing a school dress. For the girls from poorer families, a suitable item of clothing was provided by charity and, for many, it was probably the only decent dress they had. Ruth was pretty sure that that applied to Esther Robinson.

She had watched Esther's humiliation just now

18

and she had guessed only too clearly what Jane McKenzie had said. Lucy Shaw had tried to be kind – she would – but Esther would have none of it. And now the miserable wretch was sobbing and snivelling on the beach directly underneath the ledge.

Ruth tried to ignore the sounds but, each time Esther sighed and gulped, an image of the girl wiping her nose on her sleeve invaded Ruth's mind and completely overcame her own misery. She put her sandwiches, still untouched, back in her bag, slung it over her shoulder and began to climb down.

It was easy enough for someone as athletic as Ruth, and she had no fear of losing her grip and falling on to the scatter of rocks at the base of the cliff face. But, suddenly, a large white shape swooped past her, shrieking as it rose with a beating of wings. A gull. For a moment she lost her balance and one foot slithered down too far, sending a cascade of loose stones on to the beach below.

She hung on tightly and quickly regained her footing but not before she had scraped her shin. By the time she was standing safely on the beach she was hot and cross and ready to curse that stupid girl Esther Robinson. If she could find her.

Ruth stood back in the shadow of the cliff and raised a hand to shade her eyes. Everything on the beach was as it had been before. Miss Foster and Miss Williams still sat by the lifeboat house. Miss Williams was reading, but Miss Foster was leaning back against the stone ramp with her straw hat tilted forward a little. Ruth imagined that she was taking a nap.

Ruth saw that her classmates had divided into three groups of six, almost as if they were taking part in some mathematical problem.

If you take twenty schoolgirls and divide them by three, how many will be in each group and what will be the remainder?

The answer was three groups of six with a remainder of two. And, in this case, the remainder was composed of herself and Esther.

But where on earth was Esther, if not on this beach? In the short time it had taken Ruth to climb down from her vantage point the girl had disappeared.

Ruth looked out over the sand. Apart from some fisher lasses waiting for the boats to come in, a few barefoot local children and one or two sedate elderly couples with dogs, the school party had most of the beach to themselves. One of the groups of girls, the one that contained Lucy Shaw and Jane McKenzie, was straight ahead of her, about midway between the cliffs and the shoreline. The other girls had wandered into the southern part of the bay. Ruth watched as one of the groups, with much shrieking and laughter, began to pick up their belongings and move back from the advancing tide to settle again further away from the waves.

But Esther was nowhere in sight. Then Ruth heard the muffled sobbing behind her and turned to peer into the mouth of one of the caves. 'Esther?' she said. The sobbing stopped but there was no reply. Ruth stepped hesitantly into the darkness. 'Esther ... are you in here?'

'Who's that?'

'It's Ruth – Ruth Lorrimer.'

'What do you want?'

'Nothing. I came to see if you were all right.'

'Did you now? Well, I'm just fine. So haddaway and leave me be!'

'All right.' Vexed, Ruth turned to go, but stopped when the snuffling started again. She made her way into the cave. As her eyes adjusted to the dim light she could see how the craggy walls narrowed as they stretched away from her, and how the roof became lower. A single set of footprints led across the pale sand towards a huddled figure sitting at the back.

Ruth had to stoop; she leaned with one forearm against the rough stone as she bent over the miserable girl. Esther had dropped her head into her hands and Ruth stared down at the girl's tangled mousy hair. She reached out to touch her but withdrew her hand uneasily when she remembered the way Esther was always scratching.

'What's the matter?' she asked, although she knew the answer.

Esther didn't look up. 'Nowt. I just want to be on my own, so ha'ad off!'

Ruth very nearly did as she was told. She had wanted to be on her own too – alone with her thoughts and her disappointment. She hadn't asked for this situation to be thrust upon her. She sighed. Now that she had come this far she knew that she couldn't walk away.

'I saw what happened,' she said.

There was a small silence. 'Well, then?'

21

'What do you mean?'

'If you saw what happened you know what the matter is. So haddaway and leave us alone like I telt you!'

'No.'

'What are you doing?' Esther scowled up at her as Ruth began to open her schoolbag.

'I'm getting my towel out and I'm going to sit down beside you. And, anyway, what are you sitting on?'

'Me bum.'

'Well, you'll get cold; this sand's damp. The tide must come right into the caves. Where's your towel?'

'Heven't got one.'

'Your schoolbag, then? You could sit on that.'

'I left it by the far rocks... Oh, no!'

'What is it?'

'Look ... out there ... the tide's coming in. The rocks are covered.'

Ruth sighed. 'Do you want to go and try to find your bag?'

'No point. I divven't need it no more. I'm not coming back to school next term like you are. I'll hev to find work.'

'Won't your mother mind?'

'Mind what?'

'About your schoolbag?'

'Me mam won't even notice.'

Ruth wanted to ask why not but Esther had averted her eyes as she always did when the girls talked about their homes and families. Ruth sat down and opened her packet of sandwiches.

'Here, have one of these.'

22

'I've got me own.'

'I saw you drop them on the sand. They'll be inedible.'

'They'll be what?'

'Inedible. That means you won't be able to eat them. Unless you intend to lick the fillings off.'

Esther's sudden rueful grin made Ruth realize that that was indeed what the poor wretch had intended to do. But at last there was a smile on Esther's face.

'You don't half talk like a dictionary, Ruth Lorrimer,' Esther said. 'I can see why Miss Foster wants you to stay on and be a teacher.'

'A pupil teacher.'

'You'll be good at that. Better than Miss Williams.'

'Why do you say that?'

'Well, Miss Williams is scared of the lads, isn't she? She doesn't know how to control them when Miss Foster leaves the classroom. I'll bet she's glad the lads didn't come with us today but went off on their own picnic in the country. You wouldn't be scared of them, would you?' Esther continued. 'Little as you are, I bet you'd stand no nonsense. Yes, I think you'll make a champion teacher– Ruth! What's the matter? Why are you crying?'

Ruth couldn't answer her. All the misery, all her disappointment welled up and burst out in body-wrenching sobs. She should have stayed up on the ledge on the cliff; she should never have sought to comfort Esther Robinson over a few cruel words and a packet of lost sandwiches when her own wretchedness was so overwhelming.

'Ruth ... yer frightening me ... stop it ... *please*!'
Esther moved closer and put a hand on her
shoulder. 'There, there,' she said softly as if she
were talking to a bairn. 'There, there, hinny,
whatever it is that's making you fret, you just gan
on and cry it out of you.'

Ruth dropped her head and pressed the palms
of her hands against her eyes. In the dimness she
could hear her own cracked sobs echoing round
the cave. Her companion sat patiently, still and
quiet. As Ruth's crying subsided, she became
aware of sounds from the world outside. The cry
of a gull, the splash of the waves breaking on the
shore and the dragging sound they made as they
pulled back across the shingle.

'Hev you done, crying?' Esther asked at last.

'Yes, I'm sorry.'

'There's nowt to be sorry for. But at least will
yer tell us what the matter is? Has someone said
something to yer? Called you names?'

Ruth looked up in surprise. 'And what should
they call me?'

Esther removed her hand and drew back. 'Well,
yer must know they think you're a bookworm...'

Ruth dabbed at her eyes with her handkerchief.
She shrugged. 'That's not an insult.'

'...and a teacher's pet.'

'Oh, that.'

'Divven't you mind?'

'Why should I? I suppose it's true in a way. But
at least I don't abuse the situation.'

'There you go again!'

'I mean I don't tell tales. And Miss Foster is
only kind to me because she wants – wanted – to

encourage me.'

'To be a teacher like her?'

'Yes. That was the idea.'

'*Was?*'

'You're quick, aren't you?' Ruth looked at Esther in surprise. And then she astonished herself by confiding, 'I'm not going back after the holidays. I'm leaving school. I'm not going to train to be a teacher.'

The other girl's eyes widened. 'But why? I mean, you're so clever ... top of the class ... better than any of the lads. I thought it was all planned.'

'So did I.'

'Then, what's to stop you?'

'My stepmother says I have to earn my living.'

'But you'd be paid something while you trained, wouldn't you?'

'Not enough.'

'Oh, I see. They can't afford to keep you.'

'It's not that,' Ruth said vehemently. 'My stepmother wants rid of me. She wants my father all to herself, so she's found me a job where I'll live in.'

'Oh.' Esther bit her lip. She frowned as if she wanted to say more but didn't know how to start.

'What is it?' Ruth asked.

'Nothing ... it's just that some folk would be glad of a job like that. A warm bed and all found.'

Ruth heard the wistful note in Esther's voice and sighed. 'I know. But not me. I'd hoped for more.'

'But what about Miss Foster? Can't she do owt?'

'No. She can't make my stepmother change her mind.'

Ruth was silent, remembering how Miss Foster had pleaded with her stepmother. Ada Lorrimer had come to school only yesterday to inform her Ruth would not be staying on as a pupil teacher. That she and Ruth's father were not prepared to keep her or buy her the books she needed to study.

'If that's the problem, I will see that Ruth has all the books and stationery she needs,' Miss Foster had said, 'and she will have a small salary. She will be able to contribute to your household expenses.'

'And who's to buy her clothes?' Ada had retorted. 'No, she'll hev to find proper employment. In fact I've already found a job for her and that's that.'

After she'd gone, leaving Ruth devastated, for it was the first she had heard that her stepmother had already planned her future, Miss Foster had tried to rally her.

'You don't have to give up the idea of education,' she'd said. 'Remember there are evening classes and public libraries, and I will always be here to advise you, my dear.'

And it had seemed to Ruth that she had not been the only one whose vision had been blurred with tears.

She looked up now to find Esther frowning. 'And what about your dad?' she asked. 'Can't he help you?'

Ruth shook her head. 'My father would never contradict my stepmother,' she said. 'He's completely in her thrall.'

Esther grinned. 'I suppose by that you mean

he's under her thumb?'

Ruth looked at her and smiled in spite of her misery. 'Yes, I suppose I do. And now let's eat these sandwiches before the tide comes in and washes them away.'

Esther half rose in fright. 'Do you think it will? I've heard of folk being trapped in these caves. Hawway, let's gan, I divven't want to droon!'

'For goodness' sake sit down. Look out there.' Ruth pointed to where some of their classmates still sat untroubled by the advancing tide; although a sandcastle a few yards in front of them was beginning to crumble and collapse into the persistently teasing foam. 'We've got a while yet,' she said.

'Hev we?' Esther looked unconvinced.

'Yes, see how the waves advance and then retreat again. It's a gradual process; the sea won't whoosh up here suddenly.'

'Aye, well, if you say so.' Esther sat down, although Ruth could see she was uneasy, and took the sandwiches proffered. 'What shall I do with these?' she asked holding up her own sandwiches.

'We'll toss them to the gulls,' Ruth said, taking them from Esther and throwing them out of the cave on to the beach. 'I'm sure they won't mind a bit of sand mixed in with their dinner.'

After they had eaten Ruth took a drink from her bottle of water. 'Do you want some?' she asked Esther, and when the girl nodded she handed it over.

Esther took a long drink and then looked at the bottle guiltily. 'Ee, I've not left much, I'm sorry.' She held the bottle out towards Ruth.

27

Ruth shook her head. 'No, I've had sufficient. Finish it if you want to.'

As Esther did so, Ruth turned her head away to hide her expression. She was ashamed to admit to herself that she had not wanted to drink from the bottle again after Esther had done so. She reached into her schoolbag and took out the twist of paper that contained the two sugar mice.

'Here you are,' she said, holding them up by their string tails, one in each hand. 'Which would you like, the white mouse or the pink mouse?'

Esther's eyes widened. 'Ee, they're lovely! But I can't take one.'

'Whyever not?'

'Well, they're yours.'

'For goodness' sake! Tell me, white or pink!'

'Gan on, then. I'll hev the white one.'

Esther held out her hand and Ruth lowered the white mouse on to her palm. Ruth couldn't help noticing how dirty Esther's hand was – not just because she had been playing on the beach. Her skin was stained with a sort of ingrained grime as if she never washed properly.

'Aren't you going to eat it?' Ruth asked.

Esther was still staring at the mouse. 'It's so bonny – all white and sparkly. It seems a shame to eat it.'

'Well, I'm going to eat mine.'

Esther glanced up just as Ruth bit off the head of the pink mouse. 'Oh!' she gasped, and looked as shocked as if the mouse had been a real creature. 'Can I hev the paper – the bag that they came in?'

'Of course. Here you are. But why?'

'I think I'll take my mouse home and share it with Davy, me little brother – if you don't mind.'

'Of course I don't,' Ruth said, and she watched as Esther wrapped the mouse carefully in the paper and stowed it in a pocket in the folds of her grubby dress. Then Ruth asked, 'By the way, what did Lucy Shaw give you?'

Esther frowned. 'You saw that?'

'I told you I did. I was sitting on a ledge halfway up the cliff. I saw everything that happened.'

'She gave me an angel cake.'

'Why did you throw it away?'

'I didn't want it.'

'You could have taken it home for your little brother.'

Esther scowled. 'Oh, all right, it was me temper. I didn't like the way she was ... she was...'

'The word you're looking for is patronizing. You thought she was being sort of superior. Looking down on you.'

'That's right.'

'Well, I think you're wrong. It looked to me as though Lucy was being kind.'

Esther sighed. 'I know. I was stupid. I cut me nose off to spite me face, didn't I?'

'You did.'

'And you're right,' Esther said, 'Lucy *is* kind, and she's so pretty. It's no wonder everyone wants to be her friend and sit beside her.'

'Do you think so? I mean, do you think that she's pretty?'

Esther looked surprised. 'Don't you?' she asked. 'Her face is all pink and white – like the sugar mice! And her eyes are so blue – and her hair all golden and curly. She's like ... she's like a china doll.'

'Exactly.'

Esther looked vexed. 'I divven't know what you mean by that. You're a funny lass, Ruth Lorrimer. Sometimes I think you think much too much of yerself.'

'Do you? Oh, you're wrong. I don't, really I don't!'

'Then why do you sometimes say such funny things? Like you're showing off – like you know better than the rest of us!'

'I don't mean to.' Ruth was stricken. 'I just can't help myself. I can't help the way I think, you know.'

Esther looked at her through narrowed eyes. 'No, I divven't suppose you can. But I reckon you're clever enough to stop and think before yer let yer mouth run. Now, what are yer looking at me like that for?'

'I was thinking how wise you are.'

'Me, wise? Gan on! I'm hardly top of the class, am I?'

Ruth grinned. 'No, but being top of the class and being wise are two entirely different things. For example, Lucy gets good marks but I wouldn't call her wise.'

'There you go again! What hev you got against poor Lucy? What harm has she ever done you?'

'None whatsoever – and I haven't got anything against her.'

'No?'

'Well, I suppose I might be a little jealous – although I wouldn't admit it to anyone but you.'

30

'Jealous? You mean because she always has nice new clothes and a ma and pa who dote on her?'

'I don't care about clothes. It's the second thing, I suppose.'

Esther looked angry. 'Well, don't begrudge her that. You should be pleased for her!'

'Huh! You're the one who threw her cake away!'

'I know I did, and I'm ashamed of meself!'

The two of them glared at each other for a moment; then it was Esther who spoke first. 'I divven't want to quarrel.'

'Neither do I. And I'm ashamed of myself too.'

'That's that then.'

In the small silence that followed Ruth became aware of shadows moving across the walls of the cave. She looked out to see that their classmates were leaving the southern part of the bay and walking back towards the lifeboat station.

'Ooh!' the girl at the tail end cried out as a sudden wave rushed up the beach. She leaped out of the way just in time. Her companions laughed. Both Ruth and Esther watched with widened eyes as the wave lapped right into the mouth of the cave before retreating slowly.

Esther jumped to her feet. 'Quick, we've got to gan!' she cried.

'All right,' Ruth said, 'but don't panic, look. That was only one wave – they say it's every seventh, don't they? The next one won't come as far.'

They left the cave and began to walk towards the others, who had gathered around Miss Foster and Miss Williams in the north end of the bay. While Miss Williams counted heads, Ruth turned to watch the progress of the sea. It seemed the tide had strengthened. Now each wave surged forcefully right up to the mouth of the cave before dragging back just as powerfully, leaving an ever-narrowing band of glistening sand. She saw that the bay would soon be divided into two and that the caves, including the one she and Esther had been sitting in, would be filled with churning water.

'Are we all present and correct?' Miss Foster asked.

'No, there are two girls missing,' Miss Williams replied. 'Lucy Shaw and Jane McKenzie. Oh ... look ... there they are at the refreshment stall.'

'The refreshment stall? But that's ... oh, how tiresome!'

Everyone turned to look at the southern part of the bay, which was now almost cut off from where they were standing by the incoming tide. At the landward end of an old stone pier was a wooden hut that served teas, soft drinks and ices. Even at this distance the ice-cream cones Lucy and Jane were carrying were plain to see.

'I bet Jane McKenzie got Lucy to treat her to that,' Esther whispered to Ruth.

'What shall we do?' Miss Williams asked Miss Foster. 'They can't get back along the beach.'

'They'll have to go up the cliff path to the top road,' Miss Foster replied. 'Come along, everybody, we'll meet them on the promenade. Now collect all your belongings and get into twos.'

'No ... wait,' Miss Williams called. 'They're running this way.'

Miss Foster looked vexed as she strode towards

the outcrop of cliff that now divided the bay. 'Go back!' she shouted. 'Go up the cliff path. We'll bring your belongings and meet you at the top.'

But Jane didn't heed her. Or perhaps, not hearing the words properly, she simply thought that Miss Foster was angry. She was several strides ahead of Lucy and, waiting until the most recent wave began to ebb, she started to splash across the drenched sand. Ruth saw how, with each step, Jane's feet sank in, leaving deep footprints that closed up almost as soon as they were formed. Jane had almost reached the dry sand where the group waited when the next wave surged in and soaked her feet and ankles.

'You foolish child!' Miss Foster scolded; then she turned her attention to Lucy. It was too late. The wave had retreated and Lucy had already begun to run towards them.

'No, Lucy!' Miss Williams called, and Lucy hesitated.

Ruth saw Lucy's eyes widen and a look of frightened indecision cross her face as she stood, rooted to the spot, just about halfway across. Ruth stepped forward and felt her own feet sink a little. 'Run, Lucy!' she shouted. 'Don't stop there!'

Lucy seemed to shake herself and then she smiled at Ruth and started to run once more. It wouldn't have mattered which way she'd chosen to go, Ruth thought later. She had already hesitated too long. But, as it was, she'd chosen to run towards them so her look of dismay was plain to see when the wave hit her.

It was comic, Ruth supposed, and no one could

have blamed some of the girls for laughing as they did. But the next minute, Lucy's look of dismay turned to fright and then terror as the force of the wave – a seventh wave? – knocked the ice-cream cone out of her hand and then swept her off her feet. The laughter turned to cries of alarm as Lucy fell into the sand-filled foam.

Everyone expected her to get up immediately, and it looked as if she tried to, but she lost her footing and fell again and, with a second surge, the water carried her forward and threw her against the tumbled rocks at the foot of the cliffs. She must have hit her head and become momentarily unconscious for, the next time that Ruth glimpsed Lucy's face, her eyes were closed.

The wave began to retreat, taking Lucy with it, and without further thought, Ruth slung her schoolbag behind her on to the dry sand and dashed into the water. 'Wait for me,' she heard someone say, and the next moment she was aware that Esther was beside her. They reached Lucy at the same time and each grabbed hold of an arm.

Ruth felt the strong drag of the sea trying to take Lucy's limp body away from her but she and Esther pulled together and together they scrambled back and collapsed, half-laughing, half-crying, at the feet of their astonished classmates.

'Well done,' Miss Foster said. 'Miss Williams, please move the others back.' Then the teacher kneeled down and took one of Lucy's hands. Lucy opened her eyes and sat up slowly, coughing and spluttering as she did so.

'Are you all right, child?' Miss Foster asked.

'Mm.' Lucy frowned and raised a hand to

touch her forehead. She flinched. 'I bumped my head.'

'I know. You must have passed out momentarily. Ruth and Esther pulled you from the water. They saved you.'

Saved her from what? Ruth thought. Had Lucy been in danger of drowning if she and Esther hadn't dashed into the water, or would she have come round and scrambled to safety herself?

Miss Williams had obeyed Miss Foster's order and moved the others back a little. Ruth could hear her asking them to make sure they had all their belongings, telling one or two of the dilatory ones to hurry up and dry their feet properly before they put on their socks and shoes.

She looked down at her own drenched state and barely had time to wonder how she was going to get home like this, when Miss Foster said, 'Miss Williams, you must take the others back to Newcastle yourself. We can hardly have these three sitting dripping all over the train.'

'Very well, Miss Foster,' the pupil teacher said. Ruth thought that she looked relieved.

The look of relief faded when Miss Foster continued, 'But before going home yourself, you will have to go and tell Lucy and Ruth's parents something of what has happened. Don't alarm them. Say they are quite well and I shall bring them home myself.'

'Yes, Miss Foster,' Miss Williams replied, and Ruth wondered whether her look of unease was because she was imagining what she would have to face: Mrs Shaw's distress or Mrs Lorrimer's anger.

'Tell them I'll bring them home as soon as I've

35

dried them off, or at least as much as I can,' Miss Foster said. She saw Miss Williams frown, and she smiled and looked up towards a row of fishermen's cottages on the cliff top. 'I'm sure the women there will help me and I can see from the smoke issuing from the chimneys that they've got good fires going.'

'But what about Esther?' Miss Williams asked. 'Shouldn't I go and tell her mother?'

Miss Foster didn't answer for a moment and then she said, 'I suppose you should.'

'No! It's all right,' Esther called out. 'Me mam won't be bothered if I'm a little bit late.'

'Are you sure, Esther?' Miss Foster asked, and Ruth imagined that the teacher's smile was sad as well as understanding.

'Aye, I mean, yes, Miss Foster.'

'Very well. Now, you've got the return tickets, haven't you, Miss Williams? Off you go then.'

The pupil teacher began to lead the girls away but one of them, Jane McKenzie, lingered.

'What is it, Jane?' Miss Foster asked.

'Miss Foster, my feet are wet. Can't I come with you?'

'No. If you hadn't acted so foolishly we would not be in this predicament. You deserve to suffer a little discomfort until you get home.'

'But–'

'No buts. Off you go.' Miss Foster turned away from her and began to help Lucy to her feet.

'Yes, Miss Foster,' Jane said, and, scowling over her shoulder, she hurried after the others.

Ruth and Esther were still sitting on the sand. Without getting up Esther edged closer. 'Look,' she breathed.

'Look at what?' Ruth asked.

'Doesn't she look queer?'

'Who? Jane? She always looks like that. She's like the bad fairy in a children's story.'

'No, not Jane. I mean Lucy. She looks ... I dunno ... different.'

'I should think so. She's just bumped her head on the rocks and been half drowned.'

'No ... I don't mean that. I mean ... she looks sort of ordinary.'

'Ordinary?'

'You know ... her hair's all straight...'

'That's because it's wet. Did you believe Lucy's hair was naturally curly?'

'I suppose I did.'

'No. I should imagine her mother puts rags in every night.'

'And it's not just her hair,' Esther continued. 'Her face ... it's just sort of round and plain and pasty-looking.'

'That's because she's had a shock. Her natural colour's drained away. She'll look better when she's recovered a little.'

'I suppose so.'

'Of course she will. No one's going to look their best when they're half drowned, are they?'

'No, you're right.'

Esther sounded so wistful that Ruth turned her head and looked at her. And what she saw shocked her. It wasn't the look of disappointment on Esther's face as she gazed at Lucy. It was the fact that Esther herself looked completely different. Her mousy hair now hung in shining

37

wet tendrils, framing her grave, fine-boned face, which was washed clean and glistening in the sun. Her eyes, Ruth noticed for the first time, were green rather than hazel, and they were wide and lustrous.

Ruth watched as Esther raised a hand and lifted a strand of hair from her face with delicate fingers. Her movements, as she pushed her hair back in an attempt to tidy it, were graceful. Why have I never noticed before, Ruth wondered, that Esther is truly beautiful?

Chapter Two

'Keep still, Lucy, or it will get in your eyes.'

'But, Mam, it smells horrible!'

Daisy Shaw held the pudding basin with one hand and clutched a clean flannel in the other. 'Horrible or not,' she said, 'it's the best thing for that bruise. And don't call me "Mam". You know your father and I think it common. You must call me "Mama".'

'Nobody calls their mother "mama" round here. If anyone heard me they would laugh at me.'

Lucy scowled. Usually she would not have answered back like this, but her forehead was hurting and the concoction of iodine and lard that her mother insisted on applying smelled disgusting.

'If you could see your face...' her mother said. 'It would serve you right if the wind changed and you stayed like that!' Lucy didn't respond to the teasing and her mother sighed. 'I know, pet,' she said placatingly as she dabbed gently at her daughter's bruised forehead, 'I know it's difficult for you, but it's important for you to remember that we're a cut above the rest of the folk who live round here.'

Lucy sniffed and wrinkled her nose exaggeratedly to show how much she was suffering. 'Then why do we stay?' she asked. And immediately she was sorry that she had. She had brought that fretful look into her mother's beautiful eyes. Often enough she had heard her mother asking her father the very same question. She knew what the answer would be.

'Well,' Daisy Shaw said, 'your father thinks we should stay here a while longer. After all,' Lucy saw how she tried hard to smile, 'we've got a nice little house at the top of the hill, and this was a pretty village not so long ago, you know.'

'You wouldn't think so now,' Lucy replied, 'especially when the wind's blowing up from the bone yard! You've said yourself you can't bear to hang the washing in the back garden, what with the smells from the bone yard and the tannery and the soot from the factory chimneys!'

'Well, at least we've got a garden,' her mother snapped, '*and* I can afford to pay a lad to keep it in order for me!' Daisy Shaw paused to calm herself, then continued more steadily, 'I have a maid to help me, we have new clothes whenever we want them, and more than enough to eat. But, nevertheless, your father has promised me that one day – when his business affairs make it possible – we shall move somewhere more fashionable.'

Lucy saw the dreams in her mother's eyes and was silenced. She didn't have the heart to tell her that she was beginning to lose faith in her father's promises. After all, he didn't have to spend all his time here in Byker. His work took him away a lot of the time, and when he came home, Lucy imagined he was probably so content with the attractive home her mother had created that he didn't have the desire to move elsewhere.

'And now,' her mother said, 'let me finish applying this lotion. We're lucky that the skin isn't broken, so you won't have a scar. I should hate anything to spoil your beauty.'

Lucy kept still and let her mother fuss over her. In fact she had a slight headache and she was quite happy to sit here in the front parlour, in a comfortable armchair, with her feet resting on the padded velvet footstool. But ever since Miss Foster had brought her home from the picnic yesterday, her mother had insisted on treating her like an invalid and she was beginning to feel bored.

When her mother had done, she smiled down at Lucy. 'Now,' she said, 'would you like me to read to you? This romance your father brought me is set in Westmorland – mountains and lakes and a delicious love story! Or shall we look at fashion magazines together?'

Lucy smiled at her mother's enthusiasm. 'No, it's all right,' she said. 'I'd rather go for a walk. I need some fresh air. Why don't we go to Heaton Park? We could buy ices at the refreshment stall and there might be a band concert.'

'Well...' Her mother smiled as she put the bowl and the flannel down on a tray on a tea trolley near the door. She paused while she wiped her hands on a clean towel and then undid the ties of her frilled half-pinafore. Folding it over her arm she sat opposite Lucy and smiled. 'I should have liked that but I don't think we've time.'

'Time? Do you mean before Father comes home?'

'Mm.' Her mother nodded her agreement. 'Home for tea.'

'Oh, but he wouldn't mind if we were late. After all, he often keeps us waiting when he has to work late – and sometimes he doesn't come home at all.' As soon as the words were out Lucy regretted them.

She glanced at her mother. The afternoon sun slanted in through the cream lace curtains, giving a warm, hazy light. The room was comfortably furnished and spotlessly clean. The scent of the roses in the cut-glass bowl on the lace-covered table mingled with the smell of lavender furniture polish. Lucy saw a faint frown mar her mother's smooth brow as, for a moment, her smile wavered but she recaptured it and her voice was firm when she answered, 'Your father wouldn't mind. But your guests might.'

'My guests?'

'Oh, Lucy, I was trying to keep it secret, make it a surprise. But I might as well tell you, I've invited those girls to come and have tea with you – Ruth and Esther. Betty has been baking all day, and your father is going to bring the girls a present each.'

'A present?'

'A little reward – not that anything could ever be enough – for saving your life!'

Lucy frowned and found that it hurt. She turned her head and stared at the arrangement of dried grasses and flowers in the hearth. She didn't want her mother to see her troubled expression. Had Ruth and Esther saved her life? Putting it like that made the incident sound so dramatic. It had all happened so quickly. One moment she had been running across the narrow strip of sand between the sea and the cliffs, and the next she'd found herself tumbling over in the surf before the wave hurled her up against the rocks like a piece of flotsam. The next thing she remembered was Miss Foster helping her to sit up and telling her that Ruth and Esther had pulled her from the sea.

'Oh, Lucy, sweetheart!'

Lucy looked at her mother to find that there were tears forming in her eyes. 'What is it, Mam? I mean, Mama?'

'To think that we could have lost you!'

'No ... it wasn't as bad as that. I'm sure I could have saved myself if they hadn't dashed into the water like that.'

'Could you? Miss Foster said that you lost consciousness for a moment.'

'Yes ... I suppose I did.'

'There you are, you see. You could have been dragged out to sea! No, your friends were very brave. That's why I've invited them here to thank them properly.'

'Friends?' Lucy wanted to say that Ruth and Esther weren't really her friends. That in fact Esther Robinson didn't have a single classmate that she could call a friend, and as for Ruth Lorrimer, Lucy had always suspected that the girl didn't like her.

Strange that it should have been those two, she thought. She supposed that as she would never know if she would have come round in time to scramble out of the water herself, she would have to accept that they had saved her.

'When ... how ... did you invite them?' she

43

asked her mother.

'Before Miss Foster left yesterday I asked for their addresses. I was going to write to their parents. And I did. But I talked it over with your father this morning before he left for work and he agreed that he should deliver the letters in person – and invite the girls to tea!'

Lucy could imagine the conversation. The tea party would have been her mother's idea and her father would have smiled and laughed and entered into the spirit of it. Sometimes Lucy thought they were like two children, two grown-up children, constantly thinking up new ways to have fun. She knew that they spoiled her – that was part of the fun – but sometimes she wished that they would ask her first before they arranged things.

'And they said they'd come?' Lucy asked. She couldn't believe that they would want to.

'Well, I suppose so,' her mother said. 'I'm sure your father would have come back and told me if there'd been a problem. So, now, why don't you close your eyes and rest a little while I go and help Betty set the table? Then I'll come back and help you to get ready.'

'Get ready?'

'Yes, we'll wash that horrid stuff off your face with rose-water and you can put on your new clothes, the ones we bought at Beavan's. You look so pretty in them.'

'I don't think Esther and Ruth will care what I look like.'

'Perhaps not, but I do.'

Lucy knew it would be useless to protest further. She supposed she could understand her mother's need to make it obvious that they were better off than their neighbours. From being a small child, Lucy had observed that her mother was different from most of the women round here. She dressed better, she spoke better and she always insisted that they keep certain 'standards'. But, in doing so, she had made it almost impossible for Lucy to have real friends.

Oh, her classmates liked her well enough, and she knew that some of the girls even admired her – the way she dressed and the way her mother styled her hair. Girls such as Jane McKenzie were always eager to accept invitations to tea. Her mother would fuss over them and join in the gossip just as if she were one of the girls. But Lucy had sometimes felt uncomfortable when she realized that there was an element of what she could only call 'showing off' in her mother's behaviour. And had her mother never noticed that not one of the favoured guests ever invited Lucy to their own homes? And if they had, Lucy wondered if her mother would have allowed her to go.

So now she had invited Ruth Lorrimer and Esther Robinson. What on earth would her fastidious mother make of Esther? Poor Esther. Nobody ever wanted to sit beside her, for Esther wasn't just shabby: she was downright dirty. And Jane was quite right: Esther smelled. Although at least she'd had a good drenching in the sea yesterday, so it might not be as bad as usual.

And Ruth. Clever Ruth, who could be like sunlight one day and then like a brooding storm on another. Lucy had observed how Ruth some-times had to bite her lip and keep her temper in

45

check. She didn't always manage it and words would come tumbling out, hurtful words that she seemed instantly to regret. She would always apologize, and in such a way that no one ever bore a grudge.

The other girls seemed to know that there was no malice behind Ruth's outbursts. They happened because her quicksilver mind leaped ahead of everyone else's and she was so far from being arrogant about it that she was forgiven. She was even popular – but she would never have a really close friend, Lucy thought.

Like me. And like Esther. I wonder if my mother realizes what an unlikely threesome she is bringing together for this tea party.

Ruth had finished cleaning her bedroom. The small chest of drawers was empty, her few clothes and possessions were packed neatly in the carpetbag her stepmother had given her, and only her nightgown remained folded under her pillow; for she was to be allowed to spend one more night in the house where she had been born – and where her mother had died.

She turned round slowly, making sure that there was nothing that would displease her stepmother: no speck of dust on top of the chest of drawers, no smears left on the small mirror or the windows, which she had just cleaned with newspaper and water with a dash of vinegar.

There was a ragged edge on the hem of one of the faded flower-patterned curtains. The curtains had been hanging there since her mother had made them when Ruth was a small child. The last time they had been washed the material had begun to fray along the bottom edge. That was hardly Ruth's fault, but she had mended the hems as best she could. Suddenly her eyes filled with tears as she looked at them and realized that, after tonight, she would probably never sleep in this room again.

A net curtain covered the bottom half of the sash window. Ruth remembered her mother soaking the cheap white net in a bowl of cold tea overnight until it was a rich cream colour. Every now and then her mother would repeat the process, but now the net was faded to a nondescript yellowy white.

Ruth went to stand by the window. She half raised the net and looked out. The Lorrimers lived in an upstairs flat, and almost directly in front of Ruth's window there was a gaslamp. She remembered how she would lie in bed on dark winter nights and be cheered by the soft glow that shone through the curtains and seemed to warm her room.

As she had lain waiting for sleep she could hear the trams and the late horse traffic on Shields Road not far away. Then in the mornings there had been the milkman's cart, the baker and the iceman; the tread of the men's boots as they made their way down the steep cobbled street to work in the shipyards on the river.

She stood next to the windowpane and turned so that she could look downhill. It was Saturday afternoon and, apart from a few children playing, the street was quiet. The long rows of respectable terraced flats, their windows gleaming and their front steps soap-stoned, gave no hint of what lay at the bottom of the hill, where this street and those that lay parallel to it gave way to the jumble of squalid tenements and old, neglected dwellings that huddled round the River Ouseburn.

The door behind her opened suddenly and Ruth dropped the net curtain and turned. Without speaking Ada Lorrimer came forward into the room and looked round. Perhaps Ruth was imagining it, but she was sure that it irked her stepmother that she could find no fault.

'That'll do,' she said. 'You can strip the bed tomorrow before you go. And now I suppose you'd better have this. Hold your hand out.'

Ruth did as she was told and her eyes widened as she saw what her stepmother was giving her. It was a brooch that had belonged to her mother. The brooch of gilt-covered metal was in the shape of a small bow studded with paste gems. Her mother used to joke that it was made of gold and precious stones.

'What do you think, Ruth, shall I wear me diamonds today?' she used to say with a smile as she pinned it to the high neck of her blouse. But, even though it wasn't valuable, it was precious to her. Joseph Lorrimer had bought it for her as a wedding gift.

Ruth stared down at the sparkling twist of metal now lying in the palm of her hand. It was something that she had thought she'd never see again. Her mother hadn't owned much jewellery – a string of imitation pearls, a silver locket and a pair of gold hoop earrings that had belonged to her own mother had been all she'd possessed –

but once Ada became the second Mrs Lorrimer, she had claimed anything that had belonged to the first one.

Kathleen Lorrimer had barely been dead and buried six months when Ada Thirlwell had come to help out. At first it had been left to good neighbours to help the young widower look after his eight-year-old daughter, and to do a bit of cleaning and cooking for him. But then one of them had suggested that her niece, a young widow without children, who had recently returned to live with her parents, would be glad to cook and clean for him, and look after the child as well, for a small wage.

Joseph Lorrimer earned good money as a riveter in the shipyards; he could afford to do things properly, so he'd agreed.

Children know things without being told. Ruth had known from the very beginning that Ada meant to take her mother's place. Ada was small and plump but she was attractive, even in unrelieved mourning black. She always took care to look her best, especially when Joseph came home at night for his evening meal. And Joseph would go into the scullery and strip to his waist in order to wash and make himself presentable. Ruth remembered how her mother used to help him – and the laughter and 'daft carry-on' as they'd called it, before he was judged ready to join her and Ruth at the table.

Ruth wasn't allowed to wait and eat with her father any more. Ada said it was much better for the child to have a proper meal as soon as she came home from school, and Joseph, grateful that someone seemed to care for the welfare of his daughter, didn't argue with her. And, although she had a bowl of hot water ready, she didn't help him to wash. But then she would place his dinner before him and slide into the seat opposite, her head slightly bowed and barely speaking. But Ruth, sitting with her schoolwork by the fire, would glance across and see how Ada's eyes slanted up as she watched him.

Gradually the mood changed. Ada began to ask him about his day, and tell him what she had been doing, and Ruth saw that this pleased her father. Young as she was, she knew how much he missed her mother and their easy companionship. Then Ada started to linger, long past the time when she could have gone back to her mother's house a few streets away.

When the dishes were cleared away and the dark red chenille cloth back in place on the table, Ruth was allowed to sit there with her books or her drawing pad and pencils. Her father would get his pipe from the rack on the mantelpiece and sit down by the fire. Then, pushing the pipe into his tobacco pouch, he would fill it and press the tobacco down with his thumb. Ada would take a spill and lean over the fire to light it. The glow would emphasize the lights in her dark red hair and Ruth saw how her father would look and then drop his eyes quickly when Ada straightened up and turned towards him.

She would hand the spill to Joseph and then lift the kettle from the hob where it had been gently steaming, and make another pot of tea. Her father would settle back contentedly, putting his stockinged feet on the fender and drawing at his pipe, the smoke from the bowl curling up in front of him and obscuring the expression on his face. The sweet tobacco smell mingled with the thin, sharp smell of coal dust and the lingering odours of the satisfying meal he had just enjoyed.

What did her father think, Ruth wondered, the first time that Ada Thirlwell sat down in the chair at the other side of the hearth? The chair where his first wife used to sit. He and Ada would drink their tea but, strangely, they wouldn't talk, and Ruth was aware of a tension in the air between them. Without either her father or Ada actually saying so, she knew that they were waiting for the time when she would go to bed and leave them alone.

Then, little more than a year after Kathleen Lorrimer had died from influenza, Joseph had married again. And nobody blamed him. Ada was just what he needed to look after his house and his child. And if she made him happy as well, that was no more than a man deserved.

'Well, aren't you going to thank me?'

Ruth looked up to see her stepmother staring at her unsmilingly. She had folded her arms across her body in her customary pose.

'Thank you. I ... I didn't expect this.'

'Your father said you should have something of your ma's to take away with you. I decided the best thing to give you was this pretty little brooch.'

Ruth could guess how much this had cost Ada. She knew that her stepmother would have agreed to her husband's request with a smile but with reluctance in her heart. Ruth raised the brooch to pin it on her dress and, as she did so, she noticed that one of the paste stones had fallen out.

'I see,' she said.

Ada tutted with exasperation. 'And what do you see, miss? What's the meaning of that uppity look on your face? What do you mean by it?'

'I don't mean anything – I'm just pleased, that's all.' And she was pleased. She was pleased to have her mother's precious brooch even with one of the stones missing.

'Pleased? You would never think so to look at you. But then I never do know what you're thinking, do I? That's why I'm glad you're leaving tomorrow.'

This was the nearest Ada had come to admitting her feelings for Ruth, and Ruth was glad that her stepmother's dislike of her was at last acknowledged. Ada had never been like a wicked stepmother in a fairy tale. She had seen that her husband's child had good food and clean clothes and she had never raised her hand, or even her voice, to discipline her. When she was displeased she adopted a tone of cold, quiet sarcasm – but never in front of Ruth's father.

But her real cruelty had been her complete indifference to her stepdaughter's feelings. She had not offered even affection, never mind love, to the lonely child. Joseph Lorrimer had filled Ada's heart completely and there was no room in it for anyone else.

'And I'm glad to go!' Ruth felt herself flushing as she stared at the woman she now knew that she hated.

Ada's smile was tight-lipped. 'Good, I'll tell your dad how keen you are to leave him.'

'I don't want to leave my father! Just ... just...'

'Go on – say it. Then I can tell him just how you feel about the woman who's looked after you since your mother died, and how ungrateful you are.'

'No,' Ruth said. 'I won't say anything.'

She didn't want to give her stepmother any excuse to cause trouble between herself and her father. She loved her father and she knew that he loved her. She had never run to him with tales of Ada's bad treatment for the simple reason there would have been nothing to say. Ada was too clever for both of them. Joseph Lorrimer came home to a clean house, good food and a daughter who was neatly dressed and apparently well cared for.

Whatever Ada did for Ruth was 'for the best'. She had even persuaded him that the job she had found for Ruth was a much better proposition than her staying on at school as a pupil teacher. Miss Golightly wanted a 'companion'. A bright young girl to run errands, take her out in her bath chair, and read to her by the fire at night. Ruth would be well looked after and might even end up being a 'lady'.

Joseph had been completely taken in by Ada's enthusiasm and apparent concern for his daughter's welfare. Only Ruth knew that, no matter how good the position might be, Ada had simply seen it as a means of getting rid of her and having Joseph completely to herself. If Ruth quarrelled openly with her stepmother now Ada might find some means of preventing her from coming home to visit on her days off. And if Ruth couldn't see her father again she knew her heart

53

might break.

'Well, then,' Ada said at last. 'I suppose you'd better go to that tea party or whatever it is.'

Ruth was surprised. 'You mean I can go? I can go to Lucy's house?'

'I told you it would depend on how well you cleaned your room, didn't I?'

'Yes.'

Ada had said that but Ruth had not believed her. She had imagined that Ada would find some corner that hadn't been dusted or some fluff under the bed – any small fault to prevent something she imagined would give Ruth pleasure. But her stepmother hadn't even looked under the bed, she hadn't lifted the rug, nor opened the drawers. She must have decided straight away that Ruth could go to Lucy's for tea but she had wanted to keep Ruth on tenterhooks.

Ruth was careful not to show how amused she was. In fact she didn't know whether she wanted to go to Lucy's or not. She had been astonished when Mr Shaw had called early that morning with the invitation. Ada had been impressed by his smart clothes and his gentlemanly ways and had been as nice as ninepence. She had listened to his little speech about how grateful he and his wife were to Ruth and she had pretended to be proud of her stepdaughter.

The reality was that the day before, after Miss Foster had gone, she had been tight-lipped with fury at the state of Ruth's clothes. Only the fact that Joseph Lorrimer had already arrived home from work had prevented her from saying anything.

Ada followed Ruth down the stairs to the front door and saw her off from the doorstep. 'Now be a good girl and behave yourself for Mrs Shaw,' she said smilingly, for the benefit of any neighbour who might be watching. Ruth knew that everyone thought Ada the perfect wife and mother. And her stepmother's smile didn't waver as she dropped her voice so that only Ruth could hear: 'And remember to eat your fill. There'll be nowt here for you tonight. Your dad and I will have our meal in peace for once.'

Ruth could have replied that after breakfast tomorrow Ada would have her father completely to herself for every meal, but she didn't. She didn't say anything. She simply raised her head and looked Ada full in the eyes. She was given the satisfaction of seeing the woman who had made her life a misery flush and bite her lip. Then, dropping her head to hide her scowl, Ada backed clumsily into the passage and slammed the door.

Ruth stood still for a moment. Now she realized how glad she was to have been invited to Lucy's for tea. It meant that she didn't have to spend her last afternoon at home with her stepmother.

She began to walk uphill. The water cart had just clattered down the cobbled street and streams of water still flowed in the gutter, taking away the assorted rubbish as it was intended. Ruth could hear the excited cries of small children as they followed the cart and splashed in the jetting waterspouts. Then, above their laughter, she heard someone calling her name.

'Ruth ... Ruthie ... wait for me!'

She turned to see two figures running up

55

towards her: Esther and her younger brother, Davy.

'I'm glad I caught you,' Esther said when she caught up with her. 'We can gan to Lucy's together.'

'Is Davy coming with you to Lucy's?'

Ruth looked at Esther's young brother curiously. She guessed he would be about seven or eight but, although he was small, he looked as tough as any of the street urchins. Davy looked back at her with eyes just like his sister's, and Ruth saw that he had the same fine bone structure. But his hair was lank and his clothes were dirty and ragged, whereas Esther still looked reasonably clean after the soaking she had suffered the day before.

'I'll hev to bring him,' Esther said. 'Me mam's femmur.'

'Your mother isn't well?'

Ruth looked at the two of them uneasily. Disease was rife in the squalid dwellings down by the Ouseburn.

Esther seemed to have read her mind. Suddenly she grinned and said, 'Divven't fret. You'll not catch owt off Davy and me. To tell the truth, me mam's the worse for wear – she's had too much to drink and if she doesn't shake it off and hev his dinner on the table afore me da gets yem, there'll be hell to pay.'

'Oh, I see.'

'I divven't think you do. Understand, I mean.' Esther lost her smile. 'And I shouldn't hev telt yer. You'll think less of me.'

'No, I don't, really I don't. It's not your fault.'

Esther looked at her quizzically for a moment and then she shrugged. 'So yer see, I thought I'd better bring the little 'un with us. I divven't want him to get in the way if me dad takes his belt to her.'

Ruth was shocked. She couldn't imagine what it would be like to live with the constant threat of physical violence. She was amazed that Esther could talk about it in such a matter-of-fact way.

'Do you think she'll mind?' Esther looked worried.

'Who will mind what?' Ruth asked.

'Do you think Lucy's mam will mind about Davy coming with me?'

'Oh, I shouldn't think so.' Ruth said it with as much assurance as she could muster. Secretly she thought Mrs Shaw would be appalled by the appearance of the ragged little boy and she made up her mind that if Esther and Davy were turned away from the door then she would go with them.

'When Lucy's da came to our house this morning to ask me to tea he gave me mam a letter,' Esther said as the three of them set off together. 'Did you get one?'

'Yes, he gave a letter to my stepmother. She read it as soon as he had gone.'

'Do you know what it says?'

'No.'

'Wouldn't she tell yer?'

'She said my father should read it first but she was just being awkward. She likes to spite me in little ways.'

But maybe it was the letter that had persuaded her stepmother to allow her to go to Lucy's for tea, Ruth thought. She wouldn't want her husband to think she had denied his daughter this treat.

'Did yer see Lucy's da?' Esther asked.

'Yes.'

'He's very smart, isn't he? And handsome. And such a toff. Me ma kept calling him "yer worship". But I wish I knew what was in that letter. Me ma opened it to see if the reward was inside–'

'Reward?'

'Yes – Lucy's da said something about a little reward for the brave girls–'

'Oh yes.'

'Well, me ma thought it might be money. But there was nothing like that in the envelope – and she can't read so she tossed the letter on the fire.'

'I expect it was a letter of thanks for dragging Lucy out of the sea,' Ruth said.

'Aye.' Esther grinned. 'And now we're gannin' to tea!'

Ruth smiled at the obvious delight in the other girl's eyes.

'You look bonny, mind,' Esther told her. 'I like yer frock.'

'Thank you.'

Ruth had been allowed to wear the dress she was going to go to Miss Golightly's in tomorrow. It was dark blue cotton, falling from a smocked yoke; the collar was trimmed with piping. Ruth knew that even though her stepmother didn't care for her, she would be too proud to let her go to the Shaws' house looking shabby.

'And that brooch – is it real?'

'Real gold and diamonds? Don't be daft.' Ruth smiled to take the sting out of her words. And suddenly, just as Esther had confided in her, she felt like sharing something of her own. 'But it's precious to me. It was my mother's.'

Esther looked solemn. 'And yer loved yer mam, didn't yer?'

Ruth was surprised by the question but when she saw the wistful look in the other girl's eyes she simply smiled sadly and said, 'Yes, I did.'

The expression on the woman's face was a picture as she stared down at Davy Robinson. Ruth stepped back a little and observed the scene. Whoever it was who had opened the door she didn't think it was Mrs Shaw. She looked too old to be Lucy's mother, although Ruth supposed she could be her grandmother. She wore a large, spotless, white pinafore over her grey dress, and her white hair was arranged in a neat bun. Her eyes were bright blue and her cheeks were rosy. She was like an old woman in a children's picture book, Ruth thought.

'What's the matter, Betty?' Ruth heard a melodious voice call out from somewhere behind the old woman. 'Is it the girls? Why don't you bring them in?'

'You'd better come and see for yerself, Mrs Shaw,' the woman said respectfully, and Ruth placed her as a servant.

The old woman stood back and Lucy's mother appeared in the doorway. 'Well, then?' she asked, and then her eye fell on Davy.

'The lass said she had to bring her little

brother,' the woman explained. 'She says there's no one to mind him, although I don't see what difference that makes. Nobody ever minds bairns like that; they just run wild in the streets.'

'I'd better gan,' Esther said. 'Hawway, Davy, we'll gan to the park.'

Mrs Shaw's smile didn't falter and Ruth warmed to her immediately. 'Of course you won't go to the park,' she said. 'I invited you to tea and your little brother's very welcome. Now come along in.'

She leaned over to murmur something to her maid, Ruth didn't catch what it was, then she stood back to usher them inside.

The older woman raised her eyebrows but kept her counsel. Once they were inside, with the door shut, however, she took hold of Davy's shoulder gingerly and Ruth heard her say softly, 'Now, me lad, you just come with me and I'll make you as decent as I can before you sit at the table with Mrs Shaw and the lasses.'

As Mrs Shaw ushered them into the front parlour Ruth saw Davy being hurried along the passage towards the back of the house. He turned to look back at his sister but Esther had already gone ahead into the room. Ruth paused and smiled at the little boy encouragingly; he gave the impression of a prisoner being led to the gallows.

Ruth couldn't make up her mind whether Mrs Shaw was putting on an act or whether she always behaved like this. She was very pretty – perhaps prettier than her daughter; she moved gracefully and she spoke very well. Like an actress, Ruth thought, like one of the amateur players who had come to school last year to perform a Christmas entertainment in the school hall.

Mother and daughter were wearing matching sailor suits: full navy-blue skirts and white blouses with large square collars trimmed with bands of blue. They each wore a blue satin bow at the neck and matching bows in their hair. Mrs Shaw's hair was piled up on top of her head and Lucy wore her usual ringlets. Ruth thought it novel – the idea of mother and daughter wearing matching clothes – and she had to admit how attractive they looked.

Lucy smiled at them as they stood awkwardly for a moment and then Esther said, 'Ee, Lucy, you do look bonny – and yer mam does as well.'

'Thank you for the compliment.' Mrs Shaw answered for both of them. 'Now, shall we take our places?' She indicated the waiting chairs with a graceful movement of her arm. Once more Ruth was reminded of an actress or a dancer.

Esther seemed to notice the dining table and everything on it for the first time. Her eyes took in the raisin cake, the apple pie, the scones and the rock buns, the china plates of bread and butter and the little cut-glass dishes of jam. But what she said as she took her place was, 'Ee, a proper tablecloth!'

Ruth caught the look that passed between Lucy and her mother and felt uncomfortable. She wondered if they thought that she came from the same kind of home as Esther and she hated herself for caring.

Then suddenly Esther looked all round the room and said, 'Where's me brother? Yer did let him in, didn't yer?' She half rose from her place as though she was going to run out and look for him.

Mrs Shaw made one of her graceful gestures. 'Sit down, dear. Of course we let him in, but I asked Betty to take him through to the kitchen and show him where to wash his hands.'

At the same moment the door opened and the maid entered carrying a large jug of milk. She was alone.

'Where's Davy?' Esther asked her.

The elder woman smiled. 'Divven't fret,' she said as she set the jug on the table. 'Yer little brother's fine wi' me. We've decided to hev a picnic in the garden.'

'Garden?' Esther's eyes widened.

Mrs Shaw answered, 'Yes, we have a little garden at the back; a pocket handkerchief, really.' Esther frowned and Mrs Shaw smiled. 'I mean it's very small. But we keep it nice and it's somewhere to sit on a pleasant day.'

'That's nice for yer,' Esther said, 'but Davy…'

'I'll keep an eye on him and see he has plenty to eat,' Betty assured her. 'And he's more comfortable there than in here with all you lasses.'

'I suppose so.'

'I know so. Now enjoy your tea.' She turned to Mrs Shaw as if it was all settled. 'I've brought milk for the lasses but I bet you could do with a nice cup of tea, hinny. I'll fetch a pot in for you.'

Ruth had never been in a house where there was a servant before and she wondered if many maids talked to their mistresses in such a familiar way. Whether they did or not, she decided that

Betty must be fond of Mrs Shaw, for all her airs and graces.

'Now, before we begin to eat I want to say how grateful I am to you, Ruth, and to you, Esther, for saving my precious little girl.'

'Mother!' Lucy's face flushed, and Ruth grinned, but she noticed that Esther's eyes widened solemnly.

'All right, sweetheart, I won't embarrass you any further,' Mrs Shaw told her daughter, 'but I want these two girls to know that they are always welcome here. Now, shall we be polite and start with the bread and butter?'

Ruth observed that Esther, who was obviously hungry, was nevertheless hesitant and she guessed that the other girl was unsure how to act at the table. But she was quick to learn and she didn't disgrace herself.

Lucy, although she smiled politely at them, was obviously a little embarrassed by the situation. Or was it her mother who embarrassed her? Mrs Shaw was like ... like what? Ruth wondered. Like a grown-up child. That was the nearest she could come to describing the way she smiled and encouraged the girls to talk.

'Now, tell me about the cottage,' she said. 'Do you know I've always wanted to look inside one of those fisherman's cottages on the cliff top. Lucy has told me how kind the people were but, poor dear, I think she was still too overcome by her recent experience to take much in.'

Lucy glanced at her mother with exasperation but then she looked across the table at Ruth and smiled as you do when a child has amused you.

Ruth felt herself being drawn in to the warmth that existed between mother and daughter.

'You describe the cottage, Ruth,' Lucy said. 'You're good with words.'

Ruth hesitated and Esther nudged her and said, 'Gan on.'

'Well, the walls are whitewashed and very thick, and as far as I could see there were two rooms and a back scullery that opened on to a yard – where they keep the nets and lobster pots.

'At first they took us through into the largest room, which was a bedroom. I imagine they all sleep in there, the fisherman, his wife and his children; there were three big beds.'

'Nice and comfy they looked too,' Esther added. 'Real blankets and sheets and pillows – imagine that!'

Ruth saw Lucy and her mother look at Esther in astonishment. Perhaps they had no idea what life was like for Esther, living in one of the huddled dwellings near the River Ouseburn.

'We took our wet clothes off in there–'

'Everything!' Esther exclaimed, and then she bit her lip and looked down at her plate.

Ruth thought it might be because the poor girl was remembering her embarrassment at the ragged state of her underclothes. Ruth hurried on, 'And then the fisherman's wife gave us each a big navy-blue jumper to wear – she called them ganseys. They came down past our knees! Then we went back into the other room and sat by the fire while Miss Foster helped to spread our clothes out on a pulley hanging above the fire in the range. They keep the fire burning all the time,

64

that's where they cook – and it gets cold on the cliff top at night the old woman told us, even in the height of summer.'

'The old woman?' Mrs Shaw asked.

'The old granny,' Esther said. 'She was sitting up on top of the blankets on a narrow little bed against the wall. She had her boots on. She was dressed all in black, and she had a shawl tied round her old body and one of them old-fashioned white frilly caps on her head. And you should hev seen her wrinkles – she was as shrivelled as an old prune. And she was smoking a pipe! And I divven't know what she'd put in it but it smelled like horse droppings.'

Lucy giggled and her mother looked amused. Ruth realized that Esther too had a way with words.

'It did smell disgusting,' Lucy said. 'In fact I don't know what was worse – the smell of the old woman's pipe or the smell of something they were boiling in the back scullery.'

'I think that was crabs,' Ruth said. 'The fishwives sell dressed crabs from tables at their doors. Miss Foster bought one before we left the cottage.'

'Miss Foster told me that the woman was very kind to you,' Mrs Shaw said. 'Drying your clothes and giving you bread and butter and cups of tea.'

'Miss Foster tried to pay her,' Ruth said, 'but she wouldn't take any money. I think that's why Miss Foster bought the crab.'

'Well, then,' Lucy's mother said, 'all in all, it was quite an adventure. I'm sure that none of you will forget that day.'

All the time they had been talking Mrs Shaw

65

had made sure that their plates were filled and, just as they had decided they couldn't possibly eat any more, Mr Shaw came home from business. At least that's what Mrs Shaw said as she greeted him.

'Ah, Reginald, home from business, at last. You've missed the tea party after all, but I'm glad you are back in time to meet the girls. Especially as I know you have a small reward for them.'

Oh, yes, the reward, Ruth thought. That would be another reason why her stepmother allowed her to come here to Lucy's. She saw how Mrs Shaw's face filled with pleasure at the sight of her husband. She looked at him in the same way that Ruth's stepmother looked at her father. No, not quite. When Ada looked at Joseph Lorrimer with her hard direct gaze it was as if he was her prize possession, he belonged to nobody but her. Whereas Lucy's mother's face had softened, she had become like an uncertain girl, and the love that shone there was not exclusive: it took in their daughter as well.

Mr Shaw was tall and handsome with blue eyes, light brown hair, a fine open complexion and a silky moustache. He wore smart clothes, even better than those worn by the school inspector. Ruth guessed that they were a gentleman's clothes. And he smiled a lot, just like his wife. Ruth wondered what it was like for Lucy to live with parents who were so determinedly happy.

'Ah, Ruth and Esther,' he said. 'I'm so pleased to see you. And to give you these small gifts.'

He went out of the room again and came back with two wooden boxes, which he placed on the table before Ruth and Esther. 'Go on, you may open them,' he said.

Ruth looked down at her box. It was quite big. It had a name painted on the front in fancy letters: 'Lawson's'. Ruth frowned. That name meant something but she couldn't quite recall it. The box had a hinged lid and a small brass catch at the front. Esther was fiddling with hers, and she had already opened her box as Ruth recalled the significance of the name. 'Lawson's' was the name on the label of the sweet jars and boxes of confectionery in the corner shop.

'Go on,' Mrs Shaw said. 'Open your box, Ruth.'

She was aware that next to her Esther had gasped with delight, and she opened her box to find out why. It was full of confectionery. All manner of boiled sweets of different colours and flavours, laid out on a wax paper tray that was shaped to contain the individual shapes and sizes.

'That's only the top layer,' Mrs Shaw told her. 'There are two more underneath. They are my husband's top-class samples. He takes boxes such as those to the finest shops and wholesalers when he is getting orders.'

This wasn't the kind of reward my stepmother was imagining, Ruth thought. And Esther's mother would be disappointed too.

Then, 'Look, Ruth,' she heard Esther whisper with delight. 'Look in the middle – there's a white one and a pink one. Is your box the same?'

'Yes, it is,' Ruth said, and smiled as Esther carefully picked up one of the sugar mice by its little string tail.

Chapter Three

Ruth couldn't sleep. Her emotions were a mixture of sorrow and resentment. Her stepmother had sent her to bed early on the pretext that she needed a good night's rest before she set off for Miss Golightly's early the next morning. She had hoped to spend the last hours in her childhood home in her father's company, but Ada had begrudged her even that.

The sky was still light and the night was warm. Ruth had folded back the blankets and eiderdown so that she was covered only by a sheet. She lay staring at the pattern on the wallpaper: pink flowers with thin brown stems on a cream background. The colours had faded just like those in the curtains. This little room above the stairs had been neglected since her mother died. Ruth wondered if her stepmother would ever set foot in it again, or whether she would try to ignore it as she tried to ignore any evidence of Joseph Lorrimer's life before she had married him.

She thought about the events of the day and she tried not to envy Lucy even more. It was obvious that her parents embarrassed her sometimes, but Ruth wondered if Lucy had the remotest idea how lucky she was. Not because her home was attractive and comfortable, not because she had such pretty clothes, and not because there was obviously sufficient money coming in to mean that they never had to worry about paying the bills. No, she envied Lucy for the fact that her parents not only cared for each other, but they loved their daughter too.

But Mrs Shaw was not so totally wrapped up in Lucy that she couldn't be generous and kind to the girls she had invited to her home that day. Ruth didn't know when the order had been given but, when the time had come for them to leave, the old maidservant, Betty, had taken Esther aside and given her a neatly wrapped bundle to take home with her. 'The missus says you're to hev these things that Lucy has grown out of. You're a skinny little thing and they should fit you fine.'

Davy, looking as clean and scrubbed as possible, had his bundle too – of food left on the table after the tea party, as well as an apple and an orange from the fruit bowl. He and Esther had hardly stopped smiling all the way back down the hill and when they left Ruth at her door and hurried homewards she actually heard them whooping with delight.

Ruth had not been offered anything to take home and for that she was grateful. She knew it was pride and that pride was a sin, but she would have been mortified to have been judged in need of charity.

But Mrs Shaw had taken her hand in her own soft white hands and leaned towards her, so close that Ruth could smell her perfume that reminded her of rose petals. Ruth had been overcome by the genuine warmth she saw in the woman's eyes.

'I won't forget what you did,' Lucy's mother

said. 'You and Esther. And I want you to know that whatever happens to you now that you are leaving school, whatever the years bring, you will both always be welcome here.'

Esther had rhapsodized about it on the way home. 'We will gan there again, won't we, Ruth? We will call in and see them when we can?'

'Perhaps. If you think she wants us to.'

'Ah, divven't get one of yer moods, Ruthie. Of course she wants us to. Lucy's mam is a lovely lady and she really meant what she said.'

And I don't blame Esther for wanting to go there again, Ruth thought. How different it must be from her own home. And how different the three of us are, Lucy and Esther and me. But no matter what Lucy's mother says I'm not sure that we'll meet up again.

'Whisht, Davy, divven't let him hear us!'

Esther and her brother crept into the windowless room at the back of the scullery. It might have been a cupboard once, when the house had belonged to a rich merchant. But that had been hundreds of years ago and now, the once-fine old house by the River Ouseburn had become home to half a dozen families.

Some of them crammed into one room, but Esther's father was big and strong. He made better money than most of them – when he was in work, that was – so they had managed to hang on to one large room, where they ate their meals and where their parents slept, a scullery off that with its own sink, and this windowless space behind the shared staircase, where the children slept. All the families shared one privy in the yard.

Long before Esther had reached home with the clothes that Mrs Shaw had given them she had realized that she had a problem. If her mother saw the clean good-quality dresses and underwear, Esther would never be able to wear them, for her mother would take them to the old clothes market at Sandgate and sell them.

'Ha'ad on a minute, Davy.' Esther had caught her brother's arm, so painfully thin under the rough cloth of his jacket. 'Let's bide a while.'

He frowned up at her. 'What do yer mean?'

'Lissen, Davy, would you like to gan down to the river for a while?'

'What for?'

'Well, yer divven't want to gan yem yet, do yer? She'll only send yer to bed and I'll probably hev to make wor dad's dinner. We could sit and watch the boats ... eat some of them cakes and pastries.'

'The big river, you mean?' He meant the Tyne rather than the Ouseburn.

'Aye.'

'All right then.'

Instead of continuing down towards the Ouseburn valley, Esther and Davy retraced their steps a little and turned into an alley that led down at an angle towards the River Tyne. The path was steep and eventually turned into a long set of stone steps cutting down the bank between the windowless overhanging walls of ancient warehouses. Once they reached the bottom they found themselves on part of the quayside rarely used now, except by the sculler men, the boatmen who ferried paying passengers to and

71

fro across the river.

'We'll sit here on the bottom step,' Esther said. She could hear voices and laughter coming from one of the public houses not far from the bottom of the steps and, although it was early and the talk was good-natured, Esther knew from experience that it was better to keep out of the way of men with drink in them.

Her brother was happy enough as they shared the food and, for a while, Esther put her worries aside as they watched the traffic on the river.

She had been taught at school that Newcastle was one of the busiest ports in the land. Ever since she had been a small child, left to wander the streets, she had seen as many as two hundred sailing ships arrive with every tide. It was still magic to watch them – and hear the shouts of the crew as they trimmed the sails and prepared to dock. She loved to speculate about the foreign lands the ships had been to, and their cargoes of tea, coffee and spices, sugar and rum, silks and oriental rugs, furs and sealskins and the brightly painted wooden toys that were sold at the toy stalls in the Grainger Market.

Davy loved to watch the steamships. He was only eight years old but, like many of his friends, he knew the names of the ships, and where they had been and which ones had been built right here on the Tyne.

When they had finished their impromptu picnic Davy turned to his sister and grinned. 'Shall I gan to the pub and fetch us a gill?' he asked.

'Shall you *what*?' Esther said.

72

'Fetch us a glass of ale – from the pub along there.'

'You will not. What gave you such an idea?'

'I'm thirsty. Aren't you?'

'Yes I am, but we'll quench our thirst with this orange. A glass of ale indeed! And anyways, I heven't any money.'

As Esther peeled the orange she thought about why she never wanted to take a drink and how she hoped and prayed that Davy wouldn't either. Drink made their quick-tempered father even worse. She and Davy had learned when it was better to slip away and hide if he came home the worse for wear, but their mother would be left to face him. Perhaps that's why Agnes Robinson had started drinking too. Young as she was, Esther had realized that alcohol seemed to give some kind of relief – an escape from the hard life that folk lived.

Eventually a chill wind from the river drove them home. They retraced their steps, even though it might have been quicker to walk along by the river to the point where the Ouseburn joined the Tyne. But Esther wanted to put off the moment when they would enter the house. She still had no plan but, the later they were, the more likely it would be that their mother would be busy with their da's meal and they would be able to slip into the room they shared without being noticed.

In fact, as she had feared earlier, the dinner had never been made. After they had gone to Lucy's, their ma had gone on drinking. William Robinson had come home hungry from the timber yard, where he had found work as a general labourer, to find his wife slumped on the floor by the range. She was clutching a wooden spoon; a cooking pot lay upside down beside her with its contents of cheap, fatty stewing meat and potatoes spilled out on the dirty floorboards. Infuriated at the welcome that awaited him, he had begun to rampage around the room.

When Esther and Davy arrived home their mother's screams were piercing the air. One or two neighbours were in the street. Women, clutching their shawls about them, glanced uneasily at the children but said nothing. They knew it was best not to get involved.

Esther had clutched Davy's hand and they had crept along the stone-flagged passage, past the stairs that led to the other tenants' dwellings, to their room at the back of the house.

When she was certain that they hadn't been heard, Esther lifted the mattress on the bed they shared and pushed it back against the wall. She asked Davy to hold it while she laid out all the clothes Mrs Shaw had given her on top of the wire mesh, then together they let the mattress fall again. Their ma would never find them there, Esther thought. With only the bare mattress to sleep on and a rough blanket to cover them, there were no sheets to change – and even if there had been she doubted if the sheets would ever get washed.

Satisfied that none of her new belongings could be seen, Esther sat on the bed and sighed. That was one problem solved, but now, how was she ever going to wear the clothes? Her mother would hardly fail to notice the bonny clean dresses that looked as good as new. Well, at least she could wear the underwear, she thought, and she would make sure that somehow she would be able to keep it washed and fresh.

She became aware that Davy was listening at the door. 'What's the matter?' she asked.

'It's gone quiet,' he said, and he looked at her with troubled eyes.

So it had. Her mother's screams and her father's bellowing had ceased. What did that mean? She supposed she had better go and find out. She rose from the bed and went to the door.

'You stay here, Davy,' she said.

'But me mam ... I mean...'

'I know. Divven't fret. I'll find out what's happened, but I want you to stay here just in case he's still angry.'

Davy sat unwillingly on the bed and Esther closed the door behind her. As she went back along the passage she saw that the front door of the house was wide open and two of the women who had been talking in the street before were standing there hesitantly.

'There's the little lass,' one of them said when she spied Esther.

'Yer da's gone, hinny,' the other one said. 'Stormed off down the bank. We was just wondering...'

'It's all right,' Esther said. 'I'll see to her.'

'Are you sure?' the first woman asked.

'Yes.'

'Well, come next door if you need owt,' the other one said.

Esther waited until they had gone, then she pushed open the door. At first she thought the room was empty and wondered where her mother could have gone, until she heard a soft moan. She peered round, perplexed. The fire in the range was burning low and not much light came through the small dirty window.

'Esther, hinny, is that you?' The cracked voice came from somewhere low down.

Esther saw her mother at last crouching beneath the table. She must have crawled there to get away from her husband's blows.

'You can come out, Mam. He's gone.'

'Aye, I know, but you'll hev to help us. Here, that's right, give us your arm so's I can drag meself up.'

Esther felt the familiar tension knotting inside her as she helped her mother to come out from under the table, and then to rise shakily and sit heavily on the nearest chair. Esther looked at her. Her face was covered in red marks that soon would become ugly bruises. Her lips were swollen and she seemed to have difficulty in keeping one of her eyes open.

'Has he hurt you bad?' Esther asked.

Her mother sighed. 'No more than usual.' Her speech was slurred.

'What can I do?' She knew it was no use suggesting she call the doctor. They couldn't afford it.

'Gan to the scullery and soak a bit rag in cold water,' her mother said. 'I'll hold it to this eye. Then you can make us a cup of tea. I'm shaking too much with the shock of it.'

Esther knew it was the drink as much as the shock that was making her mother shake, but she did as she was told and, when the tea was made, she took a cup to Davy and told him not to fret; everything was as fine as it would ever be. She left him drinking his tea and eating the last piece of raisin cake.

When she went back to check on her mother she found her unscrewing the cap from a green bottle and she watched as she poured a generous measure of gin into her cup of tea. She stirred it round, then looked up at her daughter.

'Now, divven't stare at me like that,' she said. 'I need this to pull me round.'

Esther didn't reply. What was the use? Not long after that she helped her mother stagger over to the bed against the wall and, after closing the damper on the range fire, she went back to the room she shared with her brother. Davy had fallen asleep. She pulled the blanket over him and then, fully dressed, she slipped in beside him. She hoped she would be able to join him in slumber before their da came home.

Ada Lorrimer stood before the mirror that hung over the sideboard and arranged her best hat on top of her tortured curls. The curling tongs still lay in the hearth, resting against the fender, and a faint smell of singed hair mingled with the odours of fried bacon and eggs that Ruth's father had had for breakfast.

Joseph Lorrimer sat beside Ruth at the table. He had finished eating, and now he sat back with a large cup of tea and watched his wife getting ready. He smiled contentedly. His smile almost broke Ruth's heart. Surely he hadn't forgotten why they were up so early and where they were going?

Her father was a big, handsome man. His work as a riveter in the yards, high up on wooden planks alongside the hulls of the ships, working ten hours a day in all weathers, had weathered his skin to the appearance of tanned leather. When the winds were high he tied himself to the staging with ropes, but nothing was allowed to interfere with the rhythm of his hammer blows. When the yards were busy the racket was terrific and carried up the hill from the river far into the town.

Now Joseph Lorrimer sat in his Sunday best. His big hands, scrubbed clean, dwarfed the Sunday china, and his suit jacket rested on the chair back while he finished off his tea. His dark hair was dressed with brilliantine and his moustache trimmed. Occasionally he ran a finger round the neckline of the collar he wore under protest and his starched white shirt almost crackled when he moved. His fob watch chain – the watch and chain a gift from his new wife – looped like that of a gentleman across his waistcoat.

Ada had her best clothes on too: a decent black skirt and a white full-sleeved blouse with a piped yoke and a cameo brooch at the high neckline trimmed with broderie anglaise. The brooch was Joseph's wedding gift to Ada, and Ruth's heart ached at the thought that her mother had never owned anything so fine. But Joseph, freed from the responsibility of looking after his motherless daughter, worked all the hours he could and made good money.

He could well have afforded to let Ruth stay on at school, but he had been swayed by his wife's arguments. He genuinely believed that Ruth would be much better off in Miss Golightly's fine house at the coast rather than serving a hard and poorly paid apprenticeship as a pupil teacher.

Ada fixed the second of her hatpins into the back of her straw hat and turned to smile at Joseph. Artificial roses, violets and lilies of the valley crowded the brim, a strange mix, Ruth thought, but she had to admit the effect was attractive. And her father was enchanted.

'Shall we go?' Ada asked.

'Aye, pet,' her husband replied. 'It's a fine day. And you look so bonny in that daft hat that mebbes I'll treat you to a bit lunch in the Dainty Café on the prom.'

Her father's eyes were full of fun and Ada flushed with pleasure. Wordlessly she held out her jacket and he went over to help her put it on. Ruth stood up abruptly and went to get her coat. Neither of them had even mentioned the fact that Ruth was leaving home today.

They walked to Heaton station, Ruth trailing miserably behind. Her father was carrying her carpet bag and Ada had linked her arm through his other arm. Ruth imagined that Ada thought the pair of them a handsome couple and she was probably doing her best to ignore the girl walking a few steps behind them.

Even though it was still early on a Sunday morning Shields Road was busy with trams and other horse traffic. Ada and Ruth's father set off across the road without glancing round to see if Ruth was there. They had reached the central island where the tram poles stood before Ruth was ready to step off the pavement and follow them. Just then a tram rattled by on its way to the town centre and Ruth had to wait. By the time the tram had gone she had lost sight of them.

Ruth wondered if she should turn and run away. But where could she go? Her mother's parents were dead and her Grandmother Lorrimer would only send her back because she would never oppose her stepmother. What of Mrs Shaw? She'd said Ruth would always be welcome at her house but she meant as a visitor, not as a runaway. No ... there was no escape. She would have to go and work for Miss Golightly in Whitley-by-the-Sea.

Her father and his wife, so taken with each other, had not even noticed that she had failed to keep up with them and when they reached the station they went straight in. Ruth found them queuing at the ticket office and quietly went to stand behind them.

Once the train left the rows of terraced houses behind, it passed through fields and scattered mining villages. Ruth gazed out of the window without really focusing on the farm buildings or the giant wheels of the pit winding gear. She had been counting on having this time alone with her father. She had never dreamed that her step-mother would want to come with them.

All night she had been savouring the idea of having her father to herself for one last time. To be able to talk freely to him without having Ada listening and restricting the old easy relationship – the remembrances of times past. She had woken early and gone downstairs, hoping to sit by the fire for a while. Ada always banked it right down at night and then blazed it up when she came down to start Joseph's breakfast. Ruth knew she was being dramatic but she wanted to be alone in the room that held so many happy memories of her former life, of the times when her mother had been alive, for one last time.

But when Ruth had opened the door carefully so that she wouldn't wake anyone, Ada was already there, sitting on a cracket by the fire, waiting for her curling tongs to heat. Her stepmother was dressed only in her underwear, her corset laced tight over her petticoat, her coppery hair hanging down, straight and thick to hide her shoulders. When she turned quickly to face Ruth, her hair swung back and Ruth saw how the firm flesh at the top of Ada's arms was beginning to sag and how her full bosom strained against the white cotton.

'What do you want?' Ada's voice was sharp. She rose from the stool and snatched up a paisley shawl from the armchair and draped it round her shoulders.

Ruth stared at her, speechless; she didn't know what to say.

'For goodness' sake, can't a body hev any peace in this house!'

'I couldn't sleep,' Ruth said at last.

'Well then,' Ada gave a long-suffering sigh, 'seeing you're up, you can run along the lane to the dairy and get some milk.'

'Do we need any?'

Ada stared at her. For a moment Ruth thought that her stepmother was going to lose her temper but she went over to the sideboard. She took some coins from the top drawer.

'Take a clean jug,' she said. 'A pint will do.'

Ruth left without a word.

The dairy yard was at the top of the back lane of the street where they lived. The milk had only just arrived from the farm, and Ruth waited while the churns were unloaded. Then Mrs Bartlett took the pint scoop and ladled the fresh milk into the jug. By the time Ruth got back, Ada was dressed and concentrating on her hair.

'Make yourself useful,' had been her only greeting, 'and set the table for breakfast.'

Ruth had done as she was told, sheer misery silencing her and slowing her movements. She had not been able to eat anything, and the tea she'd forced herself to drink did little to ease the ache in her throat. Now the motion of the train was making her feel queasy.

When they left the train at Whitley station they found that although the sun was still bright there was a slight breeze; enough to ruffle the flowers on Ada's hat and make her raise one hand to steady it. Many other passengers had got off here and now they were heading for the beach, intent on a day out. Ada led them in the same direction for a while, but before they reached the promenade she turned into a wide road with tall houses on one side and a smart arcade of shops on the other.

'Here we are, Catherine Terrace,' Ruth's stepmother said, and, opening the gate of one of the houses, she led the way up the short path to the front door.

The young maid who answered the door frowned when Ada told her who they were and that they were here to see Miss Golightly. She left them standing on the front step, telling them to wait there. She actually closed the inner door and Ada flushed angrily, although Ruth guessed that her easy-going father didn't realize that they had been snubbed. Ruth herself was puzzled. Weren't they expected?

When the maid returned, still without smiling, she told them to follow her and she led them along a dark passage to the stairs, then up to the first floor. The walls were oak-panelled and the house smelled of lavender polish.

'Miss Golightly will see you,' the maid said. She made it sound as if they had asked for a favour. She knocked on the door to the room at the front of the house and then preceded them inside.

'Who gave that lass vinegar for breakfast?' Ruth heard her father say to his wife, and Ada shushed him.

Ruth was aware of going into the room and of the maid brushing past her as she went out and shut the door. She was aware of Ada talking to someone who sat in a chair by the window but she was too distracted to concentrate. She had never seen so many books gathered together in one place in her life – except at the lending library. Bookshelves lined the walls and filled the alcoves. Books were piled up on tables and there were even books lying on the floor.

'Ruth, what are you thinking about? Don't just

stand there. Come here and meet Miss Golightly.'
Ada's voice was strained, as if she would have
liked to be more forceful but was minding her
manners.

Ruth turned to look at the tableau in the bay
window. Miss Golightly was old and severe-
looking. Her clothes were surprisingly stylish – but
they were the fashions of an earlier age. In spite of
the wrinkles Ruth saw that Miss Golightly had
once been beautiful, but her large blue eyes
blinked and stared through a pair of strong, gold-
rimmed spectacles. She was seated in a substantial
wing-backed chair, while Ruth's father and
stepmother stood before her almost like subjects
paying homage to some imperious dowager
duchess. Dust motes danced in the sunlight that
streamed through the lace curtains; Ruth realized
that the air in the room smelled dusty.

'For goodness' sake, Ada, tell your husband to
bring those chairs forward and sit down,' Miss
Golightly said. Until that moment Ruth had not
realized that her stepmother was acquainted with
Miss Golightly.

Ruth's father looked around, saw the chairs in
question and moved them into the bay window.
On one of them lay an open book; he looked at it
helplessly and Ruth moved forward and picked it
up.

'Don't lose my place,' Miss Golightly said. 'Put
it on that table.'

Ruth did as she was told, but her glance lingered
on the page. As well as text there was a beautiful
illustration of a scarlet flower, a hibiscus. The
caption at the top of the page told her that the

book was about tropical plants.

'Now then,' Miss Golightly turned to Ada. 'Why have you come?'

Ada, seated now, was puzzled. She moved forward and sat nervously on the edge of her chair. 'But, Ruth ... she's to start work for you...' she began.

'Yes, yes, quite right, but I thought her father was to bring her and leave her with me. I didn't expect you to make a social visit.'

Ada flushed. Ruth thought how she must hate being spoken to like this in front of her husband and stepdaughter. 'Ruth wanted me to come,' she said. 'It's natural, isn't it? I mean, leaving home...'

Ruth was stunned by the lie. She glanced at her father to see his reaction but he didn't seem to realize how unlikely Ada's statement had been. He probably thinks we talk intimately like a real mother and daughter, Ruth thought. After all, he only has Ada's version of what happens when he's not at home.

'Fond of you, is she?'

Miss Golightly's question took Ada by surprise. Her mouth opened and nothing came out. She glanced at Ruth, her eyes flashing an appeal for help. 'That's not for me to say,' Ada said at last.

'No, I don't suppose it is,' Miss Golightly said, and she turned and looked at Ruth, who remained silent. Ruth thought she saw the faintest twitch of the old woman's lips and a gleam of amusement in her eyes before she continued, 'Well, well, I suppose if you have been looking after the child since her mother died it's natural for you to be concerned. You will want her to be happy.'

'Of course,' Ada said, although Ruth knew there was no 'of course' about it. But she saw her father look approvingly at his wife.

'Do you think you will be happy here?' Miss Golightly asked Ruth.

Taken aback, Ruth answered, 'I don't know, yet.'

'Ruth!' Ada hissed.

But Miss Golightly chuckled. 'Don't worry, Ada. That was an honest answer. I approve.' Then, turning to Ruth again, she said, 'Have you been told what your duties are to be?'

'I'm to run errands, take – I mean go for walks with you, read to you – a sort of general factotum.'

'*Factotum?* My, my. You were right, Ada. This may be just the girl I'm looking for.'

Ada frowned. Ruth could see that her stepmother didn't understand exactly what Miss Golightly was talking about but she sensed the approval in her tone and the frown became a smile. 'I told you in my letter that she was a clever girl. Quite proud of her, we are.'

Ruth's eyes widened and, once more, she saw amusement register in Miss Golightly's intelligent face. When she spoke again she addressed Ruth's father. 'You need have no fear that your daughter will be ill-treated in my home. She will be well fed and clothed and, although I expect obedience I will always be fair. Do you believe me?'

'Aye, I do,' Joseph Lorrimer said.

'Well, then,' she turned to look at Ada again, 'do you want me to offer you refreshment?'

86

'Well ... I...' Her stepmother was flustered.

And even Ruth knew that this was uncivil, if not downright rude. And although she didn't care about Ada's susceptibilities, she was sorry for her father, who had been dragged innocently into this strange situation. It was Joseph Lorrimer who answered her.

'No,' he said. 'We wouldn't dream of imposing on you. As a matter of fact I am about to take my wife out to lunch – to the Waverly Hotel.' He stood up and offered a hand to Ada. 'Hawway, pet, forget the Dainty Café. Let's make a day of it.'

Ruth was proud of her father at that moment. He was obviously puzzled by their strange reception but he had enough social awareness to know that his wife was somehow being slighted. No doubt he would believe it was something to do with the fact that Miss Golightly was of a different social class and, fiercely proud, he would not stay here to be made to feel inferior. He turned and looked doubtfully at his daughter.

'Are you sure this is all right, lass? Do you want to stay?'

Ruth saw the look of panic that crossed Ada's flushed face and she felt like crying. Not because her stepmother didn't want her – she was used to that – but because this was the first time her father had asked her what her wishes might be. Until this moment he had gone along happily with his wife's plans.

Ruth felt tears pricking at the back of her eyes and a hot lump of misery rose in her throat. She swallowed and tried to stop her voice trembling when she answered, 'It's all right, I'll stay.'

No one spoke for a moment; then Ada tucked her hand into the crook of her husband's arm and they turned to leave the room.

'Wait, Ada,' Miss Golightly said. 'I'd like to say I'm pleased for you.'

'Are you? Why?'

'I'm pleased that you have married again and that you seem to have found such a decent man.'

'Well, then,' Ada was only half mollified, 'Joseph and me will take our leave.'

At the door Ruth's father turned and said, 'Well, now, Ruthie, I'll say goodbye.' Ruth couldn't stop herself: she ran across the room and flung her arms round her father. He stooped and hugged her. 'Now then, lass,' he said awkwardly.

Ruth stepped back and smiled at him but she couldn't trust herself to speak.

'Flora will see you out,' Miss Golightly said, and she rose from her chair. Ruth was surprised to see how tall she was. She walked slowly towards the fireplace and pulled a thick twisted cord that hung from the ceiling. It had a fringed tassel on the end. 'It's a bell pull,' she said, when she saw Ruth's puzzled expression. 'Now a bell will ring in the kitchen and Flora will know that I want her.'

A moment later the young maid knocked and entered the room. Joseph Lorrimer sent his daughter one last smile, then he and Ada left, closing the door behind them.

Miss Golightly settled herself in her chair once more. Ruth noticed that her face was strained with pain when she moved. 'You think I was rude to your stepmother, don't you?' she asked.

Ruth was surprised and remained silent.

'Oh, it's all right. I saw it in your face. Well, I admit I was rude, but then I was cross.'

'Why?'

'Sit down, child – look, there's an ottoman you can drag over – you can sit at my feet and then I won't have to strain to catch those fleeting expressions of yours.'

Ruth did as she was told. The ottoman was covered in soft leather in shades of tan and brown. The pattern was faded but it looked oriental. When she had settled herself beside Miss Golightly she was aware of the scent of her perfume; it was heady, exotic. She would have expected lavender. But she was beginning to realize that her employer was someone who might always surprise her.

'I was vexed because I didn't expect to see her and, try as I might, I never liked her as well as I should,' Miss Golightly continued as if there had been no interruption. 'Does that answer you?'

'Not really.'

'Why not?'

'Because, until I came here today, I didn't know that you knew my stepmother.'

'She didn't tell you?' Miss Golightly paused. 'Obviously not. Ada's first husband was a connection of mine.'

'Connection?'

'That's a way of saying he was a relation ... family ... a distant cousin. You needn't know the precise details but my grandmother's sister made a poor marriage. You will know the expression "she married beneath her"?'

'I've heard it.'

'Well, that's what she did, but the family always looked after her and her descendants. There was always work for them at the factory. Golightly's mineral waters, you know.'

'Oh.' Ruth thought of the bottles of soda water, seltzer, lemonade and ginger beer to be found in every corner shop. This was something else Ada hadn't mentioned. It was as if, once she had met Joseph Lorrimer, her previous life had become totally unimportant to her. Until she wanted to get rid of Joseph's daughter, that was.

'You see, Ada's first husband worked in the factory, and when she discovered that he was also related to the family – my nephew runs the business now – she thought she'd gone up in the world – socially, I mean. I suppose I shouldn't blame her. She tried to behave well – sent cards at Christmas, called to see me. Perhaps I should have made her more welcome but I simply didn't take to her. I'm sorry.'

'Why sorry?'

'You may be fond of her.'

'I'm not.'

There was a moment of silence and then: 'Well, well,' Miss Golightly said. 'I think you and I will get on very well. Not because you're not fond of poor Ada, but because you are direct and honest. Do you want to know what your duties are to be?'

'Yes, please.'

'Look around this room. My household staff despairs of it. They want to be always dusting and polishing – and so they should – but they will interfere with my books. Closing them and putting them back on the shelves and then I can never find anything. So, part of your duties here will be simple housework. Or rather, it won't be quite so simple because you'll have to dust and tidy without disturbing anything. Do you think you can do that?'

'I'll try.' Ruth looked apprehensive.

'Don't worry.' Miss Golightly smiled. 'You needn't do it too often – just enough to keep Mrs Fairbridge, my housekeeper, from pulling long faces. But your other duties will be to read to me, run errands, for example to the library, post letters and maybe write them for me, take me out in my Bath chair, although,' Miss Golightly looked at Ruth doubtfully, 'you seem to be small for your age, and I wonder if you will be strong enough for that? Never mind. As you said yourself, you will be my little factotum.'

Ruth smiled, acknowledging her new employer's implied approval.

'In Ada's misspelt letter she said that you were a good scholar,' Miss Golightly went on, 'but I half suspected she was singing your praises in order to encourage me to take you off her hands.' She paused. 'You have nothing to say to that, Ruth? Very wise.

'Now, I am a little tired. You can ring for Flora and I shall ask her to take you and your belongings to your room. I'll send for you after lunch.'

'Get your things sorted out and then find your way down to the kitchen. You'll be taking your meals with us,' Flora said. 'And don't take too

91

long. Mrs Fairbridge doesn't like to be kept waiting.' Still without a smile she left Ruth in her room on the third floor.

It was an attic room, quite small, and the bed was tucked in the space under the eaves. Just as well I'm not very tall, Ruth thought, or I'd be forever bumping my head when I get out of bed in the morning.

Everything was clean and fresh. The wallpaper was pale pink with a darker pink stripe in it, the quilt was rose-patterned, as were the curtains, and the floorboards were stained a light oak colour. There was a rug for her to step on to beside the bed, a chest of drawers with a jug and a washbasin on top and a single wardrobe with a mirror set in the door. An oil lamp stood on the night table.

Ruth began to unpack her bag and put her clothes away. She could barely concentrate. Her mind was in a state of turmoil. She had been dreading coming here. Not only had she not wanted to leave her father but her hopes of becoming a pupil teacher had been dashed. She had imagined that her life was ruined. But now it seemed that her life was not going to be so bad after all.

Miss Foster had said that she would always be able to go to the library if she wished to further her education. Well, now it seemed that going to the library was to be part of her duties. And even without the library this house was full of books – and she was going to be paid to read them.

Miss Golightly was strange – Ruth thought the best word to describe her would be eccentric – and although she had been brusque with Ada, she had later tried to explain why.

It was only then that Ruth realized that Miss Golightly had talked to her as if she were an adult ... and an equal. No, not that ... she had dismissed her when she had done talking and told her that she would send for her after lunch. And she was to eat in the kitchen with the servants, not with Miss Golightly. So she was not an equal. And yet, Ruth believed that she was not quite a servant. She would have to tread carefully. She had already sensed that Flora didn't like her. Was it as strong as that? Did the housemaid's unsmiling face signify dislike?

She was done. She closed the wardrobe and moved hesitantly towards the door. She hoped she hadn't taken too long; she didn't want to cause trouble for herself on her very first day by annoying the housekeeper.

The house was quiet and, as she made her way down the stairs, a knot of tension tightened inside her. She had realized that she could be happy here after all – but that might depend on what sort of welcome awaited her in the kitchen.

'Look, Lucy, come back!'

'What is it?' Lucy stopped and turned to her mother, who had paused before one of the displays in Bainbridge's window.

'Aren't those silk shirts beautiful?'

'For goodness' sake, I thought you'd fallen over, shouting like that!'

'I didn't shout. I simply spoke loud enough to attract your attention.'

Daisy Shaw turned away to gaze at the display

once more and Lucy joined her unwillingly. The school summer holidays were drawing to an end but the weather had held and the day was warm. The smell of horse droppings, no matter how quickly the roads were cleaned, fouled the air, even in these, the smartest of the city streets. Lucy had had enough of window shopping and she sighed as she walked back to join her mother.

'They're not shirts – they're ladies' blouses,' Lucy said.

'No – look at the display card. It says, "Ladies' Silk Shirts, for cycling, boating and country walks."'

Lucy frowned. 'Well, they look just like blouses to me. All those frills and lace trimmings – I can't imagine doing anything energetic in one of those.'

'Honestly, child, sometimes I despair of you. I've endeavoured to bring you up to appreciate the finer things in life and you can't even see the difference between a blouse and a shirt.'

Lucy glanced quickly at her mother to see if she was joking. No, she thought, she's quite serious. I wonder if she knows that, no matter how much I love her, I sometimes despair of *her?* Daisy Shaw was gazing raptly at the shirts. Lucy saw one of her mother's hands rise to finger her lace collar and she knew that she was imagining wearing one of the shirts, the one with the high frilled neck and the floppy white satin bow.

'Fifty-two shillings,' her mother murmured. 'That's more than most working men earn in a week.' She sighed and shook her head. 'Ah, well, I don't suppose I shall be cycling, or boating, or walking in the country in the near future.'

Lucy tried not to smile. 'But do look at these blouses,' she said, moving to the next display. 'Don't you like that blue striped silk trimmed with lace?'

'Where? Oh, I do – and it's so much more feminine!'

'And the blue is just the colour of your eyes – and look, it's only twenty-one shillings.'

'I don't believe it! Oh, but that's still expensive. Lucy, what do you think? I mean, do you imagine your father would think me extravagant if...?'

'I'm sure he wouldn't,' Lucy assured her truthfully. For, although she sometimes heard her parents discussing their household budget, she knew that they were not exactly poor, and that her father, so long as his wife was not too extravagant, liked to indulge her. It was as if he wanted to make it up to her for all the times he had to work away from home.

Once inside the department store, Lucy had to steer her mother past all the delightful distractions such as perfume and jewellery towards the stairs that took them to ladies' wear. Daisy Shaw was even more delighted with the blouse when she saw it close up and flushed with pleasure when the young shop assistant asked her if she would like to buy a second blouse for her 'sister'.

Lucy didn't know whether to be pleased for her mother or vexed on her own behalf until she realized that the assistant was a very clever young person who knew just how to flatter a customer into spending more money than she had intended. And in this instance she was successful; in spite of Lucy's protestations, her mother bought her an

95

identical blouse.

She had noticed more and more, of late, that her mother liked them to have matching ensembles. Lucy didn't mind at all if some of the clothes were a little grown up for her, but she was beginning to be embarrassed by the fact that others were too young for her mother. She wasn't sure how long it was since she had realized that her mother was older than her father. She still didn't know by how many years and it was only recently that she had realized that her mother, no matter how much she tried to conceal it, was anxious about the difference.

'Now,' her mother said as they made their way out of the shop, 'before we go home I'm going to treat you to afternoon tea at Tilley's. Would you like that?'

'Lovely,' Lucy said, knowing and not minding that the treat was as much for her mother as for herself.

Tilley's Café and Restaurant served morning coffee, table d'hôte lunch, afternoon teas and table d'hôte dinner. By the time Lucy and her mother arrived and had climbed the stairs to the large first-floor room overlooking Blackett Street, it was almost too late for afternoon tea and the waitresses were clearing off the tables and setting them up again with clean white tablecloths, fresh cutlery and the dinner menus in silver-plated holders.

Daisy Shaw smiled winningly at the young waitress, who hurried forward, and indicated with a graceful gesture that she wished to sit at one of the tables near the window. The window tables had already been prepared for dinner but the girl

96

responded to Daisy's charm and in no time at all, it seemed, they were served with bread and butter, a dish of strawberry jam, scones and a cake stand containing most of the remaining pastries, including some delicious-looking meringues.

After a while, when her mother had eaten daintily but nevertheless as eagerly as a school child, savouring every crumbling bite of baked sugar and cream, she dabbed at her lips delicately with the linen napkin and leaned back in her chair. Her next words took Lucy by surprise.

'I wonder what will become of your poor little friend.'

'My friend?'

'Esther. She's not going back to school, is she?'

'No. She told me she'll have to find work.'

'Poor child. I wonder what she'll do. She'll hardly find agreeable employment.'

'Agreeable?'

'In a shop or an office.' Lucy's mother smiled and shook her head as if acknowledging how unlikely this was. 'I imagine she'll end up in the soda works or the bottle works – they're both near enough to where she lives. Or the ropery – oh, her poor hands!'

Lucy looked at her mother's face and saw that she was genuinely moved by the imagined hardship that would most likely befall Esther. Suddenly she realized why she loved her mother so much. She might be what some would call frivolous, but she was genuinely kind. She had always tried to impress on Lucy that they were better than their neighbours and yet, moved by compassion, she had invited Esther to call and see them whenever she wanted to.

'And Ruth – she's not going back to school either, is she?' her mother said.

'No. Poor Ruth, she wanted to, she wanted to become a teacher, but her stepmother found her a job looking after some old lady.'

'Poor child. I know what it is to have your ambition thwarted.'

'Do you?' Lucy was startled.

Her mother saw her expression and laughed. 'Oh, childhood dreams, you know.' Her smile was as lovely as ever but there was a bitter edge to the laughter. 'But now there's something I want to tell you. You know your father said that you could go back to school if you wanted to ... that you were to think about it?'

'Yes, and I'm sorry, but I still don't know. I'm not clever in the way Ruth is. I don't want to be a teacher or anything.'

'I should hope not. You'd never find the right sort of husband if you were a schoolmistress – in fact most of them don't seem to marry at all!'

Lucy sighed. She didn't want to go back to school and, if the truth were known, she didn't want to find employment. She imagined that in her case, her mother would regard agreeable employment as having a job in one of the better department stores.

'Well, dear,' her mother said, 'we've made the decision for you. Your father and I. You *are* going back to school but not that one. You are going to go to a most respectable private establishment where not only will you learn elocution and deportment – and dancing is an optional extra –

but you will be taught typewriting and office skills. Isn't that wonderful?'

'A private school?'

'Mm.' Her mother nodded and smiled.

'Can we afford it?'

The slightest of frowns clouded her mother's brow before she said, 'Your father can afford it. And besides, he always promised... I mean he said he would look after you.'

'Well, of course.' Lucy was puzzled. She wasn't quite sure what her mother meant. Her father was kind and generous; she had never doubted that he would look after her.

'Lucy – don't frown. Oh dear, I thought the news would please you. That's why I brought you here to Tilley's. I wanted it to be part of the treat.'

'The news does please me, really it does. It just took me by surprise, that's all.'

'You like the idea?'

'Yes, I do.' And Lucy realized that she did. She would enjoy learning deportment and elocution – and optional dancing. And typewriting and office skills sounded interesting. 'Where is the school? In Jesmond?'

'No. The school is at the coast, in Whitley-by-the Sea. You will go on the train each day. Won't that be fun?'

'I suppose so. I mean, yes, it will be.'

'Good. Now, would you add some hot water to the teapot, Lucy? I need another cup of tea. That's right – oh, and lift the lid and stir it a little, otherwise it will be too weak.'

Lucy poured more tea for her mother and then herself, then she turned her head to look out of the window once more. A road sweeper was busy near the foot of Lord Grey's monument and queues were forming at the tram stops. A stream of people flowed from one of the exits of the Grainger Market.

'Oh, no,' Lucy said, 'if the market's closing, we'll have to queue for ages for a tram.'

She glanced at her mother but Daisy Shaw merely smiled. She took another sip of tea and then said, 'Well then, we shall simply have to get a cab home.'

Lucy could imagine the stir it would cause amongst their neighbours if they arrived home in a hansom cab. Her father caught a cab from the Central Station sometimes when he had been working away, and she knew that that raised eyebrows. But, on the whole, it was accepted that a man with a good position might be entitled to a certain standard of life. After all, he obviously worked most of the hours that God sent.

But the same neighbours who were prepared to be lenient with her father were not so forgiving towards Daisy Shaw. Ruth knew that they thought Daisy to be a snob and that she adopted airs above her station. But what was her mother's station in life? She spoke like a lady and had brought Lucy up to speak the same way. She had always impressed on her daughter the fact that they were a better sort of folk than the other inhabitants of Byker. It was only lately that Lucy had begun to wonder why they had chosen to live there in the first place.

'I don't mind queuing,' Lucy said.

'But I do. No, we'll get a cab.'

Chapter Four

December

'Put the books on the counter, Ruth, then you can sit down while you're waiting.'

'I'd rather look along the shelves.'

'That's all right, dear.' Miss Matthews smiled as she glanced over her half-moon spectacles. 'It's a pity you haven't a subscription of your own, though. It must be frustrating for you carrying all these books to and fro for Miss Golightly and never being able to choose something for yourself. Have you got her list? Oh, here it is, in the bag.'

Miss Matthews began to check the books Ruth had brought back. She took the tickets from the narrow wooden trays on a shelf at her side of the counter, slipped them back into the little cardboard pockets that were glued inside the front covers of each book, and then placed the books on a wooden trolley. There they would wait until she had time to return them to their proper places on the shelves.

The premises that housed the Crystal Library had once been a double-fronted grocery store and, although the shop fittings had long ago been removed and replaced with bookshelves, the echoes of its former use remained in faint odours of tea and coffee, the powdery-sweet scent of biscuits and other confectioneries, and, now and then, the smell of cheese. But that was only on hot days in the summer. Today Miss Matthews wore a warm woollen shawl over her shoulders pinned together at the front with a cameo brooch.

Shoppers hurried along Park View with collars turned up against the wind. Older people walked more carefully, allowing the cold wind to cut through to the bone rather than risk taking a tumble on the icy pavements. It was hardly any warmer inside, Ruth thought.

Pale sunlight flooded through the windows and illumined the spines of the books waiting so neatly on the shelves. Miss Matthews saw that each book stood up straight with its bottom edge perfectly aligned with the edge of the shelf. Not one book was allowed to protrude any further than another. How different these shelves were from those at Miss Golightly's home, where the volumes stood or lay at all angles; some lying flat on top of others and some hidden away completely at the back of the shelf, and probably forgotten about.

Not long after Ruth had started work there Miss Golightly had instructed her to get the books in order and perhaps to catalogue them. Ruth had not liked to admit that she didn't know what 'catalogue' meant, so that night she had looked it up in the dictionary that she had smuggled up to keep under her pillow. She learned that a catalogue was a list of items usually in some sort of order, perhaps alphabetical, and with some description. Often

102

arranged under headings according to subject.

The next day she had looked round at the bookshelves and despaired. To catalogue Miss Golightly's books would be a daunting task. If she could summon up enough confidence she might ask Miss Matthews for her advice. But, in truth, she hoped that Miss Golightly would forget about it. And there was a chance that she might, for since Ruth had come to stay with her she had seemed to lose interest in reading any of her own books, and had been borrowing more and more books from the library, reading them feverishly and making notes.

Ruth was never allowed to see the notes and she couldn't imagine what they could be about, for the books she took home from the Crystal Library every week were not what her old teacher, Miss Foster, would have called textbooks. They were all novels of one sort or another, but mostly romantic novels. Ruth knew this because sometimes Miss Golightly would ask Ruth to read aloud to her.

Miss Matthews had smiled with surprise when she had seen the first of such lists that Ruth had brought her. 'Yes, we have all of them,' she had said. 'They're very popular. In fact *Thelma* by Marie Corelli always goes out the very same day it comes back in!' The way she had stressed the word 'popular' hinted that Miss Golightly had not always read such books.

Ruth watched the librarian now, a tall, thin figure in dark clothes and fingerless mittens, moving along the shelves, selecting books and cradling them in her arms like precious babies.

103

Her face was pale and her light brown hair was secured in what was intended to be a severe bun at the nape of her neck, but strands of hair had escaped the pins and hung wispily around her face. She had developed a habit of sticking out her lower lip and puffing upwards to move the wisps away from her field of vision. Ruth wondered if she knew she did this.

'Do you like that sort of book?' Ruth turned to find Miss Matthews behind her.

'What sort of book?'

'*The Master of Greylands* by Mrs Henry Wood.'

'I don't know what sort of book it is.'

'It's a detective novel, but the detective is a woman. Such fun.' Miss Matthews took the book from the shelf and opened it, glancing at the pages. 'Madame Charlotte Guise becomes a governess – but her motive is to investigate the disappearance of her husband.'

'So it's a kind of mystery?' Ruth said.

'Yes, dear. And, do you know, I love such books. And, as a matter of fact, I wouldn't be so surprised if Miss Golightly read this kind of novel. I mean, I know they can't be taken seriously, but they do exercise the mind. Whereas...' Miss Matthews replaced the book and, turning, she gestured towards the counter where she had placed Miss Golightly's order, '...those books are so – so frivolous, aren't they?'

'Frivolous? You mean because they're love stories?'

'Mm. I do. And don't you find it strange?'

'Why should it be strange?'

'That such a serious-minded, not to say, clever,

woman as Miss Golightly, should enjoy such works?'

Ruth frowned as she recalled the way Miss Golightly would listen while she read to her, her expression rapt, a look of interest and anticipation in her eyes. 'No, I don't think so,' she said. 'Perhaps she likes to escape for a while.'

'Escape?'

'From everyday life. Enter a different world, a world where everything is all right at the end.'

Miss Matthews raised her eyebrows. 'My, you are a clever child. In fact, sometimes I forget I am talking to a girl who has so recently left school. And, yes, you're probably right. Most, if not all, of the ladies who borrow books from this library want to escape, as you put it, for an hour or so.'

'And what about you?' Ruth regretted her spontaneous question as soon as she saw Miss Matthews' reaction. The librarian stiffened and drew apart as if she had suddenly remembered that the girl she was talking to might be clever, but was also a servant. 'I'm sorry,' Ruth said, 'I shouldn't have asked.'

'No, that's all right.' Miss Matthews shrugged and walked towards the counter. 'I don't mind admitting that I too am escaping into a different world when I read detective novels. A world where great crimes have been committed, but where some clever man – or woman – makes sure that justice is served and order is restored by the time you reach the last page.'

Ruth watched while Miss Matthews removed the tickets and stamped the books with the return date. She found herself wondering how old Miss Matthews was. Her face was unlined, but her hair was very slightly streaked with grey. She wasn't old – her eyes were clear and her voice was firm – but neither was she a girl. Young middle-aged, Ruth thought, and a spinster.

She wondered whether Miss Matthews was happy spending her life as the keeper of the books; dispensing information and entertainment with every volume. Perhaps she was, but she was also lonely.

As lonely as I am? Ruth mused as she packed the new books carefully into the bag. I don't live alone but there is no one I am close to. Miss Golightly is imperious and can be difficult, but she is fair and often kind. I am not treated cruelly. Mrs Fairbridge is civil and I've learned that Flora's miserable ways are due to her disposition rather than dislike of me. Poor little Meg, the scullery maid, even seeks my friendship, but she's never allowed to sit and talk for more than five minutes.

'Well, then, Ruth,' Miss Matthews said, 'off you go. I'll be closing for my lunch now.'

'Oh, I'm sorry. Have I been dawdling?'

'Don't worry, dear.' Miss Matthews walked to the door with Ruth, turned over a card hanging in the window so that the 'closed' side faced the street and then, to Ruth's surprise, came out with her and turned and locked the door.

Ruth watched in surprise as Miss Matthews selected another key from the ring in her hand and opened the door that lay in between the library and the shop next to it, a florist's. The librarian turned and smiled. 'I live upstairs,' she said. 'I make a point of going home in the lunch hour and we have a light meal together.' She must have seen Ruth's surprise for she added, 'My brother and I.'

Ruth said goodbye and began to hurry in order not to be late for her own midday meal. She found herself thinking about Miss Matthews. She imagined her hurrying up the stairs to set her brother's 'light' meal before him and then the two of them would gossip about the events of the morning. Perhaps that was why Miss Matthews had never married; perhaps she'd had to keep house for her elderly bachelor brother. Whatever the circumstance, Ruth was pleased that the librarian was not as lonely as she had imagined her to be.

And what of my own circumstances? she thought. I should be thankful that I'm going home to a hot meal, that I have a warm bed and that my washing is done for me. That I am paid a salary that, meagre as it is, is still sufficient to allow me to save a little and to take the train home on my days off, even if I am not welcome there. And, this afternoon, my duties as companion mean that I am going to a concert. My life is so much better than I thought it would be, so why is it that I am so far from being contented?

'Please come and stay with us for Christmas, Lucy. We'll have a marvellous time!'

'I can't, Julia, really I can't. I don't want to leave my mother on her own.'

'On her own? But surely your father will be there, won't he?'

Lucy frowned. It was nearly the end of term and she and Julia Wright were tidying the school stationery cupboard. They had offered to do it because it meant they would be excused from Miss Lambert's extra lesson on how to answer the telephone. Both Lucy and Julia had learned how to answer the telephone the first time Miss Lambert had brought the dummy instruments into the classroom, and they couldn't understand the girls who were reduced to terror the moment they picked up the receiver. Neither did they find it necessary to put on a funny voice as some girls did, and when this behaviour reduced the rest of the class to helpless giggles, Lucy and Julia would raise their eyebrows in exasperation.

So, this afternoon, they were cosily ensconced in the long, thin room that served as the stationery store. Shelves and cupboards reduced the floor space to a narrow strip of polished boards, but there was a conveniently wide windowledge where they could sit as they were doing now and indulge in gossip.

Lucy sat with her feet resting on a wide brown-painted hot-water pipe that ran along the skirting board, coming in through one wall and vanishing through the other. She turned to look through the window. It was late afternoon and the sky was darkening. She gazed across the frost-bound central gardens towards the tall houses beyond. The school had once been two large private houses at the seaward end of a residential square. Miss Jackson, the headmistress, who also owned the school, had been born in one of the houses and, as she had approached middle age

108

without finding a husband, her father, a successful solicitor, had bought the house next door and paid for the two properties to be converted. He and her mother had then retired to a pleasant house in Morpeth.

Miss Jackson stayed on, living in an apartment formed from the attic rooms of both houses, and running the school in an enthusiastic but somewhat haphazard fashion. Lucy had soon learned that, even though she wasn't as clever as Ruth Lorrimer, she was the intellectual superior of every other pupil in Miss Jackson's establishment. If her fellow pupils had had better brains they would have been sent to one of the schools in Newcastle.

Lucy supposed that her parents wouldn't have known this. Or more likely they couldn't afford to send her to a better school. Not that this was a bad school. The teachers did their best for the girls and it wasn't their fault if the best they could achieve for most of them would be the position of a lowly filing clerk. But a few of Miss Jackson's pupils would probably never need to find employment; they were there simply to take advantage of the lessons in deportment and French. Like Julia – who was frowning at her now.

'Lucy Shaw! I asked you a question!'

Lucy sighed. She was aware suddenly that she had slumped against the window and the cold had struck through to her shoulder. She moved forward and rubbed her shoulder with her other hand. 'A question?' she asked.

Julia spoke slowly and deliberately as if to a recalcitrant child. 'I asked you if your father would be with your mother for Christmas. A silly question, I know, but you might have given me some kind of answer instead of just staring out of the window!'

'I'm sorry, Julia. My father works long hours, even over the holidays, and especially at Christmas. My mother gets fretful while she's waiting for him.'

'And there's only you to comfort her?'

'Yes. Well, there's Betty, of course, but she doesn't live in, and my mother likes to let her get home to her own family as soon as she can.'

Julia stopped looking cross and smiled sympathetically. 'Yes, I know what it's like.'

'You do?' Lucy was surprised.

'Oh, I don't mean that my mother and I are on our own. As you know, I have an older brother, but my father may be called out at any time – at any hour. If the night bell rings, he has to go.'

'Oh...' Lucy didn't know how to respond. She knew that her friend's father was an undertaker but, instinctively, she had avoided thinking too closely about the day-to-day particulars of his trade.

'Well, anyway, will you at least ask your mother if you can come to us? See what she says?'

The sky was now dark enough to turn the windowpane into a looking-glass, and when Lucy turned her head away she saw not only her own uncertain frown reflected in the glass but also the intensity of the supplication in Julia's eyes.

Julia Wright was a large, clumsy girl who never seemed able to join in the light-hearted gossip of the others. She would often say the wrong thing entirely and, although her fellow pupils didn't dislike her, they found it hard work to have a conversation with her.

So, in spite of the fact that her family was comparatively wealthy and well-respected, Julia was often left out of things. Lucy had felt sorry for her. She had long known what it was like to feel different, although for entirely different reasons. From simply smiling and being prepared to sit beside her in class, the relationship had developed to a point where Julia considered Lucy to be her best friend. And now she wanted her to spend Christmas with her and her family.

'All right, Julia,' Lucy said at last. 'I will ask my mother, but I can't promise you anything.'

Julia's plain face was transformed by her smile. 'Don't worry. I'm sure your mother will agree. After all, she wouldn't want to spoil your fun, would she?'

Lucy wasn't so sure about that.

The lamplighter was busy in the square below, creating pools of light amidst the shadows. The central gardens had become a mysterious area of frosted shapes. Lights were going on in the houses at the other side of the square and curtains were being drawn against the chill evening air.

Running footsteps in the corridor behind them, accompanied by the ringing of the bell, signalled the end of the school day and Lucy was very glad that she had the excuse of having to rush to catch her train home.

Lucy hurried up through the town to the railway station. The air was bitingly cold and she was glad of her coat's large fur collar, which could be pulled up to form a hood, and of her matching fur mittens. As she passed a brightly lit parade of shops she paused to look in the window of the sweet shop. She didn't want to buy anything but her eye had been caught by the attractive display.

The tall shelves that filled the window were crowded with glass jars of boiled sweets: black jacks, humbugs, pear drops, aniseed balls, raspberry drops and peppermints. Here and there were taller jars containing sticks of rock with candy stripes and tins of fruit gums and scented cachous. Many of the jars bore the blue and gold labels of the firm her father worked for, including the large jar of pink and white sugar mice. She smiled, remembering the way Esther's eyes had widened as picked up the little mouse by its string tail that day in her house – the way Esther and Ruth had smiled at each other as if they shared a pleasing memory.

Lucy turned to go and someone called out, 'Have a care!'

She pulled back just in time to prevent herself falling into the lap of an old woman in a wheelchair. The person who had called out was Ruth Lorrimer.

'Ruth!' Lucy gasped. 'I've just been thinking about you!'

'Hush,' Ruth warned, and with a nod of her head she indicated the old lady. 'Miss Golightly is asleep,' she said softly. 'I'd rather she stayed that way until we get home.'

The two girls stared at each other, smiling but embarrassed. Lucy was pleased to see Ruth but she didn't know what to say. The light from the sweet shop window fell across the bundled-up figure of the old woman. Only her head and neck emerged from the cocoon formed by a bright tartan rug. Her neck was protected from the cold by a grey woollen scarf, and wispy strands of grey hair emerged from beneath the brim of a black hat trimmed with feathers. The light from the sweet shop window glinted on the twin moons of the old lady's spectacles, making it difficult to see whether her eyes were open or not.

Lucy remained silent so Ruth said, 'We've been to afternoon tea at the Waverly Hotel. But it was a sort of concert. A young man played the piano. The programme was light classical, he said. Nothing too dramatic.' She paused and grinned. 'It sent Miss Golightly to sleep.'

Lucy smiled in response and, keeping her voice low as Ruth had done, she asked, 'Do you have far to go?'

Ruth shook her head and took one hand from the chair to point at the tall row of houses at the other side of the road. 'Over there. We're nearly home.'

'So near,' Lucy breathed.

'Mm?' Ruth frowned and looked at her questioningly.

'I mean, you've been living here all this time and the school I go to is a mere five minutes' walk away.'

Miss Golightly stirred and both girls looked at her anxiously but she didn't say anything and they assumed she was still sleeping.

'Do you like–' they began simultaneously and

113

stopped and smiled and waited for the other to finish the sentence, the unspoken words hanging in the air on their frosted breath.

Eventually Lucy said, 'Yes, I like my school. And you?'

'My employment? It's not what I wanted but it's not too bad,' Ruth said.

They fell silent again. Lucy was aware of the cold striking up through the soles of her winter boots. 'I'll have to go. My mother doesn't like it if I'm late home.'

'Of course not.' Ruth smiled understandingly.

'But we must meet each other again – I mean properly. Do you come home to Byker on your days off?'

'Sometimes.'

'But you've never called to see us.'

'No ... I'm sorry. My father, you know ... I like to spend time with him.'

'Of course.'

'Does Esther come to see you?' Ruth asked.

Lucy smiled. 'Yes, she does. I think she would like to live with us! It's just as well her job keeps her working long hours.'

'Her job?'

'She works at Fowler's. As a matter of fact my mother was surprised that Esther managed to get a job in a respectable shop, but from what she tells us I think they keep her in the cellar!'

They both laughed and then simultaneously looked shame-faced. 'It's hard to lose old habits, isn't it?' Lucy said. 'I shouldn't make fun of her, especially as she looks so clean and respectable these days.'

'I'm glad,' Ruth said. 'I know how hard her life has been.'

'Are you going home for Christmas?' Lucy asked suddenly.

'On Christmas Eve – but late.'

'Oh. And I suppose your parents will want you with them on Christmas Day?'

Ruth glanced away. Lucy couldn't see her expression when she murmured, 'They're going to my stepmother's parents' house. My stepmother doesn't really want me to – I mean, I'd rather not go with them.'

'Then come to us!' Lucy said, forgetting to be quiet. 'My mother would love to have you join us.'

'Are you sure?'

'Of course I am. You know what she's like!'

'Yes, I do,' Ruth said, and she smiled as if she were remembering.

'She'll make a party of it!' Lucy exclaimed. 'I'll ask Esther too.'

'I don't suppose she'll come without her brother.'

'That's all right. Betty will clean him up if necessary.' They were both smiling again.

Then Ruth frowned. 'But what will your father say?'

'My father might not be there.'

'Not there? On Christmas Day?'

'No ... he ... he has to visit some old aunt who brought him up. She lives alone. It's a duty. He's done that as long as I can remember.'

'But why couldn't she come to you?' Ruth looked and sounded surprised.

'She lives in York. My mother says she's too old

115

to travel ... and, anyway, we don't have room for her to stay.'

Lucy saw Ruth's frown and she hoped that she wouldn't ask her why, in that case, they didn't all go to stay with her father's aunt for Christmas. The truth was that Lucy didn't know the answer. The matter had simply not been discussed over the years and, as Lucy got older, she had sensed that her mother did not wish to talk about it.

And that was why she couldn't possibly go to Julia Wright's house for Christmas. Why, she wouldn't even ask her mother, even though she had promised Julia that she would. If Lucy were not there her mother would spend a miserably lonely day on her own.

'Oh, do come to us on Christmas Day, Ruth!' Lucy said again. 'Please say that you will!'

'Yes ... I'd like that.'

Both girls smiled and began to laugh, and stopped when they heard the church clock chime the half-hour.

'Half-past four!' Lucy exclaimed. 'I've missed the train. Oh, it's all right,' she said when she saw Ruth's expression. 'Don't worry. There's another one in half an hour, and there'll be a fire in the waiting room.'

'Good,' Miss Golightly said, startling both girls out of their wits. 'I'm sick of listening to this chatter. So now that you've got your social arrangements for Christmas Day sorted out you'd better run along to the station, miss, and sit by that fire. Ruth will take me home before I freeze to death.'

Ruth had coloured. 'I'm sorry, Miss Golightly.'

She began to manoeuvre the wheelchair round so that it would face the kerb.

'So you should be. And from the tone of your voice I can tell you're wondering how much of your conversation I've heard.'

Ruth didn't answer, but she glanced at Lucy helplessly before setting off with the wheelchair.

'Take care!' Miss Golightly exclaimed. 'Do you want to tip me out of this contraption on to the road? Hold on – there's a tram coming!'

Lucy watched as Ruth waited for the horse-drawn tram to rattle by and then crossed the road with the crotchety old lady. She followed, but kept a respectful distance.

In the silence that fell when the tram had passed by, she heard Miss Golightly say, 'Well, miss, I'm glad that you consider that working for me is not too bad. Hey?'

Lucy didn't know whether that last imperious word signified anger or amusement until Ruth turned and waved. The rueful smile on her friend's face told her that all was well.

The station lamps were lit and, as Lucy hurried along the platform, she could see the cheerful glow of the fire reflected in the windows of the waiting room. The room was empty, but then she had only just missed the train so in all probability other passengers would join her within the next half-hour. Unless they chose to have a hot drink in the refreshment room in the main concourse while they waited.

Lucy had been carrying her schoolbag over her shoulder. She had just eased it off and placed it on the bench seat beside her, when an icy blast

117

informed her that the door had opened. She had been hoping for some time alone in order to think about her meeting with Ruth and what she would say to Julia, so she was frowning when she looked up to see who had come in.

'You're late today, miss. Were you kept in after school?'

'Oh, it's you, Arthur.' Lucy's features eased into a smile when she realized it was only one of the station porters. Nevertheless, she wasn't altogether pleased to see him. Now he would want to stay and talk – and he did go on so. 'No, I wasn't kept in.'

'Been a good little lass today, then? Top of the class?' Arthur laughed. His voice was rough but not disrespectful. This was his idea of teasing and he meant no harm.

Lucy knew that he wasn't much older than she was. She'd had her fifteenth birthday only a few weeks ago and Arthur was eighteen. He'd told her so himself, and he'd also told her that he had started working for the railway company as a lamp lad, 'a lampy', as soon as he had left school at the age of fourteen. It had been his job to clean and trim and light all the oil lamps at the station, including those at the front and the back of trains. Also the interior lights, which were dropped in through the carriage roofs.

He was still officially a lamp porter, although now he had a younger lad working under him. And he had begun to take on other duties: looking after both passengers and goods. Arthur had also volunteered to help look after the small gardens at each end of both platforms and to fill the flowerboxes and hanging baskets with blooms to suit the seasons. He even helped out in the stationmaster's own garden, he'd told Lucy. And he'd hinted that one day that might be his garden, along with the stationmaster's house.

Lucy watched as he half-kneeled to heap more coal on the fire. He needed a new uniform jacket, she decided. Not that it was shabby, far from it, but he had obviously grown since it was first issued. He wasn't much taller than she was, but he was stocky; his broad shoulders were straining all the seams. He'd pushed his cap back on his head and the firelight highlighted his broad forehead and glinted in his dark blond curls.

Arthur straightened up and turned to face her. His jacket was open and now she could see that his waistcoat was equally tight across his muscular chest. For some reason this unsettled her. She shivered and Arthur mistook the cause. 'Divven't worry, bonny lass. It won't be long before the room warms up.' He took a handkerchief from his pocket and wiped the coal dust from his hands.

'Thank you,' Lucy said.

She wanted him to go and yet she didn't. She loved the way he looked at her. Something in his eyes told her that he didn't regard her as a little schoolgirl. He'd actually asked her how old she was once and, when she'd told him, he'd looked disappointed. And then he'd laughed and made some joke about it not being long before she'd be sweet sixteen. When he'd added the words, 'and never been kissed,' he had flushed and looked away. Lucy had not been able to forget the feelings that had flooded through her, making her breathless and tongue-tied. Even the memories of that incident could induce a strange excitement.

Lucy knew that she looked older than her age. She was taller than her mother now and her body had developed a womanly shape. She knew that men found her attractive. Instinctively she knew how to interpret the expression in their eyes when they looked at her.

But her mother would be furious if she knew that Lucy allowed Arthur to talk to her like this. She had already begun to talk of her hopes for Lucy's future. And that future didn't include a railway porter.

Lucy was glad when the door opened and an elderly couple came in. They were smartly dressed and looked happy and excited as they talked about the variety show they were going to see at the Palace Theatre in town. Lucy learned that they planned to get a cab from the Central Station to the Haymarket and have a bite to eat downstairs in the coffee shop at Alvini's before the show.

She saw that Arthur was listening intently and then he turned to her with a smile. 'Would you like to gan to the theatre, Lucy?' he asked.

'What? I mean ... I beg your pardon. Do you mean with you?'

'I do.'

'Oh, but I couldn't. I mean, my mother wouldn't allow it.'

His smile faded. 'Of course not. You're only a bit lass. Silly of me. But one day, eh?'

'Perhaps. I don't know.'

Arthur looked at her keenly and, not seeming

to get the response he wanted, he shook his head and made for the door. Lucy turned her head and stared into the fire until she heard the door close behind him.

Esther was tired. She had been at work since half-past seven that morning and she hadn't stopped. Her back was aching and her feet were cold. Her fingers were almost numb, and several times she had dropped the scoop into the sack of sugar because she simply couldn't hold on to it. And yet her forehead felt clammy. Could you sweat when you were cold? she wondered. Could you be hot and cold at the same time? She hoped she wasn't coming down with something but the likelihood was that she was simply exhausted. And yet she was grateful to have this job.

She wiped her forehead with the back of her hand and then carried on filling the bags of sugar. A pile of folded blue sugar bags lay on the table. Esther took the bags one at a time, opened them up and placed them on the table. Then taking two scoops of sugar from the sack on the floor, she would fill the bag and place it on the scales. Then she would have to adjust the amount until the bag weighed exactly a pound. Or sometimes a half-pound. After folding the top down neatly she would place each bag in a cardboard box. When the box was full she carried it upstairs to the shop.

The cellar was cold and damp. The light from the single flaring gas jet was not enough to chase the shadows from the corners. Esther did not allow her thoughts to linger on the scratching and scuttling sounds that came from those corners. If anything was moving around down here, it remained out of sight.

Nothing was stored down here and the only piece of furniture was a large wooden table and a couple of chairs. It was Esther's job to keep the table scrubbed clean and she always seemed to be brushing flour or sugar, or whatever else she had been packing, from her clothes.

Sugar was not the only provision that Esther had to bag. Mr Fowler would carry down sacks of tea, flour, currants, raisins, sultanas, rice and salt, and Esther had learned how to deal with all of them. The worst thing was the dates that came packed solid in wooden chests. Esther needed a crowbar to dig into the box to prize the dates apart. The crowbar would get sticky so, every now and then, she would plunge it into a bucket of cold water. By the time she'd broken the lumps into three or four pounds, and then pounds and half pounds, everything was sticky, including her hair.

This was not what she had imagined her life would be like when she'd seen the notice 'Girl Wanted' in the window of Fowler's Grocery and Provision Store on Raby Street. Esther had thought that she would be standing behind the counter wearing a clean white pinafore, smiling at the customers as she served them.

The minute she saw the notice she had run straight home and boiled a kettle of water so that she could have a good wash. Fortunately for her, her mother had lain down and was gently snoring. Esther had seen the empty gin bottle but, this time, blessed it. For she was able to dress herself in one of the good dresses that Lucy's mother had given her and leave the house without being questioned. She would worry later about how she would get back in.

Fowler's was a busy shop and when she arrived Mr Fowler was harassed. He asked his wife to deal with Esther. Mrs Fowler had looked her up and down and then said, 'Come with me.' In no time at all, it seemed, Esther had left the sunny streets and was plunged into the darkness where from then on she was to spend most of her days.

The Fowlers were pleasant enough but they expected her to work as hard as they did. She was so grateful to have the job that she did her best to please. But instead of serving customers, as she had imagined she would, she could only hear them walking about above her head, and also the constant tinkle of the bell as the shop door opened and closed. It would be years before she would stand behind the counter. Meanwhile she had to serve a long apprenticeship and learn about the range of commodities sold and the use of the different scoops and knives needed to deal with them.

It didn't matter what she wore; the customers never saw her. But Mrs Fowler would inspect her nails and her hair, and Esther learned how to keep herself clean and tidy, and she protected her dresses as best she could with the pinafore the last girl had left behind when she had run off without notice.

The box of sugar was now full and Esther was just about to take it upstairs when Mr Fowler appeared.

'I'll take that, lass,' he said. 'Your brother's just arrived. You can take a break now.'

Davy had come straight from school. Not long after Esther had started work here, Mr Fowler had asked her if she knew of a capable boy to run errands and to make deliveries. 'A good lad's worth a half a crown,' he'd said.

Esther had hardly been able to believe her luck and now Davy joined her after school from Monday to Friday and all day on Saturday. He worked longer hours than he was paid for simply so that Esther could keep him with her rather than let him go home.

The situation there was bad. Her mother was still drinking and her father's temper was worse than ever. In the mornings they would all have breakfast together – although in Esther and Davy's case this meant no more than a slice of bread and dripping and a mug of tea.

After her father had left for work Esther would wash the pots for her mother, do as much of the housework as she had time for, and then slip back to the room she shared with Davy to change into one of her good dresses. She was still keeping them secret, although half the time her mother didn't seem to be capable of noticing what she was wearing.

Lucy Shaw's mother had given her more cast-off clothes since the day of the tea party. Esther had managed to keep them clean and ironed by simply taking over the duty of the weekly wash from her mother, who would sit by the fire, winter and summer, and stare into the flames with a glazed expression until roused by the need to cook her man's dinner.

If Agnes Robinson had ever had any pride in her home and family she had long since washed it away with cheap gin. In spite of the long hours she worked in the shop Esther had taken over many of the household duties and, in doing so, had probably saved her mother many a hiding. William Robinson now came home to a cleaner house than he ever had. But there was nothing Esther could do about her mother's evermore slapdash cooking; that was why she had taken on the responsibility of providing for her young brother herself.

When Esther left for work Davy would come with her. Mr and Mrs Fowler didn't mind. In fact they would more than likely find him a job, such as sweeping the pavement in front of the shop. Then they would give him a mug of hot, sweet tea to drink before he went to school. Esther would make sure that he took his bait with him rather than go home at midday. She wasn't sure whether their mam would be capable of making him anything to eat.

Esther had always looked out for Davy, ever since he was born. She had become more of a mother to him than a sister. As soon as she had seen him, a tiny scrap lying in the wooden box that served as a cradle, she had decided that he would survive; not like the two little brothers and a sister that had gone before.

Both Esther and Davy handed their wages over to their mother, but Esther had, from the start, kept sixpence of her own wages back. She gave her mother ten shillings, not telling her that her wages were really ten and sixpence. She felt no guilt. If she hadn't kept that sixpence back neither she nor, more importantly, Davy would have been properly fed.

Six pennies meant twenty-four farthings. One farthing would buy a couple of bread buns, and two a bag of scraps from the cooked meat counter. Esther took advantage of anything the Fowlers were selling off cheap and often they were kind to her. They appreciated how hard she worked, and Davy too.

Today she and her little brother feasted on a pork pie that had had its crust spoiled, and a handful of broken biscuits. Davy had brought a gill of milk for them to share, calling at the dairy on his way back from school. Esther was determined to look after her young brother now that their mam had grown so neglectful. She didn't blame her mam but she couldn't let Davy suffer.

Neither could she allow him to get in the way of their da's rage. She'd had to hold him back more than once when their da had clouted their mam. If Davy had got in the way one blow from his father's fist could have killed him. No, it was much better that her brother should be here with her where she could keep an eye on him.

After they had eaten Davy would set off on any errands that Mr Fowler had for him as well as starting the deliveries. Esther was anxious for him. He was only nine and he was small and skinny; the delivery bicycle was big and unwieldy. She always worried that he might have an accident. She'd heard how the lad from the greengrocer's had got his bicycle wheels caught in the tram lines and had toppled over. He would walk with crutches for the rest of his life. She didn't want anything like that to happen to Davy.

But Davy loved the bicycle and would almost have done the job for nothing for the chance to ride it. So Esther had taken him up and down the back lane, keeping him steady by holding on to the saddle, until the moment came when he'd shouted, 'Let go!' and he'd pedalled away grinning from ear to ear.

Davy promised Esther that he would always be careful. And he was. He enjoyed calling at all the different homes. More than one of the ladies had made something of a pet of him and they regularly gave him little treats, like a home-made jam tart or, sometimes, even a penny or two. If they did he handed the extra money to Esther. There was no need for their mam to know about that.

So even though Esther, and Davy too, worked long hours, sometimes until nine o'clock at night, and even longer on a Saturday, and even though Davy was sometimes so tired that he could hardly keep his eyes open as they walked home, Esther knew that life wasn't as bad as it could have been.

'How do you know that young madam Lucy, then?' Miss Golightly asked Ruth.
   'We were at school together.'
   'In Byker?' Miss Golightly sounded surprised.
   'Yes.'
   'In the same class?'
   'Yes.'

'She looks older than you. Sixteen or seventeen, I'd say.'

'No. I think she's just had her fifteenth birthday. And it will be my birthday in January.'

'So it will. Be careful, you're pulling!'

'I'm sorry.'

Miss Golightly was propped up in bed with a shawl around her shoulders while Ruth put the curling rags in her hair. Before she came to work here this had been one of Flora's duties and she had relinquished it gladly after showing Ruth how it was done.

Ruth had been surprised that a woman of Miss Golightly's age – actually she didn't know what that was exactly – should still be vain enough to want her hair curled. She never missed a night (and it must have been uncomfortable sleeping with all those knotted rags in her hair) and the sad thing was that halfway through the next day the curls would begin to fall out; especially if they went for a walk along the promenade and they were exposed to the sea air.

'And your friend is at Miss Jackson's school, I take it?'

'Yes.'

'That is a private school.'

'I know.'

'And yet they live in Byker?'

Ruth felt herself flushing. She knew perfectly well what Miss Golightly meant. She was surprised that anyone living where Ruth's family lived could afford to pay school fees.

'Yes, they do,' she said. 'They ... they have a nice house. Lucy's father is a salesman – the top salesman – I think, for Lawson's.'

'The confectionery firm?'

'Yes.'

'Well, well…'

Miss Golightly didn't say any more and, after Ruth had helped her to pull on her nightcap, she asked Ruth to hand her the book she was reading and dismissed her.

'I'll turn out the lamp myself,' she said. 'Now run down and ask Mrs Fairbridge for a cup of warm milk and a slice of fruit cake instead of plain bread and butter. If that young creature is only a few months older than you are I think we'd better build you up a little. Can't have them saying I'm neglecting you.'

As Ruth made her way down to the kitchen, she acknowledged that Miss Golightly had just come very close to admitting a proper concern for her. And that was more than ever could have been said for her stepmother.

'What a lovely idea!' Daisy Shaw said. 'Of course I shall invite your friends to join us on Christmas Day. You don't mind, do you, Reggie? After all, you won't be here, will you?'

Lucy saw how uncomfortable her father was, and she saw the way her parents looked at each other. To her consternation she saw her mother's eyes fill with tears. Her father stepped forward and took her mother in his arms. He kissed her brow and said, 'I think it's a very good idea. I'll bring some special presents to put round the tree. How many guests will there be? Ruth and Esther?'

129

Daisy stepped back and smiled. 'Oh, I don't suppose Esther will come without her little brother. You'd better arrange a gift for him too.'

'I shall. And I'll get the biggest tree I can – and some new baubles. We'll decorate it together.'

Her father took her mother's hand and kissed it. Once Lucy would have accepted this behaviour as evidence of how much they loved each other. But now she sensed that there was some underlying tension, that they were trying to convince each other all was well. And Lucy was shocked to discover that she didn't believe it was.

Suddenly Lucy was glad that she'd bumped into Ruth today. Not just because she'd been glad to see her – and she had been – but because it meant that her mother would have something to plan – something to distract her over Christmas.

'Sweetheart, I need a cigarette,' her father said. 'I'll go and stand at the kitchen door. I know you dislike the smell.'

'Would you ask Betty to bring Lucy and me a cup of cocoa?' her mother told him. 'And then she can go home. It's late.'

Lucy and her mother sat by the fire with their hot drinks. Betty had brought them a slice of fruit cake each; it was a 'taster' for the Christmas cake, but Lucy noticed that her mother only picked at it.

'I wonder why Ruth never came to see us. She knows she would have been welcome,' her mother said as she gazed into the fire.

'She likes to spend her time off at home with her father.'

'Of course. But you think she will come to us

on Christmas Day?'

Lucy remembered the brooding look that Ruth had tried to hide when she'd mentioned her stepmother's plans for that day. 'I do,' she said.

Tomorrow she would be able to tell Julia, quite truthfully, that her mother was inviting friends to come for Christmas Day and that, of course, she must stay. She needn't mention that they were her friends, not her mother's. And it was only then that she was forced to acknowledge that her mother had no friends of her own. No one at all.

Chapter Five

August 1893

The house was quiet. The only other person stirring at this early hour was Meg, the scullery maid, but the sun was already warming the little room above the porch. Miss Golightly had ordered Flora to clear this room, and make it into a study for Ruth now that she had been given this new duty.

Only a month ago Miss Golightly had finished the manuscript that she had been working on for nearly three years, since shortly after Ruth had come to work here, and told her that it was time to make a neat copy. And that was to be Ruth's job.

'There you are,' she'd said one morning, pointing to the pile of papers in the cabinet by her bed. Ruth stared at the cabinet. Miss Golightly always kept it locked, but now the door was open and the papers were almost spilling out on to the floor. 'I know you've been wondering what I have been writing,' her employer had said. 'Well, now I can tell you. It is a novel and as soon as you have finished copying it out I am going to send it to a publisher.'

Ruth had stared at the tottering pile in dismay. 'It's ... it must be a very long novel,' she'd said.

'Yes, it is. They'll probably publish it in three

volumes, I should think. Now don't delay. You will be excused most other duties until you have finished.'

And so she had been. Since then Ruth had spent most of her days in this little room copying Miss Golightly's work out as neatly as she could. Flora wasn't pleased because it meant that she had to do more for Miss Golightly, including taking her out for walks. Consequently, the housemaid was more miserable than ever, and even the good-tempered Mrs Fairbridge was losing patience with her. Little Meg kept out of her way as much as possible.

Poor Meg, Ruth thought. She was so pleased to see me this morning; I wish I could have stayed longer with her. They had sat at the kitchen table with a slice of toast and a mug of tea each. But Ruth hadn't lingered. Her conscience had sent her upstairs to her study as soon as she'd finished.

The room was stuffy. Ruth opened the lower half of the window enough to set the lace curtains stirring in the slight breeze, and then sat down to begin her task. But the breeze brought the salt tang of the nearby sea, and for a moment Ruth was distracted. The sky was almost cloudless and it would be a glorious morning to walk on the beach. It was her day off...

She sighed. She was going out later to meet her friends. But the appointed time was hours away. She had decided last night to get up early and work for an hour or two before going out. She sat down and resumed her work on *An Angel Betrayed*.

The wind tugged at Angelina's cloak, almost pulling her along the moorland track towards the assignation she was dreading. A sudden gust caught at her golden curls and sent them flying about her face, momentarily blinding her and making her stumble and fall. She fell amongst the cruel stones but she bit her lip to stop herself from crying out. *He* might hear her, and it would never do if he were to guess how much distress he had caused her!

Long before she reached the blasted oak she saw the figure standing, tall and proud, silhouetted against the moonlit sky. Count Hugo was waiting for her. 'You heartless knave!' she muttered under her breath. 'You wretched scoundrel! Little do you know that I will die before I give in to your demands, and that I am prepared to spend the rest of my days in this earthly vale of tears in my valiant quest to clear my name!'

Ruth laid down her pen and groaned softly. This was overdramatic, sentimental twaddle. The novel that Miss Golightly had taken so long to write was dire. Ruth stared in despair at the manuscript her employer had handed to her with such pride.

Ironically, the handwriting was beautiful, if a little childish. Clear and well-formed letters filled page after page. It was easy to read and Ruth's task should have been simple, except that every other page or so, there would be something crossed out and an extra page attached. When this occurred Ruth's instructions were to place the new text in its proper place in the story. She was forever shuffling the pages as she tried to keep track of Angelina's sufferings.

And each day, after lunch, Ruth had to report to her employer.

'How is the work progressing?' Miss Golightly would ask.

'Very well,' Ruth would answer.

'Have you come across any problems?'

'No, none at all.'

'If there's anything you don't understand you must come and ask me.'

'I will.'

'Get along then.'

After several days of this Ruth realized that Miss Golightly was growing vexed with her. She couldn't imagine why. And then, yesterday, just after she had been dismissed, Miss Golightly had called, 'Wait. What do you think of it?'

Ruth understood. Miss Golightly had been expecting praise for her work. 'It's ... it's very dramatic,' Ruth had said.

Her employer had nodded. 'Dramatic, yes. But the plot – what do you think of the plot?'

'Well ... I haven't finished...'

Miss Golightly frowned. 'No, I suppose not. And Angelina, what do you think of her?'

'She's ... she's very beautiful.'

'Does she come over as plucky?'

'Oh, certainly. Very plucky.'

'Good. Personally I can't stand these milksop heroines. Well?'

Miss Golightly had looked at her keenly,

obviously expecting more, and Ruth wished she had been prepared for this moment. She wished she could have said something that would please her employer. Perhaps that's why she fell so easily into the lie.

Miss Golightly had sighed and said, 'You're a clever little miss. I actually value your opinion. Now tell me, do you think it's well-written?'

'Oh, yes,' Ruth had said. 'It's *very* well-written.'

'Thank you,' Miss Golightly had said and she'd actually flushed with pleasure. 'Now, off you go and get back to work.'

Ruth had escaped as fast as she could. It wasn't really a lie, she'd told herself, nevertheless knowing that she had been equivocal and that her statement could be interpreted in two ways. Miss Golightly had believed what she wanted to believe, that Ruth thought the novel had style, whereas Ruth had simply been praising the handwriting.

She'd felt guilty about the deception. And that was why she was working now. Why she had risen extra early on her day off to transcribe a few more pages before going out to meet Lucy and Esther.

Long before Angelina had reached the hilltop she had sensed that Count Hugo was watching her and she straightened her shoulders and held her head proudly. After all, she was innocent. Her conscience was clear.

'You've come!' Count Hugo said, his deep voice thrilling her even though she loathed him.

'You gave me no choice,' Angelina replied.

136

'Angelina!' he cried suddenly. 'We don't have to be enemies!'

'Oh, yes we do!' the brave girl exclaimed.

'But don't you know how much I love you?'

'Love!' Angelina exclaimed and suddenly her slim form shook as her wild laughter rang out across the moor.

Ruth put down her pen. She was in danger of blotting the page. Her shoulders were shaking along with Angelina's, but it was laughter mixed with tears. Tears for Miss Golightly, who had spent years on this work in the hope that it would be published. Ruth was almost sure that this was a vain hope, and she dreaded to think what rejection would do to her kindly employer.

'It's such a lovely day,' Daisy Shaw remarked. 'Would you like me to come with you?' She was sitting up in bed, drinking the tea that Lucy had just brought her.

'Oh, but you're not ready.'

Lucy sat down at her mother's dressing table, keeping her eyes on her own image in the mirror as she put on her hat and secured it with a pearl-headed hatpin. Her eyes narrowed; the straw hat trimmed with daisies might not be secure if the wind at the coast was at all fresh. Should she secure it more firmly with a chiffon scarf tied under her chin? She became aware of a move-ment behind her. Her mother stood at her side holding two of her own scarves. They were different shades of blue.

'I think you'll need one of these,' she said.

'Which one?' She held them up and studied them carefully. 'The paler one I think; here, let me.'

Lucy watched in the mirror as her mother arranged the scarf carefully over her hat and then leaned over to give her the ends to tie herself. She smelled of her favourite rose perfume. Her mother loved the scent of roses. She sprinkled rose-water liberally on her bed linen, bathed in rose-scented bath salts, and even her cold cream was delicately tinted and rose-scented. In her nightgown with her hair falling about her shoulders, she looked vulnerable. Lucy wished she could say what her mother wanted to hear. But she tied the scarf and turned on the seat to smile up at her mother, and said simply, 'Thank you.'

'You look lovely, all in white, so fresh, so innocent,' her mother said.

Lucy rose quickly so that her mother could no longer see her image in the mirror. She could hear her own heart thudding and she hoped she had not revealed her agitation. She closed her eyes.

Her mother grasped her shoulders. 'Did you get up too quickly?'

Lucy shook her head. 'I'm all right, really. But I must go. Would you like me to tell Betty to bring your breakfast up to bed?'

Her mother sighed. 'No. I should have been up and dressed long before this, but I waited up late in case your father managed to come home. You know I hate it when he has to go away on these weekly trips. He might at least try to come home on a Saturday night!'

Lucy's eyes widened. This was the first time she had ever heard her mother say anything that came so near to criticizing her father's behaviour, although she had drawn attention to the fact that she was lonely more often than she used to be – especially now that Lucy was working.

'He probably finished work so late that he missed the last train home.'

'Yes, that'll be it.' Daisy looked away but not before Lucy had seen the flash of anger in her eyes.

'And he'll probably be on his way home now, that's ... that's why I think you should stay. You know how he likes to find you here.'

'And where else should I be?'

Lucy stared at her mother in dismay. She was out of her depth. She wanted to comfort her mother. Part of her wanted to tell her to get ready quickly and come with her to the coast to spend the day with Ruth and Esther. But she couldn't because if her mother came with her she wouldn't be able to meet Stephen.

'Oh, go on,' her mother sighed. 'You haven't said as much but I know the reason you don't want me to come with you.'

'Do you?' Lucy found herself clenching her fists and she hid them in the folds of her skirt.

'Of course I do. The three of you are young and carefree, you don't want an old – an older woman like me spoiling your style.'

'Oh, don't say that!'

'Besides, you're right. I should stay at home to welcome your father.'

Lucy was saved further discomfort when Betty

139

knocked and entered. 'Your breakfast's nearly ready, Mrs Shaw, hinny. Now why don't you just put your bit robe on and come down and enjoy it? There's no one here to see.'

As Betty helped her mistress into her silk robe, Lucy gathered up her bag and the prettily wrapped gift she had for Esther, and took her leave.

'Say "Happy Birthday" to Esther for me,' her mother called after her as she sped down the stairs.

'Now then, Davy and Joe, I want you to stay where I can see you. I'll be up there,' Esther said. She turned and pointed towards one of the seats on the promenade. 'I'll be watching you.'

'What, all the time?' Davy grinned cheekily.

'Yes, every minute,' Esther told her brother. 'So you and Joe had better behave yerselves.' She tried to put on a stern voice but the sheer happiness in the two lads' eyes made sure that her smile was as wide as theirs were. 'Now yer bait's in this bag. There's ham sandwiches, a quarter-pound of broken biscuits – chocolate ones – and a bottle of dandelion and burdock – I know that's yer favourite. Let's put the bag here between these rocks and cover everything with yer towels while yer hev a bit run around. Mind yer roll yer trousers up if you're gan to plodge.'

Esther fought the impulse to give Davy a hug. She didn't want to shame him in front of his pal. Davy was twelve years old now, and considered himself a big lad. She stood back and watched as he and Joe sat down on the smooth surface of a sun-warmed rock and began to take off their shoes and socks. At least Davy had socks, thanks to her; Joe Rutter hadn't – and was probably lucky to have the pair of tattered boots he was wearing. A lot of bairns went barefoot as well as being ill-fed. Well, that wasn't going to be Davy's fate. Not if she could help it.

'Oh, before I gans,' she said, and the boys looked up, 'are the pair of you too big to be seen with buckets and spades?'

Davy shook his head wonderingly and Joe frowned. They knew that Esther hadn't brought any buckets and spades.

'Well, here's the money to go and get a bucket and spade each,' she said. 'Gan on – that over there's a shop – can you see it? You've got enough there to get a bucket and spade each.'

The delighted grins were all the answer she needed before the lads ran off towards the beach-hut shop. Esther began to make her way up the gentle slope to the promenade, still carrying a basket over her arm. The contents of the basket were covered with a clean tea towel. She had chosen Whitley-by-the-Sea for her birthday outing because of the long stretch of sands for the lads to run about on. Cullercoats Bay, just a short walk away, might have been prettier, but she didn't want Davy and Joe going into the caves and maybe getting caught by the tide as she and her friends had once done.

It was here on the promenade at the top of Watt's Slope that she'd arranged to meet Ruth and Lucy. But she'd come deliberately early in order to give her brother and his pal as long a day

141

as possible on the beach. When she reached the promenade she tucked the basket underneath a seat to keep it out of the sun and sat down gratefully. She was tired. She was always tired, it seemed. Not only did she work long hours in the shop but she had just about taken over all the housework at home.

Home... Esther didn't know how much longer she could bear living in those squalid rooms. She kept them as clean as she could but the building was old and crumbling and, as well as the dust from the nearby timber yard, there was always the stench from the tannery across the cut.

She leaned back and closed her eyes. She breathed in the sharp salt tang of the sea and listened to the sound of the waves breaking on the shore below and the constant calling of the sea birds as they rode the currents of air, high in the cloudless sky. If only she could live here – just she and Davy. But even now that she was earning more as a counter hand, she would never be able to afford to pay the rent of anywhere decent, not for a long while.

Well, at least because of the money she was taking home they'd been able to afford another room – a former pantry, probably, when the house had belonged to a rich merchant. But that had been a hundred years ago, possibly more than that, and now, with the old shelves stripped out, it was just big enough to get a single bed in. But at least Davy had a small window, which was more than she had.

Esther had had to arrange that herself. She'd caught her father after a good meal that she'd cooked for them all and, thank goodness, he'd agreed, so long as she saw to everything that needed doing. Her mother had probably never even noticed. And that was another thing – she wasn't sure how her mother would manage if she left home.

Agnes Robinson seemed to have lost all interest in anything except where the next drink was coming from. Her father had lost all patience with her. Esther often had to come between them and try to keep Davy out of the way as well. When her brother wasn't at school Esther made sure he came to the shop, where, as well as serving behind the counter, she was now showing the new apprentice – a lad this time – how to weigh and pack the provisions. And that was another worry...

This lad, Raymond, was Mr Fowler's nephew and, as the Fowlers hadn't any children, Esther guessed that they were training him up to succeed them one day. And he obviously knew this. When his uncle and aunt were present he was respectful and ready to learn. And he was a quick learner; she had to give him that. But when Esther was on her own with him his manner changed to one of barely concealed impudence. Never mind, he was only a bairn, really, and she could put up with that, but what really exasperated her was that he had begun to tease Davy.

She had to have eyes in the back of her head almost when the two of them were in the room together. Only the other day she'd turned round just in time to stop young Raymond from tripping her brother up as he was carrying a box of groceries along the back passage to his delivery bicycle in the yard. Her glare hadn't quelled Raymond's grin and, to her annoyance, Davy's smile had been almost as wide. The incident hadn't seemed to bother him.

'Esther, there you are. But where's Davy?'

Esther opened her eyes to see Ruth smiling at her. 'Davy's on the beach with his pal, Joe,' she said. Then: 'Ee, Ruth, you do look a picture. That blue dress really suits you – and look at them bonny ribbons in yer hair!'

Ruth laughed. 'Well, you look lovely too. That pale green looks so fresh and dainty. And you're wearing a hat! Should I have worn a hat? I look like a schoolgirl compared to you. You look like a proper lady!'

'Get away with yer!' Esther said. But she was pleased. She knew Ruth well enough to know that she never paid empty compliments. 'Thank you,' she said. 'But I owe it all to Lucy's mam, as usual. She even showed me how to take the dress in to fit. Lucy had grown out of it but it was still too big for me. Ee, I'm so skinny, Ruth.' Esther shook her head. 'Next to Lucy I feel like a scarecrow.'

'You don't look a bit like a scarecrow,' Ruth said. 'You're tall and slender, and graceful too.'

Esther's eyes widened. 'You've still got a way with words, heven't yer?'

Ruth smiled. 'Whereas I seem to have stopped growing. You and Lucy are leaving me behind.'

Esther looked at her friend as she sat down beside her. It was true Ruth was small, but she was shapely. Even dressed the way she was, in a simple pale blue summer frock with no frills, she couldn't have been mistaken for a child. And it would have been a sin to cover those shining curls with a daft bit straw hat like Esther herself had done. No, whether she knew it or not, and Esther was never sure whether Ruth had any vanity, her friend had done exactly the right thing by weaving those blue silky ribbons through her hair.

Then Ruth surprised her by leaning towards her and kissing her cheek. 'Happy Birthday, Esther,' she said. 'This is for you.' She took a small parcel wrapped in silver-tinted paper from the string bag she was carrying. 'Go on – take it.'

Esther unwrapped the paper to find a small casket made of woven rush. She opened it and caught her breath. 'A work basket,' she said. 'Me own work basket!'

She stared with delight at the pink sateen lining. The under part of the lid was padded, and a corded ribbon sewn diagonally from corner to corner held in place a pair of scissors, a button hook, a bodkin and a folded tape measure. Each fitted into its own place with stitches in between. In the body of the work basket there was a ruched pocket along the back.

Esther looked inside wonderingly to find Cellophane packets containing different sizes of pearl-tinted buttons, some press studs and some hooks and eyes. In the body of the work basket there lay cards of black, brown and grey darning wools, and several bobbins of different coloured sewing threads. There were also two packets of graded needles going from the tiniest size up to darning needles and a couple of bodkins. Esther felt tears welling up and she raised a hand to rub at her eyes.

'What's the matter?' Ruth asked. 'Don't you like my present?' She sounded anxious.

'Of course I do.'

'Then why are you crying?'

'Because I'm happy. I've never had a birthday present before, and this ... this is just perfect.'

'You really like it?'

'Why do you sound surprised?'

'Because I've never bought anyone a birthday present before. Well, not since I was a little girl and my father and I went together to buy my mother a box of fondant creams. And I wasn't sure if this was the right sort of thing.'

'Well, it is. And thank you. But I hope you don't think I told you it was me birthday just to get a present.'

'Of course not.'

Esther wrapped the work box up again and, reaching under the seat, she slipped it into her bag. 'I asked you and Lucy to come because I wanted us to hev a nice day out ... something to remember, the three of us together.'

'And we will,' Ruth said. 'As soon as Lucy gets here!'

The three children grew more and more excited the nearer they drew to the coast. When Lucy had boarded the train at Heaton, they had been sitting reasonably quietly, three little boys in sailor suits, quite sweet, really, she thought, minding their manners and doing as they were told. But that happy state of things didn't last long.

There was a nursemaid in charge of them. Lucy had looked at her and realized that she wasn't old enough to be a proper nanny; she looked as if she'd only just left school – and she looked worn out. Lucy was glad with all her heart that she had not had to go into service. Fancy spending your days having to be responsible for badly behaved youngsters like this, she thought; or having to wait hand and foot on a strange old woman like Ruth did. And then there was Esther, working such long hours in that shop on Raby Street; it was almost like slavery.

Lucy knew how lucky she was to have been sent to Miss Jackson's school. Not just because that had led to her meeting Julia Wright's brother, Stephen, but also because she'd been able to get a good job. Being a typist in a solicitor's office in Collingwood Street in Newcastle was sometimes a little boring – all those long-winded documents written in old-fashioned language – but the work was clean and respectable, and Collingwood Street was close to the town centre with all the shops, restaurants and theatres. Not to mention the office just being a short walk away from the Central Station, which meant she could get down to the coast so easily to see Stephen, or he could come to town and see her, when she'd told her mother she was working late.

Also her mother refused to take one penny of her earnings from her. 'No, your father and I never intended that you should have to work for your living, but you'd be bored sitting at home with me all the time, so it's better that you should be happily occupied until you get married, as you will one day,' her mother had told her. 'And as for the money you earn, we want you to spoil yourself, buy yourself those little extras.'

One of the small boys sitting opposite had started eating an orange, and Lucy moved along the seat as far away as she could in order to avoid being spattered with the juice. The sun was shining brightly and the carriage was hot but Lucy didn't want to open a window in case the wind blew soot and grit through the opening. She would have to suffer.

She had felt sorry for the boys' young nursemaid at first but, as the journey progressed, she began to lose patience with her. The girl sat on the same side of the carriage as Lucy, while her young charges threw themselves around the carriage and at each other. Lucy felt like telling her to do her job properly but each time she looked at the girl's wan face something stopped her.

Every time the train stopped Lucy hoped they would get out, particularly when they reached the stations at the coast. But, no, it seemed they were going to Whitley-by-the-Sea as she was. No doubt because they knew there was a helter-skelter, a roundabout and some swingboats on the beach there. Lucy hoped they would go on all the rides and make themselves sick.

At last the train began to slow down as it approached Whitley station. Lucy decided she would sit back and let the little nuisances get out first. It was just as well that she did, because before the train had even come to a halt, the biggest of the three boys hurled himself at the door and opened it. The door flew away from him, the nursemaid screeched as her charge hung in space for a moment, and then they heard a gruff voice say, 'Now then!' and the lad was plucked by unseen hands out of their sight.

'Go on then!' Lucy told the girl when the train had finally come to a stop. 'Go and see what's happened to him!'

The other two lads had already scrambled out but their nursemaid remained sitting, looking whey-faced and frightened.

'Oh, for goodness' sake!' Lucy said, and she took the poor girl's arm and hauled her to her feet.

Lucy got out first and helped the girl step down on to the platform. They turned to find all three lads looking up respectfully at a big man in uniform; a porter's uniform.

'Hello, Arthur,' Lucy said.

He looked surprised. 'Lucy. Are these rapscallions with you?'

'Absolutely not. I had the misfortune to be travelling in the same compartment.' She gave the nursemaid a shove. 'This person is in charge of them. Or supposed to be.'

'Wait a minute, then. Step back a little, will you?'

Arthur gestured for them to move away from the edge of the platform, then he left them to go along the train, shutting any doors that had been left open, including their own. The guard blew his whistle and the train began to move out of the station. As it picked up speed and rattled away

149

Arthur came back to join them.

'Now then,' he said. 'I want a word with you.' He was addressing the young nursemaid and her charges. Lucy knew that he didn't mean her but she lingered curiously. Arthur was being so masterful.

'Don't you know how dangerous that is?' he asked the oldest of the boys. 'You should never open the door before the train has stopped. Those doors are heavy – I bet you got a shock when it swung away from you, didn't you?'

The lad nodded, his eyes big.

'Well, what if the door had hit someone waiting on the platform? Or what if you'd lost your footing and fallen out? What do you think this young woman would hev said to your ma if she'd had to take you home with a lump on yer head and a few of yer bones broken?'

The smallest of the boys began to whimper and turned to bury his face against the nursemaid. She put her arms round him and tried to shush him.

'What's yer name?' Arthur asked her.

'Mary. Mary Clark.' She sounded frightened but Lucy noticed that she had flushed slightly under Arthur's gaze. And as she looked up at him she turned her head so that her glance was slanted and almost coy.

'Well, Mary, I hope my words hev gone home to yer.'

'They hev, sir.' She looked almost pretty when she gave a little smile.

Arthur smiled in response. 'Yer divven't hev to call me "sir", bonny lass, but divven't forget what

I've telt yer. And as for you,' he turned his attention to the boys again and put on a stern voice and wagged his finger, 'I divven't want yer giving this lass any more trouble. Off to the beach, are yer?'

The boys nodded.

'Well, I might just stroll down there a little later and see what's what. See if you're minding what I telt yer. Right?'

They nodded again.

'Now, be off with yer.'

Lucy watched as the young nursemaid hurried away with her charges. Not one of the boys had spoken. Arthur laughed. 'Let's hope they mind my words,' he said.

'I think you've terrified them,' Lucy told him.

'Do you? Well, I hope I hev. That's a dangerous trick to play and it's not only bairns that do it. The young lads coming back from their work are the worst. They can't wait to open the door and leap out, sometimes while the train is still moving, then hurry away yem for their meal.'

The other passengers had already left the station. As she and Arthur walked towards the barrier, Lucy could hear their footsteps and the drips from the hanging flower baskets, which must have been recently watered. There were little damp patches all along the platform.

'Off to meet yer young man, then?' Arthur asked.

Lucy glanced away. 'I don't know what you're talking about.'

Arthur persisted. 'He's a good catch. The undertaker's son. There's money there.'

151

'Oh, you mean Stephen? Stephen is simply my friend's brother.'

'Oh, aye. Yer gan to see Julia and then Stephen walks yer to the station.'

'There's no harm in that.' Arthur raised his brows. 'And ... and I like him.'

'Like? That's why it takes yer so long to get to the station?'

'Mm.'

'That's why yer sit in the waiting room while two or three trains gan through without yer?'

'We ... we like to talk.'

'Talk?'

Lucy felt herself flushing as she remembered those talks. How close they had sat, how tightly Stephen had held her hand as he whispered that he would like to make her his wife but that they must keep it secret until it would be the right time to tell his parents.

'Yes, and that's no business of yours, Arthur Purvis,' Lucy snapped. She couldn't understand why she had let him question her like this. Why she had lingered. Why she felt she had to explain her actions to him. 'As a matter of fact I've come to meet two of my friends from school,' she said.

'From Miss Jackson's?'

'No, from my old school, at home in Byker. We're going to spend the day together. Now, I must be going.' She began to walk away.

'Lucy...'

'What do you want?' He didn't answer and she turned to see him staring at her. 'What is it? What's the matter?'

'Nothing. You look so bonny ... so beautiful.

152

That's all.'

Lucy knew that she was flushing, just like the young nursemaid had done. That look in Arthur's eyes was unmistakable. It was the same way Stephen looked at her. The look in itself didn't disturb her, what worried her was her own reaction, for, to her dismay, she found herself responding to his gaze just as she had when she had first realized he was interested in her.

But there could be no future for her with a railway porter. She had acknowledged that fact regretfully, whereas Stephen Wright was not only attractive, but he was also well-to-do. He would be just the sort of husband her mother would approve of.

'Happy Birthday, Esther,' Lucy said. 'Here, this is for you.'

Ruth watched Esther's delight as she took the present Lucy proffered.

'For me?' she asked.

'Of course, you goose!' Lucy said, and she laughed as she joined them on the bench on the promenade.

Ruth thought how sophisticated Lucy had become. Her mother had always dressed her in beautiful clothes and she had made sure she spoke properly but, now, since she had been to Miss Jackson's school and learned deportment and elocution as well as office skills, she was even more ladylike than her mother. But unlike her mother, Lucy did not give the impression that her manner was a performance. The daughter had much more self-assurance than the mother.

And what of me? Ruth wondered. I've never had an elocution lesson but I suppose I always tried to speak like the teachers at school – aping my betters, as my stepmother put it. And now I suppose I follow the example of Miss Golightly, I can't help it. But I don't think I shall ever achieve the confident way of talking and behaving that Lucy has. Somehow I know I shall always think of myself as neither one thing nor the other.

Esther had unwrapped Lucy's present to find a wooden box containing three bars of soap. 'Mm,' she said as she raised the box to her face, 'they smell lovely. What is it?'

'Carnation,' Lucy said. 'And my mother sends birthday wishes too.'

Ruth saw that Esther's eyes had filled. And yet she was smiling. For a moment she obviously didn't trust herself to speak, and then she said, 'Right, move your legs, Lucy, and let's get me basket. Just see what I've got for you two!'

'You've brought something for us?' Lucy asked. 'But why? It's your birthday.'

'That's right. And this is like a party,' Esther said. 'So I've brought some treats – a picnic for us to eat. Shall we gan and sit on the beach or do you want to sit here and eat?'

'Oh, not here on the promenade,' Lucy said. 'I don't think that would be proper.'

Esther's eyes widened and Ruth saw that she had no idea what Lucy was talking about, but she rose at once and said, 'Hawway, then. The beach it is, just like when we were bairns. Remember that day?'

'How could I forget,' Lucy said, and pulled

Ruth back as Esther set off ahead of them. 'I wanted to treat you both to luncheon at the Waverly,' she murmured.

'Esther wouldn't have gone; she wouldn't have wanted to lose sight of Davy,' Ruth murmured.

'Oh, is he here?'

'Davy and his friend, they're down on the beach.'

'Well, we could at least have had a snack in the beach café – I would have treated the boys too.'

Esther looked over her shoulder at them. 'Hawway, you two,' she called. 'Divven't dawdle!'

'She doesn't change, does she?' Lucy looked at Ruth pointedly, but her words were softened by a rueful smile.

Even so, Ruth was stung to answer, 'Oh, but she has changed. She's not the same girl she was at school.'

'No?'

'Well, I mean, she takes care of herself.'

Ruth had been going to say that Esther was clean now. That she always washed. But, somehow, even to call up the memory of that ragged, unwashed child seemed to be a betrayal of their friend.

Lucy looked solemn. 'You're right, of course. You always are. Esther is a very different person now in ways that really matter.' And then she smiled. 'Now, come along, we'd better catch up with her or she'll screech at us again!'

Esther watched Lucy purse her lips as she settled herself on the sand and realized that she ought to have brought a rug or something for them to sit on. Except that she didn't own a decent rug and, even if she did, it wouldn't have fit in her basket. But she could always have brought a couple of clean towels for her friends to sit on.

'Ee, I didn't think,' she said aloud. 'You'll spoil your bonny clothes.'

'No we won't,' Ruth said. 'The sand up here is clean and dry.'

They had chosen a spot near to where the grassy bank began to rise towards the promenade. It was both sheltered and sufficiently far away from the families with young children. Davy and Joe had seen them come down to the beach and now they came racing over.

'Have a care!' Esther exclaimed. 'You're kicking sand all over us. Now, what do you want? Hawway, speak up.'

Her brother seemed to have lost his tongue. Joe nudged him and said, 'Gan on, tell her, man.'

'I know what they want,' Lucy said. 'They want to go on the swingboats. Don't you, Davy?'

'Aye, we do.'

Esther knew she was flushing. 'Davy...' she said. She'd told him before they left home that she wouldn't have any money spare for the beach rides and he'd seemed to understand. Joe must've put him up to it.

Lucy rose to her feet, her white skirt swishing in the loose sand. 'Right-oh,' she said. 'I'll come along with you while your sister gets our picnic sorted out.'

'But, Lucy–' Esther began.

'I insist, my treat.'

Lucy marched away along the beach with the

boys following, and Esther glanced at Ruth helplessly. 'She shouldn't spend her own money on the bairns like that.'

'Why not?' Ruth asked. 'Oh, don't worry. I'm sure she's glad to be able to treat them.'

'Do you think so?'

'I'm sure of it.'

Very soon Lucy came back and sat down beside them. 'It was only the swingboats they were interested in,' she told them. 'Davy reckons the helter-skelter is over too quickly and the roundabout is only for little bairns, so I've left them with enough money to keep them occupied while we have our picnic.' She glanced at the white cardboard box, like a cake box, that Esther held towards her. 'What's this? A surprise packet like at the Sunday School party?'

'It's yer bait,' Esther told her. 'Gan on, take it. And here's yours, Ruth.'

She dropped her head as if she were looking for something in the basket but slanted a look up at her friends' faces, one after the other. She wanted to see their reaction to the treat she had provided.

Lucy was staring bemusedly into the open box on her knee and Ruth's eyes were wide. 'Why, Esther,' she said. 'This is marvellous. What a treat.'

'Do you think so?'

'I do. Everything's so ... so dainty.'

'Lost for the right words for once, are yer?' Esther grinned at the surprised look on Ruth's face.

'Where did you get all this?' Lucy asked. 'Not

at Fowler's?'

'Why, no,' Esther replied. 'You know that posh delicatessen on Shields Road, the German one? The one that does catering for parties and the like? Well, I popped in and telt them that I was hevin' a party – but a very small one and I wanted something special for me and me two best friends. I picked them up this morning – they're open until noon on a Sunday – and they provided everything in those boxes, even the napkins – they're paper, like – and the little wooden spoons for the trifles.'

Lucy seemed to have recovered herself. 'Esther, it looks marvellous – but I don't know where to start,' she said.

'Nor me,' Ruth added. 'Look, there's a scotch egg, cheese straws, a slice of game pie – and just look at the iced fancies, and that trifle!'

'Gan on, then. Let's get started,' Esther said. 'And when we've finished we'll gan to the beach café for a nice cup of tea.'

Later, at the beach café, Ruth insisted that Esther allow her to buy ice-creams for Davy and Joe.

'All right,' Esther said. 'But they can eat them outside, while we hev a good old gossip over our tea.'

Ruth saw how happy Esther looked, and how pretty she was in her summer muslin. The soft green enhanced the colour of her eyes. At some stage she had taken off her hat and stuffed it in her basket, and curling tendrils of hair had escaped the pins to hang around her face. No, she wasn't merely pretty, Ruth thought. Lucy was

158

pretty, Esther was beautiful. Even in Lucy's cast-off clothes.

The café was no more than a large wooden shed, Ruth thought, but it was spotlessly clean and the waitresses were forever wiping down the red and white checked oilcloth-covered tables in between customers. Esther took charge of the teapot and poured their tea.

'Ee, what a marvellous birthday this has been,' she said as she sipped her tea. 'I've never had one like it.'

'Do you feel more grown-up now that you are eighteen?' Lucy asked. 'The first of us to reach that august age!'

For a moment Esther lost her smile. She turned to look out of the window to where Davy and Joe were sitting at one of the outside tables. 'I think I've felt grown-up for a long time,' she said.

Ruth reached across the table and took her hand. 'Of course you have.'

Lucy frowned. Ruth thought that she didn't understand. No, she wasn't even listening. In fact she seemed to have lost interest in the conversation. She was staring at some point over Ruth's shoulder. Suddenly she surprised both Ruth and Esther by leaning over the table and motioning with her hands for both of them to do the same, drawing them in towards her.

'What is it?' Ruth asked.

'That man is looking at us,' Lucy whispered.

'What man?' Esther exclaimed.

'Hush!' Lucy said. 'Keep your voice down. And don't look up.'

'But if we don't look up how can we see him?'

159

Ruth asked. She thought that was a reasonable question.

'Pretend you're studying the menu,' Lucy said, and she grabbed it and lay it flat on the table between them, 'otherwise we might look foolish.'

'I'm sure we do look foolish,' Ruth said. 'With our noses touching our tea plates like this. Won't you at least describe him?'

'I was just going to,' Lucy replied, 'only you will both chatter so.'

'Gan on, then,' Esther breathed. 'Tell us about the man that's looking at us. Does he look like a bad 'un?'

'No, I don't think so,' Lucy whispered. 'Not exactly a villain. It's just that he looked so intense.' She turned her head slightly and slanted a look up over Ruth's shoulder. 'Oh, my, he still does – look intense, I mean.'

'For goodness' sake,' Ruth muttered impatiently. 'Don't make such a drama of it. If you don't tell us what he looks like I'm going to sit up and see for myself.'

'No, I'll tell you. He's older than we are – but I think you could call him young. And he's thin and pale, and he has floppy brown hair. I hate to say this but the sleeves of his jacket look a little short for him.'

'You've described him very well,' Ruth said.

'Have I?' Lucy looked pleased. Then she frowned. 'What do you mean?' She paused. 'You know him!'

'I do.'

'Well, I hope you like him because he's coming this way.'

'Ee!' Esther exclaimed. 'What shall we do?'

'Tell us, Ruth. Shall we run for the door?' Lucy asked.

Ruth saw Lucy was teasing but Esther didn't realize this and she half rose, knocking over her empty teacup as she did so.

'Stay where you are, Esther,' Ruth hissed. 'And, please, let's all sit up and try not to act like foolish schoolgirls. It's only Mr Valentine.'

'Mr Valentine?' Lucy's eyebrows rose but she didn't have time to voice her curiosity any further. She sat up and smiled brilliantly at a point above Ruth's shoulder and, hardly moving her lips, she whispered, 'He's behind you.'

Esther giggled and Ruth turned to see the young man smiling down at her. He looked faintly flushed. 'Miss Lorrimer ... Ruth,' he said. 'How nice to see you here.'

'Mr Valentine.'

'Henry, please.'

'Henry, then. But would you like to join us?'

'Should I? I – er – mean would these other young ladies mind?'

'I'm sure they wouldn't, would you, Lucy and Esther?'

'I divven't mind,' Esther said.

'Neither do I,' Lucy added, 'and, if you don't mind my saying so, it would be better if you did so at once in order to save Ruth from getting a crick in her neck.'

'Oh, I'm sorry.'

Henry Valentine looked embarrassed and Ruth gave Lucy a quick kick under the table. 'Ouch!' Lucy exclaimed, and Esther grinned and got up

161

to move the chairs around so that the young man could sit next to Ruth with Lucy on his other side.

'You settle yerself, Mr Valentine,' she said, 'and I'll just go and catch that young waitress and ask her to bring us a fresh pot of tea and an extra cup.'

When Esther returned to the table Ruth introduced Henry Valentine to her friends properly but she didn't explain how she knew him and she could see that they were bursting to ask her. She took advantage of the temporary silence imposed by the arrival of the fresh pot of tea and then took pity on them.

'Mr Valentine ... Henry ... is a musician. He plays the piano.'

'I see,' Lucy said, and from her look of vexation Ruth knew that she didn't see at all.

Henry was sipping his tea but he must have become aware of the strained silence and when he put down his cup he looked from one to the other. He smiled gently and said, 'I teach piano and violin but I sometimes give recitations at the Waverly Hotel. Nothing too heavy, just pleasant melodies to entertain the mostly elderly people who come to the concerts.'

'You mean old folk?' Esther asked.

'I do.'

'Well, yer still heven't telt us owt,' Esther said.

Henry Valentine laughed. 'You want to know how Ruth and I met, and Ruth is being deliberately obtuse if she really can't grasp that.'

'Stubborn, d'ye mean?' Esther asked. 'She always did hev her prickly moods but I thought

162

she might hev outgrown them.'

It was now Ruth's turn to look from one to the other. She knew she was being awkward. There was no reason why her friends should not know that she and Henry were friends. But that was the problem ... were they friends? She had thought of him as an acquaintance, someone she had chatted to now and then at the hotel or in the street if they happened to meet by chance.

He lived in Heaton and once, when she had been home to visit her father, she'd met Henry at the station. She'd been going back to Miss Golightly's house and he had been going to the hotel. They had travelled back to the coast together and enjoyed each other's company.

But they had never walked out together – and she could see from Esther and Lucy's expressions that they were thinking just that. By coming over to the table Henry had given her friends the impression that Ruth knew him well. And that bothered her.

Sometimes when Henry looked at her it was as if he could see straight through to her innermost thoughts and feelings. As if words were not needed between them. And Ruth was disturbed by such an assumption of intimacy.

Since her mother had died she had never shared her deepest emotions with anyone, not even with Esther and Lucy, and she did not know how to cope with a man who seemed to be able to vanquish the barriers she had erected against the world without even trying – without even acknowledging they were there.

And there was something else. Something in

163

Henry's eyes reminded her of the hunger in Ada's eyes when she looked at her father. Her stepmother's look revealed more than a simple attraction between a man and a woman. It was as if Ada wanted to own Joseph Lorrimer body and soul. Ruth knew that she had too much of an independent spirit to be caught up in such a relationship.

'Miss Golightly goes to the concerts; I have to take her.' The moment the words were out she knew how ungracious she had sounded.

There was an awkward silence and then Henry stood up. 'It's time for me to go,' he said. He turned away and then back again. 'Are you coming to the concert tonight, Ruth?'

'No, this is my day off. Flora is to accompany Miss Golightly this evening.'

'Oh, yes, the sad-faced young maidservant.'

'Sad?'

'She never smiles.'

'That's true, but I would have put that down to ill-temper.'

'Perhaps.' Henry sighed. 'And, as it's your day off I don't suppose wild horses would drag you along to the concert. Goodbye, Miss Lorrimer. Ladies.'

Ruth's eyes widened at his tone and at the way he left so quickly. She half rose and then felt herself flush when she saw the way the other two were staring at her. She sat down again quickly.

'Well, well,' Lucy said.

'What do you mean, "well, well"?'

'What has the poor man done to make you act so cruelly?'

'Cruel? That's ridiculous!'

'No it's not,' Esther said. 'You were perfectly horrible to him. And, mind, you're a dark horse. You never telt us you had a young man!'

'I didn't tell you because I haven't. Henry Valentine is just a friend – well, not even that, really. He's an acquaintance.'

'An acquaintance? Is that all he is?' Esther asked. And then she grinned. 'Well, someone had better tell the poor feller that before he makes an even bigger fool of himself.'

'What do you mean?'

Lucy tutted with exasperation. 'Ruth, you might be clever, but you're not very wise. Can't you see that the poor man is in love with you?'

Chapter Six

Ruth looked discomforted. Lucy couldn't decide whether she really didn't know that Henry Valentine was attracted to her, or whether she knew but she didn't want to admit it.

'You're a funny girl, Ruth,' Lucy said. 'Most young women would be pleased to have made a conquest.'

'Don't speak like that!' Ruth said sharply. 'You make me sound like the heroine of a cheap romance.'

Lucy was stung by her tone. 'I don't know what on earth you mean,' she said sharply. 'Or what makes you think you can scold me like this.'

'Lissen, you two. Divven't start quarrelling. Not on me birthday!'

Esther sounded so upset that Lucy immediately felt guilty. 'I'm sorry,' she said generously.

'And so you should be,' Esther responded. 'Teasing poor Ruth like that.'

Lucy was stung by the injustice of it – Esther taking Ruth's side when she had meant no harm. 'I wasn't teasing,' she said. 'I was only pointing out something that should have been perfectly obvious.'

'Well, it wasn't obvious to Ruth,' Esther said.

Lucy drew in her breath and was just about to defend herself when Ruth said, 'It's all right, Esther, I don't think Lucy meant to tease. And

I'm sorry too. For spoiling your day.'

Esther looked from one to the other and then she smiled. 'It's all right. Me day's not been spoiled. But do the pair of yer realize we've just had wor first quarrel? And the cause of it is a man.'

Lucy saw Ruth's eyes widen and then she began to smile. And so did Lucy. 'Let's make a promise never to let a man come between us again,' she said.

Esther laughed. 'I'll drink to that,' she said, raising her teacup. 'Hawway, you two.'

They were all smiling as they raised their teacups and clinked them together as if they were glasses.

'Well, now,' Esther said. 'If we're all on good terms again, I'd better be gannin' yem.' She glanced at the clock above the counter. 'Quarter to four. If we get up to the station now we might just get a train before they get crowded. Are you coming, Lucy?'

'Actually I'm not going home yet. I'm going to see ... Julia.'

'Yer friend from Miss Jackson's school?'

'That's right.'

Lucy didn't like lying to her friends, but no one knew that she and Stephen had been meeting secretly. She would have loved to have told Ruth and Esther – just as she would have liked to tell her mother – but Stephen had asked her to wait.

It wasn't that his parents didn't like her. In fact they always made her very welcome when she visited Julia, and Julia herself absolutely adored her. It was just that the more prosperous they

167

became, the higher they set their sights as far as a wife for their only son was concerned.

Lucy, as the daughter of a travelling salesman, even a chief salesman, might not be quite what they were looking for as a daughter-in-law. But Stephen was convinced that, if they were patient, and if Lucy went on visiting Julia and making herself pleasant to his mother, she would become almost part of the family. And then it would be easier for Stephen to tell them that he wanted to marry her. One day...

After Esther had paid for the tea she hurried outside to make sure that Davy and Joe had put their boots on and then they all walked together up the slope to the promenade. Lucy said good-bye, telling her friends that she and Julia had arranged to meet in the ornamental gardens nearby, so that they could go for a walk before going back to Julia's house.

'Do you want me to wait with you?' Ruth asked.

'No, that's all right.' Lucy didn't know what she would say if Ruth insisted on keeping her company but Esther saved the situation.

'If yer don't hev to go back yet, why divven't yer walk up to the station with me and the lads? We can hev a bit more gossip on the way.'

Luckily Ruth agreed, and Lucy kept the pretence going by walking into the gardens, which were situated in a slight hollow in the links. The grassy banks that surrounded the flowerbeds did not quite provide enough shelter from the sea breeze that had sprung up and Lucy shivered slightly as she sat on one of the wooden benches. She watched her friends walk away along the promenade and then disappear from sight.

As soon as she could be sure that they were far enough away Lucy left the gardens and hurried along the seafront to the Waverly Hotel. She joined the crowd of smartly dressed people who were obviously gathering for the concert. Once up the steps and into the foyer, it was easy to tag along with a group of ladies who were going to the cloakroom.

Earlier, she had made herself comfortable with the others in the cloakroom of the café, but there hadn't been a mirror there and only a cold water tap. Here she could wash properly and tidy her hair; and dab her wrists and behind her ears with the scent Stephen had given her, *Violette Printanière*, Spring Violet.

She waited until all the others had gone before slipping out again. To her dismay, as soon as she reached the foyer she saw Henry Valentine. And he saw her. He came towards her.

'Miss Shaw,' he said, 'you've come to the concert.' His eyes were fixed at a point beyond her; his smile was hopeful.

'She isn't here,' Lucy told him. 'Ruth didn't come.'

She remained only long enough to register his disappointment before slipping by him and making for the revolving glass door. Once outside she glanced back quickly and saw him staring after her. He looked puzzled. As well he might. But she certainly couldn't have stayed to explain her behaviour.

Stephen was waiting for her at the Mourning Warehouse. The undertaker's business started by his grandfather had expanded over the years so that Wright's now not only provided a decent burial but also the hire of hearses, mourning clothes, memorial cards, wreaths and flower arrangements; even catering for the wake, if that was required.

The warehouse, unlike the funeral parlour where there was always someone on duty, was closed on Sunday, and was sufficiently far away from it to be a safe place for Lucy and Stephen to meet without being observed.

A steady crowd of day trippers was now making its way back to the station, and Lucy joined the throng anonymously before slipping into the side street that led to the warehouse. The ground floor was taken up with a florist's, also owned by the Wright family, and a door at the side led to the Mourning Warehouse.

Lucy rattled the letter box; the first time they had met here, only last month, she had rung the bell and frightened herself witless when she'd heard it reverberating loudly along the passage and up the stairwell like a death knell. Stephen opened the door so quickly that it seemed as though he had been waiting at the bottom of the stairs. He smiled as he took her hand and pulled her inside. Then, closing the door swiftly, he drew her into his arms.

'Lucy...' he murmured. Then neither spoke as she gave herself up to his embrace. Long moments later, breathless with kissing, they drew apart and stared at each other solemnly. 'Let's go upstairs,' he said. 'We can be more comfortable.'

The stairs were narrow and dark; Stephen had not lit any of the gaslamps that were fixed to the wall. But, at the top, they emerged into a richly carpeted, lofty room. The dark crimson velvet drapes at the windows revealed very little of the world outside but sufficient sunlight filtered through the lace curtains to relieve the gloom.

Not that the showroom itself was gloomy, Lucy thought. It was furnished rather like a grand drawing room with large sofas and easy chairs. Instead of shop counters there were two large mahogany tables, one at either side of the doorway. Customers could sit here and ask to see bolts of cloth in black, grey, mauve or purple; in silk, wool or crêpe.

The assistants and the dressmaker were always dressed in black, Stephen had told her. There was also a selection of ready-made cloaks, coats, dresses and hats; a complete mourning outfit could be supplied immediately for any member of the family: man, woman or child. There were curtained dressing rooms where the clothes could be tried on.

Stephen's father had developed this side of the business to take advantage of the fact that respectable families, even those of relatively modest income, went into mourning for months, if not years, and would need to buy clothes long after the actual interment. He could now supply anything the bereaved family might need, from widows' caps to black-edged handkerchiefs and black-edged writing paper and black sealing wax.

When Lucy had told her mother about this side

of Julia's father's business Daisy had thought it strange that so much money was to be made from death. 'Death should be the end of it,' she'd murmured, 'all the "getting and spending". The folk here in Byker have a hard enough time keeping up with their insurance for a decent burial, let alone having to buy all that paraphernalia. A couple of decent black frocks and perhaps a widow's cap or two is all a good woman needs.' Then she'd shivered suddenly and forced a smile. 'Oh – I felt as though someone was walking over my grave!' she'd said.

Lucy remembered that conversation now. She had lied to her mother. For, of course, it hadn't been Julia who had taken her to see the Mourning Warehouse, it had been Stephen. And not one of his family had known that they'd been there.

That first time she had looked around in wonder. It was a little like an expensive gown shop, she'd thought. Stephen had made them tea in the tiny staff kitchen and the tea had gone cold while they'd held hands and then kissed on one of the sofas in the showroom.

They hadn't stayed long. They had been overcome by their own daring. Knowing very well what the consequences would have been if they had been discovered. But neither had they been able to resist coming here again at the first opportunity. Lucy's mother would think she was still with Ruth and Esther. Stephen's mother and father were visiting friends at Tynemouth and would be late home, so he didn't have to account for himself.

'Sit down,' Stephen said. 'I've got something for you.'

Stephen disappeared through the door at the back of the room, but instead of sitting on the sofa as she'd been told, Lucy wandered towards one of the dressing rooms. The curtain at the entrance was looped back and a shaft of sunlight from a window on the wall behind struck through the warm shadows and lit the full-length mirror. Lucy put her bag down on the small dressing table and moved towards the mirror.

There was enough light to reveal that her cheeks were flushed; whether with the sun and the sea air or with excitement, she didn't know. Perhaps a combination of both. She raised both hands to remove her hat and, as she did, she was aware of Stephen crossing the room behind her, carrying something. He vanished from sight and then, a moment later, he appeared behind her.

'Here, let me,' he said as he took her hat and the pin and placed them on a chair beside the dressing table. 'Turn round again, away from me.' He moved close and put his hands on her waist.

'No, it's unlucky for two of us to look in the same mirror.'

'I'm not superstitious – and nor should you be. My mother would disapprove.'

His smile took any censure away from his words, and yet Lucy knew he was serious. Stephen's parents were God-fearing churchgoers who believed that any kind of superstition was the work of the devil. They didn't even approve of having a Christmas tree or decorating their home in any way at Christmas, saying that all that nonsense was a hangover from pagan times. The only concession they made to the season was that they sent simple greetings cards to trade associates and important members of the community. But Lucy suspected that this was simply good business practice.

'Look at me,' Stephen said, and, although he spoke softly, it was like a command.

He pulled her back against his body and she raised her eyes to meet his in the mirror. He was tall, with dark hair, and his narrow face was pale and solemn. Lucy thought it was because he was constantly dealing with death and bereavement. He could hardly greet his father's customers with a jolly smile. But when he was with Lucy his grey unblinking eyes sometimes quickened with hidden fire; his glance could be compelling, as it was now. She couldn't look away.

Stephen raised his hands to her shoulders and moved his head forward, turning his face towards her neck. He kissed her on the soft skin just below her ear and she closed her eyes. She felt him move away and realized she was swaying unsteadily. Her heart was racing. She opened her eyes to find herself alone.

'Where are you?'

'Come here.'

She left the dressing room and saw that he was standing by one of the tables. On the table there was now a silver tray on which there was a bottle of something dark and red, two glasses and a plate of ratafia biscuits. 'Sit down,' he said, and inclined his head towards one of the sofas.

Lucy sank down into the velvet softness and watched bemusedly as Stephen opened the bottle and filled the two glasses.

'Is that wine?' she asked.

'Mm, Marsala.'

Lucy knew what Marsala was; the sweet Sicilian wine was her mother's favourite. 'But you don't drink alcohol,' she said.

'Who told you that?'

'Your sister. Julia told me that your father will not have anything remotely alcoholic in the house.'

'That is so. But what I do when I'm not at home is my concern.' He turned and smiled at her and, before giving her her glass, he proffered the plate of biscuits. 'I know you like them.'

'Who told you that?' she asked, and they smiled at each other.

'My sister, Julia.'

'Of course.'

Lucy nibbled on a delicious almond-flavoured biscuit and then took a cautious sip of the wine. She didn't know whether she should confess to Stephen that she had tasted it before. Her mother had allowed her a small glass now and then at the dinner table but she had never told Stephen this in case he disapproved.

As soon as she tasted it, however, she was aware that this was infinitely superior to the wine that her mother kept at home. She looked up at Stephen with genuine surprise.

'You like it?' he asked.

'It's delicious.'

'Let me fill your glass.'

'No ... I hardly...' Lucy frowned as she looked at her glass. It was almost empty. She hadn't realized how much she had drunk.

'Your hand is shaking. Give me the glass,' Stephen said. 'I don't want to spill wine on your virginal white clothes.'

Lucy handed him the glass and looked away, embarrassed by his words. What had her mother said that morning? *You look lovely ... all in white ... so fresh ... so innocent.* So innocent... She supposed she was innocent if being a virgin meant that she was so. But what about her thoughts and her desires? What about the feelings that had surged through her body a moment ago when Stephen had held her against his body and kissed her neck?

This time when Stephen handed her the glass he brought his own and sat down beside her on the sofa. They didn't speak. Lucy watched the dust motes dancing in the rays of sun that illuminated some areas of the large room, leaving other parts in shadow. The room smelled of lavender furniture polish and it was warm ... so why did she feel cold?

Lucy noticed that the hand that held her wineglass was still shaking slightly. Suddenly Stephen took the glass from her and leaned across to put both glasses on the table. But he misjudged the distance and one of them slipped off, spilling the remnants of wine as it fell. They gazed at the spreading red stain only a shade darker than the crimson of the Turkey carpet. Lucy half rose; she meant to go to the small kitchen and find a cloth to mop up the wine.

'Leave it,' Stephen said, and he seized her arm and pulled her down again. 'It will soon dry out. No one will notice.'

'What are you doing?' Lucy asked. He had pulled her into his arms and she could feel him fumbling at her waist. 'No ... don't...' she said faintly as she realized that he had pulled her blouse free from her skirt and had slipped his hand underneath. 'Stephen, you'll crush my clothes ... spoil them...'

He moved away from her, then took her hands and rose to his feet, pulling her up with him. 'Then why don't you take them off?' he said quietly.

Embarrassment caused her to laugh but then her eyes widened as she realized he meant it. She couldn't speak but she watched as his hand moved to his collar and he began to loosen his tie, and all the time he didn't stop looking at her.

She watched in silence as he removed his jacket.

'What are you waiting for? Do you want me to help you?' he asked.

'No,' she whispered and, compelled by his unblinking gaze, her hands moved to the buttons at the neck of her blouse. She began to undo them.

When Count Hugo took Angelina into his arms and crushed her against his manly chest, Angelina protested weakly – and Ruth could bear it no longer. She wiped the nib, then put the pen in its holder, then tidied the papers neatly on the desk top and sat back and closed her eyes. She was

177

tired and somehow the happy day she had spent with her friends had made her feel dispirited.

Both Lucy and Esther seemed happy with their lives. Esther worked hard and she had the added burden of having to care for her brother, and yet she was both cheerful and resourceful. Lucy ... what was it about Lucy? Although she had entered into the fun of the day, laughed and gossiped and been jolly with Davy and Joe, there had been something about her, an air of distraction. As if some part of her being was elsewhere. She had been hiding something, Ruth decided, something she didn't want to share.

Even as she thought it Ruth knew that she wasn't being fair. She was just as bad. She had known perfectly well that Henry Valentine was ... was what? Was interested in her. She would not have put it as strongly as being in love. How could he be? They hardly knew each other. Life wasn't like a romantic novel. Their eyes had not met above the heads of the elderly patrons at one of his concerts. They had simply met by chance, and since then, and talked together as ... as what? As friends?

Was Henry Valentine her friend? She supposed she had come to regard him as such, but perhaps she simply hadn't allowed herself to admit that he wanted something more. Or perhaps she couldn't believe it. In the first place he must be at least ten years older than she was, and his background was very different from hers.

Henry had told her that he lived with his parents in a large old house in Heaton, near the park. His father was a musician too – he played the violin in a theatre orchestra – and his mother had been an opera singer. Opera singer! Ruth hadn't even known what opera was and she had had to look it up in a dictionary. She had learned that an opera was a play in which the words were sung to music. She thought that strange, but she had wondered about it, tried to imagine the kind of story that could be acted out in such a way.

When Henry spoke of his parents he did so fondly. Everything he'd told her led her to believe that he came from a loving and happy home. He was talented and well-spoken and, although he was not truly handsome, he was good-looking. So why on earth was he interested in her?

Should she have gone to the concert? He had wanted her to and she would have enjoyed it, if only she'd felt confident enough to cope with Henry. So she had denied herself the pleasure – and she had been rude into the bargain.

This was her day off and Miss Golightly wouldn't have minded if she had come home late. She was not the kind of employer who wanted to make slaves of her servants. Mrs Fairbridge liked to go to bed early and she would have grumbled a little if she'd had to wait to lock up, but Ruth could have faced that problem if necessary.

So why had she chosen to hurry back and get on with transcribing this wretched manuscript? She rose from the table and closed the window. The breeze was freshening and beginning to rustle the paper. She didn't want to come into the room in the morning and find the pages blown all round.

She paused by the window and looked down into the street. It was getting late but people were still walking up from the beach and making their way to the railway station. On her next day off she supposed she ought to go home. Ada never made her welcome but her father always looked pleased and wanted to know what she'd been doing since the last time. When it was time for her to go, he always asked her if she was happy and she always told him that she was.

And she must sound convincing because he would smile and nod his head. But Ruth wondered if it was guilt that prompted his question. Perhaps, after all, her father realized that he had been manipulated by his wife into sending his daughter away from home. But he was happy to receive Ruth's reassurances and Ruth had accepted that, once she had gone, he probably forgot all about her until the next time she visited.

She supposed she ought to go down to the kitchen and have some supper with the others. She cheered up a little. The sea air had made her hungry and Mrs Fairbridge set a good table. Then she would go to her room early – but not to sleep. Not straight away. She had some writing of her own to do. She experienced the usual pleasurable shiver when she thought about the hours ahead.

Poor Angelina, the heroine of Miss Golightly's novel, was not suffering in vain. For, incredibly, the wretched girl's struggles had prompted Ruth to try to write a novel herself. And she dared to believe that she could make a better job of it than her employer.

180

Esther could hear the commotion long before they turned the corner and, when they did, the familiar group of women outside the door confirmed her fears. The women, about half a dozen of them, all poorly dressed and ragged, crossed their arms over their bodies, and gripped the ends of their shawls in a familiar pose.

One of them, Hetty Lowther, who lived with her family in the rooms above the Robinsons, turned when she heard Esther and the lads coming. Catching Esther's eye, she shook her head. 'It's bad,' she said. 'He's been gannin' his ends for near on half an hour. I divven't think you should gan in, hinny.'

'Divven't yer? Should I wait here and let him morder me ma?' Hetty's eyes widened. 'I'm sorry,' Esther said. 'It's not your fault.'

She had surprised herself with that sudden flash of rage and she supposed it was because she'd had such a lovely day at the seaside with her friends – and then she'd come home to find that nothing had changed. In fact, by the sound of her father's roars and her mother's screams, it was worse than ever. She looked down at the boys. Davy's eyes were huge in his pale face. Joe didn't even look surprised. The poor bairn is used to this, Esther thought. But she couldn't spare time to speculate on what went on in Joe's home.

'Run away yem, Joe,' she told him. 'No, wait. Why don't you and Davy play in the street for a while? Yer can gan down to the quayside and watch the boats come in.'

'I'm not gannin', Esther. I'm coming in with

181

you,' Davy said.

Esther looked down into her brother's face. The older he grew the more protective he was of their ma. And yet heaven knew why, Esther thought. Mam barely acknowledged her children's existence these days. Perhaps Davy could still remember the days long, long ago, when Agnes Robinson had held him in her arms and rocked him to sleep. Perhaps the poor bairn still longed for that bit comfort. I do me best, Esther thought, but I'm too busy working most of the time to be a mother to him. Still, I'm all he's got and I'm not letting any harm come to him.

'Now, lissen,' she said. 'Yer not coming in. I'll deal with this, right?'

'Yer sister's right, bonny lad,' Hetty Lowther said, and the other women nodded their heads in agreement. 'Gan on, run off with yer pal. Let Esther see to yer ma.'

Davy looked up at Esther, his eyes brimful of tears, and she tried to smile as she nodded. 'Gan on, pet,' she said. 'The sooner yer off, the sooner I can gan in and sort things.'

Sort things, she thought, as she watched her brother walking off down to the quayside reluctantly. Sort things? What on earth am I going to do this time? In the past she had resorted to pulling her mother out of the way and running out of the house with her – if her father didn't get to the door first. More than once she had pushed her under the table and cowered there with her, the pair of them dodging the vicious kicks her da aimed at them.

Once she had been unlucky enough to come

between them, and her father's blow had sent her spinning across the room. Luckily she had landed on the bed, but she had lain there, winded while her mother yelled blue murder. Usually her father's rages were as short as they were vicious, so if this had been going on for nearly half an hour surely his anger must be just about spent. Esther stepped through the ever-open front door into the shared hallway and put her basket down carefully beside the wall.

She straightened up, nerved herself and was just about to open the door into her family's room when the shrieking stopped. Disconcerted by the sudden silence, Esther hesitated. And then the door opened, swinging violently away from her, and her mother appeared.

Agnes Robinson looked like a wild woman. Her hair had come loose from its usual untidy bun and was hanging about her face like a witch's locks. Her bodice had been ripped from neck to hem, revealing her grubby shift and her unwashed flesh. Her shawl was tied around her waist and, as she stood, tottering in the doorway, her bony fingers picked at the knot, trying to undo it.

'Ma?' Esther said.

Her mother stared at her, her green eyes, which must once have been so clear and beautiful, were watering; her eyelids were puffed and red.

'Is that you, Esther, hinny?'

'Yes. Where's me da?' Esther could neither understand the silence nor why her father hadn't appeared raging behind her mother.

Her mother frowned. 'Yer da?'

'Yes, where is he?'

Agnes Robinson shook her head slowly as if hardly believing what she was about to say. 'He's dead.'

'Dead?' Esther was aware of the gasp that went up, almost as one, from the women on the pavement.

'Aye.' Her mother sighed. 'I've killed him. Killed him stone-dead.'

Having said those words, she suddenly seemed to come to her senses. Her eyes widened in fear and she glanced over her shoulder. At the same time her fingers had finally undone the knot of her shawl and she pulled it up, crossing it over her body, instinctively covering herself and making herself decent.

She glanced at Esther again and said, 'Divven't say owt!' Then she pushed past her and fled, scattering the startled neighbours as she went scuttling across the street to vanish into a narrow and foul-smelling alleyway.

Esther tried to follow her but found her way blocked by the assembled women who, rather than follow Agnes, had decided to come into the house.

'Stop this!' Esther pleaded as they tried to push past her. 'What are you doing?'

'To see if he's dead,' Hetty said. 'To see if she's really mordered him.'

'No!' Esther exclaimed. 'I'll go in. Wait here.' She broke free from the women and ran into the room, turning to close the door behind her. She leaned weakly against it. She could hear Hetty and the others, their voices rising with excitement, and she

184

knew they wouldn't leave until she had told them what had happened. But she couldn't bring herself to turn round and look.

She knew that she must. And, her heart beating wildly, she pushed herself away from the door and forced herself to turn. The evening sun streamed through the small window, casting light across the floor and on to the scrubbed table top. On the table there was a bread board with a loaf of bread and a knife. Esther glanced at the knife nervously and looked beyond the table to the hearth where a small fire burned and the kettle steamed on the hob.

At first she didn't see it. But as her eyes became accustomed to the shadowy light in the room, she became aware of the dark shape lying on the rug between the table and the fireplace. Her father.

She could hear the old clock ticking on the mantelshelf, the crackling of the fire as the coals shifted and settled in the grate, and her own heart beating as she crept forward. There was no sound from her father. She pressed her hand against her breast, trying to still her heart as she kneeled down and looked at him, and listened for the sound of breathing.

William Robinson lay on his back with his head twisted to one side and one arm flung up, covering his face as if warding off a blow. On the floor beside him there was a cast-iron cooking pot. Esther had a fleeting vision of her mother seizing the handle with both hands and striking at her father. She must have caught the side of his head, the side that was covered by his arm, Esther thought.

She knew she must move his arm to see what damage was done but she was afeared. Afeared to find the mortal wound that would prove her ma was a murderer, that would send her to the gallows.

She leaned forward and lifted his arm from his face and, at that moment, the door behind her burst open and a woman's voice, not Hetty's, cried, 'Well? Shall we send for the polis?'

'I tried to keep them out,' she heard Hetty Lowther say. 'I'm sorry, Esther, hinny.'

'Divven't fret, Hetty,' Esther said as calmly as she could. 'And there's no need to call the polis. Me da's alive.'

She held his limp arm and stared down at her da as the women shuffled into the room and came to stand beside her. The pan had caught him on one side of his face and the skin above his eyebrow was already beginning to swell and discolour.

'Is he breathing?' Hetty asked.

'Aye, lissen.'

The women fell quiet and then Hetty said, 'He'll need a cold rag on that eye.'

Esther let go of her father's arm and rose to her feet. 'Aye, I suppose he will.'

Hetty glanced at her keenly and then turned to the others. 'Hawway, you lot,' she said. 'Give us a hand to get him on to the bed.'

'Not me,' one of them said. 'I'm not touching that devil. What if he wakes up?'

They shuffled out. The only ones who stayed were Hetty and her grown-up daughter, Janet. Esther sank down on to one of the chairs at the table and watched as her upstairs neighbours heaved her father up and lifted him on to the bed. At one point he groaned and they almost let him fall, but his eyes remained closed and they managed to push him towards the wall.

'Gan on, Esther hinny, off you go,' Hetty said. 'I'll bathe his head, not that the old sod deserves it, and Janet will look out for Davy and take him upstairs. He can stay all night if yer like; bunk in with our Tommy. You'll hev other things to think about when yer gets back.'

'Get back? Where am I going?'

'To find poor Agnes, of course. You'll hev to tell yer ma that she didn't do for him after all. The more's the pity!' Hetty finished with an attempt at humour.

'I suppose I must,' Esther said.

Hetty frowned. It was obvious she was puzzled by Esther's reluctance. 'What's the matter?' she asked. 'Divven't yer want to relieve her mind? Tell her she hasn't mordered him? Tell her it's safe to come yem?'

'Safe?' Esther looked at her father. Even with his eyes closed he looked angry. 'Safe?' she repeated, and she and Hetty stared at each other as the same thought came into their minds.

What would William Robinson do when he came round? Would his poor downtrodden wife ever be safe from him again?

Stephen didn't see her to the station; at least not all of the way. They slipped out of the Mourning Warehouse and Lucy shrank back in the entrance while Stephen locked the door. Then they slipped quickly across the street and entered a back lane. The cobbled lanes that ran at the back of rows of tall terraced houses would lead, eventually, to Station Road.

Lucy reached for Stephen's hand and after a moment's hesitation he gave it to her. She felt furtive, slinking along hidden from view like this. She didn't like it but Stephen had reminded her that they couldn't be seen together; he was supposed to be at a friend's house. And after that he hadn't said much at all.

She glanced sideways at him as they hurried along. Was he as overcome by what they had done as she was? She couldn't tell. His features were as grave as ever. When they came to the end of the lane that led on to Station Road there was an archway. Stephen stopped in the shadows and pushed her towards the brick wall behind her. His kiss made up for his lack of words. It was almost savage in its intensity. It left her breathless and dissatisfied.

'Stephen, I...' she murmured.

'Hush. I can't come any further. You must go. Get your train.'

'But do you–?'

'Off you go. I'll watch from here but don't look back. Don't give the game away.' He gave her a gentle push.

'Goodbye, then.' She turned reluctantly to leave him.

'Wait!'

Lucy's heart rose as she turned back. 'What is it?'

'Your hat, that ridiculous hat. It's been knocked

askew. Let me put it right.' At last he was smiling at her and she stood obediently while he reached towards her and tilted her hat forward on her head. 'That's better. Can't have people thinking you've been up to something, can we?'

His smile broadened but she didn't respond. *Up to something?* Well, she supposed she had been, but she wished he hadn't put it like that, making a joke of it.

'Off you go then. And, Lucy...'

'Yes?' Was he going to say it at last?

'I'll arrange for us to be together again as soon as possible.'

Well, he still hadn't actually said he loved her but she remembered how often in the early days he had told her how he would like to make her his wife, and surely he wouldn't have wanted to marry her if he didn't love her. She smiled brilliantly at him before she turned and hurried away.

Arthur had just finished supervising the lighting of the station lamps, a job he'd used to do himself. He dismissed the lamp boy and then stood in the entrance and watched as stragglers made their way up from the beach. Here and there a father carried a tired bairn on his shoulders. A group of young lads, probably apprentices on a day out together, were laughing and shouting at each other. He'd have to have a word with them before they got on the train. Suddenly they whooped and whistled as a young woman hurried past them and Arthur saw it was Lucy.

She didn't even glance at them and Arthur

stepped back a little to watch her. She'd told him she was spending the day with her old friends, girls from school, but she was alone now, as she had been when she'd arrived.

Had she been telling the truth? Or had she really spent the day with Stephen Wright? Arthur felt the bile rising in his throat, caused by an anger that he knew he had no right to. Lucy didn't belong to him. She wasn't his lass, never had been, in spite of his dreams, and in spite of the way she looked at him sometimes.

Did she know what she was doing when she dropped her pretty head and glanced up at him through slanted eyes, he wondered. Probably not. It was just her way. She probably looked at other men like that without realizing how she could inflame a man's senses.

She hadn't noticed him – why should she? She reached the entrance and looked startled when he stepped forward.

'Arthur!' she said. 'What a surprise.'

'Why should you be surprised? I work here.'

'You know what I mean,' she said. Her cheeks were flushed and her eyes were shining.

He knew who'd put those roses in her cheeks, that sparkle in her eyes. And the knowledge made him wretched with jealousy. He turned, walked away before he betrayed the depth of his despair.

Ruth laid her notebook and pencil aside and leaned back against her pillows. She was pleased with her work, and yet she was disturbed by the emotions it had aroused. Never before had she enjoyed doing anything so much. Once she had begun she had found that the story that had started as a spark of an idea had grown and taken shape and, as it did so, the characters she had created jostled to be heard and competed with each other for more space on the page.

And the places she found herself describing... How wonderful it was to be able to bring into existence rooms, houses, streets, whole towns, that had no place in the real world. And yet Ruth knew she could make them seem real to anyone who might ever read her novel.

Novel! Was she really writing a novel? Ruth closed her eyes and thought about it. What right had she, a girl from an ordinary family in Byker, who had only been to elementary school, to write a book? What would Miss Matthews think if Ruth told her she hoped one day books she had written might join the others on the shelves at the Crystal Library? That she, Ruth, Miss Golightly's paid dogsbody, had the cheek to think she might become an author?

Ruth sighed and, putting her notebook and pencil on the table, she turned off the oil lamp. But it was a summer night and, even with the curtains closed, the room wasn't dark. And even if it had been she doubted if she could have gone straight to sleep. Scenes from the story she was writing played out in her head as if on a stage. Her characters spoke to each other with distinctive voices and acted their parts in the unfolding drama as only they could. But she, the writer, was in control.

How exciting it was to be able to make her fictional people do anything she wanted them to.

To give them clothes to wear and words to speak. To give them beauty or intelligence, humour or cunning, integrity or frailty but, above all, to make them human.

She could make them happy or sad, good or evil, she could even murder one of them and make another character clever enough to become a detective who would solve the mystery and bring the murderer to justice.

For that was the sort of book she had started to write: a detective novel. And the wonderful and daring thing about it was, her detective was going to be an ordinary young woman.

Esther drew her shawl round her shoulders and tried to keep in the shadows as she searched the huddled streets for her mother. She had no idea what she would do – what she was going to say when she found her. Agnes Robinson thought she'd killed her husband. She'd run away because she'd believed she'd be sent to the gallows. But he wasn't dead and that would bring her poor ma no relief. She'd be more in fear than ever of her brutal husband. She wouldn't want to come home.

But, even so, Esther had done her best to find her and at least tell the poor woman that she was safe from the law. She'd looked in deserted, crumbling buildings, the back yards and coal houses of occupied houses, and even in the outdoor privies. Instinctively she had worked her way down towards the river rather than going up towards Shields Road with its shops and offices, and the grander houses of Heaton beyond.

192

There were three old boathouses on the Ouseburn at a point before it flowed into the Tyne. They hadn't been used for many years. Esther had peered into them cautiously from doors in the landward end, softly calling out her mother's name. She knew that homeless folk and derelicts often slept there, but tonight there was no one in the boathouses at all.

Esther didn't know where to look next. She could hear loud voices coming from the Ship Inn across the old Glasshouse Bridge. Would her ma have gone there? She doubted it. Even if Agnes Robinson had wanted drink she wouldn't have risked such a rough place at this time of night.

Wearily Esther decided that she might as well go home. She was glad that Hetty Lowther had offered to keep Davy overnight. She hoped her da was still asleep. When he awoke she'd have to face him and tell him that her ma had gone. But where?

Esther paused while she decided what to do next. The moon was bright and the clouds seemed to be racing across the sky. There was a cold wind blowing off the river; fear gripped her as she stared down into the oily water. The thought that came into her head at that moment sent an icy shiver through her – but no, she wouldn't let herself believe that her ma had taken that way out. Nevertheless, she wondered if she and Davy would ever see their ma again.

Chapter Seven

April 1894

'I'm very pleased with you, Ruth. You have done justice to my work,' Miss Golightly said.

'Thank you.'

Miss Golightly had been reading through the manuscript ever since Ruth had finished transcribing it two days before. 'I must say,' she continued, 'I am more pleased with it than ever, now that I have seen it written out in a fair hand, with all my corrections and amendments put in place.'

Ruth didn't know what to say. Even though she had grown fond of her eccentric employer she couldn't bring herself to utter sentiments she did not feel. She glanced out of the window at the drenched street. It was only mid-afternoon but the rain clouds that filled the sky meant that it was dark. Ruth saw her own embarrassed reflection in the windowpane and that of the cosy book-lined room.

It was much tidier than it had been when Ruth had first come here. She had managed to impose some sort of order on the shelves and even begin the mammoth task of cataloguing Miss Golightly's books.

'Now, I want you to parcel the manuscript up carefully,' Miss Golightly said. 'I have plenty of strong brown paper and string. Then you must take it along to the Crystal Library.'

'The library? Don't you mean the post office?' Ruth asked.

'I mean exactly what I say. And if you had not interrupted I should have told you why.'

'I'm sorry.'

'You see, I want to ask Miss Matthews' advice. I want her to read my novel and give me her opinion.'

'Opinion? You mean of the story?'

Miss Golightly smiled condescendingly. 'A critique from Miss Matthews would be valuable, I suppose,' she said. 'But it would be redundant as I don't intend to change anything at this stage. No, what I want is for her to tell me where I should send my novel. With her experience of buying in books for the library she will have a good idea of which publisher will look at it favourably.'

'But...'

'But what?'

Ruth had been going to say that Miss Matthews might advise Miss Golightly not to send the manuscript off to any publisher but she knew that would be inadvisable. 'But it's raining hard,' she said.

'I know that, my dear, and I intend to send Flora along to the stand to fetch a cab for you.'

'Thank you!' Ruth said.

'We don't want the manuscript to get wet, do we? But there's no need to keep the cab waiting. Just pay him off when you get there. You can walk back.'

Flora looked pleased for once when she arrived

back in the cab. The errand had provided a welcome distraction from the routine of the day. She hurried up the path to the front door where Ruth was waiting with an umbrella held high. 'Come along, I've instructions to see you into the cab. And you're to keep the umbrella, although I don't know why you should,' she finished with a hint of vinegar returning to her expression.

'Thank you, Flora,' Ruth said after she had climbed into the cab. 'That's kind of you.'

The maidservant's eyes widened but she managed to smile before closing the umbrella, shaking it and depositing it on the floor of the cab. Her cheeks were flushed as she dashed back up the path and into the house. Ruth realized how very pretty the older girl was. She hoped that Flora would find another sweetheart.

She had recently learned that the reason for Flora's constantly sullen expression was caused by misery rather than bad temper. Henry Valentine had once called Flora 'sad-faced'. It had been that day at the beach last summer when they'd been celebrating Esther's birthday.

Ruth had wondered about Flora after that and, one evening, when she had been sitting over mugs of cocoa with young Meg, she had encouraged the little skivvy's chatter rather than frowning disapprovingly. She'd learned that Flora had come into service only because her sweetheart, a fisherman, had been drowned just one week before their wedding.

Ruth had been ashamed of herself for not realizing that there must be some underlying cause for Flora's behaviour. But she had also realized that her own dissatisfaction with life had caused her to shut her mind to other people's problems. Now that she had started writing her book not only was she happier, but she had also become more aware of other people's behaviour, and sensitive to the likely causes.

Miss Matthews looked at the parcel where it lay on the counter doubtfully. 'I must admit to being surprised,' she said. 'Have you read it? Can you tell me anything about it?'

'I've been copying it out for Miss Golightly. It's ... well, it's melodramatic.'

'Oh dear. Your expression tells me more than your choice of words. But I suppose I must agree. Your employer has been a good customer of the library and she's well-respected in this town. It would never do if I declined to help her and she then became a famous novelist. No one would trust my judgement ever again. What is it, Ruth? You look as though you want to say something.'

'I really hope you'll be able to suggest a publisher,' she said. 'I mean, you don't have to form any sort of judgement. Miss Golightly simply wants to know where to send it.'

'You're trying to tell me that I mustn't say it's not worth sending off to any publisher at all, aren't you?'

Ruth hesitated. 'I suppose I am,' she said at last. 'Miss Golightly would be so hurt.'

'I understand. But have you considered that she might be even more hurt if she gets a rejection letter?'

'I have. But she's already considered that possibility. She's told me of other authors, some of

197

them quite famous, who had many rejection letters before finally being published. She said the thing to do if the manuscript came back was to send it out again.'

'And again and again, no doubt. Poor Ruth.'

'Why poor me?'

'Because, if this happens, at some stage the manuscript will become tattered and torn and you will have to copy it out again. In fact, if I might make a suggestion, I think you ought to start on another fair copy straight away; from the size of this parcel, this work must have taken you quite some while.'

Ruth groaned and then covered her mouth with her hand in embarrassment. Miss Matthews raised her eyebrows and then smiled. 'Would you like to come upstairs for a cup of tea and a slice of cherry cake?' she asked.

Ruth was astonished. She had never been invited to Miss Matthews' flat above the library before. 'Do you mean now?'

'I do. It's Saturday and I feel like starting the weekend early!' She must have seen how surprised Ruth was because she laughed. 'Seriously, since it started to rain shortly after I opened this morning I haven't had a single customer; not even those with books that should be returned today. I can't blame them.

'Look, I'll put this card in the door; it directs people to ring the house bell if they find the library closed during the usual opening hours. Is that umbrella big enough to shelter both of us? And the precious manuscript too?'

'I think so.'

'Wait! Don't open the umbrella until I've got the door open! And don't look at me like that – I know as an educated woman I shouldn't be superstitious, but I am.'

Miss Matthews had never seemed so light-hearted. It made her look younger. Ruth sheltered them both with the umbrella while the librarian locked the shop door and they hurried the short distance to the house door. She had it open in a trice and they stepped inside.

'That's right, leave the umbrella in the stand and you can hang your coat up,' she said as she hurried up the stairs ahead of Ruth. She waited at the top and took the manuscript. 'I'll put this in my room,' she said. 'And then I'll make a pot of tea. That's the door to the sitting room. Go in and sit by the fire.'

Miss Matthews disappeared and Ruth opened the sitting-room door as she'd been told. But before she went in she paused. She had just remembered. Didn't Miss Matthews live here with her elderly brother? Would he be sitting by the fire, and would he be surprised to see her?

The room was empty. It was also extremely clean and tidy. Everything shone, even the leaves of the houseplants. The scent of lavender polish mingled pleasantly with something else. Ruth was unexpectedly reminded of her father and recognized that something else as the smell of pipe tobacco.

Where was Miss Matthews' brother? Ruth hoped the old gentleman wasn't ill in bed. Should she ask Miss Matthews or leave the librarian to broach the subject first? As she was wondering what to do, the librarian came in bearing a tray.

'Move that little table up for me, Ruth, will you? That's right. We'll sit by the fire and toast ourselves.'

Before settling down Miss Matthews removed the cinder guard and built up the fire, which had been burning low. Then, for a while, with the fire crackling and the rain still beating against the windows, they talked of nothing in particular, such as what a dreadful few days it had been, and how the tides had been so high that the waves had crashed right over on to the promenade.

Several foolish young men had gone down to look and one of them had been almost swept away. Fortunately two of his friends had grabbed on to him and held on tight. They had fallen over backwards and had all received a good soaking. And serve them right, Miss Matthews said. 'My brother would never have been so foolish.'

Ruth was startled. She had a momentary vision of the respectable old gentleman on the promenade with the young pranksters. The scene played itself in her head. Old gentleman engulfed in the wave, arms raised, walking stick waving desperately; monocle and top hat flying. She almost laughed out loud and had to cover a suspicious snort by saying loudly, 'Of course he wouldn't!'

She was disconcerted by Miss Matthews' reaction. Her hostess gave her such a strange look. Was it surprise? Or was Miss Matthews puzzled? But in any case she changed the subject by asking Ruth if she'd like her teacup filled up and another slice of cake.

'Yes, please,' Ruth said, and for a moment neither of them spoke as Miss Matthews poured the tea and cut the cake.

'I never thought,' the librarian said. 'Should you have gone straight back to Miss Golightly's?'

'No, that's all right,' Ruth replied. 'Miss Golightly's nephew and his wife are coming to have dinner with her tonight so she told me I was free from duties for the rest of the day.'

'And what will you do?'

'I'll go to my room and do some wr– reading.' Ruth had almost mentioned her writing but Miss Matthews, sipping her tea, had not appeared to have noticed the apparent stumbling over her words.

'What are you reading at the moment?'

'Oh – *David Copperfield*. Miss Golightly has all the novels of Charles Dickens.'

The second sentence was true, at least, and as for the first, Ruth had taken the book from the shelf, and even carried it to her room, but she had only glanced at it. All her spare time was taken up with her own writing at the moment but she didn't want to admit to that. She was sure that Miss Matthews, kind though she was, would be surprised and perhaps even scornful if she knew that Ruth was writing a novel.

Soon they became engrossed in talk about books and favourite authors and neither of them noticed that the sky was growing darker and the rain heavier. At last the sound of the wind rattling the windowpanes caught their attention. They stopped talking for a moment and looked out towards the wet roofs of the houses and shops opposite.

Smoke from the chimneys whirled skywards and blew away in the wind. A sudden gust seemed to shake the very room they were sitting in. There was a crash and Miss Matthews jumped up from her seat.

'Was that thunder?' she asked.

'I don't think so,' Ruth replied. 'It sounded like something downstairs.'

'Do you mean from the library?'

'No, it sounded like a door slamming.'

Before they could wonder further the door opened and a tall young man walked into the room.

'Roland,' Miss Matthews gasped. 'You're early.'

Ruth observed how flustered she was, almost as if she were a servant who had been caught slacking. But her expression changed to one of relief when the young man turned to Ruth and smiled brilliantly. She felt herself flushing. Not just because he was the handsomest man she had ever seen, but also because of the wild thoughts that had flooded into her head.

Who was Roland? Why had he come here to see Miss Matthews? What on earth could be their relationship when he obviously had a front door key?

And then another shock. 'Guinevere?' he said as he turned back to face the librarian. It was obvious that he was asking who the visitor might be – but, *Guinevere*!

Then the woman who Ruth would never be able to think of as dull Miss Matthews again said,

'Roland, this is Ruth Lorrimer.'

He raised his eyebrows. 'Yes?'

'Ruth works for Miss Golightly. She brings her books and orders to the library.'

'Of course.'

He turned and offered a hand. Ruth wasn't sure whether she should rise to take it or remain sitting but she rose anyway as some instinct prompted her not to show how intimidated she was.

'Ruth, this is my brother, Roland,' Guinevere Matthews said, and Ruth wished that she had remained sitting as all her preconceptions about the librarian's brother vanished like the smoke from the chimneys.

Lucy set off for Whitley-by-the-Sea as soon as the office closed at noon, supposedly to see Julia, but really because she expected that Stephen would come home when he too finished work at lunch-time. Stephen usually had Saturday afternoon free, but not always. Lucy didn't feel that she could actually ask Julia what her brother's plans were.

Julia was alone when Lucy arrived. Her brother and father were out at business and her mother was visiting friends. Julia expressed surprise.

'I wasn't expecting you today,' she said.

Lucy knew that meant that she hadn't been invited. Of late she'd noticed that their friendship had not exactly cooled, but had become more formal. Instead of her being welcome to call by whenever she wanted to, Julia, no doubt on the instruction of her mother, would say, 'Why don't you come for tea next Saturday,' or, 'Shall we meet in town for a change? At Tilley's? Then we can do some window shopping.'

As far as Lucy could remember the last time she'd been to the Wrights' imposing villa at the north end of town near the links, Julia had said, 'We'd better leave it for a week or two. My mother has a lot of social calls to make and I'm expected to accompany her. I'll drop you a line when we can meet again.'

Well, Julia hadn't dropped a line, and Stephen hadn't been in touch either. Stephen couldn't write to her, of course. Her mother would have recognized that the handwriting was different from Julia's and would have wanted to know who the letter was from. Stephen usually telephoned Lucy at the office. It was one of Lucy's duties to answer the telephone and, as long as she kept the call short and was discreet, her employer, Mr Hetherington, didn't mind her having the occasional personal call.

But now, after an initial awkwardness, Julia gave every impression of being pleased to see her.

'But you look like a drowned kitten!' she said. 'You'd better come up to my room and make yourself respectable.'

Lucy was pleased to avail herself of the luxuries on offer in Julia's dressing room. Julia had been exaggerating; her umbrella had kept her more or less dry but her curls had come out in the damp air and the bottom of her skirt, fashionably long enough to sweep the ground, was muddy.

'Let me help.' Julia brushed and sponged the hem as if she were a lady's maid while Lucy unpinned her hair and did the best she could with it.

Julia offered her curling tongs but Lucy declined. 'No, thank you. My hair's so fine the tongs will make it frizzy. My mother says I must only use rags.'

'You're so lucky,' Julia said, surprising her.

'Why lucky?'

'To have a mother who is interested in such things. My mother likes me to be clean and tidy, and even to adopt the latest hairstyles and fashions, but that's only so that people will know we can afford them. She hasn't any idea of what suits me or how to help me.'

'But she buys you all those magazines,' Lucy said, indicating the pile of *The Ladies Journals* on a table. 'You can look at the illustrations and get some idea from them, can't you?'

Julia sighed. 'I know. I shouldn't complain. But if only she would look at the magazines with me and we could have fun together the way your mother and you seem to have. You are lucky, you know, to have a mother like that. A mother you can talk to like a friend.'

'I know I am,' Lucy acknowledged. She hoped Julia would change the subject.

For friends confided in each other, didn't they? Friends told each other about their hopes and dreams. Of late she had actively been avoiding conversations with her mother – because of Stephen. And, also she had been neglecting her. Her mother was more and more left on her own because of the impossible hours that her father worked. Daisy had explained that the more senior he became in the firm, the more responsibilities he had, and the more he was paid. They shouldn't complain.

And it was true; life was full of even more little luxuries these days. Lucy's mother had a generous clothes allowance, and so did she. But what her mother really wanted was to move from the little house in Byker Village to somewhere more fashionable. She hardly ever reminded Lucy's father of his old promise these days, but Lucy could tell that she had never forgotten it.

After spending a more or less pleasant hour 'beautifying' herself, as Julia put it, the two of them settled in the upstairs sitting room. Julia rang for the maid and ordered a pot of tea, a plate of cold roast beef sandwiches, cakes and biscuits. Lucy, having come straight from the office, had not had any lunch but she found she couldn't eat anything. She was too strung up. She sipped the tea and nibbled on a sandwich while she watched Julia devour everything in sight.

Julia would have to be careful, Lucy thought, or she would grow stout like her mother. Mr and Mrs Wright were like Jack Sprat and his wife. Thankfully Stephen took after his father. He was lean and muscular and very, very strong. Lucy closed her eyes as she remembered the last time he had taken her in his arms. Even the memory of it swamped her senses. It was getting more and more difficult for them to be sensible.

Stephen had told her that he would make sure that she never became pregnant. He told her that he would practise coitus interruptus, that is, he would withdraw from her just before he reached his climax. She knew it was difficult for him, and it sometimes left her unfulfilled, but they would have to go on like this until they were married.

'What are you thinking about?' Julia asked.

'Thinking?'

'You were miles away.'

'Was I? I'm sorry.'

'Was it somewhere nice?'

'Perhaps.' Lucy tried to affect an amused smile and she rose quickly and walked to the window. Time seemed to be passing so slowly.

It was still raining and a sea fret had rolled in to hover over the hummocky grass of the links. Lucy watched a tram making its way towards the bandstand. When it stopped at the terminus only one passenger got off. A man smartly dressed in an overcoat and a bowler hat. She held her breath until the man crossed the road and then began to walk in the wrong direction. It wasn't Stephen.

'Would you like to stay for dinner?' Julia asked her.

'I'm not sure.' Lucy pressed her fingertips on the cold glass and watched as the horse was unhitched and led round to the other end of the tram. 'My mother will worry if I stay too late.'

'It's a pity you don't have a telephone at home, then you could let her know. But if we eat now you wouldn't be very late.'

Lucy remained standing with her back to Julia, pretending to look at the scene outside. 'But don't you have to wait for your family?'

'No, I shall be on my own tonight. My father is working late and Stephen is going straight to his friend Sydney's house.'

'Oh.'

'At least he says he is. It's my opinion that there's a woman involved.'

'What makes you say that?' Lucy was glad that Julia couldn't see her face, witness her shocked expression.

'Well, many a time when he's supposed to have been at Sydney's he hasn't been there at all.'

'How do you know that?'

'Sydney's sister, Iris, told me. We compared notes one day and came to the conclusion that our brothers were providing alibis for each other.'

'I see.'

'Are you all right, Lucy? Your voice sounds shaky.'

Lucy summoned a smile and turned to face Julia. 'I'm quite all right. Just a little tired. It's hard being a working girl, you know. Unlike certain ladies of leisure I know, I have to get up early in the mornings and slave away over a typewriter and a telephone.'

'You're teasing me.'

'I'm not. I do work hard.'

'Well, nevertheless, let me tell you I envy you, being able to get away from home and have a life of your own. I hate being stuck here with nothing much to do. I'd like you to know that I've begged Papa to let me come and work for him.'

'Have you?' Lucy was genuinely surprised.

'I have. After all, that's how he met my mother. She worked in his office before they married – and for some time after.'

'But your father doesn't want you to work?'

'Actually, I don't think he'd mind. It's Stephen who objects.'

'Why on earth would your brother object?'

'I used to think he was just being awkward, but now I think it's because he wants it all his own way.'

'What do you mean?'

'Well, the business will be his one day when my father – well, you know – when my father is put to rest in one of his own coffins!' Julia giggled and Lucy was shocked. She supposed the nature of her father's business might have made Julia insensitive to the usual taboos.

'Why should that make a difference?' Lucy asked.

'I think Stephen imagines Papa might decide to leave part of the business to me – you know, the Mourning Warehouse, for example. Stephen wants everything. He keeps saying things like, they should find a prosperous husband for me, someone to look after me, but it isn't my welfare he cares about – he just wants me out of the way!'

'My goodness, Julia. I had no idea.'

'Of course you hadn't. How could you have?'

Julia looked puzzled and Lucy laughed and tried to make a joke of it. 'I meant I had no idea that you could be so passionate about something. You're usually such a lovely easy-going companion.'

'Am I?'

'Yes. That's why I love coming to see you.'

Poor Julia flushed with pleasure. 'Then you will stay for dinner, won't you?'

'I'd love to, but I really must get home. I left this morning while my mother was still in bed. I don't like to neglect her.'

'Is your father working away again?'

'Mm.' Lucy felt like adding that he was more away than at home these days and that it was making her mother anxious and fretful, but she didn't want to be disloyal.

'Very well, I understand. But at least let me treat you to a cab. I can telephone for one and tell them to put it on our account.'

'Thank you. I'd be grateful.'

During the short ride to the railway station Lucy thought about her conversation with Julia and she hoped that her friend had not noticed her discomfort when she had been talking about Stephen perhaps using his friend to give him an alibi. Lucy herself was the reason he needed an alibi. But where was he, tonight? Was he really at Sydney's house? She could hardly have asked Julia to find out from Sydney's sister if that were so. But if he wasn't there, where was he? And why did he seem to be avoiding her lately?

No, that wasn't true. He wasn't avoiding her. He still wanted to see her and when they did meet he was as passionate as ever. It was just that they didn't meet quite as often as they used to.

When she arrived at the station Lucy realized there was a twenty-minute wait before the next train to Heaton, which was the nearest station to where she lived. The small refreshment bar was open but there was a lively party of young men and women there. They were dressed for a night out and Lucy guessed they might be going to the theatre in Newcastle; or perhaps a theatre in North Shields, a couple of stations away.

Lucy bought a cup of tea at the counter and asked if she might take it to the waiting room.

'All right, pet.' The woman behind the counter smiled and nodded towards the boisterous young people as she poured the tea. 'I wish I could come with yer. That lot's giving me a headache. They're harmless enough but, if you see the porter tell him Gladys wants him to call by. Mebbes he could hev a word before they gets on the train. High spirits like that can lead to accidents. There you are; bring the cup back, mind.'

Gladys had been generous; the cup was full to the brim and Lucy carried it carefully. She held her furled umbrella under her arm and when she reached the waiting room she pushed the door with her free hand. She sensed the welcome warmth of the fire straight away, but she remained standing in the doorway when she saw the two people at one side of the fireplace.

The man and the woman hadn't heard her come in and they remained locked in an embrace. Lucy felt her cheeks burning as her body adjusted to the warmth of the room, so different from the draughty platform behind her. But it wasn't just the fire that made her burn. She gazed fascinated at the tableau before her. The man was broad-shouldered; the woman was small and slight. He held her so tightly that she seemed to melt into his body.

Lucy could see neither of their faces but she didn't need to, at least not to identify the man. The uniform, the cap that lay on the floor at his feet, the broad shoulders, and the thick dark blond hair. It was Arthur.

The fire crackled and hissed as stray raindrops made their way down the chimney. The woman's

211

coat steamed slightly and Lucy could smell the damp fabric, the odour mingling with that of the burning coal.

Suddenly Arthur pulled the woman into the curve of his body more forcefully and she moaned with pleasure. Lucy recognized the sound only too well.

'Oh!' Lucy gasped involuntarily and the cup she was holding rattled in the saucer. Arthur released the woman and stepped away from her. He glanced at Lucy and surprise mingled with embarrassment, then turned to dismay.

But Lucy hardly noticed. She was staring at the girl. For it was only a girl who stood there, although when Lucy examined her closely, she saw that she was older than she had at first thought. For even though she was now dressed in what was surely her best coat, with a ridiculous hat, probably handed down from her mistress, clinging precariously to the back of her head, Lucy recognized her immediately.

The woman who had been returning Arthur's kisses so enthusiastically was the young nurse-maid who had been in charge of the unruly boys on the day of Esther's birthday party last summer. What was her name? Mary Clark.

'Lucy,' Arthur said, and his cheeks were as bright as the blaze in the hearth.

'Gladys wants to see you,' she blurted out. She couldn't think what else to say.

'Right,' Arthur said. 'Well, then ... Mary, lass...'

'I'll come with you,' the girl said. 'I'll wait in the refreshment bar.'

'Right,' Arthur said again, and Lucy realized

that he was too embarrassed to ask her to move out of the way.

She moved well away from the door and the two of them hurried past her. 'Wait,' Lucy said, just as Arthur gripped the door handle. He stopped and came back towards her. Lucy saw the young nursemaid scowl with annoyance.

'What is it?' he said, and she could see the torment in his eyes.

'Would you take this cup back for me?'

'But you heven't drunk it.'

'I know. I don't want it.'

Arthur shook his head and reached for the cup and saucer. His hand brushed hers and Lucy was glad that she had her gloves on for she knew she couldn't have borne to feel his bare flesh.

When they had gone Lucy stood and gazed down into the fire. She was too unnerved to sit and she didn't know why. She loved Stephen, didn't she, so why had she been so dismayed to see Arthur kissing someone else? Could she be jealous? No, that wasn't possible. Unless it was because her pride had been hurt. She supposed she had always believed that Arthur was sweet on her. He had hardly made a secret of his feelings. Indeed, she had believed that he was hurt and angry when she had started meeting Stephen – although he had no right to be!

She admitted to herself at last that she had enjoyed Arthur feeling that way about her and had been truly sorry that the differences in their backgrounds had prevented her from responding as she'd wanted to. But whatever the truth of the matter, it was all changed now. Arthur had found someone else. That soppy, useless little excuse for a nursery maid Mary Clark. And Lucy had to admit that she didn't like it.

What a disappointing day this has been, she thought, and she sighed with weariness. She wished she hadn't sent the tea back with Arthur. She could have done with a hot sweet drink but she couldn't have faced returning the cup to the refreshment bar and maybe finding Arthur's new sweetheart sitting there and simpering up at him.

When the train steamed into the station Lucy saw Arthur having a word with the party of young people. They laughed and agreed good-naturedly to do as they were told. Lucy chose a carriage well away from them, but she couldn't resist glancing back and was disconcerted to see Arthur coming towards her as he made sure that the carriage doors were shut properly.

As she boarded the train she was aware of Arthur looming up behind her and shutting the door. Flustered, she didn't see the stretched out legs of the gentleman who was already sitting in the compartment she chose. 'I'm sorry,' she said as she stumbled and then righted herself.

He glanced up from the paper he was reading and nodded politely enough. But he looked vexed. The lady sitting beside him smiled as if embarrassed by his manner and murmured, 'That's all right, dear.'

They were the only other occupants of the compartment and Lucy observed them surreptitiously on the journey home. They were middle-aged, perhaps a little older than her mother, Lucy thought, and respectably dressed. Maybe they had been visiting family or friends; they didn't look as though they were going into Newcastle for a Saturday night treat at the restaurant or theatre.

He studied his newspaper without comment. Not a bit like her father who would read interesting items aloud to her mother. The woman gazed out of the window into the gathering dusk rather sadly, as though wishing her husband, for husband he surely was, would talk to her. But Lucy noticed how close together they sat, and how, in spite of his seeming neglect, he patted her hand after he had turned the page of his newspaper. Will Stephen and I be like that? Lucy wondered. When we have been married for years and years? I hope not.

And, yet, what will we talk about? It was only then that she realized that she and Stephen did very little talking when they were together. All the time they stole was taken up with lovemaking. Even afterwards, when they were full of the wonder of what they had just done, there was little time for sweet talk or endearments. She dropped her head when she felt tears pricking at the back of her eyes and a sharp ache of misery lodge in her throat.

She sensed the woman's eyes on her and looked up to find her looking at her questioningly. Suddenly Lucy felt the craziest urge to confide in this kind-looking stranger how unhappy it made her that in spite of his ardent lovemaking, Stephen had never actually told her that he loved her. And how, of late, he had grown more and more remiss about making arrangements for them to meet again. And how, when he did contact her, he took it for granted that she would fit in with his arrangements, never asking her if it was convenient.

But, of course, I could never do such a thing, Lucy acknowledged. Even if we were alone, she and I, in this compartment, I could never tell this complete stranger what sort of person I am, letting a man make love to me without a wedding ring on my finger nor even the definite promise of one. No matter how kind she looks, this woman would be shocked by my behaviour. As I should be.

The woman smiled shyly and dropped her gaze. Lucy hoped she had not upset her by looking hostile. The man, oblivious to the interplay, rustled his newspaper and Lucy's attention was caught by the front page:

'TRAIN CRASH IN YORKSHIRE', the headline said. 'THREE DEAD, MANY INJURED'.

Morbidly fascinated, Lucy leaned forward a little and read as much as she could make out. What a miserable day this had been.

'The rain is easing off, thank goodness.' Roland Matthews stood by the window and gazed out into the darkening street.

'Then I suppose I'd better go.' Ruth began to rise from her chair but Roland turned and gestured for her to stay.

'No, finish your tea,' he said. 'Then I'll walk you home.'

'Oh, there's no need.'

'It's getting late. I think I should.' Miss Matthews' brother came back to join them at the table. 'Don't look so worried,' he said.

'But I feel I'm inconveniencing you.'

He smiled. 'You're not. I have two more calls to make and it wouldn't be out of the way. Now would you like another slice of seed cake?'

'Yes, please, it's delicious.'

Miss Matthews smiled with pleasure at Ruth's compliment and Ruth was relieved to see her expression. She had been worrying over the fact that the librarian had hardly said a word since her brother had come home and, after an initial moment of surprise, had asked Ruth to stay for tea.

Miss Matthews had looked taken aback but she had immediately bustled about, setting the table with the most delicious home-baked fare.

'My sister always prepares too much,' Roland had said, smiling. 'She thinks I'm still a greedy little schoolboy. She's been looking after me since our mother died when I was a small child,' he explained. 'My father was lucky that Guinevere was old enough to take over the running of the household and care for both of us.'

'Father died only two years ago,' Guinevere Matthews added sadly. 'We were a happy little family.'

As they took their seats Roland told Ruth, 'Guinevere gets up at some unearthly hour every morning to make sure that food is prepared and the housework done before she gives me my breakfast and goes downstairs to the library. I'm a lucky man.'

While they enjoyed their meal Ruth learned that Roland Matthews worked for an insurance company and he didn't always have to work on Saturday afternoon, but sometimes it was the only time to catch the gentleman of the house at home.

'And evenings too,' Miss Matthews added. 'My poor brother often has to go out to visit clients in the evening and in the most inclement weather.'

'Yes, well, sometimes I have the sense to let the inclement weather drive me home, like today. And I'm very glad of it for otherwise I might not have met your friend Miss Lorrimer.'

Ruth had been almost overcome with pleasure at his words. Not only did Roland seem to mean that he was pleased to have met her but he had called her Miss Matthews' friend. As Ruth responded to Roland's easy smile she was taken unawares by her own reaction to his physical beauty. Fortunately his glance never lingered for very long, and soon she found herself replying to his light-hearted banter. Superficial but enjoyable; any challenge was to her wit, not to her emotions.

Now, as she nibbled her second piece of seed cake, trying to be ladylike, she reflected that perhaps Miss Matthews had barely spoken because Roland had not given her a chance. Ruth had learned more about the librarian in the last hour than she had in all the months she had been coming to the library.

Miss Matthews' parents had opened the Crystal Library when Mr Matthews senior, a schoolmaster, had come into a small inheritance. Mrs Matthews loved reading and was an incurable romantic, hence the names, Roland and Guinevere, she'd given her children. 'She got them from some poetry book or other,' Roland had said.

His sister had shaken her head at his words and smiled sadly. 'My brother doesn't read very much,' she'd said quietly.

'Well, you read enough for both of us,' he'd replied, and laughed.

'I feel I should help you with the washing-up,' Ruth said as Miss Matthews began to clear the table.

'No, that's all right, dear. But while Roland prepares his paperwork you could help me carry these through to the kitchen.'

Roland sat at a tiny desk in a corner near one of the windows and began to sort through papers and documents in his briefcase. Ruth loaded a tray and followed Miss Matthews into a tiny kitchen-cum-scullery at the back of the house. Everything was scrubbed and clean. Green and white gingham curtains framed the tiny window and matching curtains hung from the bench top to the floor, covering the shelves and also the space under the sink – just like in the scullery at home, Ruth thought.

Miss Matthews lit the gaslamp and the dusky view of the back yards and lanes vanished as the window became a looking-glass to reflect the scene within, which was cosily domestic. Ruth watched Miss Matthews fill the kettle and place it on the gas stove. That was unlike home: Ruth's stepmother heated water and did her cooking on a coal-fired range.

'My pride and joy,' Miss Matthews said when she turned and saw Ruth watching her. 'We used

219

to have a range in the living room like everybody else but Roland insisted that I should have the latest gas stove installed in here and a more attractive hearth placed in the living room. It was very good of him.'

Ruth wondered fleetingly whether Roland Matthews had been thinking of his sister's or his own comfort. After all, having a proper sitting room was probably as much for his own comfort and convenience, but unwilling to think any less of him, she dismissed the thought as quickly as she could.

She watched Miss Matthews put on a large apron and realized that she was uncomfortable at seeing the librarian in this strange new role. Guinevere Matthews was an educated woman, who acted and spoke like a lady, and yet here she was, in the kitchen about to start washing dishes just like Ruth's own stepmother.

And, going by what Roland had said before, the Matthewses didn't seem to have any domestic help in the form of a maid. For if there had been even a daily maid-of-all-work, these dishes would have been left on the bench to be tackled by that maid first thing in the morning.

When Ruth and Roland were ready to go Miss Matthews accompanied them down to the front door.

'I'll read Miss Golightly's manuscript carefully and try to give her the right advice,' she assured Ruth.

Roland stepped out first and unfurled a large umbrella. 'We'll share this one,' he said. 'Take my arm.'

Ruth did as she was told, and as they made their way through the lamp-lit streets she tried to control her breathing. It was disturbing to be so close to this handsome man. Furthermore, a man who seemed determined to be charming. I must say something, she thought. But what? If this were Henry Valentine we would talk about books or he would tell me about music, which is his passion. But Roland Matthews doesn't read and I have no idea what enthuses him.

'Do you like your work?' she asked suddenly.

'Selling insurance? Yes, I do,' he replied. 'And I'm good at it.'

'Oh.'

He laughed. 'I know. It's not proper to praise oneself, but I've never understood why one can't be truthful. It's not as if I'm boasting or exaggerating.'

'I don't know very much about insurance,' Ruth ventured.

'Why should you? Basically, insurance is a safeguard against loss or failure. Rich men protect their property or their businesses, and even the very poor make regular payments to ensure they'll have a decent burial.'

'And you collect these payments?'

Roland remained silent and Ruth risked a glance up towards his face. He was frowning. 'Yes, I do,' he said at last. 'And I advise people about the sort of contract they need and persuade them to buy more insurance. But soon, I hope, I will be promoted, and then I shall have my own desk in a comfortable office in Newcastle and I won't have to pound the streets quite so much – oh, watch out!'

As he spoke Roland took the umbrella with his other hand, slipped his arm around Ruth and lifted her clear of a large puddle that had formed on the pavement. He swung her forward as he leaped the puddle and set her down on the other side.

Ruth felt her heart pounding. In that moment of intimacy she had learned how strong he was – and how little she had control of her emotions. She was trembling as she took his arm again. Fortunately they did not have far to go.

Roland insisted on seeing her right to the front door and held the umbrella over them as she rang the bell. It was late and Mrs Fairbridge knew who it would be, so she sent Meg to answer. The girl's eyes opened wide when she saw Roland and she and Ruth stood together on the doorstep as they watched him turn and hurry away.

'Who was that?' the little skivvy asked.

'Oh, no one important,' Ruth breathed as she turned and fled upstairs. When she reached her room on the top floor she closed the door and leaned back against it, trying to catch her breath. It was a long time before her heart achieved its regular rhythm. And Ruth was grateful that, smitten with Roland Matthews as she no doubt was, she found she had enough intelligence to realize that the attraction was prompted by his supreme good looks and that she retained enough of her sense of humour to be able to laugh at herself.

Well, well, she thought, I'm just as bad as the wretched Angelina.

The shop stayed open until eleven o'clock on Saturday night so Mr and Mrs Fowler had gone to their flat upstairs for a rest. Raymond was putting the orders up and, as the bad weather had kept the customers away, Esther was taking advantage of the quiet time to dust and tidy the shelves and clean the counters. Only poor Davy was out in the rain.

Esther had bought him a second-hand waterproof cape and a sou'wester for days like this. With the hat pulled forward to keep the rain out of his eyes and the broad flap at the back protecting his neck, it was only his poor hands that got cold and wet.

Davy had already had a soaking on the way to work. He had run up Raby Street to Fowler's shop; it wasn't too far, but far enough for him to get drenched. Esther had taken him into the back shop and dried him off as much as possible with a rough towel. She'd given him a hot mug of tea and a bit of bread and cheese and he'd set off with his first load cheerfully enough.

But Esther was worried that with his damp clothes he might develop a chill. When they got home, she'd decided, she would warm up a pan of broth and maybe add a dash of the cheap draught sherry she kept hidden for emergencies.

The groceries were well-protected, of course, with the tarpaulin cover specially made to fit over the basket of the carrier bicycle. Esther was thankful that there were only two more deliveries to be made tonight. Then she and Davy could go. Raymond was going to stay on to help his aunt and uncle until the shop closed.

Esther looked out into the street. The rain had thinned to a relentless drizzle. It would be a miserable walk home. She sighed.

'Tired?' Raymond asked.

'No.'

He laughed. 'You don't hev to be afeared of admitting that to me.'

'Why should I be frightened?'

'In case me uncle thinks he should get someone who isn't dragging herself around all the time.'

'That's not true! I don't drag meself around!'

'Suit yerself.'

Raymond carried on slicing ham and Esther glanced at him surreptitiously as she polished the counter. Mr Fowler's nephew, who had come to work in the shop straight from school, was going on sixteen, but physically he was like a grown man. He was tall and muscular with red hair that he kept well brilliantined so that it looked a shade darker.

In his shopkeeper's apron, and with his shirtsleeves kept neat with metal armbands, he looked very smart. The trouble was he knew it. He knew how the young lasses round here were only too pleased to fetch their mothers' shopping just so's they'd get a chance to talk to Raymond Fowler. And some of them weren't exactly young lasses, either; nor single. Esther thought those women ought to be ashamed of themselves.

And Raymond was sharp, she had to admit it. He learned quick and he missed nowt. Dragging herself around. That's what he'd said and he was right. She was mortal tired. What with working the hours she did and looking after Davy and keeping house for her father – and trying to keep him sweet. Well, that was all enough to tire out any normal body, even someone who didn't spend half the night scouring the streets of Newcastle.

It was eight months since her mother had run out of the house believing that she'd murdered their father. On most nights, when Davy was safely asleep and her father snoring, Esther put on a dark cloak with a hood that pulled up to cover her head and she went out looking for her. She knew that, even if she found her, it was unlikely that Agnes Robinson would come home. She would be too frightened of what her husband would do.

But Esther wanted to set the poor woman's mind at rest – tell her that she wasn't going to hang. And she also wanted to be able to reassure Davy that his mother was alive and well; as well as she could be if she had joined the ragged army of homeless on the streets. So, not daring to tell her father and unwilling to tell Davy in case his hopes were raised, Esther visited the soup kitchens, the temporary hostels set up by well-meaning citizens in abandoned warehouses, the alleyways and the shop doorways night after night. No wonder she was tired.

Esther looked up to watch the rain streaming down the shop window. She could make out lighted windows in the houses at the other side of the road. Suddenly there was a blurred flurry of movement racing past the window followed by the sound of something crashing to the ground and someone called out in pain. Davy!

Esther raced out of the shop and peered through the rain. Davy had come off the delivery bike a few yards downhill and he was lying in a tangled heap with the bicycle on top of him. She hurried towards him.

'Davy!' she cried as she stared down at him. 'What hev you done?'

He moved slightly, trying to get up, but the bicycle impeded him. He groaned and then somehow wriggled over so that he could stare up at his sister. 'What do yer mean, what hev I done? I've come off the bike – can't yer see?'

'Divven't be so impudent.' Esther knew she sounded cross but in a funny way that was because she was relieved that he seemed to be all right. Although she still didn't know whether he'd broken something. 'Here, let's get you up.'

Ignoring the water streaming downhill in the gutter, Esther half-kneeled and reached for the frame of the bicycle.

'Wait a minute,' a voice behind her said, 'I'll do that.'

Esther turned her head and squinted up through the rain. Raymond Fowler stood behind her, holding a large umbrella. 'Hawway, lass, divven't waste time, take this.'

Esther resented the way he talked to her but she rose and took the umbrella. She wasn't looking for a quarrel. Not with the boss's nephew.

'Come on now, Davy,' Raymond said to her brother. 'Move yer arm. That's right – that one. Now, let's ... get ... this bike ... that's it.' Raymond lifted the bicycle free and Davy began to get to his feet. 'Divven't get up too quickly, lad. Are you all right? No bones broken?'

'I divven't think so,' her brother said. But Esther thought he looked femmur.

'How did it happen?' Raymond asked.

'The cobbles is wet – slippy, like. And me hand slipped on the brake.'

'Easy enough, I suppose, in this weather,' Raymond said. And then his tone hardened. 'Right then, gan and pick the basket up. It's a good job there was nowt in it or you'd hev had yer wages docked.'

The basket that fitted into the carrier frame had fallen free and tumbled down the street. As Davy set off across the wet cobbles he lost his footing and Esther darted forward. But he righted himself before she reached him.

Raymond laughed. 'Like a mother hen, aren't yer, the way yer look out for that lad?' He laughed at her.

Esther felt her anger rising but she choked it back. When Raymond had first come to work for his uncle, who had no children of his own, she had been instructed to show him the ropes. He'd been a quick and willing pupil and it wasn't long before he didn't need her advice at all. Esther could see the day when the lad, young as he was, would know as much about running the business as his uncle did and she wondered if this would pose a threat to the job that meant so much to her.

And she never knew quite where she was with him. For sometimes he would tease and then he would take her by surprise and act as if they were friends. And, just now, she had been astonished by the gentle way he had dealt with Davy. Until the lad was on his feet, that was.

'I'm sorry, Esther,' Davy said as he came back with the basket. 'I divven't want to cause trouble for yer.'

'That's all right, pet,' Esther said. 'As long as yer not hurt.'

'And as long as the bike isn't damaged,' Raymond said.

Esther turned towards him angrily. But she was taken aback by his grin. He wasn't being sarcastic; his smile seemed genuine. 'Gan on,' he said as Davy replaced the basket and took the handles of the bike from him. 'Take it round the back to the yard and yer sister can make you a mug of tea afore yer gans out again.'

'Out again?' Esther said.

'Aye, there's two more orders to deliver and I divven't intend to take them meself.'

'Of course not.' Esther sighed. There was no point in protesting. Raymond was right, the orders would have to be delivered and it was Davy's job to deliver them. It was just that whenever his uncle and his aunt went upstairs it seemed more and more natural for Raymond to take charge. There was no denying that he was capable; but he was only a lad, after all.

'Lissen, Esther, it's Sunday the morrer and the lad can hev a lie in. You an' all. Right?'

She nodded but she didn't speak because there he went again, talking to her as if she were the one who was more than two years younger.

'And divven't look at me like that.'

228

'Like what?'

'As if yer divven't like me.'

For a moment he seemed uncertain of himself. Esther had never seen him like that before. Then he laughed. His self-assurance came back and he stepped closer; Esther backed off.

'It's all right,' he said. 'I just want to share the umbrella. Yer wouldn't begrudge me that, would yer? I must look like a drowned rat.'

Indeed he did. His hair was dripping down over his forehead and his shirt was plastered damply against his shoulders and his upper arms. Esther felt a twinge of guilt. It was her fault – hers and Davy's – that Raymond was in such a state.

'Take it,' Esther said, and she thrust the umbrella into his hands before hurrying back into the shop. In that moment as she'd looked at him in the rain something had changed between them and she didn't know what to make of it.

The smell of frying fish was tempting. Lucy hesitated at the entrance of the fish-and-chip shop on the corner of Heaton Road. She knew that she had neglected her mother of late and this would be a nice treat for her. Lucy looked inside at the small queue at the counter. She wouldn't have to wait too long. She went in.

The two young women ahead of her in the queue turned, nudged each other then looked her up and down. Their glance was hostile and Lucy knew it was because she looked so nice; so well-dressed in comparison to their own shabby selves. Well, there was nothing she could do about that. It wasn't her fault that her father had a good job and was able to provide well for his wife and daughter. And she worked hard herself in that dusty office. If she wanted to spend her money on fashionable clothes she was entitled to, wasn't she?

As soon as she'd made her purchase she hurried home. But, what with carrying her umbrella in one hand and the newspaper-wrapped parcel of fish and chips in the other, she couldn't hold her skirts up from the rain-soaked pavements. She knew she would have to spend hours brushing the hem clean, and she wondered if she would be able to persuade Betty to do it for her.

Shields Road was busy and Lucy had to wait for a succession of trams and cabs to pass before she could cross. The horses' hoofs sent up sprays of filth, and Lucy stood well back before dashing across and nearly colliding with a delivery lad on a bicycle. He swerved to avoid her and brought his bike to a stop. He turned to look at her and she thought she heard him call out but she hurried on. She didn't want to get into an argument with a cheeky youngster.

Once home, and still juggling with the fish and chips and her umbrella, Lucy managed to bang on the front door. She was taken aback when Betty answered it. Her mother was a thoughtful employer and she usually let their maid go home early on a Saturday if Mr Shaw was not coming home for dinner. Perhaps her father had arrived home after all, Lucy thought fleetingly, and then all reasonable speculation was driven from her mind when she heard the dreadful cries coming from the living room.

'Betty ... what is it? What's happening?' she asked.

The overhead gas mantle in the passageway revealed that the old woman was white-faced and shaking. Her eyes were red-rimmed as if she'd been weeping. Lucy realized from the small gasping sounds that she was making that she still was.

'My mother?' Lucy asked. 'Is my mother...?'

At that moment the figure of a woman emerged from the door of the sitting room and came rushing along the passage towards them. She was shrieking like a madwoman, her hair was wild and her face was ravaged with grief. It was her mother.

'Lucy!' her mother cried. 'Where have you been? Where were you when I needed you?'

Lucy shrank back from the accusation in her mother's eyes, but Betty took hold of her and, pulling her inside, she shut the door. Then she earned Lucy's gratitude by placing her solid body between them.

'Whisht, Mrs Shaw, hinny,' the old woman said soothingly. 'Whisht afore you do yerself a harm.'

Their maid took hold of her mother's shoulders and turned her round before guiding her back towards the living room. 'Divven't just stand there,' she said over her shoulder. 'Put that parcel in the scullery and come in.'

Lucy suddenly became aware that she had been clutching the fish and chips tight to her body. She could feel the heat of them coming through the paper and she wrinkled her nose at the thought that they might make her clothes smell. But she did as she was told and, treading warily past the living-room door, she left the fish and chips and her umbrella in the scullery before going hesitantly into the living room.

Thankfully her mother had stopped the dreadful screeching. She was sitting in an armchair by the fire with her arms wrapped around her body as she rocked backwards and forwards moaning softly. Betty had got down on her poor old knees in front of her and she was looking at her helplessly. Lucy noticed distractedly that the pages of the morning paper were scattered over the floor, some of them crumpled.

Betty looked up. 'I'm glad yer home, pet, but it's dreadful news I hev to tell you.'

'Is my mother ill?' Lucy asked.

'Aye, ill with grief.'

'Grief? But why?'

As the old woman began to rise painfully to her feet Lucy's eyes strayed to the newspaper on the floor and she saw the same headline that she had read earlier. She was still staring at it when Betty took her in her arms.

'It's yer mam that should tell you this, hinny, but she's in no fit state. It's yer dad—'

'No!' Lucy was aware of the panic in her voice. 'There's been an accident—'

'A train crash!'

'Aye, pet,' Betty sounded puzzled but she went on, 'in Yorkshire. Yer dad was on that train. He was killed outright.'

Chapter Eight

A queue had already formed outside the soup kitchen at the old hospital; Esther walked by, scanning their faces anxiously. She had learned to keep her head down and to glance up sideways rather than stare. Not only would that have been ill-mannered, for even these poor unfortunates deserved to be treated with respect, but also it might have drawn rough comments and caused trouble. She didn't want to be responsible for any wretched creature being turned away.

Since she had started looking for her mother at night she had seen many a sight to make her heart break. It was not just the old and the crippled that lived on the streets, but children too. Many of them were orphans who survived as best they could. The sight of them made her more determined than ever to look after Davy as long as he needed her. And, also, of course, to find her mother. Although she still had not decided what she would do if she did.

Sometimes she dreamed of finding some better rooms for them to live in together. But she wasn't sure how she could afford that, and worse, her father would be bound to find them. That was what was preventing her from moving out right now, she and Davy. And even if her father didn't come after them, she knew she would be filled with guilt at leaving him to fend for himself.

Whatever he had done, he was still her father and if he didn't have a wife to keep house for him then a daughter should.

The doors of the soup kitchen opened and a groan of pleasurable anticipation went up from the waiting crowd as the delicious smell of the evening's meal wafted out into the cobbled courtyard. Esther hung back and watched as the poor folk shuffled forward. Some of them would be desperately hungry and yet they kept in an orderly line, confident that they would not be turned away.

When the last few stragglers had entered Esther turned to go; her mother had not been among them. She decided that she would go straight home. She couldn't face searching the usual shop doorways, not tonight; she was tired and the damp air had chilled her to the bone. She would go home and go to bed. It was Sunday the morrer and she and Davy could sleep a bit longer, thank goodness. Sometimes Esther wondered if she would ever get enough sleep again.

'Yer ma's asleep now, Lucy, hinny, and I think you should gan to bed an' all. But drink this first. You need it.'

Lucy looked up from the newspaper she had spread out on the table. 'What is it?'

'Hot sweet tea – with a drop of brandy,' Betty said. 'Yer ma keeps it for what she calls "medicinal purposes".'

'Thank you.' Lucy managed a weak smile. 'And what about you?'

'Aye, I'll hev a drop.' Betty tipped a generous

slug of brandy into her tea and sat down. She looked exhausted.

Lucy gave the old woman a chance to drink a little and then she said, 'Tell me what happened today.'

'Yer poor mother had one of her bad days for a start...'

'Oh, no.' Lucy felt guilty. She guessed her mother's mood would have been caused by what she perceived as her daughter's neglect.

Betty sighed. 'Aye, she was out of sorts from the minute she woke up. I took her breakfast up on a tray and, after she'd eaten it, she went back to sleep for a while. Then, when she did get up, she didn't settle.

'At one point she was all for going into town and calling for you at the office. She said she'd persuade you not to gan to yer friend's house and that a little bit shopping and tea at Tilley's would cheer her up.'

'But she didn't go?'

'No, pet. I persuaded her not to. I knew you wanted to gan to the coast and see Julia and I thought it quite right that you should. Yer ma, bless her, shouldn't expect you to stay at home with her. You're just a young lass and you need a bit fun.'

Lucy dropped her head and stared into her cup of tea. She felt hot with shame, and she hoped dear old Betty would never know that most of the times she'd said she was going to see Julia she'd really been going to meet Stephen. And what they got up to would not be classed as an innocent bit of fun.

'Well, anyways,' the maid continued, 'we spent the afternoon sorting through her wardrobe. Yer ma laid aside a few outfits that she says she'll never wear again and she asked me to clean them and alter them to fit yer friend Esther. Although that lass is quite capable of altering them herself now.

'Ee, when I think of what a little ragamuffin she was when I first set eyes on her – she's come a long way. And she looks after that brother of hers better than their ma ever did. You know, Esther will make someone a grand little wife one of these days.'

Betty stared into the mid-distance, her tired old eyes not really focusing. It was as if she was trying to distract herself, to think about something more pleasant for a while. She shook her head slowly, then picked up her cup and finished her tea in one long draught.

'I'll hev some more of this, if you don't mind, Lucy, pet,' she said, and reached for the teapot. 'Do you want a fill-up?'

'No, thank you.'

Lucy didn't comment when Betty laced her tea with another slug of brandy. She reckoned she deserved it. After a moment's silence she said, 'But you were telling me...'

Betty looked at her and frowned. 'Telling you?'

'About ... about my father ... about how...'

'Oh, aye.' The old woman's sigh seemed to come from her boots. 'The paper. She'd never read the paper. After tea I offered to stay until you came home, keep her company, like.'

'Oh.' Another stab of guilt.

'I said we'd sit by the fire and she could read the paper to me. She often did that, you know. Yer ma has a lovely voice; she makes the little bits and pieces from the newspaper sound like proper stories. Sometimes she has me laughing fit to bust, and sometimes she has me crying...'

Lucy watched her eyes fill with tears. The old woman's lips began to tremble. 'I'm sorry, Betty, but you have to tell me. You have to tell me why my mother thinks that my father is dead.'

Betty wiped her eyes with a handkerchief and all the while she was stuffing it back in her pocket she stared at Lucy, frowning. 'But it's there in the paper,' she said. 'On the front page – the train crash – the derailment they called it – there, look.'

'I am looking.'

When Betty had persuaded her mother to go upstairs Lucy had gathered up the loose pages of the newspaper from the floor and spread them out on the table. Her mother had been able to tell her very little beyond the fact that her father had perished in the train crash and, once she was alone, Lucy had wanted to make sense of it. But far from explaining things, the newspaper report had left her more confused.

'There's a list of names – the unfortunate victims ... the dead and the injured,' Betty told her now.

'I can see that. But my father's name isn't here.'

'It must be.'

'Did my mother read it out to you?'

'Yes ... no ... she got as far as the names and then screamed. I asked her what on earth was the matter and, at first she didn't make sense. She was going on so that I thought she was losing her wits. And then I guessed, of course. I know your pa's head office is in Yorkshire – the factory an' all – and I guessed. I asked her if yer pa was among the injured and she said he was among the dead.'

Lucy smoothed the crumpled newspaper with both hands. She had read the headlines and the first paragraph on the train coming home, of course, but then the print got smaller and it would have been rude to lean any closer to her fellow passenger in order to read more.

Now she scanned the whole report again, feverishly. Perhaps there were two lists of names, although she couldn't see why there should be. 'Show me, Betty,' she said at last. 'Show me where my father's name is.'

'I canna.'

Lucy looked up to see Betty smiling sadly. 'Why can't you?'

'Lucy, pet. You know very well I canna read.'

'Oh, of course. I'm sorry.' Lucy realized that the problem was not going to be solved. At least not tonight. Well, not entirely. She looked once more at the list printed in the newspaper, trying to make sense of it. Reginald Shaw's name was not there. But there was a Reginald. Reginald Lawson. Lucy stared at the name. Lawson was the name of the firm her father worked for. When he was travelling on business he had cards and samples with him. That could be it. In the confusion after the derailment it would have been easy to make a mistake.

But no ... among the injured there was a Mrs

238

Lawson ... and a Miss Lawson. Mr Reginald Lawson's wife and daughter, the newspaper explained.

'I don't understand!'

Lucy didn't realize that she had crumpled the newspaper up and was holding it to her breast until Betty rose and came round the table to prise it gently from her hands.

'I know, hinny. It's too much to bear, isn't it? You divven't want to believe it but it's there in black and white.'

'Black and white...' The printed names seemed to leave the paper and circle round in front of her eyes. Mr Reginald Lawson's wife and daughter were only slightly injured, the paper said. But Mr Reginald Shaw, Lucy thought, who worked for Lawson, had not been travelling with his wife and daughter. Mr Reginald Shaw's wife and daughter were here in their house in Byker Village while the remains of poor Reginald whoever-he-was had been taken to a mortuary in York.

So who were the two ladies who had been treated by a doctor at the site of the accident and then taken by coach to their family home on the North York Moors? Lucy shook her head.

'No, I don't understand,' she said. 'I don't know what the answer is.'

'Answer? I divven't know what you mean, pet. But I do know that you should gan to yer bed. Now, come along, I'll take you up. And divven't fret, I'll not gan yem the night. I'll be comfy enough in the armchair and I can help your ma in the morning.'

'Will you?'

'Of course, pet.'

Lucy allowed the kindly woman to take her upstairs and help her undress and see her into bed as if she were a child. But, after Betty had left her, she lay sleepless as she tried to repress the dreadful suspicions that were beginning to worry away at her peace of mind. She realized that mixed with her grief was a feeling of anger; anger at the deception and at the lies that must have been told over the years if what she suspected was true. For, of course, if it were true so much was then explained.

Finally, as she willed herself to sleep, she heard sounds from the next room. Her mother moaned and then began to sob. But Lucy didn't go to comfort her. Let Betty do that, she thought wearily, and was grateful to hear the old woman climbing the stairs. She only hoped that by morning her mother would have calmed down enough to explain things to her. Until then she would cling to the forlorn hope that the newspaper had made a mistake.

The moon was bright but, coming back from town, Esther kept to the shadows. As a lone young woman out at this time of night she didn't want to attract attention and, rather than walk across Byker Bridge with its modern lighting, she hurried down the foul-smelling alleyways that led to the Ouseburn Valley.

Although it was long past midnight there were still raised voices and boisterous laughter coming from the Mushroom Inn. The ramshackle old building, with warm light spilling on to the boat landing, was in stark contrast to the nearby Dead House. Esther paused, as she always did when she passed the city mortuary.

Had her mother ended up here, a nameless bundle of old bones? Would it serve any purpose if she went in to enquire or would she have to resign herself to the fact that Agnes Robinson had long ago been buried in a pauper's grave with a number instead of a name marked in the ledger to record her passing?

Just before she reached the old Glasshouse Bridge she had to pass the Ship Inn. Two men staggered out, one supporting the other, and she drew back quickly. They headed for the bridge. Esther stayed pressed close to the side wall of a nearby house. She would let them get well out of the way. They were drunk and seemingly jolly but there was no telling which way the temper of a man could go when he had the drink in him. She knew that only too well.

She watched as they stopped on the crown of the bridge and one of them leaned over the parapet and began to heave the contents of his stomach into the burn. Eventually they went on their way and Esther, holding her cloak tightly round her, hurried across the bridge and up the cobbled bank to her home.

The house was quiet but Esther held her breath as she tiptoed past the room where her father would be sleeping. Before going to her own room she decided to look in on Davy. She knew he would be sleeping but it was something she always did. She opened the door of his room just enough to peep in and she waited for her eyes to adjust to the dim light.

She had hung some curtains that Lucy's ma had passed on to her at the small high window but the moonlight filtered through the gap and fell across her brother's bed. He wasn't in it! Or rather he was, but instead of lying sleeping as he should have been he was sitting on the edge of the bed in his nightshirt, his fists clenched as they rested on his knees and his eyes wide with terror.

He was trying to tell her something. He looked straight at her, he moved his eyes to the side and then back. He did it again. Esther's nerves knotted with fear. Davy was telling her that someone was standing at the other side of the door. No sooner had she realized that than the door was yanked open and, as she was still gripping the door handle, the force pulled her into the room. She turned to see her father standing there, his face a mask of cold fury.

'Run for it, Esther!' Davy yelled, but how could she? Even if her father had not already gripped her arm, she would never have left her brother alone with him when he was in a mood like this.

'Where the hell hev you been?' her father yelled.

'I telt him...' Davy sobbed. 'I telt him you've been to yer friend's, to Lucy's house!'

'Shut up, you!' their father shouted. 'I telt yer to say nowt!'

'Davy, whisht,' Esther said. She was pleased he'd had the sense to let her know what he'd said but she didn't want him to anger their da any further.

'Is that right, then?' Her father gripped her

arm, swung her round and pulled her in close so that her face was close to his. 'Hev you been to Lucy's house?'

Esther gagged at the foul smell of her father's breath. 'Yes,' she whispered.

'Liar!'

Before she had the chance to pull away he raised his other arm and brought his hand down across her face. She felt her neck twist with the force of the blow and she began to fall but her father yanked her upright.

'Divven't hit her!' Davy screamed, and he leaped off his bed.

'Stay back – stay back, Davy! I'm all right.'

'One step further, lad, and I'll take my belt to you!' their father bellowed. 'Now tell me the truth, my lass. Where hev yer been?'

'Just ... just walking.'

'Aye, that's more like it.'

'What do you mean?'

'You know damn fine what I mean. Do you think I'm stupid? Do you think I heven't noticed all them bonny new clothes? How come you can afford clothes like that? I divven't buy them for you.'

'I've got a job – I earn me own money. I buy me own clothes.'

'Oh, aye. You're a shop girl. Shop girls can't afford clothes like that.'

'And I get things from Lucy and her ma. They give things to me.'

'A likely story. They live up in the village, don't they?'

'Yes.'

'Well, folk round here don't buy good stuff like that. Oh, no, miss, you've found other ways to put clothes on yer back, heven't yer? Walking the streets, that's what you do. You've been sneaking out at night when respectable working folk are abed, haven't yer?'

Esther stared back at him. What could she say? She couldn't tell him the reason that she walked the streets at night. Since the day her mother had left he had cursed his wife's name. He had threatened to do her injury if she ever showed her face again. How could Esther tell him that she had been looking for the poor woman?

'Heven't yer?' Enraged by her silence her father shouted louder than ever and Davy begin to sob. 'It's no use trying to deny it. You've been seen.'

'Seen?'

'Aye, more than once. Laughing at me, they were.'

'Laughing at you?'

'For God's sake, divven't keep repeating what I say like a bloody parrot. Two of the fellows I work with were heving a fine old time, eyeing me up and nudging each other. And when I asked them what the hell was so funny, they telt me that they'd seen you many a night sneaking back home like a dirty alley cat.'

'No! It's not what you think.'

'Divven't talk back, just lissen. I divven't want to put you out – although you deserve it – but it's got to stop. No more gannin' out at night, right?'

Esther nodded, wordless. Her father seemed to have calmed down and she thought she knew why. But now she just wanted him to go.

'Do you understand?' he asked, and she thought he looked uncomfortable.

Esther nodded.

'Right, then.'

Her father released her arm and backed away. He hesitated as if he were going to say something more but then he left her and went back along the stone passage. Esther watched him go. She could hear low voices, words she couldn't make out, echoing down the stairwell. Her father had roused the upstairs neighbours with his shouting.

She waited until she heard his door close before she stepped out into the passage and peered up into the gloom. Hetty Lowther and her daughter were leaning over the banister. 'It's all right, Hetty,' she said softly. 'Me and the bairn's all right. You can gan back to bed.'

'Are you sure, pet?'

'Aye, I'm sure.'

'What was all that about? What set the old devil off at this time of night?'

'Nothing in particular. You know what he's like.'

'Aye, I suppose so.'

Hetty and her daughter shuffled off along the upstairs landing but Esther could tell that their curiosity had been aroused. What am I going to do? she thought. I divven't want to give up looking for me mam but now me da'll be watching me like a hawk. I daresn't gan out and leave Davy alone to face the consequences...

'Esther?' It was Davy and he sounded frightened.

Esther went back into his room and shut the

door. She sat next to him on the bed. 'What is it, pet?'

'I telt our da that you'd gone to Lucy's because that's the only place you ever gan.'

'You did right, pet. You were trying to help.'

'But you didn't gan there, did yer?'

'No.' She couldn't lie to Davy.

'So where were you?'

'Like I telt our da. I was out walking.'

'In the middle of the night?'

'I couldn't sleep.'

'Did yer hev toothache?'

Esther smiled. 'Aye,' she lied. 'Just like you had that night last week. You couldn't sleep either, could yer?'

The anxious lines on Davy's face softened. 'I didn't know what to say when he asked me,' he said. 'I didn't know you'd gone out. You didn't tell me.' An accusing note had crept into his voice again.

'Well, I didn't want to waken you, did I?'

'What did our da mean? About you walking the streets to put clothes on yer back?'

Esther felt the heat rising. 'He meant he thought I was a loose woman,' she said angrily. 'Someone who turns a coin by selling her body. You know what that means, don't you?'

'Yes.' Davy sounded shocked.

'Well, he's wrong,' Esther said. 'I would never do anything like that.'

'But Da said it's not the first time you've been out when I'm asleep.' Again the accusing note.

What should she do? Should she tell him and raise his hopes that his ma might be found? No, she couldn't do that, it would be too cruel. 'You know, pet, I hev a lot to worry about.'

'Do you?'

'Yes, me job at the shop's tiring and that Raymond's a right handful.'

'I know. He doesn't half tease you. He's a proper card.' To her surprise Davy began to smile.

'Do you like him?' She was amazed.

'Aye, I do.'

'But he torments you.'

'We-ell,' Davy looked thoughtful, 'he used to but it's teasing, really. And he's always fair.'

'I suppose he is. You know, Davy, you're more grown-up than I thought you were if you'd worked that out. More grown-up than I am!'

'Aye, and yer still heven't telt us why yer gans out at night.'

Esther gave him a sharp look. He was growing up indeed. 'I gans out when I'm troubled and I can't sleep.' Well, that was part of the truth, wasn't it? she thought.

'Well, you shouldn't.'

'Why not?'

'Because the streets aren't safe for a lass on her own. And if anything happened to you what would become of me?'

'Oh, Davy! You're right. I must hev been mad!'

They looked at each other for a moment and then her brother flung himself into her arms. She held him close and they both began to weep.

'Promise me you won't go out again, Esther. Promise me you won't leave me.'

'I promise, pet. Now, you'd better get to sleep.'

Esther knew that she would have to try to keep that promise, at least until Davy was old enough to be told the truth. And perhaps then he would come with her when she searched for their ma at nights. As she settled in her own bed she wondered why she did it. After all, their ma had hardly been a good mother to them. But she had not been deliberately cruel, unless neglect was a form of cruelty.

In spite of the hard work involved in keeping a job going as well as doing the housework, life had actually been happier since she'd gone. Their da was a hard man but, as long as the house was kept in reasonable order and his meals were set on the table he didn't cause much trouble. Unless he'd had too much to drink. And then Esther and Davy simply kept out of his way.

Esther knew very well why he was allowing her to stay. It was because she was a better housekeeper than her ma had been. He enjoyed an easier home life than he'd done for years and he was selfish enough to want that state of things to continue.

But Esther had just realized that she was selfish too. Selfish enough to want a life away from his tyrannical ways. A life where her little brother was always in fear of their da's rough justice dealt out with the back of his hand or his belt.

Well, she'd stop going out at nights – she could do with the sleep – but she was also determined that she would start looking for a way that she, and Davy along with her, could leave this place and find a happier home elsewhere.

Daisy Shaw sat at the table, staring at her piece of toast. She had not dressed, and she was toying with the frills of her robe with nervous fingers. Lucy watched while Betty, who had stayed the night as she'd promised, tied her mother's hair back with a ribbon and then busied herself pouring tea for the three of them.

Lucy herself had not slept much and she had washed and dressed early. Unlike her mother, she had managed to eat the scrambled egg that Betty had made and was now enjoying a second piece of toast and marmalade. She had acknowledged to herself that she was full of anguish over the death of her father – for she had accepted that he was the man who had died in the train derailment – but the unanswered questions were preventing her from grieving properly.

'Aren't you going to eat that?' Betty asked her mother.

'I'm not hungry.'

'Nevertheless, I think you should eat something, Mrs Shaw, pet. You've got to keep your strength up.'

'Why?'

Their maid frowned. 'What do yer mean, "Why?"?'

'Why should I keep my strength up?'

Betty shook her head sadly. 'For the funeral, of course.'

'There won't be any funeral.'

'Whyever not?' Betty was so surprised by the statement that she sat down at the table.

Lucy had also been taken unawares and she paused with her toast halfway to her mouth and

249

stared at her mother.

'Lissen, Mrs Shaw, pet, I know you're upset,' the maid said, 'but you're talking nonsense. There's got to be a funeral. The poor man will hev to be laid to rest.'

Lucy's mother sighed. 'He will be. What I meant was the funeral won't be here, and he won't be laid to rest by me.'

'But why not? Oh, you mean his family will want to see to things,' Betty said, nodding as if the penny had dropped. 'You mean that rich aunt of his in Yorkshire?'

'Yes, I mean his family.'

Lucy realized that this had not been a straight answer to Betty's question but she held her tongue.

'So you and Lucy will be off to Yorkshire, then?'

'I don't think so.'

Her mother's answer had been a low whisper and Betty leaned forward and frowned as if she hadn't heard aright. When she saw the tears begin to form in her mistress's eyes again and then well up and spill down her cheeks, she realized that she had.

'You mean they won't invite you?'

'That's right.'

'But that's scandalous! I mean, I'm not daft, I worked out long ago that his family and you didn't get on. You never went to visit and not one of them ever came here. I thought it was because they didn't approve of you.'

Her mother made a moaning sound and her eyes widened. She dropped her head into her hands.

'I'm sorry, pet, I divven't want to offend,' Betty continued, 'but I mean, you being an actress an' all. But not to hev you to the funeral!'

Daisy Shaw started weeping in earnest and Betty heaved herself to her feet and went to comfort her. But Lucy was rooted to the spot with shock. Her mother an actress? And Betty knew this? Well, no one had ever told her!

But that explained many things, of course. Her mother's beautifully modulated voice, the way she moved so gracefully, her mobile face, and the way her eyes could express so much of her emotions. And perhaps even her extravagances and her undoubted frivolity.

Lucy watched as Betty helped her mother over to the armchair, lifted her feet on to the padded velvet stool and wrapped a rug around her carefully as if she were made of porcelain.

'Lissen, Lucy,' the old woman said when she had done. 'Can you see to her for about an hour while I gan down yem?'

'Of course.' In fact Lucy wanted to be left alone with her mother.

'I'll be back to make the Sunday dinner, but I must put in an appearance in case me daughter-in-law thinks I've pegged it and starts celebrating. Ee, Lucy, hinny,' Betty said when she saw her surprised expression, 'you've got to make a joke of it or it would drive yer to drink, it would. I hope I heven't offended yer talking like this when ... when there's a death in the house.'

Lucy shivered at the words. 'No, you haven't offended me.'

'Now before I gans I'll close all the curtains –

251

that's proper – and divven't you answer the door, hinny. It'll only be nosy neighbours when they see the windows. I'll let meself in the back door.'

Betty put on her coat and hat but she seemed reluctant to leave her mistress. She stood and looked at her uncertainly but Lucy's mother kept her eyes closed. Her expression was drawn and anxious, as if she'd fallen into a troubled sleep. Lucy was certain that she was awake.

Lucy got up and put her arm round their maid. 'It's all right, Betty, you go home. I'll look after her.'

'I don't know what she'll do,' Betty muttered under her breath as Lucy walked into the scullery with her. 'She loved him so. Too much, I used to tell her. I was glad when you came along. Gave her something else to think about, someone else to love. She'll be depending on you now, Lucy, pet. You know that, don't you?'

'Yes, I know that.' And the words filled her with foreboding.

She'd been right about her mother feigning sleep. Her eyes were open when Lucy went back into the living room but she was staring straight ahead.

'Mother?' Lucy said.

'What is it?'

Lucy took the newspaper from the sideboard where she had left it the night before and spread it on the table. She sat down. 'How did you know that my father had died in the train derailment?'

'It says so in the paper.' Her mother's voice was flat.

Lucy looked down at the paper. 'The dead are

named as Thomas Hogget, the train driver, Sergeant Peter Barrass and–' Lucy paused and took a breath – 'and a Mr Reginald Lawson.'

'Your father.'

'Ah.'

Her mother sighed. 'I hoped that you need never know.'

Lucy found that she was clenching her fists. She had an almost uncontrollable urge to shake her mother. She was aware that her voice was wavering as she asked, 'Never know what?'

'Lucy... I...' Her mother's voice broke pitifully. 'Lucy, I can't talk about it now.'

'I'm sorry but you must.'

'Must?' Her mother looked directly at her, her beautiful eyes widening with surprise. 'You're telling me I *must*? I don't know how you have the heart to speak to me like this!'

Lucy suppressed a surge of exasperation. She knew how heartbroken her mother must be and yet she felt that she was putting on an act. Or perhaps she can't help it, Lucy thought. That's the way she is. She tried to keep the impatience out of her voice.

'It's only fair,' she said. 'Don't you think I have a right to know why my father and I don't have the same name?'

Daisy Shaw stared at her for a moment as if deciding something and then her whole body seemed to shrink in on itself. She became smaller and more vulnerable. 'We-ell,' she said, 'I suppose you can guess why?'

'You and he were never married?'

'That's right.'

'But why?'

'Your father was already married.'

'Oh, of course. And his wife and daughter were with him on the train. It says so in the newspaper.'

'Yes, they were.' For a moment her mother's expression became waspish.

'I have a sister.'

'What are you talking about?'

'It's obvious. If my father had another daughter, then she's my–'

'*Half*-sister. But he never meant for you to meet her. In fact he hoped that you would never find out that ... that...'

'That I'm a bastard.'

'Lucy! Don't use that word. The proper word is...' Her mother looked at her helplessly.

'Illegitimate. And if I am illegitimate, what does that make you?'

'Don't be cruel!'

'Cruel?'

'You sound so angry.'

'I am angry.'

'I don't know how you can speak to me like this when your father is lying dead in a mortuary. When ... when we shall never see him again. When our life together, our happy life, has been brought to an end.'

Her mother stared at her and now the tears, completely unfeigned, were streaming down her face. In spite of her mother's way of expressing herself Lucy knew very well how much she had loved her husband and she saw that she was heartbroken. Lucy felt the moisture on her cheeks and realized that she was weeping too.

'I'm sorry, Mother. I am, really,' she sobbed. 'But surely you understand, not only have I learned that my father is dead but also that "our happy life", as you put it, was a sham.'

'No! It was never a sham. What makes you think that?'

'Well, isn't it obvious? My father, your husband, had another family, a legitimate family, a family who was with him on the train, whose existence is reported in the newspaper while you and I are unacknowledged. I know how much you must be grieving – I'm grieving too – but I really think you owe it to me to explain why I can't even go to my father's funeral.'

Her mother turned her head away. Here, where the wind blew up from the river, it could be cold whatever time of year it was. Her mother shivered and, without speaking, Lucy rose, then kneeled by the hearth to place more coals on the fire. Then she sat in the other armchair, facing her mother.

'I think you should tell me what you can before Betty returns,' she said. 'She thinks you're married, doesn't she?'

'Yes.'

'Well, you may need my help if she asks any awkward questions. We should both tell the same story, shouldn't we?'

With those words Lucy realized that she had accepted the situation – the fact that her life had been built on lies – and it sickened her. But, to her surprise, she found that she was not so shocked that she would not be able to carry on the deception. Better that than face the shame of people knowing that her mother was a mistress rather than a wife and that she herself was illegitimate.

'You're right,' her mother said, and she seemed a little calmer. 'You ought to know the truth, partly because you're entitled to, but also because I don't want you to think too badly of me. I love – I loved him so very much, you know. And he loved me.'

'Yes, I do know.' Lucy tried to ignore the anxious uncertainty in her mother's eye.

Lucy remembered all the times her mother had fretted when he hadn't come home as he had promised. All the times her whole face had filled with joy when he did come home. All the times when, although she could never say that she had been neglected, her mother had hardly seemed to notice her presence when her father was in the room.

And her father? What of him? Of course he had loved her mother, but even when she had been a child Lucy had come to understand that his feelings were not so intense. He had been affectionate and kind and full of fun, almost as if he had been playing a part. As if he had cast himself in a role and was determined to extract the utmost enjoyment.

Playing a part? Lucy had just learned that her mother had been an actress. Was that how they had met? At the theatre?

Her mother sighed and tried to smile. 'I don't know where to start.' She was silent for a moment, the only sounds being the ticking of the clock on the mantelpiece and the shifting of the coals in the hearth. And then she said, 'I'm not from these parts, you know. I was born in Brighton – that's on the south coast – and I had – still have, as far as I know – five younger sisters.'

Lucy's eyes widened at this news. Now, as well as a half-sister, she had learned that she had five aunts.

'We all followed our parents into the theatrical profession. I made my debut when I was twelve years old as one of the fairies in *A Midsummer Night's Dream*. My father was playing Oberon and my mother Titania.'

For a moment her mother's eyes shone as if the memory was happy but then they filled with tears again. 'My poor darling parents, they were more enthusiastic than talented, I'm afraid. They never played on the London stage. We toured the country constantly and one by one, my sisters found husbands and not only left the company but left the theatre altogether. No doubt gratefully.'

'But you didn't marry?'

'Oh, I had the chance – more than one. But I had this foolish notion that I was going to be a great actress. A household name. I didn't want to become a provincial housewife.'

The hint of a smile again. 'My sisters are living in small towns scattered all over the British Isles.'

'And you haven't kept in touch with them?'

'No.' The faint smile vanished and her mother's expression became bleak. 'Nor my parents.'

'But why?'

'Because ... because they disapproved of what I did.'

'You mean because of my father?'

'Yes. People have the mistaken notion that theatrical folk have loose morals.' Her mother coloured slightly. 'Well, some of them do, but not my family. By the time I met Reginald all my sisters were respectably married. They wrote to my parents regularly, informing them of their growing families, and we would visit them whenever our company appeared in the towns where they were living.'

Her mother fell silent but Lucy could see her hands clutching at the rug that Betty had placed over her.

'You miss them, don't you?' Lucy asked softly.

'I do.' Her mother sighed. 'I would so much have liked them to meet you. But, Lucy, do you know I don't even know if my mother and father are still living.'

She stared at Lucy with huge eyes. Even if she was acting Lucy knew the emotions to be real. But she had to go on. She asked, 'Where did you meet my father?'

'Right here in Byker. We were appearing at the Grand. A musical comedy, a piece of nonsense about a princess who falls in love with a common soldier.'

'You were the princess?'

'No.' Her mother frowned. 'I was her maidservant. But your father said I should have been the princess. I was far more beautiful and had the better voice.'

'Then why weren't you given the part of the princess?' Lucy couldn't help asking.

'Because I wasn't married to the actor-manager!'

258

Daisy Shaw's eyes gleamed with humour, and instinctively Lucy slipped off her chair and kneeled at her mother's feet. She took one of her hands and said gently, 'Tell me, tell me how you met my father.'

'He was on one of his business trips, staying at a nearby hotel. He was lonely that night and came to the theatre on his own. He told me he fell in love with me as soon as he saw me. He waited outside the stage door and when I came out he pressed some flowers into my hands. A huge bouquet of red roses.

'Oh, that sort of thing had happened to me before. But, I don't know, there was something different about your father. He wasn't like the usual stage-door Johnnie. As soon as I saw him, so young and so handsome, you'll think me crazy but I–'

'You fell in love.'

'Yes. At first sight, as they say. I did. Really. And he came to the theatre every night after that – then followed the show round the northern theatres. My parents had no idea that we were meeting.'

'How did you manage that?'

'When my parents were resting in the afternoons we'd go for coffee and cakes, or walks in the park – if there was a park. And, oh, Lucy, I'm ashamed to say I even sneaked out of our lodgings at night when everyone was sleeping. My poor mother, she had no idea.'

Daisy Shaw had flushed at the memory of her deceptions and it made Lucy feel uneasy. She knew only too well what it was to deceive your mother. What about her and Stephen? She had to move the story on.

'So, eventually he asked you to – well, to live with him.' Her mother gasped, softly. 'And you agreed. But what happened to your ambition?'

'Do you know, Lucy darling, I said goodbye to all that the moment I knew that your father wanted me to spend my life with him. And to be perfectly honest I think I had begun to suspect that fame and fortune were not going to come my way after all.'

'But what exactly did he ask you? I mean, he couldn't offer marriage, could he?'

'No. He was honest with me from the start. He was already married to his childhood sweetheart. A mistake, he told me.'

'Of course he did.'

'Lucy!' Her mother sounded shocked. 'I don't know how you can be so cynical. But you must believe me, if I hadn't been so much in love I would never have accepted this ... this arrangement.'

'He promised you more, didn't he?'

'I don't know what you mean.'

'When I was growing up you always led me to believe that we were not always going to live here. That we might move to somewhere more fashionable.'

Her mother looked truly anguished. 'I know. At first he used to talk of divorce. He said that when Annabel, his little girl, was older, he would free himself from his marriage and marry me. But until then we should live here, tucked away from anyone who might know his family.'

'And you believed him?'

'I did. And I really think he meant it. At first. But he is – I mean he was the heir to the business, you know. And his wife's family are important wholesalers. He grew to realize that he might be ruined if he ... if he followed his heart.

'But, nevertheless, he promised that he would always take care of us. He opened a bank account for me, you know. Every month he would pay sufficient funds into it to keep you and me in comfort.'

'I see.'

Suddenly her mother cried, 'That's enough. I can't talk about this any longer. All these memories ... they're too painful.'

With a flash of intuition that sometimes comes when emotions are heightened Lucy knew the full extent of her mother's pain. And it wasn't straightforward. For not only was Daisy Shaw grieving over the tragic sudden death of the man she loved, but she was also wretched because she had suspected for some time that she had already lost him in one sense.

Now Lucy realized that her father's more frequent and longer absences from the little house in Byker could only have meant that he was tiring of the charade; tiring of his beautiful but older mistress and wanting to spend more time where he belonged – with his lawfully wedded wife and legitimate daughter.

And what about me? Lucy wondered. Was he tiring of me...?

'All right,' she said. 'We'll stop now. In any case, Betty will be back soon to start cooking the meal.

We'll talk later.'

Lucy thought she saw her mother suppress a fleeting expression of panic. She sensed that not only was there more to discover about their situation but that her mother was reluctant, perhaps even afraid, to reveal it. She heard the sneck lift as Betty opened the back door and she rose gratefully, pushing her uneasy suspicions to the back of her mind.

Strangely, in spite of her genuine grief at her father's death and the shock of everything she had just learned, she found that she was hungry. She would leave her mother to grieve alone for a while and go to help Betty make the Sunday dinner.

Chapter Nine

Lucy clung to the rim of the sink in the scullery as wave after wave of nausea shook her body. At last, when the retching had brought up only bitter-tasting bile, she righted herself and stood for a moment gazing miserably out of the window into the rain-drenched back garden.

She began to sluice out the sink. She had woken early, feeling sick, and raced downstairs in her nightdress rather than use the chamber pot, but the rain had dissuaded her from going out to the back-yard privy.

She hadn't stopped to put her slippers on, and now the cold struck up from the stone-flagged floor and hurt her feet. When the sink was clean she crossed to the back door and opened it. Her head was aching and she needed fresh air. But the damp air carried with it the smell of hundreds of coal fires and also the stench from the bone yard and the tannery.

Lucy wrinkled her nose in disgust. Even though they lived at the top of the hill, whether or not they could enjoy their back garden depended on the way the wind was blowing. No wonder her mother had wanted to move away from this part of town. Now Lucy doubted she ever would.

Closing the door again, she filled the kettle and took it through to place it on the hob of the living-room fire. It was early; Betty wouldn't be here for at least another hour. She would make herself a cup of tea. Weak tea, she thought instinctively, and didn't know why.

While she waited for the kettle to boil, Lucy kneeled down and raked the fire. Betty had left it banked down but fit to last the night. They had to keep the fire going all year round, because the back boiler warmed the water and the single oven of the small range was used for baking. Even though they had a new gas stove in the scullery, Betty had not yet been persuaded to use its oven. She had at least agreed to use the hob for the pans rather than fill the living room with cooking smells.

A short while later, as she sat cradling her cup of tea, Lucy thought how comforting it was to gaze into the glowing coals and watch the steam from the kettle curl upwards. She had wrapped the rug around her shoulders and pulled up the padded footstool. The feel of the velvet was sensuous under her bare feet and she dug her toes into it like a cat making a bed for itself.

She knew she deserved what had just happened to her. She had made a pig of herself yesterday over the Sunday roast; in contrast to her mother. Betty had tried her hardest to tempt her mother to eat. She'd made barley soup, roast shoulder of lamb with mint sauce, browned potatoes and spring cabbage, followed by steamed ginger pudding and custard.

These were all favourite dishes of Daisy Shaw but, unfortunately, just as she started her soup, she'd remembered that Reginald had loved them too. Actually, Lucy's father had been the easiest man to please at the table and would eat anything that Betty had prepared for him, but now his widow convinced herself that these dishes were his absolute favourites, and as the poor man would never savour them again, neither would she.

She picked at every course, making Betty more and more anxious and Lucy more and more angry. She couldn't have explained her anger to anyone, let alone herself, but she reacted by eating everything that was put before her and asking for more.

Dear old Betty had been pleased with her. 'That's right, bonny lass,' she said. 'You get yer strength up. It's going to be dark days ahead.'

On hearing those words Lucy's mother almost collapsed. She allowed herself to be led up to her room where they gave her a cup of hot sweet tea, laced with brandy. Betty offered to sit with her but she asked to be left alone.

Downstairs again, Lucy asked Betty to join her at the table and eat some of the food that would otherwise have been wasted. The old woman did so gratefully. Lucy suspected that Betty's daughter-in-law kept her on short rations and the old woman depended on the meals she had at the Shaws' house.

Lucy had sent her home early although Betty had been reluctant to go. Not only did she want to stay and help but Lucy guessed the poor old thing wouldn't be welcome at home.

And that was unfortunate, Lucy thought this morning as she stared into the fire, because she wasn't sure if her mother would be able to afford to keep Betty on. The conversation she'd with her mother after Betty had gone home yesterday had left Lucy feeling more and more uneasy.

She had taken a tray up at tea time and tried to ask her some questions. Her mother answered reluctantly at first and then got more and more flustered.

'How can you?' her mother had screamed. 'How can you ask me about such everyday matters when your poor father is hardly cold in his grave?'

'My father is not in his grave yet,' Lucy had retorted, 'and, even when he is, I shall never see his resting place.'

Her mother had pulled the bedclothes over her head and refused to speak.

Lucy had left her alone and gone downstairs to attack the table that Betty had left set up for tea. She had filled her plate with slices of cold ham, pease pudding, lettuce and tomatoes and then finished off with three currant scones and two slices of rice cake washed down with several cups of hot sweet tea.

No wonder I woke up feeling sick this morning, she thought as she stirred herself to go up and get dressed. But rather than take a jug of hot water up to her room she decided to get washed at the kitchen sink. But as she leaned over to rinse the soap suds from her face she felt the bile rising once more. She was leaning over, clutching the rim of the sink with both hands and gagging at the sour taste left at the back of her throat and in her mouth when the door behind her opened and Betty walked in.

'Lucy, hinny, what's the matter?'

Lucy cupped her hands under the cold tap and raised them to her mouth. She rinsed it out and reached for the towel. Betty put it into her hands. By the time she had dried her face Betty was hanging her damp coat on a hook on the back of the door. She turned and looked at Lucy speculatively.

'Well, then, pet. What's this?'

'I've been sick.'

'I can see that.'

Lucy saw the old woman's expression change to one of uncertainty.

'I had too much to eat last night,' Lucy told her. 'My mother was ... my mother was difficult, and I was angry– Oh, I don't know...' She shook her head.

'Aye, it can take you like that, I suppose. Grief. It can make you angry and you want to comfort yerself.'

Betty seemed to have made her mind up about something but her reaction had left Lucy feeling uneasy. When she had first come in the old woman had leaped to some kind of conclusion. Fear made Lucy's heart thud suddenly and she felt herself sway.

'Poor little lass,' she heard Betty saying as she put her arm round her and guided her into the living room. 'Sit down while I make yer mam's breakfast. Could you stand a cup of tea?'

'I'm not sure.'

'Well, I'll make you one and you must try and drink it, pet. You've got to pull yerself together and be strong for yer mam, you know. She's going to need you more than ever.'

267

Lucy felt a surge of panic at Betty's words. In spite of sitting by the fire her skin felt cold. She had already accepted that her mother needed her help. But what would happen if she wasn't in a position to give it?

'I don't understand why even our petticoats have to be black!'

Lucy stared rebelliously at the pile of black taffeta underwear her mother had chosen for them. Daisy Shaw turned from the cheval glass and looked at her sadly. 'Imagine,' she sighed, 'if we were to lift our skirts from the mud in the street – don't you think it would seem frivolous to show white or pink frills when our outerwear is deepest black?'

'I suppose so. But even our stockings?'

'Of course.' Her mother's tone was abrupt. She had lost patience and Lucy held her tongue. She didn't want to upset her mother, particularly since coming into town to buy their mourning clothes at Bainbridge's seemed to have lifted her spirits a little.

Lucy marvelled again that someone who was genuinely heartbroken, as her mother was, could still enjoy choosing new clothes, trying them on and posing in front of the mirror in the dressing room as if they were the very latest fashions. As indeed they were. Lucy had seen enough of the goods on display at Wright's Mourning Warehouse to realize that her mother was choosing only the best gowns, coats and underwear as well as all the necessary accessories. No matter what the price.

'As the widow,' her mother paused and flushed slightly, 'as the widow,' she said again more firmly, 'I shall have to wear black for a year and a day, you know.'

As she spoke she stepped gracefully out of a gown made from parramatta, a dull merino-like cloth made from wool and cotton. The sales girl had assured them that this was correct but she had added with an encouraging smile that after a year, silk gowns could be worn and they need not be black. Violet, pansy, lilac, scabious and heliotrope would be perfectly acceptable.

Lucy wasn't even sure what some of those colours were but she could see that her mother was enchanted. Dangerously so. For who was going to pay for all this? She wondered if she should remind her mother that she had once expressed an opinion that one or two decent mourning dresses were all a widow should need, but decided that would be cruel as well as provocative. She sighed.

Mistaking Lucy's solemn expression her mother said, 'Don't worry, sweetheart. Nobody will expect you to stay in full mourning for as long as I do. As a young working girl you will have a greater freedom – so long as the clothes you choose are sober and respectable. Now, what about some veils for the funeral?'

'But we're not going to the funeral!'

'I know that, you know that,' her mother said bitterly, 'but everyone else, including Betty, will see us leave the house by hansom cab in a day or two's time dressed as if we were going to your father's funeral. If they cared to follow us, which

269

they won't, they will see us alight at the Central Station and board a train heading for Yorkshire. We shall, of course, be carrying as much luggage as would be expected for our stay with your father's family. I've told Betty that they want to bury him and she'll pass that on to anyone who is nosy enough to ask.'

'But you've already told Betty that you're not on good terms with my father's family. She doesn't expect us to go to the funeral.'

'And you saw how scandalized she was! No, it won't do, Lucy. If I'm going to protect my reputation – your reputation – I shall have to invent a small reconciliation. A letter shall arrive inviting us to go to Yorkshire.'

'Letter?'

'Yes. I've already written it. We'll post it while we're in town today.'

'But the postmark?'

'You know Betty can't read.'

Lucy shook her head. 'But where on earth are we going to go when we're supposed to be with my father's family?'

Her mother shrugged. 'Does it matter?'

She glanced away, but Lucy noticed that the movement was evasive. 'Mother! You're not thinking of actually going to the funeral, are you?'

'No, of course not,' Daisy Shaw answered.

But Lucy wasn't so sure.

She watched moodily while her mother paid for everything they'd bought and asked for it to be delivered that very evening. The staff in the mourning department were used to such requests and the young assistant ushered them out respectfully.

'Good,' her mother said, as they emerged into the watery sunshine, 'it's stopped raining. As soon as I've been to the bank, we'll have a light lunch at Tilley's.'

'I didn't know we were going to the bank,' Lucy said.

'Mm. I shall check my account. You know your father opened an account for me long ago and he paid something into it each month. I shall have to find out from the manager what arrangements your father has made for this ... for this eventuality.'

'Are you sure that he did make arrangements?'

'When I gave up my career to set up house with him he promised me that I should always be taken care of.'

The words were meant to be reassuring but Lucy was troubled by the tone. It was almost as if her mother was trying to convince herself, as well as her daughter, that all was well.

A little later, as Lucy followed her mother up the stairs to Tilley's first-floor restaurant, she had to stop more than once to catch her breath. The trying on of clothes after a sleepless night and that dreadful sickness early that morning had left her feeling out of sorts.

After breakfast Betty had been given the tram fare into town and been dispatched with a letter to Lucy's employer to tell him what had happened. She had returned with Mr Hetherington's sympathy and instructions to take the whole week off. Lucy could regard this week as her annual holiday.

271

But that was a holiday without pay. Could she afford it?

Her mother had been distracted when she had emerged from the bank manager's office. She gripped Lucy's hands but all she would say was that she needed sustenance and that they would talk over their coffee cups at Tilley's.

Lucy was surprised when her mother asked the waitress to show them to one of the tables at the back of the room. She usually liked to sit by the large windows and watch the passing scene below. As they took their seats at a table half hidden by a screen she saw Lucy's expression and said, 'I shouldn't like any of our neighbours to see us dining out when we are in mourning.'

Lucy nearly retorted that it was highly unlikely that any of their neighbours would be taking lunch at Tilley's but she held her tongue. She sensed that her mother was seriously disturbed and she wished that she hadn't guessed why.

But, disturbed or not, Daisy Shaw told the waitress that they would have the full table d'hôte menu and to follow they would have coffee and a dish of marzipan fancies. While they waited for their soup Lucy couldn't stop herself from blurting out, 'Can we afford this?'

'What a peculiar question. Of course we can.'

Her mother smiled brilliantly, but Lucy noticed that her eyes were almost too bright and her voice was strained.

Lucy watched her mother tear at her bread roll until her side plate was covered with doughy crumbs and then slide her spoon into the tomato soup time after time without filling it. If she

272

raised the spoon to her mouth she barely sipped its contents. Lucy had finished her own soup long before her mother signalled to the waitress to come and take their dishes away.

It was the same with the second course. She ate one of the lamb chops, left the other, and didn't touch the cabbage or the creamed potato at all. But in spite of her sorrow and anger over the circumstances of her father's death Lucy found that she was enjoying the meal.

When she had finished her sherry trifle her mother, who had eaten only the glazed cherry from the top, looked at her and said sharply, 'No wonder everything we have just bought for you had to be slightly bigger than usual.'

Lucy dropped her spoon; she felt the heat rising. 'What do you mean?' she asked.

'Well,' her mother looked thoughtful, 'you are young, and I suppose you could still be developing into womanhood. Perhaps you are going to be a little more full-breasted than I am. But, there again, I've noticed how your appetite seems to have increased. Perhaps it's because you have to go out to work. You'll have to be careful. You don't want to lose your shapely figure, do you?'

Lucy didn't answer and her mother didn't pursue the matter. She stared into her coffee and didn't seem to notice that she had put three spoonfuls of sugar in. She kept stirring it round and, when she finally drank it, she complained that it tasted foul and, furthermore, it was cold. Nevertheless she left a more than usually generous tip for the waitress.

Instead of waiting at the tram stop near the

273

monument they walked down Grainger Street to the Central Station. 'I want to buy a newspaper at the kiosk there,' her mother explained.

'But we can get a paper here, from the boy on the street corner.'

'Not the paper I want,' her mother said sharply. 'I hope there's one left. I should have thought of this earlier.'

At the station Lucy had a wild urge to run away and take the train to Whitley-by-the-Sea. Stephen didn't know that her father had perished in the train crash. He would be sympathetic, wouldn't he? He would take her in his arms and comfort her and she would be able to tell him, not only of her sorrow but also of her other fears.

But what would he do if she told him that she had only just discovered that her parents had never been married? That she was illegitimate? Would that make any difference to his feelings for her? And, as she considered this, she suddenly knew with dreadful certainty that, even if it made no difference to Stephen, it would make all the difference in the world to his parents. They would never allow their son and heir to marry her now.

Well, then, she wouldn't tell them. But that meant she would probably have to deceive Stephen too. Again her emotions swung from sorrow to rage as she looked at her mother buying her newspaper. The *Yorkshire Post*. Of course. Her spirits sank even further. But the paper remained unopened, clutched in her mother's hands, until they got home and then, asking Betty to make a pot of tea, Daisy Shaw spread the newspaper out on the table and turned the pages until she reached the Births and Deaths page.

When she saw her mother's tears begin to fall and spread across the columns of newsprint, she knew that she had found what she had been looking for. The notice given of her father's funeral.

'I can't believe we're doing this!'

'Hush, Lucy. Keep your head down and talk quietly.'

'No one can hear us. What with the rain and the howling gale.'

'Nevertheless, you are raising your voice,' her mother said, 'and it's not appropriate.'

'Not appropriate? This whole venture is inappropriate. We shouldn't be here.'

Lucy caught her breath as she struggled to keep the large umbrella in position over both of them. She had to use both hands, which meant that she had no means of controlling her veil. Fortunately it was full enough and heavy enough not to lift up. Instead it was being flattened against her face so that every time she opened her mouth to speak she got a mouthful of damp black lace.

For a while she remained silent as they made their way up the winding street, which had been transformed into a rushing stream as the rain cascaded down over the cobbles. But even in this foul weather Lucy could see that this was what the postcard manufacturers would call a picturesque village, with its old stone houses and bow-fronted shops.

They had left Newcastle Central Station at an unearthly hour in the morning and taken a train to York. Once there they had booked in at a respectable guesthouse and then gone back to the station. A branch line across the North York Moors had brought them to this rugged part of the country where her father was to be buried. The reason that the funeral was to be held here was that the Lawson family lived in an imposing manor house perched on the windswept moor top nearby. Her mother had pointed it out from the train. It was more like a castle, Lucy thought, but her mother had told her that it wasn't an old building at all.

She said that Reginald's grandfather had had Moorside Hall designed and built deliberately to look as though it had weathered the centuries, with extensions and additions built in the style of different historical periods. He reckoned that since his family had been making sweets, lozenges, comfits and candied peel since at least 1765, and had become very rich in the process, they had as much right to live in style as any tribe of impoverished aristocrats.

Lucy had not been able to resist asking her mother how she knew all this.

'Your father told me, of course,' she said.

'But neither of you ever told me.'

'How could we?'

They travelled in silence for a while and then, as the train began to pull into the station and her mother tugged her veil down to cover her face, Lucy said, 'You've been here before, haven't you?'

Her mother's veil fluttered in agitation. 'Why do you say that?'

'You knew exactly where the Lawsons' house was.'

'Mm.'

'How did you know?'

'I've been there.'

'You've been there? You've met the family?' Lucy knew she sounded incredulous.

'No, of course not.'

Her mother remained silent as they descended on to the platform and made their way to the exit. They were not the only passengers dressed in mourning black. Daisy lingered so that they were at the back of the queue waiting to hand in their tickets.

'Well?' Lucy said.

Her mother inclined her head towards the people in front of them and murmured, 'We'll talk later.'

Lucy, seeing the door of the waiting room, suddenly took her mother's arm and guided her towards it. There was no one inside but the brightly burning fire reminded Lucy of another station waiting room – and other circumstances.

'What are you doing? Why have you brought me here?' Her mother sounded vexed.

'Because I want you to tell me now. Is there any more I ought to know before we go to the church – which will be full of my father's family and friends.'

'Don't worry. Dressed like this with our faces obscured by the veils we could be anyone.'

'Even his mistress and his illegitimate daughter!'

'Lucy! Don't … not today.'

For all the histrionics her mother was capable of, Lucy knew that, now, her anguish was genuine. 'I'm sorry,' she said. 'It's just that I feel I'm treading on quicksand. Not knowing what I'm going to discover next is terrifying.'

'There's nothing more to discover. I've never met any of your father's family. He never knew that I came here.'

'Then why did you? Were you going to confront him in his home and did you lose your nerve?'

'I don't think I was going to do that. Even now I'm not sure. It was when I was expecting you. I was so lonely in that little house in Byker. I had no friends; I couldn't tell my family. In fact, my family had cast me off as beyond redemption. One day I just set off determined to find the place and … and, oh, I don't know.'

Her mother lowered her head and her voice faded. 'I just wandered round the village, walked across the moors, looked at the house from a nearby hillside and thought how beautiful it was with the sun glinting on the windows. I thought of your father inside there with … with his family.'

'But you went home?'

'Suddenly I saw a carriage come round to the front door. A couple came out of the house, followed by a maidservant. The maidservant was carrying a small child, a girl. The couple got into the carriage and the maid handed them the child. Even from where I was standing I could see what a happy family they were, how close they sat, how the man … your father … leaned over to play with the child.'

Her mother fell silent but Lucy could see her trembling. Outside they heard the guard shout and the train draw away from the station. The hiss of steam and the rattling of the wheels over the tracks receded into the distance.

'Of course I went home,' her mother said. 'What else could I do?' She sighed deeply. 'Your father had promised that, whatever happened, he would look after me – look after us. He knew I was with child. I thought that if I marched up to the house there and then it might ... it might upset things. He might – I mean, his father might insist that he cut all ties.'

'You didn't trust my father to stand up for you.'

Even before the words were out Lucy regretted them but, instead of a cry of anguish her mother simply raised her head and said, 'We should go to the church now. Mingle with the other mourners. We'll take a seat at the back and we'll probably never even be noticed.'

So here they were, battling their way up the hill behind the respectful crowd. It was a large church for such a small village, which was just as well considering how many people had come to pay their last respects to Reginald Lawson.

'I wonder how many of them will be going back to the Hall,' her mother murmured as they paused in the shelter of the lich-gate.

'Mother, you wouldn't!'

'No, of course not. I just wondered, that's all.'

They followed the crowd up the path to the church door where a sober gentleman directed them to leave their umbrella with others in the

279

porch. Then they took their places in the pew at the back. Lucy went in first and edged along until she was sitting half behind a stone pillar. Her mother had no choice but to join her. The organ was playing solemn music and, taking their cue from the rest of the congregation, they kneeled to pray while they waited for the service to begin.

Glancing sideways, Lucy saw her mother's mouth moving in silent prayer. They had never been regular churchgoers and the only prayers Lucy knew were those that had been taught and recited every morning at school. She had no idea what she was supposed to say to a supreme being who had treated her so cruelly. But she kept her hands together, her eyes closed and her head down.

Her senses were assaulted by the smell of the massed flowers mingling with the damp, musty smell of the congregation's clothes. It made her feel sick. Miserable, cold and wet as she was, Lucy found herself indulging in speculation that she knew to be hysterical.

She imagined her father's family gathered in a grand room in Moorside Hall after the funeral. A bewhiskered legal gentleman in old-fashioned clothes was setting his papers out on a highly polished table. The family, stiff and formal, sat bolt upright on uncomfortable chairs and glanced nervously, first at the bewhiskered gentleman and then, furtively, at each other while the wind hurled rain at the mullioned windows.

And then the legal gentleman would begin to read the will. Her father's will. And when he had finished a heavily veiled woman would rise from her seat at the back – possibly half-hidden behind a large potted plant – and thrust herself forward whilst demanding piteously to be told what was going to happen to her and her poor child.

There would be a horrified silence. Then servants would be summoned and the woman and her poor child would be seized and flung out into the elements, where they would have to make their way across the moors and possibly perish and never be heard of again.

Lucy found herself laughing and sensing her mother's incredulous shock she turned the sounds into sobs. She felt guilty when her mother put an arm around her shaking shoulders and shushed her like a child. 'There, there, sweet-heart. Hush now. You must stand up. The service is about to begin.'

And then they rose and sat and kneeled and sat and rose in a bewildering sequence, trying always to do exactly as everyone else was doing. They sang hymns and chanted what were to Lucy half-familiar words until, finally, her mother whispered to her to sit down and wait while the church emptied.

At no time did Lucy have any sense that they were here to say farewell to her father. While they waited, her mother took hold of her gloved hand and it was only when she gripped it so tightly that it hurt that Lucy looked up and saw that the coffin was being carried out. Then it was her turn to put her arm around her mother and murmur words of comfort. Fortunately, sitting at the end of the pew and half-behind the pillar as they were, no one saw the gesture.

When the church had emptied they slipped out and stood huddled for a moment under their umbrella, watching the procession wend its way to the newly dug grave. Seeing that no one was taking any notice of them they followed, but they hung back under the overhanging branches of some gnarled old elm trees.

Lucy was conscious that her feet were cold and wet and that the bottom of her skirt was soaking. She closed her eyes and imagined herself at home, sitting by the fire in their warm and friendly little house in Byker with her mother and father laughing and talking together in their own intimate way. She felt an ache of sorrow in her throat and her eyes filled as she accepted that that world had gone for ever. And, furthermore, no matter how happy she had thought herself, it had been a world built on lies and deceit.

She tried to imagine her father's other life. She opened her eyes and the tears spilled out. She gazed through the blur of tears at the crowd surrounding the grave. The vicar, in his white vestments, was intoning words from his prayer book and everyone's head was bowed.

She heard one of the women cry out and saw another woman move to comfort her. The sobbing woman was tall and elegant; her body was full but well-shaped, womanly. The woman comforting her was taller and, even though her face was obscured by a veil, as was the other's, the graceful lines of her body declared her to be young.

That is my sister, Lucy thought with certainty.

And she is comforting her mother, who is my father's widow and who has every right to be here at his graveside while my mother does not. And what of me? Have I the right to be here?

The sobbing woman seemed to collapse a little, and an older, heavy-set man stepped close to support her. My grandfather, Lucy thought. And the stout woman on his other side is my grandmother, and I have never known them. Nor am I likely to.

'Don't you think we should go now?' Lucy asked her mother. 'Before the party begins to leave and we are noticed?'

'Perhaps.'

But her mother made no move to leave the churchyard. Instead she began to walk further under the dripping trees, where last year's leaves lay mouldering and damp in the long grass. The voices at the graveside receded, drowned out by the soughing of the wind in the branches and the cawing of the rooks. Lucy followed miserably, longing to seize her mother's arm and drag her away. She hated being here. She hated being part of such a shoddy enterprise. The smell of the rotting vegetation was making her sick.

At last they fetched up against an ancient moss-covered wall that sheltered the graveyard from the wild countryside. The breeze was fresh and Lucy lifted her veil then raised her head to watch some large birds circling high over the moors. It had stopped raining and, as she furled the umbrella, she realized how beautiful it was here.

This was where her father had grown up, far away from the smoky industrial city on the River

Tyne. And he had never told her about it. Instead he had led her to believe that his existence centred on the little house in Byker. She began to realize why, in spite of her mother's pleadings, he had never wanted to move into something grander.

His life with them had been secret. It had been another life, perhaps a delightful escape from reality, a fantasy. He would not have wanted it to echo his 'proper' life as the son and heir of a successful businessman and husband of a no doubt well-connected and entirely suitable woman.

'Your father had no brothers and sisters so I suppose your half-sister, Annabel, will inherit everything one day when the old man dies.'

'I don't want to know any of this,' Lucy said, knowing that she didn't really mean it but wary of exposing her feelings. 'I've lived all my life so far without knowing and I want it to stay that way.'

Her mother didn't reply and, after a while, still without speaking, she led the way back through the trees. They must have been away for some time for there was no one left by the graveside save for two men in shirtsleeves, gravediggers, busily shovelling the heavy wet soil on top of the coffin. One of them was whistling but he stopped when he saw them and touched his cap.

Now, with the sun trying to break through, the smell of the floral wreaths and the exposed soil was overpowering. The men stopped working and waited respectfully as Lucy and her mother stood at the graveside. Suddenly her mother lifted her veil, arranging it over her hat, and then opened her handbag and took out a single red rose wrapped in white crepe paper and tied with a red satin bow. She raised the rose to her lips, kissed it and then threw it into the grave. It landed on an exposed corner of the coffin.

It may have been genuine but it was a highly dramatic gesture and Lucy was furious. She saw one of the men nudge his companion and she could guess at the sort of gossip that would get around the village and eventually back to the Lawson family home.

She turned and began to walk away. Her heart was thudding painfully as she made her way between the tombstones and, not looking properly where she was going, at one point she tripped and almost fell. She saved herself by grasping at the wings of a carved stone angel and, as she paused for a moment, breathing heavily, her mother caught up with her.

'Why did you leave me?'

'Do you know what you've done?'

'What are you talking about?'

'Throwing the rose into the grave like that.'

'My last gift to your father. What's wrong with that?'

'The gravediggers saw you. Saw both of us. What will they think?'

'I don't care.'

'No, you don't, do you? You don't care that the story will be all round the village.'

'Story?'

'Don't pretend you don't know what I mean. Now everyone here will know that two women came to the funeral, two women who were not part of the family party, and yet one of them threw a red rose into Reginald Lawson's grave. A red rose! What do you imagine his wife will make of that?'

'She can make of it what she likes.'

Her mother's voice was waspish and Lucy looked at her incredulously. 'You want her to know, don't you? You want her to suspect that her husband had a mistress.'

'Don't use that word!'

'Why not? That's what you were. And you want his poor wife to believe that he had another woman and possibly a daughter too.'

'Poor wife! There's nothing poor about Geraldine! Your father told me that she set her cap at him when he was barely out of school and both families thought it a good match, so that was that.'

'Didn't he want to marry her?'

'No – I mean he didn't care one way or the other. She was beautiful and rich and there didn't seem to be any reason to displease his father. But, oh, how he regretted it later.'

'Were they unhappy together?'

'Happy, unhappy, it makes no difference. I mean he regretted it once he had met me.'

'I see.'

But in truth Lucy didn't see. How could she understand a man who would marry someone just to keep his family happy and then set up home with someone else, someone that he must have known his family would have been opposed to him marrying in the first place? He had happily betrayed both women. She tried very hard to

286

despise him and found she couldn't. She had loved her father. He had been a warm-hearted and easy-going parent. Whenever he came home he had lifted her mother's spirits and her own almost immediately with his sense of fun and enjoyment.

And yet … surely her mother's spirits had been low in the first place because of the way she had been living. And that was his fault…

Her mother turned away and began to rearrange her veil.

'So now you want to add to Geraldine's sorrow,' Lucy said. 'Is it a kind of revenge?'

'Maybe.' Her voice betrayed a certain satisfaction. 'While he was alive my very existence – your existence too – was kept secret. If I had walked up to the house that day all those years ago things might have been different. But because I didn't, that woman and her child have been shielded from the truth.' She raised her chin and although her face was now obscured by the filmy black lace, Lucy could see that the set of her jaw was firm. 'Well,' she said, 'now they'll know.'

Sickened, Lucy turned and began to walk away. 'We should go now,' was all she said. 'It must be time to catch the train back to York.'

They had decided that they would stay only one night away from home, mainly because they couldn't afford to stay any longer. Daisy hoped that would be sufficient to satisfy any curious neighbours. Betty had been taken in by the letter that Daisy had written herself and would tell anyone who asked that Mrs Shaw and Lucy were staying with Mr Shaw's family.

The guesthouse was comfortable and the landlady, seeing the way they were dressed, treated them kindly. When Lucy remembered what her mother had done the woman's considerate behaviour made her feel guilty. And then cross with herself for feeling guilty. After all, she had been entirely blameless throughout this harrowing episode.

The tiny room she shared with her mother was on the top floor of the tall old house and, all night long, Lucy lay sleepless, listening to a nearby church clock strike every quarter of an hour. If she sat up in bed and peered through the gap in the flower-patterned curtains she could see the moonlight illuminating the face of the clock. It seemed to stare back at her. Her mother whimpered in her sleep as she turned restlessly in the double bed they shared. Lucy fell asleep eventually at daybreak and was soon woken by her mother shaking her crossly.

'Wake up, Lucy,' she said. 'I don't know how you've managed to sleep so soundly. I haven't slept a wink all night.'

They ate breakfast in the guesthouse dining room, along with two men who looked like commercial travellers, who eyed their black clothes and then talked quietly to each other while glancing at them now and then speculatively.

Lucy heard the words 'funeral' and 'Lawson' mentioned and hoped that word had not already got round the business world about her mother's histrionics at the graveside. But the men's glances remained respectful so she persuaded herself that it had not. As they got up to go they bowed politely and said, 'Good morning.' Her mother nodded graciously.

When they were alone in the dining room her mother said, 'We can't go home yet. We must at least spend the day here in York. We'll take our bags to the left luggage office at the railway station and then walk around the city. Have lunch somewhere nice, perhaps. We needn't wear our veils now that the funeral's over.'

In spite of the circumstances Lucy might have managed to enjoy their day as sightseers, if she had not been so sick immediately after breakfast. Luckily her mother had not questioned why she had been so long in the bathroom and, by the time they had packed their bags and were on their way to the station, the colour had returned to her face and she felt quite well again.

But as they explored the maze of winding alleys and cobbled streets that surrounded York Minster, Lucy accepted that the significance of her physical symptoms could no longer be denied. When they got home, in mourning or not, she would have to tell Stephen that they should be married as quickly as possible.

Chapter Ten

May

Roland hurried along beside Ruth as she made her way towards the railway station. 'Why do you have to go home?' he asked.

'Because I told my father I would.'

'When did you tell him?'

'I wrote to them. They'll be expecting me.'

'Then take me with you. I'd like to meet your parents.' He took her arm.

'I can't, not yet.' Ruth stopped walking and stared up at Roland Matthews with wonder in her eyes. She could hardly believe this conversation was taking place. And hardly believe that this handsome man had sought her out as much as possible ever since the day she had met him in the clean and tidy little apartment above the Crystal Library.

'Why do you say not yet?' he asked, and he smiled at her quizzically.

'Well...' This was awkward. 'Roland, we hardly know each other...' She stopped and looked at him in hurt surprise when he snorted with laughter. 'Why are you laughing?'

He let go of her arm and placed one hand on his chest, making a dramatic gesture with the other and in a falsetto voice he proclaimed, *'Roland, we hardly know each other!'*

'Don't tease,' she said.

'I'm sorry. But do you know what you sounded like?'

'No, and I don't think I want to.'

'You sounded like a blushing heroine in a romantic novel.'

'I thought you never read them.'

'I certainly don't. Nor anything very much, if the truth were known. I've watched my poor sister Guinevere waste her life by burying her nose in countless dusty volumes and I decided long ago that I'm more interested in the real world.'

'I know, you've told me that more than once,' Ruth said uncomfortably. 'So if you've never read one, what makes you say I sound like a character from a book?'

'Because when I was too young to be able to protest, my sister used to take me with her to the reading circle. I used to have to sit and listen to all sorts of rubbish. And, even worse, certain members of the reading circle were also members of the amateur dramatic society, including Guinevere, and you can imagine the sort of plays they chose to put on.'

Ruth thought that being in both the reading circle and the dramatic society would be rather fun but she didn't say so. She knew Roland well enough by now to predict what sort of response that would bring. She realized that they didn't share interests but she wondered if that mattered when the attraction between them seemed to be so vital.

If she could believe what he said and did, he seemed to be as drawn to her as she was to him.

And she had to admit he was attractive and fun to be with. And, of course, she couldn't help noticing the way other girls looked at him – and possibly wondered what on earth such a handsome man could see in her!

'Well, can you?' he asked.

She decided to make a joke of it. 'I can,' she said. 'And I'm sure you had a lot of fun laughing at your sister's friends, but now I really must go and catch my train.'

Roland frowned and, for a moment, she feared that she had angered him. When his smile reappeared it didn't reach his eyes. 'Very well,' he said. 'Off you go.'

He turned to walk away and Ruth placed a hand on his arm. 'Roland, I'm really sorry but it's so long since I've been to see my father. You do understand, don't you?'

She was relieved to see his expression soften a little. 'Yes, I do. How long do you intend to stay there?'

'Oh, I'll have my lunch there – and then stay an hour or two.'

'Do you suppose your parents would mind if you came back here for tea with Guinevere and me?'

'No, I don't think they'd mind.' Ruth knew very well that her stepmother would be only too pleased to get rid of her – but what if her father wanted to talk? To ask her about her work ... whether she was happy?

'I'll see you later, then.'

'Wait ... I can't promise.'

But Roland didn't wait. She wasn't even sure if

he'd heard her as he hurried away. Ruth was left with her feelings in turmoil. She was ecstatic because Roland seemed really to care for her – otherwise why would he be so possessive? – and anxious because she had obviously angered him. Oh, he had smiled and waved cheerfully enough but his clipped tones had betrayed his displeasure.

She stood and watched him, even wondering whether she should abandon her plan to go home to her father's house. If he turns round and waves again I'll stay, she thought to herself. But he didn't and the sound of the train steaming into the station made her turn and run towards the ticket office instead.

At the coast the skies had been clear and bright and the air fresh and tangy with the cool breeze from the sea. Once home in Byker, it was warmer but the air smelled old, somehow, and it was heavy with soot and the stench of waste from the industries crowding the riverbank.

Nevertheless there were children playing in the street. A few small lads were playing tag while three little girls played hopscotch. They smiled at Ruth as she went by and she was inordinately pleased that they remembered her. These days, when she came home, she felt more and more like a stranger. As she drew nearer to the front door of her old home she was aware that one of the little girls had detached herself from the group and was running after her.

Ruth had already knocked on the door and was standing waiting when the child arrived, face flushed, her hair ribbons coming loose and her hair straggling across her face.

293

'Hello, Susan,' Ruth said, glad that she could remember the child's name.

Susan pushed her hair back from her face and, to Ruth's consternation, wiped her nose with the back of her hand before she said breathlessly, 'They've gone out.'

'Who's gone out?' Ruth asked.

'Yer mam and dad. First thing this morning.'

Ruth hated to hear Ada spoken of as her mother and she would have corrected a grown-up, but Susan had not even been born when Ruth's real mother had been alive. 'Are you sure?' she asked.

'Aye, they were dressed in their Sunday best but they wasn't gannin' to church.'

'How do you know that?'

'Because they stopped to talk. Me mam and me was coming back from Fowler's with the milk and the bread. Me mam said how nice yer ma looked and were they going visiting.'

'And what did they say?'

'Yer da said they were going to hev a day in the country – catch the train to Rothbury, hev a nice bit dinner at the hotel.'

'But they knew I was coming!' Ruth blurted out without thinking.

She saw Susan's expression. The child's eyes were round with surprise and so were the eyes of her friends who had come to join her.

'You can come and ask me mam if yer don't believe us,' Susan said.

'Oh, no, pet, I believe you. I was just ... just surprised.'

Ruth knew she wouldn't have gone to ask Susan's mother even if she didn't believe the

294

child. She didn't want any of her former neighbours to know that her father had gone out for the day when he knew she was coming home to visit. But did he know? It wouldn't be past her stepmother not to have told him about the letter.

The post would have come after her father had left for work in the shipyard. She had a sudden vision of Ada opening the letter, reading it and then, her face narrow with spite, crumpling it up and throwing it on the fire. Ruth wouldn't put it past her to even make some remark about the fact that they hadn't had a letter lately and how it was a shame Ruth didn't keep in touch.

Ruth heard someone call her name and she looked up the street to see Susan's mother coming down towards them.

'Well hello, Ruth, hinny. What a surprise.'

Oh no, Ruth thought. What shall I say?

'Yer dad and Ada's gone out for the day, didn't you know?'

'Yes, I knew,' Ruth said. She saw Susan draw breath and hurried on before the child could prove her a liar. 'But I'm on the way to visit Esther – you know, Esther Robinson – and I just knocked on the off chance they hadn't left yet.'

'No, you've missed them. They set off sharp so's they could make a day of it. What a shame.'

Susan's mother's smile was unaffected and Ruth thought she had accepted her story, for the moment, anyway.

'Well, I'd best be off, then,' Ruth said, and turned to walk down the bank.

'You're going the wrong way,' the woman called.

'What do you mean?' Ruth stopped and asked

in surprise.

'Esther's doing a Sunday morning shift at the shop this morning. Didn't she tell you?' Susan's mother was frowning now.

'No, she didn't. Perhaps it was a last-minute arrangement.'

'Likely it was. Will yer gan up and see her there?'

'Yes, and if Susan and her friends would like to keep me company we'll see if Fowler's still sell sugar mice.'

'They do!' Susan cried, and the excitement in her face showed that she'd probably forgotten that Ruth had acted as if she'd had no idea at all that her father would be going out for the day.

'That's kind of you,' the child's mother said. 'But send them straight back, now, those two little 'uns are me sister's bairns and they've got no sense. I don't want them straying on to Shields Road.'

'Don't worry, I'll bring them as far as the corner, watch them down the bank.'

'Well,' the woman laughed, 'You'd better pick yer skirts up and hare off after them; they're halfway there!'

Ruth smiled and set off. She called to the three children to slow down, but she stayed a few paces behind them. She had her thoughts to sort out. She had never intended to visit Esther, but now she was glad she was going to.

She hadn't seen much of either of her friends recently. Every spare moment had been spent with Roland Matthews. Of late Miss Golightly had seemed to be tired for most of the time. At first Ruth had thought that her employer had exhausted herself writing her novel but then the doctor had started to call regularly and, on his advice, Miss Golightly had begun to take more naps during the daytime and go to bed earlier at night.

Ruth was given certain tasks, such as tidying the bookshelves and dealing with the correspondence, but when she had done she was allowed to please herself: she could read in her own room or go out. She had chosen to go out, but until today she had not come home.

'Hello, stranger,' Esther said when Ruth followed Susan and her cousins into Fowler's. Ruth felt guilty when she saw how pleased her friend was to see her. 'What can I do for you?'

'Well, for a start you can give these three a sugar mouse each.'

Ruth watched the three little girls' faces as Esther reached for the glass jar, took the lid off, and asked, 'Now then, which colour do you want?'

She placed the jar on the counter and glanced at Ruth as the children stared at the sugar mice inside it. 'Remember?' she asked. 'You followed me into the cave and offered me one of your sugar mice.'

'Of course I do.'

'Which one did I choose, white or pink?'

'You chose the white mouse – but you took it home to share with Davy.'

Ruth was transported back to that day in Cullercoats Bay when she and Esther and Lucy, the most unlikely allies, had been thrown together

297

by the surge of a wave. Instead of the grocery shop odours of coffee and bacon and cheese, she could smell the salt tang of the sea. The clip-clop of the horses' hoofs and trundle of wheels on nearby Shields Road faded to be replaced by the cry of gulls, the pounding of waves on the shore and the long drag back over the pebbles.

Ruth took the money from her purse and paid for the sugar mice. Esther offered to wrap them in a twist of paper but Susan and her cousins shook their heads. They had all chosen pink mice and, clutching them in their grubby hands, they hurried to the door and set off home.

'Wait a moment – I promised to watch them down the bank,' Ruth said, and left Esther replacing the jar on a shelf behind the counter.

'Did they say "thank you"?' Esther asked when she returned.

'They forgot.' Ruth smiled.

Esther laughed, then, 'Poor Lucy,' she said puzzlingly.

'Poor Lucy?' Ruth half-smiled, thinking that Esther was referring to the time the two of them had dragged Lucy from the sea and Mr Shaw had rewarded them with a box of sweets each.

She saw that Esther was frowning. 'Of course. You divven't know. How could you? You've not been near the place for weeks, now.'

Ruth sensed that she was being criticized. 'I ... I've been busy.'

Esther sighed. 'I know, you work hard for that old woman and I don't suppose you get much time off.'

'Well...'

'Anyways, I telt Lucy to write to you – as a friend you had a right to know – but she's been acting real strange. It's the grief, I suppose.'

'For goodness' sake, Esther, tell me what's wrong.'

'Hev you nothing better to do than gossip, my lass?'

Ruth found herself rudely pushed aside as an old woman shoved her way to the counter. There was no need for it, there were no other customers and there was plenty room, but she held her tongue when she saw Esther's tolerant expression.

'Now then, Mrs Briggs,' her friend said. 'What can I do for you?'

'You can take that smirk off yer face for a start. I've a mind to tell Mr Fowler on yer. I would never hev got away with that kind of lax behaviour when I was a counter hand.'

'I'm sure you wouldn't, Mrs Briggs.' Raymond Fowler emerged from the back shop and Ruth saw that, like Esther, he was smiling. 'I shall talk to Miss Robinson but, meanwhile, would you like me to serve you?'

The old woman looked at him suspiciously through constantly blinking eyes. She was clutching a ragged old shawl around her hunchbacked body with bony fingers that were none too clean. Ruth saw that her clothes were grubby and the tongues of her boots lolled out because she had lost their laces.

Esther stepped back from the counter as Raymond leaned down and brought a newspaper-wrapped parcel out from a shelf beneath it.

'Here you are, Mrs Briggs,' he said. 'I hev your

299

order all ready for you. We don't like to keep valued customers waiting. Would you like the lad to carry it home for you? I'm sure I can spare Davy for a minute or two.'

'That's all right, bonny lad,' she said. 'I can manage if you'll just put it in this bag for me.'

She produced a string bag from the folds of her clothing and Raymond proceeded to put the parcel inside. 'There you are,' he said. 'Shall I just put it on your account?'

'Please do.' The old woman drew herself up and, for a moment, there was a hint of a former graciousness. 'And remember to tell your uncle about this lass gossiping when she should be working,' she said.

'I will.'

The old woman hobbled out of the shop. Ruth watched her go and then turned to see Raymond Fowler and Esther smiling at each other. Esther didn't seem at all put out by Mrs Briggs' criticism and Raymond obviously had no intention of reporting the matter to his uncle.

How Raymond has grown, Ruth thought. And how manly he looks, although he is surely at least two years younger than Esther.

'Mrs Briggs doesn't have an account, does she?' Ruth asked.

Esther shook her head slowly and her smile became sad. 'No, she doesn't, although Raymond thinks she did, once.'

'She did. A long time ago,' Raymond said. 'I've been going through the old books and I discovered the Briggs family were good customers. Her husband had a well-paid job in the yards and her five sons worked on the railways. There was a lot of money coming in to that household and they lived well.'

'What happened?'

'Tragedy after tragedy,' Raymond said, and his usually confident demeanour faltered. 'Her husband died when the rigging of a ship he was working on collapsed. No pension, of course. At first there were her sons to take care of her, although two of them had already married and left home. But they helped out as much as they could. Then the younger ones decided to emigrate.'

'And leave their mother?' Ruth said.

'They wanted her to go with them to Canada but she wanted to stay near the grandbairns.'

'And that was strange,' Esther said.

'Wanting to stay near her grandchildren?'

'No, I don't mean that. According to folk round here, she never heard from those three sons again.'

'Surely they wouldn't forget all about their mother?'

'You wouldn't hev thought so, would you?' Raymond said. 'Perhaps the ship went down. Perhaps they never got to Canada, or if they did, perhaps they died in some disaster over there.'

'But that's dreadful,' Ruth said.

'There's more to come.' Raymond sighed. 'The remaining two brothers were in the same maintenance crew. They were killed in a shunting accident. No pension, just like their da, and, even if there had been, they'd both left a wife and bairns. One of those families ended up in the workhouse. The younger of the two wives married again and moved away.'

'So how does Mrs Briggs survive?'

'She earns enough to pay the rent for one miserable room by minding bairns for working women,' Esther said. 'Although I wouldn't leave a child of mine in that house.'

'And folk are kind,' Raymond added.

'Like your uncle,' Ruth said.

'My uncle?' Raymond looked puzzled for a moment and then he grinned.

'Mr Fowler doesn't know a thing about this arrangement,' Esther said. 'Mrs Briggs only comes in to the shop when she knows Raymond will be in charge. He gives her a bit tea, sugar, bread, cheese, scraps of cooked meat. And he kept it secret, even from me until Davy saw what he was up to.'

'Well, I couldn't hev you knowing what a nice fellow I was, could I?'

Raymond Fowler grinned but, when he looked at Esther, Ruth saw the yearning in his eyes. He's in love with her, she thought, and young though he might be, what a wonderful match he would make.

But as she watched them, Esther moved away from him as if suddenly wanting to put distance between them. She knows how he feels, Ruth thought, but it's as if she can't believe it. In her eyes Raymond is just a lad, not much older than her brother. She can't believe it would be right to respond to him. How sad.

'You can go now, if you want, Esther,' Raymond said.

'Go? I'm supposed to work until noon.'

'Aye, if me uncle comes down I'll say we were quiet – which we are. He won't dock your pay.'

'But Davy?'

'He's still got to put up one more order and deliver it. When he's done I'll send him down to Mrs Shaw's. That's where you're gannin', isn't it?' Esther nodded. 'Gan on then,' Raymond said, 'here's yer pay. Take yer friend up to the German café on Shields Road, treat yerselves to coffee and cake, and tell her all the news.'

The flowerseller's basket provided a burst of bright colour on the corner. The streets were drab and tired-looking and the spring sunshine was barely warm enough to take the chill off the strong breeze blowing up from the river. Ruth and Esther were glad to take refuge in the little coffee shop.

On the short walk up from Fowler's, Esther had told Ruth of the tragic way Lucy's father had died, but not much more, and they were subdued as they took their table. The shop was double-fronted and had started as a delicatessen that sold foreign cheeses, salamis, sauerkraut and pickled cucumbers from large barrels kept under the counter.

But they also sold pastries and delicious cream cakes and it was because of this that Frau Kruger had put a few tables in the front of the shop near the window and started serving pots of coffee and tea along with a choice of delicious snacks. Esther ordered coffee and almond slices for both of them and they waited until they were served before they took up their conversation.

'So it seems he hadn't provided for them,' she said.

Ruth frowned. 'But Mr Shaw was chief sales representative for Lawson's, wasn't he? And he seemed such a loving father. I can't believe that he would leave Lucy and her mother destitute.'

Esther shook her head. 'I must admit I divven't understand it. Lucy doesn't say much but she seems to be real angry with him – and she's at odds with her mother, an' all, although I can't understand why. It's not poor Mrs Shaw's fault, is it?'

'Hardly.'

For a while they sipped their coffee and nibbled on their almond slices. They looked out of the window at the traffic on Shields Road. It wasn't very busy; there was a Sunday quietness and, apart from the trams, there was only the odd pony and trap or cyclist. Groups of people, dressed in their sober best, were either on their way to or from church or to visit families. The feathers in the women's hats were fluttering in the breeze.

'So, anyways, I suggested that Mrs Shaw might take Davy and me in as lodgers,' Esther resumed the conversation. 'They need the money and I could help with the housework now that they've had to pay Betty off.'

'Oh, no. Poor Betty.'

'Ee, she's taken it bad. She said she would stay on without pay if she could – I mean I divven't think poor Mrs Shaw knows how to boil an egg – but Betty has to hev paid work or that witch of a daughter-in-law of hers would probably send her to the workhouse!'

'So what's Betty doing now?'

'I was able to help out there.' Esther flushed slightly. 'I found her some cleaning jobs with some of the shop's customers. Poor old thing, down on her hands and knees scrubbing all day at her age instead of being in charge of a cosy little house, but it's better than nowt, I suppose.'

'And are you really going to lodge with the Shaws? I mean, is there room for you and Davy?'

'I'll hev Lucy's room and she'll hev to share with her ma. We're going to put a single bed in the front parlour for Davy – we'll get it at the sale rooms, of course, and I'll pay for it.'

'Has Mrs Shaw agreed to this arrangement?'

Esther smiled. 'I can see you're surprised – and to tell the truth she had to be persuaded – but Lucy convinced her ma that it was either that or she'd hev to go out and find a job.'

'I knew nothing about this – believe me.'

'Feeling guilty, are yer?'

'Why should I feel guilty?'

'Because you heven't been up to see us for so long. Oh, I know you divven't gan to yer pa's very often but you've even stopped dropping in at the Shaws' house. Lucy and me thought it was because of that young man.'

'What young man?' Ruth's hand shook as she replaced her cup in the saucer.

Esther's smile widened. 'So that's the truth of it, is it? You've finally taken pity on poor Henry Valentine.'

Ruth's agitation subsided and she was able to say quite calmly, 'No, I'm afraid not.'

'You mean you heven't been walking out with Henry instead of coming to visit yer old friends?'

'I haven't.'

'Well, then, what's the reason for neglecting us?'

'Oh, Esther, I'm sorry. It hasn't been so very long, has it?'

'No, I suppose not. It's just that so much has happened it seems like years to me – and probably to Lucy too.

'Do you want to come with me to see them now? Me and Davy's hevin' a bit dinner there. There'll be enough for you. Davy's taking the food down from the shop and I'm cooking it, of course!' Esther smiled. 'And then we're going to discuss the arrangements – when I'm to move in and all that.'

'But what about your father, Esther? Has he agreed that you should leave home?'

'Home! Some home that is. No, he hasn't agreed because I heven't telt him yet.'

'Oh dear.'

'You're thinking he'll cause trouble? Well, you're right, but I'm not going to give him cause. The only reason he wants me to stay at home is because I've been keeping house for him ever since me mam ran off.'

Esther paused and, from her expression, Ruth could see she was dwelling on unpleasant thoughts. Esther had never explained why her mother had gone, nor where she had gone to. An uncharacteristic reserve in Esther's manner kept Ruth from asking about it.

'Well, anyways,' Esther sighed and continued,

'I've given notice to the landlord that me and Davy don't need the back rooms any more, so that'll be less rent for me da to pay, and I've arranged with Hetty Lowther, the upstairs neighbour, to keep his place clean, do his laundry and cook his meals. I'm going to pay her.'

'Can you afford to?'

'Just about. Me and Davy between us do all right, and I work extra hours whenever I can.'

'I think Lucy is lucky to have you as a friend.'

'It works both ways.'

'What do you mean?'

'I can get me brother and me out of that hellhole at last.' Esther finished her coffee and placed the cup back in the saucer decisively. 'Well, are you coming to the Shaws'?'

'Yes, I'd like to see Lucy – and her mother – but I won't stay for the meal.'

'Are you sure? You know Mrs Shaw. She likes company, even in her present circumstances.'

'Yes, but you'll have a lot to talk about, won't you? She might be embarrassed to have to admit to someone else that her circumstances have changed.'

'You're right. But then they might be hurt if you don't stay.'

'I'll say I have to get back to Miss Golightly's.'

Surprisingly Esther grinned. 'After you've met with Mr Valentine that is.'

'No! I've told you. I'm not meeting him, really.'

Ruth knew she had flushed and she couldn't meet Esther's eye as her friend stared at her across the table. 'No? Well, I'll believe yer, although thousands wouldn't. But from the look on yer face yer meeting someone, aren't yer? And it's my bet it's a man, or yer wouldn't hev gone such a bonny shade of pink!'

Ruth didn't answer and Esther shrugged as she rose to her feet. 'Ah, well, keep yer secret, but I'm glad that at least you're going to show yer face.'

As they walked to the Shaws' house together Ruth imagined that Esther had only just refrained from finishing off her sentence with the words, 'at last!' But she acknowledged that she deserved the criticism and she was relieved that Esther had dropped the question of who she had been spending time with.

Roland had been put out by the fact that she hadn't agreed to take him to her father's house but he'd asked her at least to have tea with him and his sister when she returned. When she left the Shaws' house she would take the tram into the city, she decided, and do a bit of window shopping, perhaps find somewhere to have a light lunch. She needed time to herself, time to think, time to work out exactly what her feelings were before she returned to the coast and went to have tea with Roland Matthews.

Lucy's mother looked stunning in black. Ruth saw that she had lost weight but that only made her look more elegant. Her daughter, however, looked pale and lumpy. Those were the words that sprang into Ruth's mind. In fact, Lucy's face was more than pale, it was pasty, and there were dark smudges, purpling almost like bruises, under her eyes. Her hair was as carefully curled and arranged as it always was but it somehow lacked lustre, and her womanly figure looked as though it had been stuffed into a dress at least one size too small.

Perhaps it was grief that had wrought the change. Lucy certainly seemed to have been deeply affected by the death of her father. And yet Esther was right: there was an air of suppressed anger too. No doubt she had a right to be angry if Reginald Lawson hadn't left his family provided for but Ruth was shocked by the abrupt way she dealt with her mother. As Esther had said, it was hardly poor Mrs Shaw's fault.

Ruth felt guilty at the way that both Mrs Shaw and Lucy greeted her so warmly. In spite of their grief and Lucy's strange air of suppressed anger they had been genuinely pleased to see her and neither of them had reproached her for staying away.

Esther had gone straight into the kitchen and soon she set up the table with a large plate of sliced cooked ham, dishes of salad and boiled potatoes and a large plate of bread and butter. 'There wasn't time to do a proper roast,' she said, 'but we'll all feel better when we've got this lot inside of us. And I've got a nice slab of fruit cake for afters. Davy, divven't just stand there, arrange the chairs – and get one for Ruth an' all.'

Ruth was tempted by the sight of the food but she still felt uneasy. For all their welcome, she sensed that Lucy and her mother were seething with unspoken resentments – at least Lucy was. Daisy Shaw had an air of stubborn defiance about her that sat oddly with her grief. What had gone on between these two to set them so at odds when they should have been supporting one another?

Could Esther really not sense that there was a mystery here? Perhaps not. Perhaps it was the curse of a writer always to read more into the way people looked at each other, to hear the words that were intended even if they were not spoken. Ruth smiled at her own conceit – a writer indeed. She had not even finished her first attempt at writing a novel; had not even decided if she really dared to submit it to a publisher.

Esther, seeing Ruth's smile, mistook the reason. 'So, you are staying to eat with us, then?'

'No, thank you, but I can't. You know, I...' She looked at Esther, hoping that she would remember that they had already agreed that it was better that she didn't. And what they would say.

'Oh, of course, you hev to get back to Miss Golightly's, hevn't yer?'

'Yes, I'm sorry.'

Mrs Shaw hugged her. 'That's a pity,' she said. 'Lucy is going down to the coast to see her friend Julia. You could have travelled together.'

In spite of her level tone, Lucy's mother didn't look pleased and Lucy's face flushed unattractively. It was obvious to Ruth that this proposed visit was a bone of contention between them. Daisy Shaw confirmed this when she shook her head sadly and said, 'I've told her that it's too soon to go gallivanting–'

'It's hardly gallivanting, Mother, visiting my old school friend!' Lucy's voice was sharp. There was a hard edge of ill-feeling to it that Ruth had never heard before.

'Well, I know,' her mother said, 'but I thought you would want to spend more time with your mother ... in the circumstances.'

Ruth heard Lucy's intake of breath and was apprehensive but Esther soothed matters by saying, 'It'll be good for Lucy to go and see her friend, Mrs Shaw, we agreed that, didn't we? And, anyways, who says yer'll be alone? Davy and me'll be here with you. Davy's going to chop some firewood and clean all the shoes and you and me are going to sit by the fire and hev a good old chinwag until it's time fer me to make yer supper.'

Ruth's eyes widened when Esther went over to Lucy's mother and put her arm round her. 'Now, come and sit at the table,' she said, 'and I'll pour you a nice cup of tea. Davy will see you out, Ruth.'

'Of course. Goodbye. I'll come again, soon, I promise.'

At the door Davy shook his head like a wise old man. 'Like cats in a bag, those two these days,' he said. 'Always fighting. It's a good job wor Esther knows how to handle them.'

Ruth smiled at him. 'Will you like living here?'

His eyes widened as if she had asked a stupid question. 'What do you think? Mrs Shaw is a real lady and Lucy's all right when she's in a good mood. And our Esther'll look out fer all of us. And this place is like a palace! Do yer think I'd want to stop at me da's house when we can move in here?'

'No, of course you wouldn't.' Instinctively Ruth

leaned down and hugged him.

'Give over, Ruth. I'm not a bairn, you know.' Davy drew back and looked up and down the street. He seemed relieved to discover that there was no one about. He grinned. 'I might be small fer me age but there's one or two lasses round here I fancy me chances with. If they was to see what you'd just done they might think we're courting!'

Ruth resisted the urge to tousle his hair and smiled in return, before taking her leave.

'Ta-ra, then,' he called after her. 'And mind you keep your promise to come back soon. Me sister thinks a lot of yer, yer know, and Lucy and her ma think too much of their own concerns to be real friends to her.'

As she walked back to the station Ruth pondered how wise Esther's little brother was. He must be about twelve years old, she thought, even though he looked no more than ten. He was obviously bright as a button and she suspected that he owed his air of confidence entirely to his sister. Esther had always looked after him as well as any mother and it was good to see that he appreciated this.

And now Esther seemed to be taking on yet more responsibilities. She was going to move in and look after Lucy and Mrs Shaw. Oh, officially she was taking lodgings there, and she would be paying them for the privilege, but it seemed to Ruth that Esther was really going to be taking over Betty's duties – as well as working full time in Fowler's.

Suddenly Ruth felt pinpricks of moisture on her face. Raindrops spotted the pavements and the breeze strengthened, blowing the rain against the shop windows. She didn't have an umbrella. Rather than stand at the tram stop on Shields Road she decided to hurry to Heaton station and get the train into town.

A few minutes later, breathless with her exertion she ran into the ticket hall and collided with Henry Valentine.

'I beg your pardon,' they said in unison and stepped back, their eyes widening as they realized who it was they had just bumped into.

'Ruth!'

'Henry!'

They paused, each waiting for the other to speak and then they both laughed self-consciously.

'What a surprise,' Henry said.

'Mm.' Ruth was surprised to find how pleased she was to see him.

'Have you been visiting your father?'

'Yes. But unfortunately I must have got the days mixed up – they weren't there.' Ruth couldn't meet his eyes. She didn't want him to guess that she suspected her stepmother had arranged to go out deliberately.

'What a shame. So what are you going to do?'

'Do?'

'For lunch. I presume you were expecting to have a meal with them?'

'I thought I'd go into town and find a café.'

'All on your own? Come home with me!'

'Oh, no, I couldn't.'

'Why not? My mother would be delighted. She's always telling me that it's time I found– I mean she's always telling me that my friends are

313

welcome.' Henry blushed furiously and Ruth felt a surge of compassion. But she didn't know what to say to ease his embarrassment. 'Do say you'll come, then we can travel back to the coast together afterwards,' he added.

'Are you playing the piano at the hotel tonight?'

'Not tonight. I'm going to church. That's where I've just been.'

'To church?'

Ruth was startled; she found she could not quite imagine that Henry was so devout that he would attend services more than once in one day.

He laughed softly. 'The organist at St Paul's is away on holiday. I'm standing in for him.'

'Oh, I see.'

'Come along then.' As he spoke he took her elbow and guided her to the door. There he stopped and looked up into the sky with dismay. 'It's raining.' He glanced round at her. 'But of course it is. I should have realized that straight away – when we bumped into each other there were raindrops sparkling in your hair.'

His look was so intense that it made her laugh nervously. 'And no doubt the feathers in my hat are drooping miserably,' she added, trying to make a joke of it.

'Shall I run and get a cab?' Henry asked.

Ruth imagined the two of them in the confined space of a hansom cab. 'Is it far?'

'My parents' house? A few minutes' walk – it's on Heaton Road.'

'Then there's no need for a cab. We can hurry.'

'Take my arm.'

Ruth grasped his arm and hurried along with

Henry as she was told. The passing traffic trundling through puddles threw up small cascades of dirty water and they began to laugh as they dodged to the side of the pavement every time they heard the clatter of hoofs and the trundle of wheels coming up behind them.

When they reached the tall house on Heaton Road they were breathless with laughter. Henry opened the gate and stepped back to allow her to precede him. It was only then that she realized she could not remember the exact moment when she had agreed to come home with him.

'You shouldn't have written.' Stephen's glance was cold.

'Why not?'

Lucy's tone was defiant. She chose to ignore the way he was pursing his lips. The letter, sent to him at home, had at least achieved the desired result. He had come to meet her at the Mourning Warehouse.

'I need to see you on a matter of some urgency,' she had written, borrowing the phraseology from some of the letters she had typed for Mr Hetherington.

She had been pretty sure that Stephen would come. And if he hadn't then she had been determined to go to his home; ostensibly to see Julia, but really to confront him.

Stephen glanced at her in surprise. He was not used to her speaking to him like this; she knew that up to now she had been docile and easily led. 'Julia might have recognized your handwriting,' he said.

'Did you?'

He frowned. 'What do you mean?'

'Did you recognize my handwriting?'

'No, of course not. You've never written to me before.'

'Exactly.'

'Lucy, I haven't the faintest idea what you're talking about. Look, sit down. I'll pour you some wine.'

She wanted to refuse. She hated the way he was trying to control her – to keep her in her place. But she was tired, she hadn't slept properly for weeks now, and, in truth, she would welcome a glass of wine.

'Very well.'

She sat on one of the red plush sofas and tried to control her breathing. Stephen left her alone in the showroom and went to seek the wine. She stared at a catalogue left open on a nearby table. The illustrations were of gracefully posed women in various mourning attire. She was aware that in her own black robes she looked nowhere near as elegant. And she knew why.

Stephen returned carrying a cut-glass decanter full of deep red liquid, two glasses and a dish of biscuits on a silver tray. Or rather silver-plated, Lucy thought inconsequentially. Here it was all for show, all to impress the customers, who, vulnerable in their grief, would be persuaded to spend more than they could afford on the funerals of their dear departed.

'Here, Marsala, your favourite,' he said, 'and ratafia biscuits.'

She knew he was patronizing her but she

controlled the urge to take the biscuits and hurl them across the room. That would only anger him and she needed him to be in a good mood before she broke the news.

'I'm sorry about the letter,' she said. 'But I had to see you.'

Stephen didn't sit beside her. He balanced the tray on one hand, like a waiter at the Waverly, she thought, while he half stooped to close the catalogue and move it aside. Then he placed the tray on the table. She had made no move to help him.

He drew up a chair before pouring them each a glass of wine. 'I would have telephoned you at work as I usually do.'

Lucy took a welcome sip from her glass before she replied. 'When exactly?'

'I don't know exactly when.' His voice was laced with irritation and he raised his own glass to his lips and frowned down into it as he drank.

'You haven't telephoned for some weeks now,' she said.

'I know, I'm sorry, but Julia told me that you had written to her about your father's sad demise.'

'Don't speak to me like that!'

'Like what?' He looked surprised.

'You're using the words of an undertaker.'

'I am an undertaker.'

'But I'm not one of your clients! I wrote to Julia knowing that she would pass the news on to your mother – to you – and I thought you might have contacted me to at least say how sorry you are.'

'I am sorry but I thought you would want to

have time to grieve.'

'You didn't think you ought to comfort me?'

Stephen put his glass down on the table and spoke with patience as if to a fractious child. 'Comfort you? How? I imagined that the last thing you would want would be to come here, of all places, and make love. Not so soon after the death of your father.'

'Of course I didn't want that!' Lucy protested. She felt the heat rising. His words had angered her but they had struck an unpleasant chord.

She dropped her head and stared at the floor. In spite of her grief at the death of her father she had been shocked to discover that she missed the sheer physical excitement of being in Stephen's arms. In fact her body craved his touch. His neglect had hurt her on more than one level. 'I ... I just wanted you to hold me – to say that you cared.'

She heard him catch his breath and she looked up in alarm to catch the strangest look in his eyes. She felt panic rise within her. For of course, he had never actually said that he cared. But he had told her he wanted to marry her, hadn't he? When they used to sit in the waiting room at the station. Surely she hadn't been mistaken about that? And he had told her how much he wanted her ... but he had never told her that he loved her...

'You're right,' he said at last. 'I've been remiss. Of course I should have been in touch. I made a mistake. Will you forgive me?'

Lucy stared at him. He was sitting with his back to the window. His face was in shadow and she

318

couldn't see his expression. He made no move towards her and she sensed a weary detachment about him, as if he had searched for the correct thing to say only in order to avoid further aggravation.

'Of course,' she said. She knew she sounded pathetic and she felt like crying. She took a long sip of the wine.

'Would you like some more?'

Without waiting for an answer Stephen leaned forward and filled her glass. She noticed that he had hardly touched his own.

'Well, now that you're here, what shall we talk about?' he asked. 'Are you and your mother managing? Has your father left you well provided for?'

'No, he hasn't.'

'I beg your pardon?' Stephen sounded genuinely shocked.

'I said my father hasn't left us well provided for and we're not managing very well at all.'

'Oh, I see.'

But she could tell that he didn't see and, to her horror, it occurred to her that he was probably thinking that she'd come here to ask for financial help. His next words confirmed it.

'Is there anything I can do? A small loan – I mean, a gift–'

'Stop it!' Lucy found herself screaming. 'I didn't come here to ask for money. I have a good job, thanks to my parents paying for my education, and my mother has accepted that she's going to have to take lodgers. We'll manage. But not for very long if you don't marry me.'

'I beg your pardon!' Stephen rose so quickly that his chair fell over. 'You want me to marry you?'

Dismay at his response surged over her like a cold wave. For a moment she floundered, staring at him helplessly. 'You ... you have to,' she said when the restriction in her chest eased a little.

'*Have* to?'

'Yes.' Anger at Stephen, and anger at herself for having being so blind, so trusting, spurred her on. 'You have to.'

'And why is that?'

'To give our child a name.'

'That's impossible.' He glared at her.

'Impossible?'

'You can't be with child. I took precautions.'

'It wasn't safe. I ... I've been to a doctor.'

She had bought a cheap ring at a pawn shop and called herself Mrs Shaw. Why hadn't she thought of another name? But in any case the doctor had not been fooled and had made no attempt to hide his expression of amused disdain.

But when he had told her what she had dreaded to hear she had broken down and sobbed. After that he had been quite kind. He had questioned her closely and Lucy, burning with shame, had told him that her 'husband', for she kept up the pretence, had believed that by withdrawing before his climax he would not make her pregnant.

The doctor had shaken his head. 'He's been careless,' he'd said. 'It's risky relying on that method. Now off you go and tell him to make an honest woman of you.'

320

Lucy felt sick with embarrassment at the memory.

'It isn't mine.'

'What?' Lucy stared at Stephen in disbelief. Her intuition had told her that this would be difficult but she hadn't expected this.

'The baby isn't mine. You've been with someone else.'

It was no good; she couldn't stop the tears from spilling over. Hot tears that coursed down her cheeks and soaked into the black lace frills of her high collar. 'Stephen, how can you say that? Of course I haven't been with anyone else. You must know how much I love you.'

His stern look faltered. She thought he was going to come to her, take her in his arms. But then he seemed to pull himself together. 'Love?' he said, making a question of that one word. 'What has passed between us has nothing to do with love.'

'But I thought–'

'Don't play the innocent with me, Lucy. You knew perfectly well what I wanted from you and you were more than willing to go along with it.'

'Because I loved you!'

'For God's sake, stop this whining. It doesn't become you. You've been caught out–'

'*We've* been caught out.'

'Oh, very well. I'm not going to abandon you.'

'You're not?' Lucy rose from her seat, hope and joy dispelling all her misery.

'No. I can't afford the scandal; not now that I'm to be married.'

'Married!'

For the first time since he had let her in and brought her upstairs Stephen looked uncertain. 'Yes ... married. I never led you to believe that I was going to marry you, did I?'

'Yes you did!'

'When?'

'Almost the first time you walked me to the station from your parents' house, and you did so more than once.'

Lucy bit her lip as she tried to remember the last time Stephen had mentioned making her his wife. It had been just before ... before...

'Oh, yes,' Stephen said, and he sounded surprised. 'But I thought you'd forgotten about that.'

'Forgotten! How could I? Especially after ... after what we did.'

'If you were the sort of girl I intended to marry we wouldn't have done that.'

Lucy stared at him in horror. She was overwhelmed with a sense of shame. 'How cruel!'

'I'm sorry. I shouldn't have said that. I never would have said it if you hadn't gone on about having to marry you. I honestly believed that you knew what was what.'

'That you only ever intended me to be your mistress!'

'No, not at first but after I discovered what your background was, everything changed.'

'I beg your pardon!'

'I was attracted to you from the start. When my sister brought you home I honestly believed that there might be a future for us – a respectable future–'

'You mean that we would be married?'

'Yes.' Stephen looked uncomfortable. 'But knowing my parents' hopes for me–'

'Hah!'

'Knowing that the girl I chose would have to please my parents, I made enquiries about you.'

'You did what?'

'Don't worry, I was discreet. When I found out your circumstances, naturally I was disappointed.'

'What did you find out?'

'Exactly who your father was – and the illicit little nest he had in Byker with his mistress.' Lucy flinched. She'd had time to get used to the idea but it was painful to hear someone else describe her mother in such terms. 'Lucy, I've known for a long time that you are illegitimate.'

'Then you knew more than I did.'

Stephen looked astonished. 'Really? You didn't know?'

'I only found out after my father died. My mother never told me anything.' She sighed. 'So that's why you thought you could treat me the way you did,' she said bitterly. 'Like mother like daughter, I suppose.'

'You must believe me – I thought you knew your situation. Otherwise why would you have allowed me to make love to you?'

Lucy sank down on to the sofa and covered her face with her hands. She closed her eyes. She had 'allowed' Stephen to make love to her because she thought that he loved her. She had genuinely believed in the beginning that he intended marriage. Of course, she had been worried that

323

he had seemed to be in no hurry to make his courtship public, but she had believed that he had been waiting for the right time to tell his parents.

How could she have known that Stephen was the kind of man who divided women into those you married and respected, and those you used simply for physical pleasure. She groaned.

'And I suppose this girl you are going to marry will be the sort your parents will approve of?' she asked. Although she knew what the answer would be.

'Of course.'

'And what about your child? It is your child, you know.'

Her eyes remained closed so she sensed rather than saw him moving towards her. He sat beside her and reached for her hands. He pulled them away from her face and when he spoke, he spoke kindly.

'Listen to me, Lucy. You shocked me with your news and I've been unkind.'

'Unkind!'

She tried to snatch her hands away but he kept tight hold. 'No, look at me, this is important.' Unwillingly she turned her head and met his gaze. 'The baby will be cared for. I'll give you an allowance; enough to live comfortably. And I'll come and see you – you and the child.'

'And my mother!' Lucy felt hysteria rising.

'No, of course not. You should get your own place. I'll come as often as I can. We can go on as before.'

Lucy kept quite still for a moment and then she

324

withdrew her hands from his. He was smiling at her – thinking that she had agreed to his plan. She began to shake her head slowly from side to side.

'No,' she said.

'Lucy?'

'No.'

'What do you mean "no"?'

'We won't go on as before. And you won't come to visit me.' She rose and began to back away from him. 'And I don't want your money.'

'Don't be ridiculous. How will you manage?'

She didn't answer. She had reached the door that led to the stairs and she turned away from him, opened it and began to hurry down. Before she had reached the front door she heard Stephen pounding after her. 'Lucy! Wait! You're not going to cause trouble, are you?'

She half turned to ask, 'Trouble?'

'You're not going to tell my sister – or my parents? It wouldn't do any good, you know. Lucy! What are you going to do?'

Lucy began to laugh. She opened the door and ran out into the street. She knew he wouldn't follow. He would be too afraid of them being seen together. She hadn't answered him. Let him stew. But, in any case, how could she have answered him when she hadn't the remotest idea what she was going to do?

Chapter Eleven

Esther had done her best to make the meal an enjoyable occasion. Lucy's mother had responded to her attempts at conversation about the spring weather and the new popularity of Scotch plaid fabrics. Esther had even drawn Davy into the conversation with questions about his favourite football team, Newcastle United.

But, as the meal progressed, Esther had grown more and more annoyed with Lucy, who had remained stubbornly silent and had seemed determined to ignore and snub her mother at every turn. Esther had felt like telling her friend that she was very lucky to have a mother who cared so much and who made every effort to be kind to others. But she knew it was not her place to say anything so she'd held her peace.

As soon as Lucy had left them to go to the coast, Daisy Shaw fell silent. It was as if she had used up all her energy for the moment. She looked washed out, Esther thought. She settled her in the armchair near the fire and left her there while she and Davy cleared the table and washed the pots. When they'd finished Esther made a pot of tea and put it on a tray, along with cups for the three of them.

Daisy looked up and smiled distractedly. 'That's kind of you, Esther,' she said.

Esther poured the tea. 'Do you mind if Davy

joins us?' she asked. 'Only I divven't like leaving the bairn in the scullery on his own.'

Lucy's mother brightened for a moment. 'Of course he must join us and you really shouldn't call him a bairn, Esther. Your brother is not a little child.'

'That's what I keep telling her!' Davy said, and he grinned.

'You're only twelve,' Esther said. 'And as far as I'm concerned you're still a bairn.'

Daisy shot him a sympathetic smile but then she sat back in her chair with the cup of tea Esther gave her and looked pensive again. Esther was overcome with a feeling of fondness for her friend's mother that bordered on love. She wished she knew how to smooth the frown from that beautiful brow; how to solve whatever problem it was that was driving a wedge between mother and daughter, the two people, along with her brother, Davy, and her friend Ruth, that she loved most in all the world.

'Hawway, Esther,' Davy said suddenly, 'divven't sit there dreaming, give us me tea.'

'I'll hev less of yer cheek,' Esther said, but nevertheless she smiled. 'Here, take the cracket.' Esther pulled the small wooden stool forward before she handed him his cup, 'and sit by the fire quiet, like, while me and Mrs Shaw hev a chinwag.'

'Aye,' her brother replied. 'I'll behave meself. Raymond gave us his newspaper, he'd finished with it. I'll hev a read and you can gossip away to your heart's content.'

Davy set his cup down carefully on the floor by

the fender and drew a rolled-up newspaper from his back pocket.

'Now take care, divven't spill that tea,' Esther said.

Davy simply grinned and began reading the paper.

He was a good lad, Esther thought, as she sipped her own tea, and he deserved this chance of a decent home. She knew how lucky she was to be moving in here, although of course she was sorry that she and Davy were benefiting from someone else's sorrow.

Mrs Shaw was staring into the fire, her eyes unfocused. What was she thinking, poor lady? Of the happy times there had been in this little house? No matter what had happened, no matter what was going to happen, Esther realized that she envied Lucy all the happy memories that she must have.

And what on earth was the matter with the lass that she should be behaving so badly when her mother needed her most? Fancy traipsing off to the coast to see Julia Wright when she could hev been sitting here drawing comfort from her mother's love and her true friend's concern for her. She simply didn't know how lucky she was to hev a mother who cared.

Suddenly Esther thought of her vain quest for her own mother and she wondered why she had bothered to search for a woman who had neglected her bairns so woefully. And then she felt guilty. Of course she would search again whenever circumstance allowed. It wasn't her mother's fault. Who knows, if she had had a better husband, a kind caring man like Mr Shaw had been, she might hev behaved altogether differently. She was taken unawares by an ache of grief in her throat and she felt the tears gathering in her eyes.

'Are you crying, Esther?' Mrs Shaw's voice broke into her thoughts. 'That's kind of you.'

'Kind?' Esther brushed the tears away with the back of her hand.

'To care so much for Lucy and me. But we'll manage, you know, now that you are going to move in here to help us.'

'Aye ... well ... would you like another cup of tea?' Emotion was almost choking her and it was all she could think of to say.

'No, I don't think so. I'd like to go upstairs and lie down for a while. Are you going to stay awhile? You know you're welcome.'

'Aye. I promised Lucy I'd hev something on the table for when she gets back.'

'That's good of you.'

'No, it isn't. I'd rather be sitting here than in that slum me father calls home. And...' Esther faltered, 'I was wondering if it would be all right to move here permanent by the end of next week. I should hev everything settled by then.'

'Of course you may, dear. Now, would you take this cup?'

The cup rattled in the saucer and Esther noticed that Mrs Shaw's hand was shaking slightly. She took it from her and put it on the table and then turned back to find that Lucy's mother had risen but was standing with her eyes closed and both her hands pressed on to her breast. Her face was white as milk.

'Mrs Shaw, what's the matter? Davy – what happened?'

'I divven't know.' Her brother had risen and the newspaper had fallen to the floor. His eyes were huge. 'She just got up and then she stumbled,' he said. 'I thought she was going to fall down but she righted herself before I could catch her. It happened that quick.'

'I'm all right, Esther,' Mrs Shaw said.

'You divven't sound right and you look right femmur.'

'Shall I gan for the doctor?' Davy asked.

'No ... really ... I just stood up too quickly. I haven't been sleeping properly, you know.'

'Of course you heven't. Davy, will you get the tray and take these cups into the scullery?' She wanted to keep him occupied; he looked as though he'd had a shock. 'And Mrs Shaw, I'm going to help you up the stairs.'

Esther put her arm round Lucy's mother's waist and realized how much weight she had lost. Not like her daughter, Esther thought fleetingly. Mrs Shaw grasped one of her hands.

'You're a good girl, Esther. I think the angels must have sent you.'

'Now divven't talk like that.' Esther was embarrassed.

'No, I mean it. I've never forgotten, you know.'

'Forgotten?'

'How you and Ruth saved Lucy's life that day. How you dragged her from the sea.'

'If we hadn't somebody else would hev.'

'Would they? I don't know.'

'And I divven't think she would hev drowned,

you know. She would hev come round and got up herself.'

Mrs Shaw was shaking her head. 'No, you saved her, you and Ruth. And now you've come here to help me.'

'Aye, help you up to bed. Now come along.'

But Mrs Shaw didn't move immediately. She took hold of one of Esther's hands and examined it. 'Poor Esther.'

'Now what are you on about?'

'You're young and beautiful and yet your hands are rough and work-stained.'

'Well, that can't be helped.'

'Yes it can. I must give you some of my own hand cream and show you how to take care of yourself.'

'You've already helped me that way.'

'How? Oh, you mean the clothes? They were only cast-offs – but how beautiful you look in them.' Suddenly Mrs Shaw moved away a little and took Esther's face in both her hands. Esther noticed how smooth they were and how her skin smelled of roses. 'There's another way I could help you, Esther, if you'd let me.'

'And what's that?'

'You know how I've brought Lucy up to be a lady? To dress well and to...' she hesitated, 'to speak properly.'

'Aye, she was always better than the rest of us, even at school.'

'Would you like me to teach you how to speak properly, Esther?'

'Oh ... I divven't know...'

'You mean, you *don't* know, not divven't.' Daisy

331

Shaw's smile softened the criticism. 'Well? It would give me so much pleasure.'

'We'll see,' Esther said. 'And now, it's off to bed with you.'

The older woman allowed her to lead Esther towards the door. 'You'll wake me up when Lucy comes home, won't you?'

'Aye – I mean yes, I will.'

They both smiled and then Lucy's mother looked serious. 'I've been worried about her, you know. I know she's grieving and I know she's angry with me.'

'Why should she be angry?'

For a moment Daisy Shaw let her gaze slip and then she said, 'Oh, it's a natural part of grief, I'm told. But it's not just that. I think ... I think there's something she isn't telling me.'

They looked into each other's eyes and now it was Esther who could not hold the other woman's gaze. She pictured Lucy and how, unlike her mother, she seemed to have gained weight rather than lost it. She thought of how abrupt Lucy's manner had become and how her mind seemed to be dwelling on other things all the time.

'No,' Esther said. 'I'm sure you're wrong.'

But the truth of it was that Esther was far from sure. She had just realized what it was that was worrying Lucy's mother so much and now she was worried too.

'Don't you like the pudding, Henry?'

'I do, Mother. The pudding is delicious.'

'Then why won't you have a second helping?'

'I've had sufficient.'

'Oh, no. You don't eat enough. You're far too thin. He's too thin, isn't he, Ruth? Tell him he's too thin – you must have noticed!'

'Well, no, I hadn't... I'm sorry.'

Ruth watched Henry's mother nervously to see if she had displeased her. She thought that perhaps she should have agreed with her hostess but she had caught Henry's warning look.

'Oh, I expect you think he's perfect,' Mrs Valentine said with a sigh. 'No doubt you wouldn't change a single thing about him.'

'Mother!' Poor Henry's face was the colour of the red wine in the decanter.

'Cordelia, my love, you're embarrassing the lad. No doubt he's wishing that he'd never brought his young lady home to meet us,' Henry's father said, and now it was Ruth's turn to blush.

She should have guessed that coming home for Sunday lunch with him would cause his parents to imagine that they were walking out together.

'I thought you liked ginger pudding.'

Fortunately no one was looking at Ruth. Cordelia Valentine had returned to the subject of second helpings.

'I do, Mother, I do. It's just that I've had sufficient.'

'Especially when it's served with lemon sauce.'

'You might as well give in, Henry,' his father said. 'Your mother is not going to give up until every scrap is eaten.'

'Oh, very well, but just a little,' Henry said.

'Good. And what about you, Walter? Will you have some?'

'Of course, my dear.'

'Good.'

While Henry's mother busied herself giving her husband and son second helpings of the steamed pudding, Ruth caught the look that passed between father and son. A look of fond exasperation. This scene must have been played out many times, Ruth thought, and yet both men were prepared to indulge Cordelia, even if they had to suffer the consequences.

Ruth was grateful that her own polite refusal of a second helping had been accepted. Although the manner of its acceptance had both startled and embarrassed her.

'Of course, dear, I understand,' Mrs Valentine had said. 'You want to keep that graceful figure of yours. Henry told me how lovely you were but I had imagined it was the natural exaggeration of a young man smitten until I saw you.'

Ruth had been unable to suppress an affronted glance across the table at Henry, but he had been unable to meet her eye.

What strange people these were, Ruth thought, as Henry and his father manfully coped with their second helpings of pudding drenched in lemon sauce. Strange but engaging, with their lack of conventional formality.

Walter Valentine was an older version of his son, with the same floppy brown hair, but he was of a heavier build, verging on stout. And no wonder if today's meal was anything to go by.

They had started with clear soup and delicious freshly baked rolls, gone on to roast pork with apple sauce and vegetables, and then Mrs

Valentine had produced the ginger pudding. Or rather a dishevelled young maid had appeared with the pudding and the sauce while Henry's mother had watched her son eagerly as if waiting for his reaction. Henry had obliged, showing himself well pleased but had then let her down by refusing seconds.

But that was forgiven now and Mrs Valentine busied herself pouring thick black coffee into tiny cups while her unfortunate husband and son ate up every scrap as they had been commanded.

'Turkish coffee,' she said as she passed the cup to Ruth. 'I was introduced to it during my season in Paris and I have savoured it ever since.'

Ruth looked at her helplessly. She had not got used to her hostess's way of talking: the strange vocabulary, the extravagant expressions. Henry dabbed at his mouth with his napkin and smiled at her.

'My mother sang at the Opera House when she was young.'

'Ah, those days.' Mrs Valentine laid a hand on her breast and smiled sadly. 'Those dear, long-gone days.'

Her husband immediately captured her hand in his and said, 'What a fortunate man I was that you gave up such a promising career for me.'

His wife stared at him searchingly and, although once more Ruth had the feeling that this scene had been played out before, she could have sworn that the tears in Henry's mother's eyes were genuine. It was then Ruth saw how beautiful Mrs Valentine must have been. She was still attractive: tall, perhaps taller than her husband, and with a full but shapely figure. Her fair hair was parted in the centre and drawn back in a severe, classical style, revealing her fine-boned face. And those limpid eyes must once have been captivating.

She was startled to see Henry's father draw his wife's hand to his lips and kiss it before they both turned their attention to their coffee. She sipped her own coffee and found it bitter.

'You'll need sugar,' Henry said, and he took up the sugar basin and came round the table to join her. He pulled up a chair and then reached for his own cup. 'Let me,' he said as he stirred two spoonfuls of brown sugar into her cup. 'This coffee is an acquired taste. My mother has it sent specially.'

'From Paris?' Ruth asked.

'No, from the Army and Navy Stores in London, although my father has tried to persuade her that she should try the coffees on sale at Pumphreys in the Bigg Market.'

'Did she regret giving up her career?' Ruth couldn't help asking. She had lowered her voice. 'I'm sorry, that's personal.'

'That's all right. We are unconventional in this house – as you must have already gathered. No, she didn't. She had a fine soprano voice, still has, but she made a love match and considered herself blessed.'

'But surely ... if you can sing ... it must be a trial not to.'

'Oh, my mother still sings. The occasional concert, filling in when visiting companies need an extra singer or two. And, of course, she gives lessons, as we all do.' Ruth shook her head. 'What is it?' Henry asked.

'I've never met people like your parents before ... or you.'

'I'm sure you could grow to like us.'

'Oh, I do!'

Straight away Ruth wished she hadn't said that. She wished Henry was better at guarding his emotions. He looked so pleased, as if he were reading a significance into her words that she had not intended.

'What are you children talking about?' Henry's mother was looking at them keenly. 'Me, I'm sure. Don't you know that's rude?'

Ruth glanced in alarm at Henry but he laughed. 'You know you like people to talk about you, Mother. And I'm telling Ruth what charming people we are,' he said.

'If a trifle bohemian!' his mother added with a pleased smile. Then she said, 'You will come and visit us again, won't you, Ruth? Walter and I are so pleased to have met you at last.'

Ruth was dismayed by the 'at last'. 'Oh ... well...' she floundered. 'I don't get much time off and when I do, I like to go and visit my father.'

Henry's mother frowned. 'What's the matter? Have we frightened you?'

'Oh, no. I've enjoyed myself, really. It's just that I would like to come again but I don't know when I will be able,' she finished lamely.

She had sensed Henry's distress but she refused to look at him and she remained quiet as the family discussed some arrangements for later that evening when Henry had returned from church.

'We might as well take our leave now,' she heard Henry say to his mother and soon they were on their way to Heaton station.

It had stopped raining for the moment although the sky still looked threatening. There were pools of water on the pavements, and Ruth concentrated on holding her skirts to avoid getting them wet and muddy.

'You're angry, I can tell,' Henry said as he took her arm to guide her across the road.

Ruth shook her head. 'No.'

'But you are, and I know why. My mother's words have made it plain that I have talked about you at home, that I have confided in my parents how I feel about you.'

'Please don't go on.'

'I'm sorry. But you can see we are not an inhibited family. We talk about everything that concerns us.'

'And you think that includes me?'

'I beg your pardon. I don't understand.'

Ruth wasn't sure that she understood either. 'I mean whatever ... however you regard me, the way you have talked, your mother must think that I feel the same way as you do.'

'And you don't.' His words were half statement and half question. Ruth couldn't bear to hear the pain in his voice.

'Oh, Henry. What can I say?'

'It's all right. Don't say anything. Just listen.' Ruth was surprised at his firm tone. 'We get on well, you and I, we're the same kind of people.'

'How can you say that? You live in a big house, your parents are cultured. Your mother is an opera singer–'

'Was once.'

'Your father a distinguished musician.'

'He plays in a theatre orchestra.'

'They are wealthy.'

'They work hard.'

'Don't interrupt! And you–'

'What about me?'

Ruth shot him a steely glance and he shrugged and smiled.

'You are educated.'

'Yes, I went to a good school. So what?'

'Henry! And you're talented. And I? I left board school at fourteen–'

'That doesn't mean that you haven't got a good brain.'

This time she hurried straight on. '–and whatever Miss Golightly chooses to call me, I'm nothing better than a servant.'

'Don't talk like that.'

'Why not? I'm sure you haven't told your parents that I am a servant girl!'

'I've told my parents exactly what you do. You're Miss Golightly's companion – but so much more.'

'And where my father lives?'

'Yes.'

'And that he works in the shipyards?'

'Yes. Ruth, I can hardly believe we're having this conversation. You've met my parents now. Do you really think they are the sort of people who would think such things important?'

Henry's words silenced her and she stared ahead, frowning. She knew instinctively that, just like their son, Henry's parents would care little for social convention. It was Ruth herself who had seized on the differences between them and had tried to erect a barrier.

Because, from the moment she had first met Henry and he had looked into her eyes in that intense way of his, she had felt threatened. She had known immediately that this man seemed able to know what she was thinking without a word passing between them. People called that being able to read your mind – but it was more than that – she felt that he sensed her emotions too – and perhaps could even guess at her dreams.

And that was dangerous. Ever since her beloved mother had died and the father she adored had shut her out so completely, Ruth had shied away from revealing too much about herself to anyone. Her friends accused her of being moody but it was all part of her attempts to control any situation she found herself in. Never to reveal herself.

Ruth had been a defenceless child, ready to love anyone who was kind to her, and her stepmother had been the cause of so much pain that the child had learned to keep her emotions to herself and, as she had grown, she had vowed never to allow herself to be so vulnerable again.

She had been silent too long and a flash of awareness, a vibration in the air between them, told her that Henry was going to press his point.

She schooled herself to sound unconvinced as she said, 'Would they be happy if you wanted to walk out with the maid who waited on us at table?'

'No.'

'There, you see!'

'They wouldn't be happy because Sally is engaged to be married to a very large young man who might take offence and come along and have it out with me.'

'Henry! I'm being serious.'

'And so am I. But what's the point?' They had reached Heaton station and they could hear a train pulling in with a hiss of steam. They hurried through the ticket hall, boarded the train and took their places in the compartment before Henry finished what he was saying.

'For no matter how serious I am about you,' he said, 'it's plain that you do not feel the same way about me. Or do you? It's not the difference in what you perceive to be our stations in life that's bothering you, is it? There is something troubling you, something that is preventing you from accepting what is plain to see. We are the same kind of people in the most important way, and one day I hope you'll realize that.'

Ruth didn't reply. There was nothing she could say. They travelled back to the coast in silence. But her conscience was far from clear. She shouldn't have gone home with Henry. She still wasn't sure why she had.

Later, sitting with Miss Matthews and Roland at their table in the tiny apartment over the Crystal Library, Ruth was even more confused. As she consumed Guinevere's neatly cut cucumber sandwiches and raspberry jam tartlets, she kept glancing surreptitiously at Roland.

She tried to work out what it was about him

341

that attracted her. Well, of course he was hand-some. She'd never seen a more attractive man. And he was good fun – so long as things were going his way.

But that wasn't his fault, Ruth acknowledged. It was obvious that his elder sister had indulged and spoiled him from the moment she had become responsible for his upbringing. And he was not always kind to his sister. Ruth had seen him snap at her if he imagined she had not been listening to him – Guinevere often had an air of distraction – or if the household arrangements were not exactly to his liking. But he could always be coaxed back into a good mood, and then he would not exactly apologize, but go out of his way to make it up to her.

And then Roland caught her eye across the table and smiled brilliantly. Her hand shook and she put her cup down quickly; it rattled in the saucer. She felt her heart racing as she acknowledged the reason why Roland disturbed her so. It was sheer animal magnetism; uncomplicated physical attraction of the sort that had bound poor Angelina, the heroine of Miss Golightly's novel, to Count Hugo, even when she believed him to be a villain.

Ruth returned Roland's smile.

Just before Lucy reached the station at Whitley-by-the-Sea she heard the guard's whistle and the slamming of carriage doors that told her the train was about to depart. It was no use running; the distance was too far and she was already out of breath.

She slowed down and tried to regain her composure as she sauntered the rest of the way. She had left Stephen in a fury, had told herself that she never wanted to see him again; but she couldn't help looking back to see if he had followed her. Of course he hadn't.

What was she going to do? After his initial disbelief – his disgusting accusation that she must have been with another man – he had seemed to accept that the baby she was expecting was his. But he had made it clear that he had no intention of marrying her. He never had – at least not from the moment that he had discovered that her parents weren't married and that she was illegitimate.

Lucy felt despair and rage rising to choke her. Despair because she was expecting a child and would remain unmarried, and rage both at Stephen and at her parents, whose fault this was.

Why on earth had her mother agreed to live with her father, a married man, in the first place? Why had she settled for being a mistress rather than a wife? Her mother had offered no explanation other than the fact that she had fallen hopelessly in love and that her father had led her to believe that one day, when his legitimate daughter was grown and married, he would leave his wife, ask her to divorce him, and marry the woman he truly loved.

How could her mother have been so naïve?

Lucy believed that her father had never had any intention of leaving his family. The arrangement had suited him perfectly. And how old was Annabel, anyway? When Lucy had glimpsed her half-sister at the funeral she had guessed her to be not much older than she was.

When Reginald Lawson had first persuaded Daisy Shaw – Lucy had learned that Shaw was her mother's maiden name – to set up home with him, had he told her how long she would have to wait until his daughter was grown up and married? And when her mother went to Yorkshire that day and watched Reginald's family from the hillside, hadn't she realized how hopeless her situation was?

And that was exactly the sort of arrangement that Stephen had just offered her. How dare he? No, she would never accept such a humiliating position in life. Never! But how much more humiliating to have to tell her mother that she was expecting a baby and that she would have to bring the child up without a father. Ironically, she suspected that her mother would find this shameful.

But did she have to have this baby? Lucy knew about abortion. She even knew where a certain woman lived who would solve her problems for a few shillings. But she'd also heard the horror stories of girls who had died along with the unwanted child and she didn't know if she was brave enough to go ahead with something like that. And besides ... could she do it even if she were? The poor little morsel hadn't asked to be created just as she herself hadn't...

With her eyes downcast and hardly looking where she was going Lucy sensed that people were walking towards her. Passengers from the train that had just departed she guessed. She moved aside and stopped. Only to realize that someone was blocking her way.

'Hello, Lucy. You've just missed the train.'

Lucy focused her gaze on the person standing before her. 'I know that, Arthur.' Her tone was caustic. He coloured and looked down. She felt ashamed. 'Look, I'm sorry. I'm just cross with myself.'

'For missing the train?'

'Yes. Now I'll have to wait for half an hour and I'm cold and wet and miserable.'

'Aye, it's turned chilly and the rain's drizzled on and off all day.'

'You do have a knack of stating the obvious, Arthur.'

His smile vanished and he looked sullen. 'Well, if that's how you feel, good day to you. I'm off yem.'

Lucy was astonished. Arthur had never spoken to her like that before. She looked at him properly and saw that he had an overcoat on over his uniform. It looked cheap but it was stylishly cut and so was his hair.

'Wait, Arthur,' she said, and she put a hand out hesitantly to grasp his arm.

Instead of looking at her he looked at her hand as if he was deciding whether to shake it off. 'What do you want?'

'I'm sorry. I didn't mean to offend you.'

'Didn't you?' He looked up and Lucy saw the suspicion in his eyes.

'No.'

'Well, in that case I divven't know what you'd be like if you did set out to offend.'

'I've told you – I'm not myself.' The sob in her voice wasn't contrived and Arthur's eyes suddenly widened as he looked at her, taking in her black clothes as if remembering the significance.

'Of course you're not. Your father ... it's not been long, has it? I'm sorry, bonny lass, I should hev understood.'

They stood and looked at each other hesitantly and then Lucy said, 'Well, anyway, I'd best go to the waiting room and sit down. I'm ... I'm a little tired.'

'Aye, there's a fire in there, you'll be comfortable. Hawway, I'll walk along with you.'

'But you were on your way home, weren't you?'

'Aye. But there's nowt there that won't keep.' She thought he sounded weary.

Arthur walked with her through the station towards the waiting room. The skies outside were grey and the station was shadowy. It was not yet time to light the lamps. A cold wind winnowed along the platform, chasing a discarded scrap of paper; it looked like the wrapping from a bar of chocolate. There was no one else in sight and Lucy thought how desolate the place looked.

Suddenly a sense of hopelessness overwhelmed her and she started to cry softly, hardly making a sound as the tears streamed down her cheeks. She heard Arthur's intake of breath before his arm went round her as he guided her towards a door.

'Whisht, lass,' he said as though to a child. He took a key out of his pocket with his other hand; then he took his arm away from her as he opened the door and she felt strangely bereft. She

346

followed him into the room unquestioningly, then stopped, uncertain where she was going in the dimness inside.

'Wait there,' he said as he closed the door behind them and moved towards a hearth where a fire burned low.

She concentrated on the small area of light and watched as Arthur removed a cinder guard and stooped to heap more coal on the fire. The coal smoked for a moment and then, as Arthur took a poker and rearranged it, the light flared. Lucy looked around the small room wonderingly. It was a sort of office with a high desk and stool near a window that looked out on to the platform. There was room for one cupboard and there was a map and a timetable pinned to the wall. On the floor near the fire there was a hearthrug and, to the side of the fireplace there was a comfortable leather armchair.

'What is this place?' Lucy asked when Arthur stood up.

He wiped his hands on a clean white handkerchief and smiled. 'My office.'

'*Your* office?'

'Aye, I'm head porter, didn't you know?'

Lucy shook her head and Arthur sighed. 'Well, of course you didn't,' he said. 'It's been a long time since you had the time of day for me.'

'That's not fair.' In spite of her misery Lucy was stung enough to be indignant.

'Not fair? And why's that?'

'Because it seems to me that you haven't had the time for me – now that you're walking out with that little nursemaid.'

Arthur looked discomfited. 'Oh, aye, Mary.'

'I mean, she's your sweetheart, isn't she? She wouldn't be too pleased if you and I were to gossip like we used to, would she?'

'I suppose not. But is that the reason you avoid me? Because you don't want to upset Mary, or is it because you're too taken up with Stephen Wright?'

'I've told you before, I don't care for Stephen Wright in that way. Not one jot!'

'I know you did but I thought you must hev changed your mind and decided to marry him.'

Now it was Lucy's turn to be astounded. 'What on earth made you think that?'

'This is a small town. Word gets round. And the gossip is that Stephen is courting serious. He never gans out with his old pals any more. One of them, Sydney Fletcher, let slip that Stephen was on the lookout for a nice little property for him and his bride-to-be.'

'And you thought that was me?' Lucy wiped the tears from her cheeks with her fingers and forced herself to laugh. She hoped the laughter didn't ring false.

'Aye, I did. After all, you've been coming here to see him all this time.'

'No, I come to Whitley to see Julia. You know that.'

Lucy's heart was thudding so violently that she imagined Arthur would be able to hear it. She had only just learned from Stephen that he was going to be married and yet, according to Arthur's words, it must have been common gossip for a while.

348

Why hadn't Julia told her? Well, she had hinted at it, she supposed, and perhaps, as Stephen's sister had no idea that Lucy had been seeing Stephen in secret, she would not have thought it would interest her at this sad time after her father's death. She might have thought it insensitive to mention a wedding at a time of mourning.

Lucy put on her brightest smile and forced herself to look at Arthur. She was glad that the room was in semidarkness. Apart from the fire, the only light was that coming through the window from the station platform where one or two of the lamps had now been lit. The lamp boy must have started his evening's task.

'Fancy you thinking that,' she said.

'Well, you can't blame me, can you?'

'No, I suppose not.'

'Look, I'm sorry if I've angered you ... upset you,' Arthur said. 'Why don't you sit down – here by the fire.' He drew the chair nearer to the hearth. 'I'll gan and fetch you a cup of tea from the cafeteria.' He came towards her and put his arm round her again, drawing her towards the armchair.

'But is there time? I mean the train...?'

'Forget the train. There'll be another one along later, and more after that. I'm not letting you gan yem until you're in better fettle.'

When Arthur left her Lucy sat and gazed into the flames, trying not to think too closely about the lies she had just told. Trying not to think at all. The chair was comfortable and the fire was warm. She closed her eyes and allowed herself a few moments' respite from her cares and worries.

'There you are,' Arthur said when he returned with the tea. He set the tray down on the desk and took his overcoat off, hanging it on a hook on the back of the door. 'By, it's nice and warm in here the now,' he said, and he smiled. 'Do you want to take off your coat?'

Lucy raised a hand to the buttons of her coat but paused uncertainly.

'You better had,' Arthur said, 'or you won't feel the benefit when you gans out.'

His words reminded her of what Betty, their dear old maid, used to say when Lucy was a little girl, and she smiled. 'All right.' She stood and removed her coat. 'Where shall I put it?'

'Here, give it to me. And your hat, too. Make yourself comfortable.'

Lucy removed her hatpins, took off her hat and then pushed the pins into the felt before handing the hat to Arthur. He gazed at it for a moment and grinned. 'Daft little thing,' he said, 'with those feathers and little shiny bows.'

'Do you like it?'

'Aye, I suppose so.'

Arthur hung her coat beside his own and put her hat on the desk. Then he vanished behind the desk to emerge a moment later with a small packing case. He set it down on the hearth rug and then placed the tray on top. 'This will be our table,' he said, smiling again.

Lucy adjusted the combs in her upswept hair as she gazed at the contents of the tray. As well as two large mugs of tea with steam rising, there were two plates with a pork pie and a currant bun on each.

'Oh, Arthur, I couldn't...' she began.

Arthur sat down cross-legged on the hearth rug and grinned up at her. 'Well, suit yerself. But I'm famished. I was on me way home for me tea, you know, when we bumped into one another.'

'I'm sorry.'

'What for?'

'I've stopped you going home.'

'I telt you. There's nowt spoiling there.'

He sounded cynical and this prompted Lucy to ask, 'Where do you live, Arthur?'

'Do you really want to know?'

'Of course. Why shouldn't I?'

'You've never asked me owt like that before.'

She was glad of the firelight that warmed her cheeks and would make her heightened colour go unnoticed. 'Well, I'm asking now.'

'In lodgings just a short walk away. The house is clean and respectable but that's about it.'

'I'm sorry.'

'Divven't keep apologizing, lass.'

'I'm – I mean, have you no family?'

'I'm an orphan. I was fetched up in a home. It was more like a prison, as if the poor little beggars that ended up there was responsible for their own situation and guilty of being a nuisance to the parish.'

'I'm so s–'

'Divven't say it!' He grinned up at her. 'I survived, didn't I? And at least I was well fed and schooled properly – at least schooled in a manner so that I'd know me place and work hard for me living.'

Lucy stared at him with widening eyes. All

351

these years she had known him and she had known nothing about him. He returned her gaze and then looked down, embarrassed, as if he'd given away too much.

'Look at us sitting in the dark,' he said. 'I'd better light the lamp.'

He half rose but Lucy raised a hand to stay him. 'No, I like it like this, sitting in the firelight with ... with you.'

'Do you?'

He sounded so pleased – pleased yet astonished, his voice almost breaking with pleasure – that she felt guilty. For she knew what she was going to do. She wasn't quite sure when she had decided, or if she had made any conscious decision at all. Perhaps it was when he had put his arm round her to lead her towards the door of his office – or perhaps the moment when he had taken his arm away and she had missed the comfort of it. But the chance to solve her problem had presented itself and she was going to take it.

'Yes, it's cosy,' she told him. 'Just you and me in the firelight. Don't you like it like this?'

He'd caught something in the softening of her voice, in the way she had lowered her head and half smiled. His own voice was husky when he answered, 'I like it fine.'

Lucy let the moment lengthen and then she straightened her head and widened her smile into something less seductive. 'And, do you know what?' she said. 'I am hungry, after all.'

'That's good,' he said. But, to tell the truth, she got the impression that he had lost interest in the food.

As they shared their meal and drank their tea together in front of the fire, Lucy was overwhelmed with a sense of her own power. Power she had never had when dealing with Stephen Wright. Oh, he had desired her, and if she had known at the beginning how badly he was going to behave she would have behaved very differently herself. She would never have allowed him to seduce her that day in the Mourning Warehouse.

Had Stephen seduced her? She tried to suppress the uncomfortable knowledge that she had been just as eager for their lovemaking. But now she knew that she should have been much wiser. She should have made him wait. Wait until she had a ring on her finger. She was as foolish as her own mother had been! Well, now she intended to salvage the situation.

The next train steamed into the station before they had finished their impromptu picnic. Lucy pretended to panic and started to rise but Arthur bade her be seated again.

'You can get the next one,' he said. And then he looked concerned. 'Will your ma be worrying?'

'No, that's all right. I didn't tell her what train I was catching home. But she'll want me home before dark.'

'Divven't worry. I'll see to it.'

When Lucy had finished eating she dabbed at her lips with her handkerchief and with her face half obscured by the clean linen square, she asked, 'Do you see much of Mary, then?'

Arthur took his time before he replied. 'I suppose so.'

Lucy laughed softly.

'Why do you laugh?' He looked offended.

'I didn't mean to. But, Arthur, if you could have seen yourself. And what kind of an answer is that, anyway?'

'I divven't know what you're talking about.'

'Oh, don't frown. It's just that you didn't sound much like an eager suitor.' She saw his frown turn into a scowl and she hurried on, 'I mean, I thought you and Mary were lovebirds...' she paused, waiting for a confirmation or a denial, but he looked away and remained silent, 'and ... and when I ask you if you're seeing her, all you can say is, "I suppose so".'

She held her breath, hoping that she hadn't gone too far. The last thing she wanted was to hear him say that he and Mary Clark were regular sweethearts, but all he did was stare at her. Then, almost imperceptibly, he smiled and said, 'Mary and I gans out now and then. Now stop blathering, lass, and drink your tea.'

Her eyes widened and she had to look down quickly to conceal her surprise. The way he had spoken to her just now revealed none of the old deference. Arthur's confidence had suddenly grown. He had read the signals right and he was slipping in to a new way of dealing with her. It was what she'd hoped for and surely she needn't be ashamed when she would be making Arthur happy – giving him what he'd always wanted. And what of her own feelings? She'd liked Arthur from the start, hadn't she? It was just that she had schooled herself not to think of him this way...

She raised her mug of tea to her lips and tried

to conceal her feelings of excitement and anticipation.

Lucy had enjoyed the pie and the bun so she was annoyed when a sudden sharp pain announced the onset of the indigestion that had been troubling her. She pressed a hand on her upper chest and took a few deep breaths, willing herself not to burp.

'What is it?' Arthur asked. He looked alarmed.

'Oh, nothing. Just the warmth of the fire, I think.'

'You looked pained just now.'

'No ... really. But I am hot.' She sighed with relief when she felt the indigestion ease.

'Shall I fetch a glass of water?'

'No.' She shook her head and made fanning motions in front of her face with one hand. 'But I think I'll just loosen the neck of my dress. These black clothes are so constricting.'

She dropped her head and raised her hands to the back of her high-collared dress. The buttons were small and her fingers felt swollen with the heat. 'I can't quite manage this, Arthur,' she said. 'Would you help me?'

She heard his indrawn breath and she didn't dare look up. But she could see the packing case that had acted as a table for them and she sensed the movement beyond it. He had risen to his feet. She kept her eyes down and saw his legs and feet as he walked towards and then slightly behind her. She withdrew her hands quickly when she felt his fingers on the buttons.

'That's right,' she said. 'Just the top two or three so I can pull the collar away from my neck a little. What is it? Why have you stopped?'

'Some of your hair – just a wisp – it's caught in one of the buttons.'

She turned her head sideways a little and pushed one of her hands up her neck and back to gather up the stray hair and push it upwards. She felt the sharp tug as she freed it from the button. 'There,' she said.

Arthur didn't say anything but she could hear his breathing quicken as he undid another couple of buttons. She put her hand up and eased her collar forward. 'That's better,' she said. And waited.

She felt her nerves coil into a painful knot in the growing silence and then, at last, she felt Arthur's fingers on the sensitive part of her neck just below the hairline. 'Such bonny bright hair,' he murmured. She remained quite still as first he played gently with the wisps of loose hair and then began to stroke her flesh. 'And such soft skin – like silk, it is.'

Although Arthur's hands were clean, his skin was hardened by work and his skin was rough. At first Lucy gasped and held her breath. She had expected to ache for Stephen's touch, but when Arthur put his hands on her she found herself surprisingly responsive. She relaxed and began to enjoy the sensation.

'Undo a few more buttons,' she whispered. Arthur stopped stroking her neck. She could sense his surprise but she didn't turn to look at him. 'Go on, I'm so warm – I might faint.'

The irony was that she really did feel like fainting. She could feel her heart thudding and when, after a moment, Arthur did as he was told, she let out a long ragged sigh.

And then he took her by surprise. She felt his mouth on her neck and his hands gripped her shoulders as he began to kiss the bare flesh with the softest of kisses. She rose quickly and as she did so her dress fell a little, revealing her shoulders.

'I'm sorry,' Arthur gasped.

She turned to face him; his cheeks were flushed and his brow finely beaded with sweat.

'No, don't be sorry.'

She moved towards him with her arms half raised and he reached out and clasped her to his chest. She clung to him while he kissed her; amazed at her own response. When he moved away from her she clutched at him and tried to pull him back.

'No...' he breathed. 'Wait...'

Arthur moved to the door and locked it, then he returned and took her in his arms again. Their kisses grew more urgent and soon they sank down on to the floor, eager in their embraces and half laughing as they helped each other remove their clothes. And then there was no holding back. Lucy's passion had risen to such a height that she was barely conscious of the shadow of the flames dancing on the ceiling above them or of the hiss and roar of a train entering the station.

'Are you sure you'll be all right?' Esther asked Mrs Shaw.

'Of course I will.'

Lucy's mother had slept for a while and then

come down, obviously expecting to find that her daughter had come home. She hadn't.

'But I don't like leaving yer,' Esther said. She frowned. 'Where on earth can Lucy hev got to?'

'Oh, don't worry about my daughter,' Daisy Shaw said. 'She'll be happy with her friend Julia. She won't have given a second thought to her poor mother sitting here all alone.'

'I'll stay. I'll wait until she gets back.'

'No, Esther. You need to get home to bed. I know you'll have to get up early for work in the morning.'

'I could stay and keep Lucy's ma company,' Davy said, and both women looked at him.

'But you're in need of your sleep too,' Mrs Shaw said.

'I could sleep on the sofa in the front parlour. After all, that room's going to be me bedroom when Esther and me move in here, isn't it?' he said. 'So why don't I just stop here now?'

Esther smiled. 'That's a good idea. Would you like that?' she asked Lucy's mother.

'Do you know, I would. Your brother is such a sensible young fellow and he's good company, too.'

'That's settled then,' Esther said. 'I'll find him a pillow and some blankets and then I'll make us all a bite of supper before I go.'

A short while later, after Esther had washed the pots, she told Davy not to be a nuisance and not to stay up too late. Then she paused and looked at Mrs Shaw uncertainly. She was not stupid and she knew very well that Lucy's mother could put it on – could exaggerate the way she acted and talked – but, in Esther's opinion, the poor lady had every right to be vexed with her daughter. And hurt too. But then she suspected that, apart from grieving for her father and worrying how they were going to manage, Lucy had something else to worry about. She hoped that she was wrong but she feared she wasn't.

'What are you thinking?' Mrs Shaw asked her.

'Thinking?'

'You were in a brown study just then.'

'Was I?'

'Mm.'

'Oh, it's nothing. I was just thinking how cosy you look, you and Davy by the fire, and I hev to go out in the rain.'

'Is it raining again?'

'Aye, can't you hear it on the window? And the wind's getting up too.'

'You must take an umbrella. There are one or two in the hallstand. One of my – one of Mr Shaw's would be best. Nice and big.'

'Thank you, I will. And now I really must be off.'

But before she left Esther crossed the room swiftly and bent to kiss Mrs Shaw's brow. 'Good night and God bless,' she said.

'Good night, dear. I'm so glad that you're coming to live here.'

Once out in the rain-drenched streets Esther didn't head for home. Or rather for the hovel that wouldn't be her and Davy's home much longer. She walked along to the top of Shields Road and caught a tram into town.

She hadn't planned to do this but the

opportunity was too good to be missed. With her brother safe in the Shaws' house, she could go and look for her mother, for she hadn't given up hope of one day finding her. Never mind that she would have to get up early and go to work, she could surely spare an hour or two searching amongst the huddled groups of homeless people taking shelter from the rain in the arcades and the shop doorways.

He'd offered to wait up with her but Daisy Shaw had sent Davy to his bed on the parlour sofa and she'd remained sitting by the fire, waiting for Lucy to come home.

At last she heard the key in the lock and a moment later, to her surprise, the soft murmur of voices. She looked up in astonishment when Lucy came into the room followed by a well-set-up young man in a cheap overcoat.

'This is Arthur, Mother. Arthur Purvis,' Lucy said. 'It was late so he thought he'd better see me home.'

'Indeed!' She knew her voice was sharp and she had to fight to control her anger. Not only was Lucy late home but she had brought this stranger into the house at this time of night.

'Divven't be angry with Lucy,' the young man said, and Daisy Shaw winced at his rough way of speaking.

'Angry?'

'Aye, you hev a right to be. But it's purely my fault that she's stayed out so late.'

'Is it?' Daisy was at a loss. 'I thought ... my daughter told me that she was going to visit Julia.'

'And that she did. But we met up when she was on the way home and we got to talking.'

'Talking? Till this time of night?'

Neither Lucy nor the young man answered her but she saw the look that passed between them and her heart sank. Surely not. Surely there was nothing between them? But if there wasn't why could neither of them meet her eyes suddenly?

And what was she to make of Arthur Purvis? Oh, he was handsome enough, and clean, well-groomed, even a bit of a dandy with his velvet collar. But his speech betrayed that he was a man of the working classes. Surely her beautiful, educated and well-spoken daughter could have aimed higher than that.

'Lucy, haven't you anything to say?'

Her daughter shook her head. 'There's nothing else to say. I met Arthur and we've been talking.'

The young man in question glanced from mother to daughter and back again before saying, 'Well, I'd best be off, then.' Daisy frowned when she saw Lucy nudge him and push him forward. 'Oh, aye,' he added, 'but I hope I'll be seeing you again soon, Mrs Shaw.'

Daisy drew herself up in the chair. 'Do you? Why?'

The young man flushed and seemed at a loss for words. He glanced round at Lucy, who stepped forward, her eyes blazing. 'For God's sake, Mother, don't act so superior,' her daughter snapped. 'You will be seeing Arthur soon whether you like it or not because tonight he has asked me to marry him and I have accepted.'

361

Chapter Twelve

July

'Should I take the post up now, do you think?'

Flora, who had seemed so unwelcoming when Ruth first started working at Miss Golightly's, had now become a friend. Not the sort of friend that Esther and Lucy were – neither Ruth nor Flora ever talked about anything personal – but they were quite happy to gossip at the table or when they were sharing the mammoth task of dusting the old lady's bookshelves.

Miss Golightly hardly ever went into her upstairs sitting room these days. Most of the time she rested in bed but, occasionally, she would make the effort and ask Ruth to help her dress, then push her along the corridor in her Bath chair.

But even if her employer had never visited her sitting room Ruth would not have given up on the task of keeping her books in order, and compiling a catalogue of them.

But, most days, after Flora had collected Miss Golightly's breakfast tray, Ruth would go to the bedroom to help her deal with the morning's mail, read the newspaper to her and get instructions for whatever shopping she required. Then, after lunch, while Miss Golightly was taking a nap, Ruth would carry on with the cataloguing before escaping to her own room to work on her manuscript.

Usually Flora would not have asked whether she should take the post up. She would have placed whatever letters there were on the breakfast tray. But, today, there was a parcel. It lay on the hallstand where Meg had placed it along with an official-looking envelope. Flora looked at the parcel dubiously. 'More books?' she said.

'No, I don't think so,' Ruth replied. 'Just take Miss Golightly her breakfast. I'll take the parcel up when I report for duty.'

'What about the letter?'

'Leave it – I'll say the post was late.'

Ruth took her breakfast with the others in the kitchen. She was subdued. She had guessed what the parcel was and she hoped that Miss Golightly was strong enough to be able to deal with a disappointment. For she was sure that she would be disappointed, if not heartbroken, when they opened it.

Her employer was sitting up in bed, propped up against a mound of pillows when Ruth entered the room.

Flora, who was just leaving with the tray, paused to whisper, 'She said she thought she'd heard the postman's knock and I just had to play dumb. Put her in a right mood. I only hope it's something nice you've got there!'

Ruth's heart sank. Miss Golightly had her spectacles on and she was staring at the parcel keenly. She knows what it is, Ruth thought, and she's in a state of excitement. If the news is bad, and I suspect it is, this won't be good for her.

Ruth delayed things as long as she could. She closed the door behind Flora and took as long as possible to draw up a chair.

'Hurry up, child,' Miss Golightly said. 'Open it up. It's from the publisher, isn't it?'

'It could be,' Ruth said, taking time to examine the postmark. 'It's from London.'

'Tsk, tsk,' the old lady tutted with irritation. 'What's stopping you?'

'This string ... I mean the knot ... and the sealing wax ... it's difficult.'

'For goodness' sake just cut the string. Here, take the scissors from my bedside cabinet.'

Miss Golightly leaned sideways and opened a drawer in the cabinet, then she thrust a pair of scissors towards Ruth. 'Oh, don't look so shocked. I know I've always told you to save string and wrapping paper but some occasions call for exceptions.'

Ruth cut the string but before she opened up the wrapping paper she asked, 'Shall I read this letter to you first?'

'What letter?'

Ruth held the envelope towards her and Miss Golightly peered at it. 'Postmark?' she asked.

Ruth checked. 'Newcastle.'

'Give it to me.' Ruth did so and Miss Golightly took up her magnifying glass and peered at it. 'No, I know what this is. Been waiting for it. From my solicitor. Copy of my last will and testament. In view of my state of health it was time to make sure everything was as I wanted.'

Ruth was shocked. She knew that her employer had been poorly for some time – Dr Collins had been calling almost daily – but she had not allowed herself to think that the old lady's life was in danger. This made her task even more upsetting. She opened up the paper and, sure enough, Miss Golightly's novel nestled inside.

'It's the letter that's important,' her employer said.

'I beg your pardon?'

'You're thinking that they've rejected my novel, that's why they've sent it back. But that may not be the case. They may want me to make some adjustments, cut things here, add things there. You know what I mean.'

'Yes, I think I do.'

Ruth took up the letter that was enclosed and skimmed through it as quickly as possible before she began to read it out loud. It was a rejection, of course, but she thanked heaven that whoever had written it had been kind.

'Thank you for sending us your delightful novel,' the letter said. 'We were very taken with the story but, unfortunately, you write with such an individual style that we do not think it is quite suitable for us. We hope that you will have success in placing it elsewhere.'

When she finished reading there was a long silence. Ruth hardly dared look at Miss Golightly but, when at last she did, she saw that the old lady had her eyes closed. Eventually she sighed and said, 'Elsewhere...'

Ruth remained silent.

'No suggestions, no corrections; they suggest I should place it elsewhere.'

'That's what the letter says.'

'Are you disappointed, Ruth?'

Ruth was surprised at the question. 'Me? Yes, of course.'

'I thought you would be. After all the work. I am very grateful to you, you know. I could tell you enjoyed helping me.'

'Oh, I did!'

'Well, then. We must start again.'

'Again? You mean you are going to write another novel?'

'No. Well, yes, I will in time. But, first we must examine the manuscript and see what state it has come back in. You may have to make another fair copy.'

'Another copy?' Already? This was even worse than Guinevere Matthews had suggested.

'Of course. What did they say? "We hope that you will have success in placing it elsewhere." They wouldn't say that if they didn't think it was publishable, would they?'

'I ... I don't suppose so.'

'Very well, Ruth, we will send Angelina out into the world again!'

Miss Golightly's smile didn't fool Ruth. She could see the tears glinting in the old woman's eyes and she had to blink rapidly to clear her own eyes.

'I think I would like to rest until lunch time,' Miss Golightly said. 'And as it is your afternoon off we'll draw up a plan of action tomorrow morning. What do you think?'

'Of course. Anything you say.'

'And is your friend Esther coming for lunch with you again today?'

'Yes, she is. And I'm grateful to you for allowing it. Thank you.'

'Oh, it's Mrs Fairbridge you must thank. I shouldn't have suggested it if I hadn't known that she would agree. She rules the kitchen, you know.'

Miss Golightly had sunk back into her pillows and now she closed her eyes. 'Off you go,' she said, and her words were like a tired sigh. 'Oh, put the manuscript on the bedside table, would you?'

Ruth did as she was told. Her employer's gentle breathing told her that she was already sleeping. Ruth leaned over and carefully removed Miss Golightly's spectacles; she placed them on top of the manuscript and tiptoed out of the room, closing the door quietly behind her.

'What about her lunch tray?' Mrs Fairbridge asked when Ruth told the cook-housekeeper that Miss Golightly was sleeping.

'I should send it up as usual,' Ruth said. 'But just something light. A bowl of soup would be fine.'

'Poor old thing,' Flora said. 'She's fading away, isn't she?'

'Don't gossip, miss,' Mrs Fairbridge admonished. Her tone was sharp but Ruth could tell that she was hiding her own disquiet. All the household staff liked and admired their mistress, and not just because this was a pleasant house to work in.

When Esther arrived the mood was quiet but, as they relaxed round the table in the kitchen, they began to talk as usual.

'So, you're off to visit your married friend again, are you?' Mrs Fairbridge asked as Ruth, Esther, Flora and Meg tucked into generous helpings of steak and kidney pie and mashed potatoes.

Esther and Ruth nodded. They couldn't speak, their mouths were full.

'And you were all at school together and you're still friends?'

They nodded again.

'That's nice. A woman needs her friends, don't ever forget that.'

For pudding they had apple charlotte and custard. 'This is delicious,' Esther said. 'I wonder if you'd give me the recipe?'

'I've already written it out. I knew you would ask.' Mrs Fairbridge smiled at Esther. Ruth knew that the older woman approved of Esther. She liked her gentle manner and she couldn't help but be flattered by the way Esther would ask her questions about her recipes and the best way to order things in the running of a house.

Esther had first come to spend her half-day with Ruth not long after Lucy had married Arthur Purvis. Not knowing which train she would be catching, they had thought it wise for her to call at the house. She had arrived earlier than was expected and Ruth was still eating lunch with the rest of the staff in the kitchen. Mrs Fairbridge had immediately instructed Meg to pull up an extra chair and invited Esther to join them. The routine had been the same ever since – as had what followed.

The first time they had visited Lucy in the

terraced cottage near the station, they had not known what to expect. The terrace itself was attractive, with a central garden running the length of the row of houses that was shared by all the tenants and householders. Each cottage had its own tiny front garden, and that belonging to their friend's house was well tended and attractive.

They had paused at the gate, suddenly finding themselves nervous, and not knowing quite how Lucy would receive them. Her mood had been uncertain of late.

'It's so small,' Ruth had said as she surveyed the narrow dwelling with the trellised porch.

'Well, there's only the two of them for now,' Esther had replied, and then she'd flushed. 'But it looks very nice,' she'd added after a moment when neither of them had been able to meet the other's eye.

That first afternoon when Lucy had answered the door she had stood for a moment as though unwilling to let them enter and then she had shrugged and gestured for them to follow her. Ruth had wondered if they were unwelcome but, once inside, she understood her friend's reluctance. The place was a tip.

Without hesitation Esther had quietly set about tidying and cleaning Lucy's house for her while Ruth sat and talked. At first the conversation had been stilted. No one, it seemed, wanted to talk about the hasty wedding at the register office, an occasion that had been overshadowed by Daisy Shaw's air of sad resignation. An air that had lingered even when she invited them home for a most generous wedding breakfast. So they talked about the weather, the local shops here in Whitley-by-the-Sea, and Lucy's neighbours, many of them railway families.

Esther, her cleaning done, had set the table and, as if by magic, produced a meal for the three of them. She had brought some treats from the shop, and by the time they were on their second cup of tea and the fruit cake had been devoured, the atmosphere had been almost as easy as in the old days.

They had left before Arthur was due to return from work, knowing it was not good manners to be sitting gossiping when a working man came home for his evening meal – although there was no sign of such a meal being prepared. That afternoon had set the pattern for all the visits that followed.

But today Ruth was fretful. Perhaps it was because she had been upset by poor Miss Golightly's disappointment over the return of her novel, but, on the way to Lucy and Arthur's cottage, she found herself speaking quite sharply to Esther.

'You really shouldn't let Lucy take you for granted like this, you know.'

Esther was stung by Ruth's tone. 'I'm not sure what you mean,' she said quietly.

'Cleaning her house for her every time we go.'

'But I don't mind, really I don't.'

'Well, you should. You work hard at that shop, then you go home to clean up and cook for Mrs Shaw–'

'But I live there! And Davy too. It's only fair

that I should do my share of the work.'

'You do much more than your share. And besides, you pay rent, don't you?'

'Well, yes, but–'

'There's no "buts" about it. She should be looking after you.'

'She does.'

'I don't see how you can say that. Does she wash and iron your clothes? Of course she doesn't. More likely you do her laundry. And does she have a meal ready for you when you get home?'

'No, but–'

'There you are.'

'Let me finish. She's helping me in other ways.'

'Which ways precisely?'

'For goodness' sake, you're talking like Miss Foster did at school!'

Ruth was surprised by the flash of anger in Esther's green eyes. Esther, usually so quiet and easy-going, had changed of late. Not only had she grown more confident but there was something else about her, Ruth couldn't pin it down.

'I'm sorry, I didn't mean to interrogate you.'

'There you go again. What did you have for pudding?'

'I beg your pardon?'

'I had apple charlotte but you had your old favourite, dictionary pudding, didn't you?'

Ruth stopped walking and stared at her in amazement. Esther stopped too, and Ruth saw that she was smiling. 'Oh, Ruth,' she said. 'Do you remember that day you came after me into the cave? I didn't tell you at the time but I was so pleased that you did. I mean, the cleverest girl in the class, and you actually cared enough to come after me. And you're still clever – brainier than ever. I don't know what exactly you do in that job of yours but you talk like a real educated lady these days.'

'I'm sorry.'

'No! Divven't – I mean don't apologize. It's right that you should want to better yourself.'

And with that small slip of the tongue – the quick replacing of 'divven't' with 'don't', Ruth realized what it was that Mrs Shaw was doing for Esther. For a long time now – since the first time they had visited Lucy's home, in fact – Daisy Shaw had been helping Esther by giving her good quality cast-off clothes and encouraging her to be clean and smart, but now she was taking it one stage further. She was teaching her to talk more like herself and Lucy.

'Is that what you want, Esther?' Ruth asked.

'What are you talking about?'

'Do you want to be just like Lucy?'

Esther's flush told Ruth that she knew what she meant. 'No.' She turned away and started walking ahead. 'I don't want to be just like Lucy – or you – or anybody else. I want to be just like myself. But a better kind of self. You're so clever, I'm sure you know what I mean.'

'Of course I do.' Ruth hurried after her. 'And I'm pleased for you, really I am. I was just worried that Mrs Shaw was taking advantage of you.'

'Oh, she does that all right.'

'What?'

Esther was smiling again. 'I'm not daft, you know. Lucy's mam used to be on the stage. Did you know that? She was an actress. She telt – told – me all about her wonderful career and how she gave it all up for love.' As she spoke Esther placed a hand on her heart and spoke in an exaggerated way. Ruth couldn't help laughing.

'Oh, I know what she's like,' Esther continued smilingly. 'She certainly puts it on. I mean, she really is heartbroken, there's no question about that, but she can't help being the drama queen. Have you heard that expression? That's what her own daughter called her one night. Lucy was angry with her, but I can't be angry. I love her too much.'

'And don't you think Lucy loves her?' Ruth asked solemnly.

'I'm sure she does. But there's something between them. Something festering away. Something went wrong just after Mr Shaw was killed in that train crash but I don't suppose either of them will ever tell us what. Too much pride. And now, of course, Lucy's married and doesn't even live at home. I don't know if they'll ever make it up properly.'

And I wonder if you want them to, Ruth thought. But she suppressed the thought immediately. No matter how happy Esther was living with Mrs Shaw, being coached by her and treated almost like a daughter – almost, but not quite. Ruth couldn't imagine Lucy cooking and cleaning for her mother the way Esther did. No, no matter how much Esther was enjoying the present situation, Ruth could never imagine her taking advantage of it. She had too much integrity ever to put herself between mother and daughter.

'So you see, Ruth, I really don't mind Mrs Shaw taking advantage of me. I'm happy to do what I can. I'm even happy to spend my half-days cleaning her daughter's house for her just so that I can go back and say, truthfully, that everything's fine.'

Lucy took ages to answer the door and, when she did, she looked dreadful. Her complexion was not just pale, it was puffed and doughy and there were bluish circles under her eyes. She had obviously made an effort with her hair; it was curled and teased into the latest style. But, perversely, this only emphasized how exhausted she looked.

Ruth and Esther exchanged concerned glances before following Lucy along the narrow passage to the kitchen.

Lucy promptly sat down at the table and Esther vanished into the tiny scullery where Ruth could hear her filling the kettle. She brought it back and placed it on the hob on the range fire. 'Ruth, why don't you clear the table?' she said.

The table was littered with dirty dishes, probably from breakfast time, and perhaps even supper the night before. There was about half of a large loaf on the bread board and crumbs scattered across the stained cloth and on the floor.

'I'm sorry,' Lucy murmured, 'I meant to tidy up before you came but I'm just so tired.'

'Never mind that now,' Esther said. 'We'll have a cup of tea and a slice of the fruit cake I've brought and then Ruth and me – I mean, Ruth and I – will tidy up for you while you rest a while.'

Ruth glanced at Esther sharply. She had never helped her to do any of Lucy's housework before but there was a new air of confidence about Esther and she looked as if she would brook no argument.

By the time she had scraped off the plates and left them stacked ready to wash on the bench in the scullery, Esther had turned the tablecloth over, smoothed it out and set up a tempting little meal of ham sandwiches and slices of rich, dark, fruit cake, all brought from Fowler's, no doubt. Ruth hoped that Esther was allowed a discount.

Lucy seemed to enjoy the meal but she wasn't very talkative. Every now and then she would wriggle around on her chair as if she was trying to make herself more comfortable and settle in a new position with a great sigh.

Eventually Esther said, 'Listen, Lucy, would you rather we didn't come here to see you?'

'Why do you say that?' Ruth saw that the question had genuinely shocked her.

'Well, you never seem to be very pleased to see us.'

'Oh, I am.' To Ruth's consternation she saw that Lucy's eyes were sparkling with tears.

'Well,' Esther said, 'you never have very much to say for yourself.'

'But that's because I don't know what to say!'

Esther frowned. 'You never had any problems gossiping with us in the past.'

'But don't you see? That's it precisely. Those days are gone. My life has changed completely. You and Ruth still have your whole lives before you and I ... I am stuck here in this miserable little house with Arthur for the rest of my days!'

Ruth was shocked by the anguish in Lucy's voice and the raw misery betrayed by her trembling hands as she clutched at her cup of tea.

'Here,' Esther said gently, 'put that cup down afore you spill your tea.' She reached across the table and took the cup herself and placed it in the saucer. 'Why, it's gone cold. Ruth, will you top up the pot with a bit hot water? Then throw this out and pour Lucy a fresh cup.'

Ruth found herself doing as she was told. She was quite happy to let the new Esther take charge of this situation. Faced with all this emotion she found herself at a loss. It's funny, she thought, I'm good at writing about the way people feel but I don't know how to cope with it in real life.

When they were settled with fresh cups of tea Esther leaned towards Lucy and asked, 'Don't you love Arthur? Is that why you're so unhappy?'

Lucy stared down into her cup. 'Do you think I'm unhappy?'

'You're behaving as if you are.'

'Couldn't it just be because I'm ... well, you know ... because I'm pregnant?'

'Well, it could be that,' Esther said. 'Goodness knows, I watched my poor mother's misery often enough. But I think it's more than that, isn't it? Particularly after what you've just said about being stuck here with Arthur for the rest of your days.'

'Poor Arthur,' Lucy said, and shook her head as if in despair.

At this Ruth couldn't contain herself. 'What do you mean, poor Arthur? If he's responsible for ...

I mean, he's only got himself to blame and he did the right thing by marrying you, didn't he?'

For a long time Lucy said nothing. She held her cup with both hands and kept her head lowered. And then she drained the cup and placed it in the saucer before she looked up at them. 'Yes,' she said, 'Arthur did the right thing and I should be grateful to him.'

'Nonsense!' Ruth exclaimed. 'Why should you be grateful? Surely the truth of the matter is he should be ashamed of himself!'

'Ashamed?' Lucy whispered, and her eyes revealed such a depth of misery that Ruth was taken aback.

An uneasy suspicion stirred in her mind. For some reason she remembered the day of Esther's birthday picnic and how Lucy had been quite adamant that she did not want Ruth to sit with her while she waited for her 'friend'. No, Ruth thought … it's my writer's imagination again. She resolved to say no more. She sat back and accepted Esther's admonishing look meekly.

'Whisht, Ruth,' Esther said. 'Don't upset her further.'

'No, it's all right,' Lucy said. 'But, Ruth, Arthur is a good man and I won't have a word said against him. In fact he deserves better than this. He works hard and he comes home to a wife who can't cope and an untidy, uncomfortable house.'

'But it needn't be like that,' Esther said. 'I know you won't be feeling grand at the moment but, if you listen to me, I could help you work out a sort of routine to take care of the house. And I've been writing down some easy recipes so that you could at least have a nice bit dinner waiting for him when he gets home.'

'Have you, Esther? You won't make a perfect housewife of me, you know.'

'All right.' Esther smiled. 'Forget perfect. I'll settle for better than you are right now. And we'll start by getting tonight's dinner on, shall we?'

'But I haven't thought... I mean I haven't been to the shops yet.'

'And you've nothing in the pantry?'

'No. Well, not much.'

'That doesn't matter. I'd thought of that and I've brought enough to get a bit stew on the go. Pass my bag over, Ruth. That's right, put it on the table.'

Ruth watched in wonder as Esther brought several parcels out of her bag. She opened them up to reveal some kind of meat, 'neck end' she said it was, a couple of onions and a few carrots.

'Have you got potatoes in?' she asked, and when Lucy nodded, Esther bustled them all into the scullery. Then, in next to no time, it seemed, there was a large pan simmering on the range and a delicious smell wafting round the house.

'Now that was easy enough, wasn't it?' she asked when they were sitting round the table again with another cup of tea.

'I suppose so,' Lucy said doubtfully.

'Look...' Esther paused and Ruth thought she looked embarrassed, 'It's not money that's the problem, is it?'

'Oh, no. We started off well; Arthur has some savings and he earns enough to pay the rent and keep us in reasonable comfort.' Lucy sighed. 'It's just not what I was used to. And it's so silly that I can't go on working until ... well, you know, as long as possible. But Mr Hetherington was adamant. He won't employ married women. He thanked me for having been a good employee, gave us a wedding present – an Irish linen tablecloth and napkins – then wished me well and that was that.'

'Shame,' Esther said. 'It seems a silly rule, doesn't it? Well, anyway, here's a shopping list for the week. You should be able to afford everything that's on it and, if you follow my instructions for each day, Arthur should be a happy man – whether he deserves it or not!'

Ruth was concerned to see Lucy's eyes fill with tears. But then she saw that she was smiling. 'Oh, Esther,' Lucy said. 'You're wonderful.'

'Me? Wonderful? Get away with you!'

'Yes, you are. You do all the housework and cooking for my mother, you work full time in Fowler's and then you spend your half-day sorting me out. You make me feel ashamed.'

'And me too,' Ruth said.

Lucy and Esther looked at her in surprise. 'Why do *you* feel ashamed?' Lucy asked.

'Because I'm so ignorant.'

'Ignorant? You?' Esther said.

'Mm.'

'But you were the cleverest girl in the class,' Lucy said.

'Not just the cleverest girl,' Esther added. 'You were better than every one of the lads, as well.'

Ruth smiled. 'That may be so. But Esther has just shown me how little I really know. Until

379

today, for instance, I had no idea how to make a pan of stew.'

Esther laughed. 'As if that's important!'

'But it is important,' Ruth said. 'I may have been top of the class at school and Lucy had a good job in an office, but neither one of us knows how to keep house properly or cook a meal for ourselves, let alone a husband.'

Esther smiled and shook her head. 'Didn't your stepmother ever teach you anything about housework, Ruth?'

'She made me keep my own room clean, and sew buttons on, or darn my stockings. Any job she gave me was designed to keep me out of her way. She couldn't abide to have me near enough to her to teach me how to cook. And, besides, she wanted to do everything for my father herself. She would have hated it if he'd ever praised me for anything.'

'Well, I shouldn't worry too much about it,' Esther said. 'In your present position you have everything done for you, and if you marry Henry Valentine you'll probably be able to afford a servant or two.'

'Marry Henry Valentine? What on earth made you say that?' Ruth asked. She was astonished. She thought her friends had forgotten all about that nonsense.

'Well, you never mention him,' Esther said.

'That doesn't make sense,' Ruth retorted.

'Yes it does, in a sort of way. You're a dark horse, Ruth. You never mention his name and yet Lucy and I both think you're seeing someone. You have a certain look about you sometimes. As if you're thinking about something ... someone ... about...'

'Thinking about a man,' Lucy finished the sentence for Esther. 'That look in your eyes is unmistakable.'

'And I suppose we thought it must be Henry because it's so obvious that he cares for you.'

Ruth looked from one to the other. 'You've been talking about me behind my back!'

'Not exactly,' Lucy said. 'We just bring the subject up now and then. And there's no harm in it, is there?'

'Yes, there is. Because it's nonsense. I'm not seeing Henry. In fact he's gone to London. He went ages ago.'

Ruth saw the look that passed between her friends. She knew they wanted to ask her if there was someone else but they didn't dare. Ruth knew how fierce she could look and she glared at them until they glanced away uneasily. She didn't know why she just couldn't have told them the truth; that there was someone else she thought about day and night.

Perhaps it was because she was still uncertain whether Roland felt the same way she did. Oh, he was attentive enough, the way he teased and flattered. He was even jealous of her time. He had objected yet again to her spending this afternoon with her two old friends, even though he would be at work. But he had never declared himself. She bit her lip and laughed inwardly at herself for coming up with that expression – *declared himself!*

She'd been reading too many novels. And that

381

was an activity that Roland despised. How could she love a man who didn't understand what books meant to her? And furthermore, what would he say when she told him that she was writing a book herself?

Did she love him? When she was lying awake at night imagining what it would be like to be held in his arms, to be kissed and caressed and whispered to in the way that she wanted, she thought it must be love. But he had never told her that he loved her. Was that what she was waiting for? She knew in her heart that, until then, it was best if she told her friends nothing at all.

'Come back, Ruth!' Lucy said, and Ruth looked up to find that her friends were smiling at her.

'Mm?'

'From the look in your eyes, you were miles away,' Esther explained.

'I'm sorry,' Ruth said. 'And I'm sorry I was cross just now. But I'm really not walking out with Henry, you know.'

'But why has he gone to London?' Lucy asked.

'To study at the Royal Academy. And, before you ask, we're not writing to each other. In fact I don't even have his address.'

While the three of them tidied up the kitchen and set the table ready for Arthur's evening meal, Esther gave Lucy various cooking and house-keeping hints and Ruth was happy to remain silent.

She thought about the letter she had received from Henry shortly after that day she had gone home with him for Sunday lunch.

My dear Ruth, *he had written*
I am going to London to study at the Royal Academy of Music. In order to support myself I have obtained part-time employment teaching piano at a girls' school and I shall also undertake various casual engagements in the theatre, provided by friends and colleagues of my father.

I do not yet know where I will be living but, when you wish to contact me, you can always get the address from my mother.
Sincerest regards,
Henry

The letter had been unsettling. Not just because it opened up the prospect of a new and strange life for Henry – the Academy, the girls' school, and the 'various' casual engagements in the theatre – but because of that word in the last paragraph. 'When.' Not 'should' or 'if'. 'When you wish to contact me', Henry had written. Was he so sure that she would?

Ruth had crumpled up the letter and tossed it in the wastebasket. But, before Meg had come up to clean her room, she had retrieved it, and stuffed it at the back of a drawer. She did not know why she had been unable to throw it away.

They had had to stoke up the fire in the range in order to cook the pan of stew, and the little room became more and more stuffy, even with the window open. Ruth and Esther were dressed in lightweight summer fabrics but poor Lucy, in her heavy mourning black, became more and more distressed.

After mopping her brow yet again with her handkerchief she said, 'Whatever the conventions are, surely it's too much to expect me to be as uncomfortable as this. I've a good mind to come out of mourning here and now.' Her tone was defiant, as if expecting her friends to argue with her, but they were sympathetic.

'You could always get yourself some nice mauve muslin,' Esther suggested. 'I would help you make it up.'

'Would you? That would be marvellous!'

'But what would your mother say?' Ruth asked.

'I don't care. She can't tell me what to do now. I'm a married woman.'

'And Arthur?'

Lucy looked at Ruth and smiled. 'Oh, Arthur wouldn't stop me. He just wants me to be happy.'

'Listen, Lucy,' Esther said, 'I wouldn't help you if I thought it would upset your mother. I respect her too much.'

'Do you?' Lucy's air of surprise was exaggerated and scornful, and Esther looked vexed.

'Yes, I do, and I'm not going to argue with you about it. But you're wrong if you think your mother wouldn't want you to be comfortable. In fact, she suggested herself that I might like to help you make some more suitable clothes for ... for your condition.'

'Oh, I see.'

Ruth guessed that, perversely, Lucy had now lost some of her enthusiasm but nevertheless she agreed that Esther should bring some paper patterns with her next time they came, and

384

together they would go shopping for some fabrics.

'We could go to the Mourning Warehouse, couldn't we?' Esther said. 'It's just nearby, isn't it?'

'No, we'll not go there,' Lucy said. 'I've heard they charge scandalous prices. And, anyway, I've a better idea. Why don't the three of us go into Newcastle? We could go to Bainbridge's or Fenwick's – or one of the stalls in the Grainger Market and then we'll have tea at Tilley's. Yes, we'll have an afternoon in town – that will cheer me up enormously!'

'Very well,' Esther said.

But Ruth was doubtful. 'Are you sure that's wise?' she asked.

Lucy looked at her in surprise. 'Wise? What do you mean?'

'Well, I mean ... your condition.'

Lucy laughed. 'I'm expecting a child, I'm not ill. No, you two shall carry all my parcels, and if I feel tired I shall take a cab back to the Central Station. You can't dissuade me, I'm determined to go. Next week, then. I'll look forward to that.'

When they left Lucy's house Ruth walked with Esther to the station.

'Has Lucy always been as mercurial as this?' Lucy asked.

'There you go again,' Esther chided.

'I mean moody ... swift to change her mood. I can't remember.'

Esther sighed. 'You were the moody one. You still are. Lucy and I never know if anything we say is going to send you off into one of your sulks.'

'Sulks?'

'Well, not exactly sulks, but you go into a sort of brown study sometimes.'

'I know and I'm sorry.'

'That's why we put up with you.'

'What do you mean?'

'Well, you always seem to know when you've been a bit difficult and you say sorry and you try to make up for it. But you're right about Lucy.'

'Oh dear.'

'No, you don't have to worry. It's part of being pregnant. And, besides, she's had a lot to bear, what with her father dying so tragically and his not seeming to have provided for them very well.'

'Yes, that's strange, isn't it? I mean, I thought Mr Shaw had a very good job. Mrs Shaw was always keen to tell us that he was the senior sales representative for Lawson's. Surely he should have left them something.'

'Perhaps they never managed to save anything,' Esther said. 'I know Mrs Shaw well enough by now to see how extravagant she can be.'

'That must be it,' Ruth agreed. 'Poor lady. Is she finding it very difficult?'

There was a pause before Esther answered. 'Yes, she is. The only money coming in is the rent I pay for Davy and me, and Lucy sends her what she can out of duty.'

'Can she afford to help her mother?'

Esther shook her head. 'I don't know how she manages it. I mean, Arthur has a good job but he can't be making a fortune. I didn't know about his savings, but there's a baby coming and what will happen then?'

'Oh, there *is* Arthur. We'd better change the subject.'

Ruth had intended to wait with Esther until her train arrived, so while they had been talking they had entered the station and walked along towards the end of the platform where there was a seat beside one of the garden areas.

'Well, hello!' Arthur was in his shirtsleeves, gardening tools were propped up against the seat and a large bunch of blue and white bell flowers lay on the ground beside him. 'I can gan yem now, I suppose,' he said.

'What do you mean?' Esther asked.

'I finished me shift a while back so I decided to do a bit gardening. Keep out of the way of the womenfolk.'

As he spoke Arthur picked up his jacket from the bench seat and slipped it on. His face was ruddy from exposure to the sun and he looked the picture of health – and happiness.

'I didn't realize we were keeping you from going home,' Ruth said.

'No, lass, that's all right. These afternoons with her old friends mean a lot to Lucy. I'm grateful to you for coming by, especially as her ma doesn't see fit to call very often.' His smile had vanished and he frowned as he collected the gardening tools.

'Mrs Shaw would come,' Esther began, 'it's just that ... just that she's still grieving and she doesn't go out much at all, you know.'

'Oh, aye?' Arthur looked at Esther steadily. 'If that was the case wouldn't you think she'd take comfort from spending time with her only daughter?'

Esther hesitated and Ruth said quickly, 'Perhaps she doesn't like to come too often because you're newly married. Perhaps she thinks she'd be intruding.'

'Perhaps,' Arthur said, and he shrugged. 'Well, whatever the truth of it you're a pair of nice lasses and I'm glad Lucy has you for her friends. And that's why I stay out of the way whenever you come to call.' Arthur took the gardening tools and locked them in a small shed at the back of the platform and then he returned with a sheet of newspaper, which he wrapped around the flowers. 'And don't think I don't know that you help her with the housework – and the cooking an' all,' he said.

'That's Esther,' Ruth said. 'I'm not very good at that sort of thing.'

'No?' Arthur said. 'Well, neither is me poor wife. But I can be patient. After all, I don't suppose Lucy dreamed she'd end up marrying a fellow like me and have to fend for herself. I know how lucky I am. And luckier still to know there's a bairn on the way. Do you know she must have fallen pregnant straight away? I was over the moon, I can tell you.'

Ruth and Esther glanced at each other, surprised by his words and not knowing what to say.

'Are those flowers for Lucy?' Ruth asked, to end the embarrassed silence.

'Aye, who else?' He laughed. 'I'd get me head in me hands to play with if I gave them to anyone else!'

Still laughing, Arthur bade them good day and

set off for home carrying his flowers.

'Now why did he say that?' Ruth asked when he was out of earshot.

'Say what?'

'About Lucy falling pregnant straight away. Surely he realizes that we all think she was pregnant before they got married?'

'That'll be why,' Esther said.

'I don't understand.'

'He's protecting Lucy's reputation. He doesn't want her friends to think less of her.'

'Perhaps,' Ruth said, 'but I don't think so. A man like Arthur would never be very good at dissembling. I think he really believes what he said. And that's a puzzle.'

'And not the only one,' Esther added. 'We still don't know why Lucy and her mother are at odds with each other, do we?'

'Do you think Lucy will ever enlighten us?' Ruth asked.

Esther shook her head. 'She may look like a china doll – well, when she's not pregnant she does – and she's not as brainy as you are, but Lucy Shaw is deep. Sometimes I think she could outfox both of us.'

Soon after that the train steamed into the station and Ruth and Esther stood back to allow the passengers to descend.

'For goodness' sake, watch what you're doing, lad!' a woman called out as one of the carriage doors flew open and a young man leaped out even before the train had come to a halt. He raced off, nearly knocking the woman over and she screamed after him, 'Young hooligan! I'll

389

report you to the stationmaster.'

But she turned and climbed into the carriage when she saw that he had been stopped by one of the porters. 'There'll be a serious accident one of these days,' she muttered to Esther, who entered the carriage after her.

Ruth waited on the platform and waved Esther off, then she began to walk slowly back to Miss Golightly's. The sun was still warm but a slight breeze was blowing up Station Road from the sea. Ruth wondered if she should go down to the sea front and walk along the promenade for a while. Usually she saw Roland after saying goodbye to her friends but he'd told her that he was working late tonight and would not be able to meet her.

She thought about Arthur, going home to Lucy, and wondered if he would be pleased with the meal that was waiting for him. She thought about Esther going home to the Shaws' house where she would no doubt prepare the meal for Mrs Shaw and young Davy.

Am I feeling sorry for myself? Ruth wondered. I shouldn't. I have a good position with a kindly employer, I live in a comfortable house, I have my own room, and Mrs Fairbridge provides good meals for us. Flora and Meg are pleasant companions. But they are not really friends. We don't have much in common.

But then I consider Lucy and Esther to be my real friends and what do the three of us have in common? We barely spoke to each other until the day of the school picnic. Lucy was so much better off than the rest of the class; so well-dressed and well-spoken. She was her mother and father's darling, but she didn't behave like a spoiled child. She was kind and tolerant. Much more tolerant than I ever was. Everyone wanted to be her friend. And yet none of her special little group ran into the sea to save her that day…

And Esther. Poor Esther. Nobody wanted to be her friend. She was ragged and dirty and always scratching. Girls like Jane McKenzie thought it clever to make fun of her. I never tormented her and yet when I went into the cave that day to see why she was crying I was wary of sitting too close. And yet, once she was washed clean and Mrs Shaw began to take her in hand there was no doubt that she was the most beautiful of the three of us. And she is so practical and hard-working. She wants nothing better than to make a decent home for her brother and anyone that she loves.

And me. What kind of a person is Ruth Lorrimer? I had such hopes. I was going to be a teacher but my stepmother said I had to leave school. When she found me a job as a companion to an old lady it was because she wanted to get rid of me. Ada wanted my father all to herself. And she's succeeded. I hardly ever see my father now. And yet my life has not been so bad after all. I am hardly a conventional kind of servant. The work I do for Miss Golightly has allowed me to read more books than I ever thought existed … and to hope that I may even become a writer myself.

But, for all my new knowledge I still can't say what it is that Esther and Lucy and I have in common. Unless ... unless it is because we are all outsiders. We were all different in our own way from the rest of the girls in our class at school. Lucy was set apart by her comparative wealth and Esther by her poverty. And me? I have to admit that I knew I was cleverer than the rest of them. I knew I had a better brain and I wasn't going to settle for an ordinary kind of job to work away the years until I got married.

And now what has become of us? Lucy, who had such a happy childhood, has lost her father and is hardly speaking to her mother, who thinks her precious daughter has married beneath her. And I suspect that Lucy only married Arthur because she had to. Does she love him? I don't know.

And me? I wanted to go to college and become a teacher and instead I am following an even more unattainable dream. A dream that the man I believe myself to be in love with would almost certainly disapprove of.

Only Esther, who had the least promising start in life, seems to be making a success of things. If you can call working in a shop being successful. And yet she is happy. She is the only one of the three of us who seems to be content.

Deep in thought, Ruth had hardly noticed her surroundings, and now she found herself at the gate of Miss Golightly's house. It was not late but the terrace faced east and the sun was already low in the western sky, causing the tall houses to cast shadows right across the road to the arcade of shops opposite.

A horse and trap stood in the road nearby, the

horse and the groom looking equally patient, as if used to waiting.

Ruth opened the gate and then paused, looking up at the house uncertainly. Something was wrong. It took her a moment to realize what it was. Every curtain was closed against the evening light. Why?

It was Meg who opened the door, her eyes round with a sort of excited awe. 'She's gone!' she said before Ruth had a chance to step over the threshold.

'Who's gone? Where?'

'To heaven, I hope!'

'But–'

'Miss Golightly!'

'Miss Golightly has–'

'Aye. But hawway in, we mustn't keep the door open so that her poor old soul won't try to come back home again. And Mrs Fairbridge made me close all the curtains in the house, an' all.'

Ruth stepped inside and Meg closed the door, making a show of shutting it quietly. Then she turned to Ruth and continued in hushed tones barely above a whisper, 'It was Flora that found her when she took her tray up with a bowl of soup – you know, like you said she should. Well, anyways, Flora couldn't rouse her – I mean, she was sitting up and there was some kind of papers all over her bed. Her specs had slipped down her nose and her eyes was closed, and she was clutching at the papers.'

'Her manuscript,' Ruth said softly, but Meg didn't hear her.

'Anyways,' the little scullery maid continued,

393

'Mrs Fairbridge went up and she tried to prise the papers from the mistress's fingers – and she still didn't open her eyes and Flora telt me Mrs Fairbridge held a mirror to the old lady's mouth – it was open – and then she sent Flora for the doctor.

'And Dr Collins brought Flora back in his trap – and he's still here. He's in the drawing room, writing some papers. Anyways, he says Miss Golightly must hev dozed off and then passed away in her sleep. All peaceful like. He telt Mrs Fairbridge it was a good way to go. But peaceful or not, Flora telt me that when she found her, the old lady's cheeks was wet with tears.'

Chapter Thirteen

August

The young woman who stood in the doorway could have been his wife thirty – no, forty years or more ago. She was fair-haired with blue eyes and a complexion that reminded him of a china doll. She would have been truly beautiful had her features been more refined. She reminded him of a healthy country girl – just as his wife had all those years ago.

Hannah had been a true country girl, the daughter of a prosperous farmer who had known her duty. She had fallen pregnant almost as soon as they had been married; in fact they had probably conceived on their wedding night. What a pity that the complications that developed during her confinement had meant there could be no more children; only the one son.

This young woman was with child, he suspected, although the attractive mauve muslin gown she wore had been cut skilfully to obscure the rounded curves. She made a pretty picture, standing under the rose-covered arch of the trellised porch, but after an initial curious smile, her eyes had widened with surprise and her lips had pursed with suspicion. She seemed to be lost for words.

'Are you going to invite me in?' he asked.

'I don't know you.'

'Don't you?' He had seen recognition flare in her eyes and he knew that she must have seen him on the day of the funeral. Nevertheless, he handed her his card and said, 'Josiah Lawson, Reginald Lawson's father, which makes me, I believe, your grandfather.'

Her expression was unreadable. She didn't speak but simply backed away into the shadows of the narrow passage. At first he thought she was going to slam the door in his face, but then he saw her make a slight beckoning motion and he stepped inside. She led him into a small front parlour. It was a pretty room, furnished to a higher standard than he had expected, but there was a film of dust on the mantel and the roses in the vase on the table drooped and shed their petals on the lace cloth.

'Will you sit?' she asked, gesturing towards a chair beside the fireplace, but she made no move to relieve him of his hat. After he had taken his place he kept it on his knee.

'And you?' he asked.

Reluctantly, it seemed, she took her place at the other side of the hearth and then he saw how clever she had been. She had offered him the chair facing the window so that the sunlight streamed in on his face, whereas she sat with her back to the light and he could not easily make out her expression. He smiled to himself as he shuffled round a little so that at least the shaft of light was not blinding him.

'Why have you come here?' she asked.

There was a fan made of folded paper arranged

in the empty hearth and he stared at it for a moment before lifting his gaze and replying with a question of his own. 'Did you not expect me to?' he asked.

He heard her quick intake of breath. 'Why should I expect it?'

'Is that not what you desired? You and your mother? Was it not your intention to provoke this visit?'

'I don't know what you're talking about.'

She sounded snappish and he sensed an underlying anger. But he got the impression the anger was not entirely directed towards him.

'You came to my son's funeral.'

'He was my father.'

'And that's why you came?'

He saw her scowl and once more felt that there was something that she was angry about. 'I don't understand you,' she said.

'You want me to believe that your only motive was to pay your last respects to your father.'

'Is that so hard to believe?'

'No, of course it isn't. But it was your behaviour afterwards that is almost unforgivable.'

'*My* behaviour!'

So that was it. It was her mother she was angry with. 'I'm sorry,' he said. 'I think I understand.'

'Do you? Can you have any idea what it was like for me to discover that my father was not married to my mother? That he had another family? And that he had not even provided for us?'

'Ah, so that's it.' He thought he understood the reason for her anger and in spite of his own outrage at how the two women had behaved, he could not help feeling sorry for her. 'You mean you really had no idea of your true position?'

'*Position?*' Her eyes gleamed angrily.

'That you were illegitimate?'

He saw her fists clench in the folds of muslin. 'I did not. Neither my mother nor my father had ever discussed it with me. Although my mother has since told me that my father had every intention of leaving his wife one day – asking her for a divorce – and coming to live with us permanently.'

'I doubt that very much.' He had not meant to sound so forceful and he watched as she raised her chin and stared at him defiantly.

'Are you calling my mother a liar?'

What could he say? It was more than likely that Reginald had told the woman such a tale, perhaps to keep her sweet, but he did not think that his son could have meant it. 'No,' he said, 'possibly your mother believed that was true. It's just that I don't think my son would ever have left his wife and daughter. He loved them, you see.'

'How could he? He loved us ... my mother ... and me!'

How much easier it would have been if he could have contradicted her. Perhaps Reginald had loved his mistress and his child, who could say? He had been a happy child who had grown up into a good-natured man. He had worked hard and never complained that his life had been set out for him from the start. He hadn't expected to live the life of a young gentleman of leisure – which the family could well have afforded to let him do. He had started in a lowly

398

position in the firm and had agreed that the best way to get to know the business was actually to work in it just like any other employee.

So who could blame him for taking a mistress to comfort him on his nights away from home? Josiah had guessed long ago that his son had alternative domestic arrangements and had accepted it. Far better a long-term mistress than a series of more questionable women who brought the risk of scandal and disease. But who could have foretold that the boy would die before making proper provision for the woman? And that the creature would turn up at the funeral and make such a show of herself – risking scandal after all?

But what was he to make of this young woman? Surely she was an innocent party, even if she was staring at him so belligerently.

'How did you find me?' she asked him.

He shrugged. 'It wasn't difficult. I hired an investigator.'

'But why?'

'I had to see you. To tell you that you must never do anything like that again.'

'Like what?'

'Show yourselves near the family home. Make life difficult for my son's widow and his daughter. Obviously there was gossip in the village after your mother's action in the churchyard. Throwing a rose into his grave! What on earth did she think she was doing?'

The young woman didn't answer him and he could see that she looked uncomfortable. He wondered if she had been an unwilling player in the charade.

'As I said, it must never happen again.'

'Have you told my mother this?'

'No. I came to you. I have no wish to see her. I fear I should not be able to control my anger. Geraldine is a good woman; I do not want her hurt by prurient gossip. And Annabel loved her father–'

'My father.'

'Whatever the truth of the situation, I do not want her to think less of him.'

'Why should they be protected?'

'I'm surprised you ask. They are his family.'

'But so are we!'

'I mean they are his legitimate family.'

'Ah, so they are allowed feelings and we are not!'

'I'm not going to argue with you. I've come here to tell you that you must stay away, and you must convince your mother that it will be in her best interests to do so. The allowance I am about to settle on you depends entirely on the promise that neither of you will ever try to contact the family again.'

'I don't understand. Are you paying us to keep away?'

'If you must put it like that. I shall give your mother an allowance – say, thirty pounds annually – for as long as she remains single. If she marries, it ceases. And you ... I will give you five hundred pounds – call it a wedding gift – and one hundred pounds a year for life.'

She stared at him open-mouthed. He could hardly suppress a smile at her astonishment –

and at his own decision. For in truth he had intended to settle only half that amount on her, but her spirited response to this meeting had taken him unawares and had filled him with begrudging admiration.

'Why are you doing this for me?' she said at last.

'Because you are my granddaughter and I am concerned about what will become of you.'

There, he had said it, the words that he had never intended to say, and now that he had said them he knew that she would remain in his thoughts for the rest of his life. He rose to go.

'You'll keep your promise?'

'I haven't made one.'

'But you will?'

'What if I don't want your money?'

'Don't,' he shook his head, 'don't say that, Lucy. You have not married well and I believe you are expecting a child. I should not like to think that my – that you were living in poverty.'

'While my sister lives in luxury,' she said softly as she too rose to her feet.

'Annabel is your half-sister and she does not know of your existence. She must never know.' He tried not to be affected by the pain in her eyes. 'I must go.'

'Wait – does ... does your ... does my grand-mother know of my existence?'

'She has guessed.'

'And did ... did she not want to see me?'

'No. I'm sorry, but she would rather banish the thought from her mind. She too is devoted to Annabel. Now, I must go. You will get a letter from my solicitor. So will your mother. I will arrange things so that you have your first payment as soon as possible. But remember, if you do not adhere to the conditions, the allowance will stop and, furthermore, I will take steps to recover the initial payment. Goodbye, Lucy.'

Neither spoke again. Lucy saw him to the door and then stood and watched as he walked away. At the end of the terrace a hansom cab was waiting; it set off in the direction of the station. The distance was short – it had hardly been worth hiring a cab – but Josiah Lawson would not have known that when he arrived.

Lucy wondered if Arthur would see him; whether he would wonder why such a fine top-hatted gentleman had come to Whitley-by-the-Sea that day. She wondered if Arthur would tell her about him when he got home. When the sound of the cab had rattled into the distance she closed the door and went through to the kitchen to make a cup of tea.

It would soon be time to start preparing Arthur's meal but she needed to sit and think for a while. She would have to work out what she was going to say.

They sat in the grand dining room on the ground floor, the room that had never been used for as long as Ruth had been working in Miss Golightly's house. Mrs Fairbridge had prepared for the visitors light refreshments of daintily cut cucumber sandwiches and tiny iced cakes. The solicitor's young clerk had consumed most of them while at the same time managing to cast sheep's eyes in Flora's direction.

To Ruth's astonishment Flora seemed equally smitten, although what on earth she could see in his tall, bony frame and shabby, half-starved appearance, Ruth had no idea. But then if she could fathom what it was that made two human beings take to each other she would be better able to understand herself, wouldn't she?

They were seated round the table, the visitors and the late Miss Golightly's servants alike, although Mr Douglas Golightly, who was Miss Golightly's nephew, the solicitor, Mr Harris, and his young clerk had taken up positions at one end and Mrs Fairbridge, Flora, Meg and herself at the other.

Every now and then it was Flora's duty to get up and fill the visitors' teacups. The young clerk had had at least three cups of tea and Ruth's eyes had widened when she saw what had happened the last time. While Flora was pouring the tea he had slipped a note into the pocket of her pinafore. She saw Flora's colour heighten and the tiny smile that played about her lips. Well, well, Ruth thought, I only hope his intentions are honourable. And then she smiled to herself as she realized that that phrase could have come straight from a novel.

'This is very kind of you, Mrs Fairbridge,' Miss Golightly's nephew said. 'We didn't expect it.'

Mrs Fairbridge looked pleased but she didn't say anything. Ruth knew how anxious the cook-housekeeper had been about this meeting, as they all had. On the day of Miss Golightly's funeral the mourners had come back to this house where Mrs Fairbridge had provided 'the funeral meats', as she called them.

Miss Golightly's nephew had taken her aside and asked her to stay on at the house with Flora, Meg and Ruth until it was decided what was going to be done with the property. Their wages would be paid as usual. He'd told her that there was also the matter of his late aunt's will, and that he was sure her faithful servants would have been remembered.

Mrs Fairbridge had relayed all this to the others that night and they wouldn't have been human if they had not been wondering exactly what provisions had been made for them. Ruth had remembered the long legal-looking document that had arrived only hours before her employer had died. Miss Golightly had told her that it was her last will and testament. Poor old lady, she'd thought. She can have had no idea how soon that will would come into effect.

'Well, then,' Douglas Golightly said. 'It's time to get down to business.'

Ruth felt Meg tug at her sleeve. 'What does he mean?' she whispered. 'What business is he going to do?'

'He means he's going to tell us what is going to happen,' Ruth told her quietly. 'To the house and to us.'

'You mean we won't be staying here?'

'I shouldn't think so.'

'Oh, no,' Meg's voice rose to a thin wail. 'I divven't want to gan yem.'

Mrs Fairbridge frowned in Meg's direction and Ruth, who knew that Meg's family lived in dire poverty and that her father was a drunken tyrant, took hold of the girl's hand. 'Hush,' she said. 'We'll soon know what is going to happen.'

'Ahem,' Douglas Golightly said. 'If you're ready. First I would like to thank you all for serving my aunt so well. She was very lucky in her servants and if my wife and I had decided to keep this house then it goes without saying that your positions here would have been secure.'

'What's he talking about?' Meg whispered, and Ruth shushed her again. Mrs Fairbridge coughed nervously.

'However,' Miss Golightly's nephew continued, 'we already have a home in Gosforth where we are very happy so, regretfully, I have decided to sell this house. I am only telling you this because my aunt made it quite clear that you had all become more than simply servants. I think she regarded you as her friends.'

Ruth saw the solicitor shake his head as if he could hardly credit what he had just heard so she surmised that this sort of thing was unusual. But then Miss Golightly had been a most unusual person.

'Mrs Fairbridge,' Douglas Golightly continued, 'may I ask you to stay on here and look after the house until it is sold?'

The cook-housekeeper nodded but Ruth saw that she was frowning.

'And you may keep the staff to help you, of course. Although in their own interests they ought to start looking for new positions.'

'Thank you, sir.'

'You will all be paid your usual wages even

though your duties will be less onerous. And now I am going to be quiet and let Mr Harris inform you of your bequests.'

Ruth saw Mrs Fairbridge and Flora glance at each other and smile slightly and then she realized that her own name had not been mentioned. Meg was tugging at her sleeve again and this time she shushed her more forcefully.

Mr Harris put on his spectacles and held his hand out imperiously. His clerk handed him some papers and the solicitor shuffled through them as if reminding himself of their contents. He's putting on a show, Ruth thought. He's enjoying this; keeping people waiting.

When he spoke his voice was thin and cracked like stale water biscuits. His tone was condescendingly superior as if he were speaking to backward pupils. 'I'll make this as simple as possible,' he said. 'Miss Golightly wanted me to tell you that she was very grateful for the way you made her life as comfortable as possible. She has written excellent references for each one of you to enable you to find further employment, and she has made bequests as follows. Ah ... these are her own words: "To Mrs Fairbridge, who has been the kingpin of this household, and who may wish to retire now, one hundred pounds."'

Mrs Fairbridge gasped and Flora and Meg looked at her with round eyes.

'"To Flora, who has carried out her duties diligently, even though she had never intended to enter domestic service, twenty-five pounds."'

Flora flushed with pleasure as Mrs Fairbridge nodded at her approvingly.

'"And to little Meg,"' the solicitor continued, '"who, I am sure, has found herself confused at times, five guineas."'

For once Meg was speechless.

Mr Harris put his papers back on the table and adjusted his spectacles, which had slipped down his nose. 'That is all, except that Mr Golightly,' he gestured towards Miss Golightly's nephew, 'has asked me to inform you that you will receive a final settlement of a month's wages when the house is sold. You may go now.'

Mrs Fairbridge and Flora rose and hurried to the door, no doubt anxious to get along to the kitchen and discuss their good fortune. But Meg stood with one hand on Ruth's shoulder and said, 'But what about Ruth? Isn't she getting anything?'

Mrs Fairbridge and Flora turned round at her words and stared as if they had only just realized that Mr Harris had said nothing about Ruth.

Mr Harris looked vexed. 'That will do, young lady,' he said. 'Now please leave the room with the others.'

Meg looked as if she were about to protest but Ruth rose and took her by the arm and guided her towards the door.

'No, wait, Miss Lorrimer,' Mr Harris said. 'I have not quite finished. But what I have to say to you, Miss Golightly wished to remain private and confidential.'

'Should Flora clear the table, sir?' Mrs Fairbridge asked from the threshold. 'I don't like leaving all these dishes.'

'Oh, very well,' the solicitor said. 'But be quick about it.'

407

Mrs Fairbridge directed Flora and Meg to gather up the dishes, and when it became obvious that they might have to make a return journey, Mr Harris said, 'Oh do hurry up – look here, Atkins will help you.'

The young clerk leaped to his feet with alacrity and gathered up any dishes that were left. He looked only too pleased to be helping.

I wonder if he knew of Flora's bequest, Ruth thought. His clothes are shabby and he looks underfed. Perhaps he thinks that a parlour maid, who is not only pretty but has a decent little sum of money coming to her, might be a good marriage prospect.

When the door closed behind the others Mr Harris shuffled his papers again and cleared his throat. 'Miss Lorrimer,' he said. 'I have asked you to stay because your situation is not quite the same as that of the other members of staff.'

Ruth looked at him in surprise. What on earth could he mean?

'Uhum ... er ... no, indeed.' And then the cracked voice seemed to dry up altogether.

Ruth glanced at Douglas Golightly, who smiled encouragingly. 'It seems my aunt has written a novel, is that correct?'

'Yes,' Ruth murmured, and judged from the way Mr Golightly was looking at her with raised eyebrows, something further was called for. 'Er ... it's very, um, interesting,' she said.

'And where precisely is the manuscript?' Mr Harris asked.

'I put it back in Miss Golightly's bedside cabinet,' Ruth told him. 'It's still there.'

'The work is completed?'

'Yes, Mr Harris. It has been submitted to a publisher. It was ... returned.'

'No good, then?' Miss Golightly's nephew asked ruefully. 'But at least we may take it that my aunt got that out of her system?'

'Oh, I wouldn't say that,' Ruth said. 'In fact that very morning – the day that Miss Golightly died, that is – she spoke of sending it off to another publisher.'

'Ah!' Mr Harris nodded as if satisfied that he had enough information to go ahead. 'Well, then, when Miss Golightly amended her will the novel was still with the publisher. She wanted to cover all eventualities, but all you need to know is that, as the situation stands, you are still in Miss Golightly's employment.'

'But how can that be?'

'I shall try to explain,' the solicitor said, injecting a weary patience into his voice.

Does he think I'm stupid? Ruth wondered. Does he think he has to translate Miss Golightly's instructions as if to someone who is illiterate?

Evidently so, for when Mr Harris continued he spoke slowly and enunciated each word carefully.

'You are to be employed by the Golightly family for another two years. During that time you will help Mr Golightly here to deal with any correspondence arising from his aunt's writing endeavours. Also Miss Golightly has left many short stories and poems that she wants you to copy out and arrange in some kind of order. She – er – believes they may be valuable some day.

'But your main task will be to resubmit the

manuscript of her novel as many times as required to achieve publication.'

Ruth thought that the solicitor's voice was becoming drier and dustier by the minute. He looked up at her suddenly over his half-moon spectacles as though he had heard her thoughts.

'And, er, ahem,' he said, 'Miss Golightly has made a note that you should be able to consult with a certain Miss Matthews at the Crystal Library about which publishers will be suitable. Is that correct?'

Ruth nodded.

'At the end of two years, if the novel has not been accepted for publication, you are, of course, free to seek other employment. Although Miss Golightly expresses the hope that you would continue to try to find a publisher in your own time and, of course, my office will reimburse you for any expenses you incur. Does that meet with your approval?'

'Of course. I'll try my best.'

'Good. That's that, then,' Mr Harris said.

'Ahem, not quite,' Mr Golightly said. 'There's the question of Miss Lorrimer's remuneration – and her bequest.'

'I was coming to that.'

The solicitor shuffled his papers again, no doubt to conceal his irritation at being interrupted, and Mr Golightly actually winked at Ruth. She suppressed a surge of laughter and stared into the near distance at the motes of dust dancing in the shaft of sunlight.

The lower half of the sash window was open a little and even the combined fragrances of the lavender polish applied by Flora to all the furniture, and the large bowl of potpourri in the hearth, could not vanquish the odour of horse droppings from the busy road outside.

'Well, then,' Mr Harris said at last. 'You are to be given a lump sum of seventy-five pounds, which, in my opinion, is more than generous, to keep you for the next two years. Miss Golightly expects that you will go home to live with your parents, but makes no stipulation.

'Miss Golightly has also left a list of dictionaries and other reference books which you may take to help you with your work and which need not be returned to the estate and, as well as those books, you may choose up to one dozen other books before Mr Golightly disposes of them as he sees fit.'

Ruth was overwhelmed. Like the others in this house she had lain awake at nights wondering what on earth she was going to do next. And now she knew. She had been entrusted with Miss Golightly's novel and she was to be paid extremely generously.

Seventy-five pounds was much more than she needed to keep herself, and she hoped that the sum reflected some kind of warmth on her late employer's part. She had certainly grown fond of the eccentric old lady. She hoped those feelings had been returned.

'Is there anything you want to ask me?' Mr Harris said.

'Yes,' Ruth replied. 'I wonder if I might stay here until the house is sold?'

'Why would you want to do that?'

'Because … because it would be easier to work in a familiar place … at my desk with all the usual books around me.'

'Well, I suppose so–' Mr Harris began.

'Of course you can stay for a while,' Mr Golightly said. 'There's no harm in it and I'm sure you'll make yourself useful to Mrs Fairbridge, as well as helping me to sort out all my aunt's books, won't you?'

'Yes, I'd like to.'

'That's settled then. Now, would you go and ask Mrs Fairbridge to make us another pot of tea?'

'And find out what's happened to Mr Atkins,' the solicitor said. 'Tell him to come back here at once!'

Howard Atkins was happily ensconced in the kitchen drinking tea and hungrily devouring Mrs Fairbridge's fruit scones and home-made plum and apple jam. It seemed that the cook-housekeeper had known the young man's late mother when they were girls, and she kept repeating how distressed her old friend would have been to see how undernourished Howard was.

She also stated how proud his parents would have been that he was following a gentlemanly occupation, and had already quizzed him about his lodgings. He told her they were nearby, and his marital state; she smiled speculatively when he said he was single. Mr Atkins was revelling in the attention and, judging by the looks that passed between him and Flora, he was wondering if he was going to be even happier in

412

the near future.

Meg was goggle-eyed. 'He wants to gan out with her,' she whispered to Ruth. 'He asked her if she liked Shakespeare, and when she said yes, he asked her if she would like to accompany him to a production of *Romeo and Juliet* that the local amateur players will be performing. He said they would no doubt make a noble attempt – those were his words. Flora said she'd love to gan with him but, yer know, Ruth, I divven't think she knew what he was talking about!'

'Hush,' Ruth whispered when she saw Mrs Fairbridge frowning at them. 'Mr Atkins,' she said, 'I'm sorry to interrupt your conversation but Mr Harris would like you to return to the dining room.'

'Oh dear.' Poor Mr Atkins looked startled. He rose in one swift ungainly movement, forgetting the tea plate balanced on his knee. Flora caught it before it landed on the floor.

'And Mr Harris has asked for another pot of tea,' she told the housekeeper.

'Of course. Tell Mr Harris it's on its way, Howard,' she said. Then she smiled archly. 'I'll send Flora in with the tray.'

A month later a buyer was found and preparations began to empty and clean the house. Everyone helped, even Flora, who had not made any great effort to find a new position. Flora was unwilling to expose Howard to the rough-and-ready atmosphere of her parents' home where her tall, sturdy fishermen brothers might have made fun of his sickly physique and gentlemanly

413

ways, so Mrs Fairbridge was delighted to act the part of a mother and keep an eye on things to see everything was done properly.

Ruth learned only now that there never had been a Mr Fairbridge. The title of 'Mrs' was a courtesy title given to most senior members of household staff. It always had been a happy establishment but, in these last few weeks the formalities seemed to unravel even further.

When they were all exhausted after a day's packing and cleaning they sat over supper and talked to each other about their future lives. It seemed clear that Flora was soon to be married, and as for the cook-housekeeper, she told them that she wanted nothing better than to retire to her widowed brother's farm at Shiremoor and help him cook and clean for her nephews.

Only Meg had no idea what was to become of her. She showed a real terror at the idea of going back to live with her family and she had begged Flora that, if she was going to marry Mr Atkins, she should take her on as a maid. But Flora had told her that she doubted if she and Howard would be able to afford a maid at first and, when they could, she had a young sister of her own who would soon be leaving school and would need to find employment.

More than once Ruth had found Meg with tears streaming down her face as she emptied cupboards or scrubbed the floors. Then one day she was able to tell her that she might be able to help her, but that she should keep looking for a job, just in case.

Ruth had very soon copied out Miss Golightly's

manuscript again, for the first copy had looked a little dog-eared and, with the help of Miss Matthews, had chosen another publisher to send it to. While she waited for a response she began to sort out Miss Golightly's books, listing them all and making notes to help Mr Golightly when he came to sell them.

She had asked Mrs Fairbridge if it was all right for Miss Matthews, the librarian, to come to help her in this task, and permission was granted. Miss Matthews had been overwhelmed.

'My dear,' she had said the first time she stood and gazed at the wall-to-floor bookcases, 'the poor woman had no discrimination.'

Ruth had frowned.

'I mean,' the librarian continued, 'there are some extremely valuable volumes here – and there's also some total rubbish!'

Ruth felt moved to defend her employer. 'Miss Golightly loved reading and if the books gave her pleasure perhaps we shouldn't criticize.'

'Oh, I'm not criticizing,' Miss Matthews said. 'I admit to enjoying reading a little "rubbish" myself sometimes. It's just that even with the library budget to help support my reading habit, I've never been able to indulge myself in the way your late employer did. And, you know, some of these books – the light romances and the detective stories – are not worth very much. I wonder if Mr Golightly would like to donate them to the library.'

'I'll ask him,' Ruth told her. 'I'm pretty sure he'll agree.'

Then Miss Golightly's novel was rejected for a

second time. Ruth took it along to the Crystal Library to consult with Miss Matthews once more.

The letter of rejection had been quite terse. Even rude, suggesting that the author should abandon hopes of publication and take up painting or embroidery. Feeling a little like a traitor, Ruth showed the letter to Miss Matthews, who shook her head sadly.

'Well, I've heard of authors who have had worse rejections than this and yet still gone on to be published eventually,' she said.

'Have you?' asked Ruth. 'Really?'

'Yes, really. But in this case ... well, I don't know what to say. Except...'

'Go on.'

'Well, have you never thought of rewriting the novel?'

Ruth frowned. 'What exactly do you mean?'

'Well, editing it, I suppose you'd call it. I mean to say, it is a jolly good story – not the sort that I usually read – but it's an exciting tale and it fairly races along – or rather it would if the overblown language didn't trip it up on nearly every page.'

'I know what you mean,' Ruth said.

'Well, you could put that right, if you wanted to.'

'But then it wouldn't be Miss Golightly's book, would it?'

'Yes it would. It's her story, her creation, and you would never have to tell anyone, would you? You could let her family believe in her talent – that would be a marvellous memorial for her, wouldn't it?'

'I suppose so. You're right. I will do that. As soon as I finish my own novel I'll do my very best for poor Angelina.'

'*What* did you say, my dear? Your *own* novel?'

Ruth had been nervous about telling Miss Matthews about her endeavours. She had been worried that the librarian might pour gentle scorn on the idea of an elementary school pupil aspiring to be a novelist. But the more she had come to know her, the more she realized that would not be the case. Now she was delighted with the way Miss Matthews was looking at her. She was surprised, yes, but it was a pleased surprise.

'I ... I've been writing a novel of my own, quite different from Miss Golightly's. It's a mystery story; there's a detective, a woman detective. I got the idea from one of my old school friends, Lucy. When she left secretarial school she got a job working in a solicitor's office. Well, of course, she said that most of the work was boring but–'

'Oh, Ruth, I know what you're going to say! A young woman like that might come across secrets ... puzzles ... mysteries! And, of course, your heroine would set out to solve them. What a clever idea!'

Ruth was pleased that Miss Matthews seemed so enthusiastic. 'Do you really think so?' she asked.

'Of course I do. Are you going to let me read it?'

'Yes.'

'When?'

'You can start today, if you like. I'm just about finished and, before I write the last chapter, I'd like your opinion ... if that's all right?'

417

'Of course it is!'

'And will you help me decide which publisher to send it to?'

'I'd be delighted.'

'But...'

'What is it?'

'Please don't tell anyone about it.'

'I won't, not if you don't want me to. In any case, who should I tell?'

'Well ... Roland.'

'Ah, I see.' Miss Matthews' smile faded.

She didn't ask why Ruth didn't want Roland to know about her novel; Ruth saw that there was no need. Guinevere Matthews adored her young brother, but she knew his character. She seemed not to have minded that Roland and Ruth had been walking out together but, one day, when Roland had been working late again, and she and Ruth had been waiting for him to come home for his tea, she had approached the subject falteringly.

First of all she had assured Ruth of her friendship and then she had gone on to say how much she loved her brother, all the time looking more awkward, until she said finally, 'But you and Roland have very different characters, you know.'

When Ruth had stared at her aghast, Miss Matthews had taken her hand and said, 'But, after all, what does an old maid know about these things? I promise you, I won't mention the subject again.'

'By the way, Ruth, did you know that Roland will be moving out soon?'

'Moving out?' Ruth was stunned.

'Ah, I thought he hadn't told you.'

'But where is he going?'

'My clever young brother has been promoted. His new position is in the insurance company's head office in Newcastle and he is going to take a flat in Heaton. He's been looking at properties after work at nights.'

'He's not really been working late, then?'

'Oh, yes, the nature of his work means that he has to keep awkward hours, but he has also been looking for a suitable property. But, please, Ruth, don't say anything. And don't be hurt. I think Roland must want it to be a surprise for you.'

But Ruth was hurt. And vaguely troubled. How could anyone who was supposed to be a friend, perhaps more than a friend, spend time with you and not tell you something as important as the fact that they were planning to leave their childhood home?

Had Roland grown bored with her? Had he found someone else? Whatever the answer was, Ruth realized how little she really understood the man she imagined she was in love with.

With Miss Golightly's manuscript sent off again and her own nearly finished work with Miss Matthews, Ruth was restless and unsettled. She realized that, whatever happened, there would come a time eventually when she would have to start looking for a new position and she had no idea what she wanted to do – apart from write.

Miss Matthews had promised to ask around to see if any of the ladies who subscribed to the library required a companion, but they both knew that the sort of duties that Ruth would be expected to fulfil would be much more menial than she had been used to as Miss Golightly's companion.

She would be expected to fetch and carry, to groom the cat and walk the dog, to read the newspaper or the latest romantic novel aloud to her employer, and perhaps to write a letter or two. But in such a household she would never find the mental stimulation and the encouragement she had found in Miss Golightly's house. And now she would soon have to leave the house in Catherine Terrace. Where should she go?

Ruth had not seen her father and stepmother since Miss Golightly's funeral. She had been surprised when they had arrived at the church but then she remembered Ada's tenuous family connection.

Mr Douglas Golightly had been equally surprised when Ada and Joseph Lorrimer had arrived at the funeral tea. But he had been the soul of politeness when Ada reminded him that her first husband had been a distant relative – and that Ruth was her stepdaughter.

'She's a credit to you,' he had said. 'And you must have missed her. I expect you must be very pleased that it won't be long now before Ruth can come to live at home again.'

Ruth had had to turn her face away and hide her amusement at Ada's expression of dismay and alarm.

And now, with the cleaning and packing almost finished, Mrs Fairbridge had given them all, including herself, the day off. Flora had gone to spend the day with her family in Cullercoats; Mrs

Fairbridge had told her it was time to tell her mother and father about Howard. Meg had said that she would rather stay alone in the house than go to visit her parents, so the housekeeper had taken her with her to her brother's farm. Ruth had come home to Byker.

Ada greeted her with a sour face and the words, 'You might have told me you were coming. It would have been easy enough for a girl with your education to write a letter.'

Ruth ignored the sarcasm and replied simply that she hadn't known she could come until that very morning.

'Good job there's enough to go round,' Ada said. Then remained purse-lipped when she noticed Joseph's frown.

After they finished lunch Ruth helped Ada clear the table and wash the dishes. They sat with cups of tea. Ruth and Ada were still at the table but Joseph sat in his usual place by the hearth, even though the fire was banked low. This way he could lean forward and knock the ash from his pipe into the grate and put his slippered feet up on the brass fender.

'Well, I'm sorry you're out of a job, pet,' her father said, 'especially as you were happy there.'

'I still have some work to do ... paperwork. It could take a year to finish ... or longer.'

Ruth did not feel it was necessary to explain to her father and stepmother about Miss Golightly's manuscript. Indeed, she had promised Miss Golightly's nephew that she would tell as few people as possible about his aunt's novel. She had guessed that he was embarrassed, perhaps imagining how bad it might be.

'And you'll be living there at the house until you've finished?' Ada asked.

Ruth turned towards her stepmother, who had got out her mending. When they had washed the dishes together she had said hardly a word, but Ruth could tell Ada was seething with unease.

It's funny, Ruth thought, I have always thought of this woman as Ada. Young though I was when she came into our lives, I never wanted to call her 'Mother'. I think my father would have liked that, it would have eased his conscience, but Ada herself didn't encourage it. I think she would have preferred me to call her Mrs Lorrimer. But that would have been awkward. And as a small child I could hardly have addressed her as Ada. So instead we settled for something even more awkward – nothing at all.

'I shall live there only until the new owners move in,' Ruth answered.

'And then?'

'Mr Golightly expected that I should come home.'

'That's impossible,' Ada snapped, and Ruth knew that this was the moment the woman had been dreading.

'Why impossible?' her husband asked. He looked surprised. 'It would be nice to have the bairn home for a while.'

'She's not a bairn, Joseph, and she won't thank you for calling her that.' Ada put on a false smile as she pretended concern for Ruth's sensibilities. 'But the reason it's impossible for her to come home is that we haven't got the room.'

'But her old room is empty.'

Ruth sat back and watched as her father, for once, tried to oppose Ada's will. She wondered what had prompted this rebellion. Perhaps he had truly missed her.

'It won't be big enough,' Ada said. 'Not if Ruth has to bring books and paperwork home. She needs somewhere where she can put a desk if she's going to do the job properly. Isn't that right, Ruth?' Ada looked up sideways from her darning. Only Ruth could see her cold challenge.

'Yes, that's right.' She could have said that the dining table would do to spread out her papers. After all, she used to do her homework there. But she knew she would have hated that as much as Ada would. Having to lay out her papers each time in between meals, not being able to leave her work set out. Also she would have Ada breathing down her neck at all times as she went about her housework.

And then there was her own writing. She would need peace and quiet and total privacy. She dreaded to think what Ada would say if she thought Ruth was writing a novel of her own.

'No, you'll have to find lodgings – somewhere with a bigger room. I dare say Miss Golightly has left you enough money to take care of that?'

'Yes, she has.'

Ada sniffed. 'And is that all?'

'What do you mean?'

'Did she leave you any little token – you know, a gift of some sort?'

'Yes.' She saw her stepmother's eyes glint with anticipation. 'Miss Golightly left instructions that

I was to choose some books.'

'Oh, books.'

Ada shook her head and went on with her
darning. Ruth could have told her that there were
no restrictions, that she would be able to choose
any books that she wanted and that some of them
were quite valuable. But she remained silent.
For, after all, she doubted if she would ever sell
them, and if Ada knew they were worth anything
at all she might try to put pressure on her to do
so.

'You could always move in with your old school
pal, I suppose,' Ada said. 'I've heard she's bought
a house.'

'You mean Lucy?'

'Of course. Who else? The talk is that her da's
will was sorted out at last and he's left Lucy and
her ma quite comfortable. I've heard there was
some sort of insurance.'

'It seems there was.'

Ada paused, waiting for Ruth to say more and,
when she didn't, she went on, 'It must have been
quite a tidy sum.'

'Why do you say that?'

'Well, for goodness' sake! Buying her own
house!'

'It's just a small house.'

'But at the coast.'

'Her husband works there.'

'And Mrs Shaw. She's taken on that old woman
to clean and cook for her again. But it's funny,
isn't it, that she doesn't want to move in with her
daughter.'

'No, I don't think so. She probably likes her

own house.'

Ruth knew that wasn't true. Esther had told her that Lucy's mother had been hurt that Lucy hadn't even suggested that she move in with her and Arthur. It seemed there was still some coolness between mother and daughter and Esther still hadn't fathomed why.

'But that might be good for you,' Ada said.

'I don't know what you mean.'

'Well, you could take a room at Lucy's house.'

'I could I suppose, but I probably won't.'

'Whyever not?'

'Yes, why not, pet?' her father asked. 'I would like to think you were with your friend.'

Ruth smiled at her father. 'Well, for a start I'm not sure that Arthur would like to have a lodger in the house. But, even if he did, they are expecting a child and I don't think I'd get much peace and quiet to get on with my work.'

Ada gave an exaggerated sigh. 'Well, you're obviously determined not to listen to my suggestions. But, have it your own way. My conscience is clear; I've done my best to help you.'

Ruth stared at her stepmother in disbelief. Did she really believe what she was saying? The only thing that mattered to Ada was keeping Joseph to herself. That's why Ruth had been found the job with Miss Golightly in the first place.

'So, will you stay at the coast?' Ada asked.

'I expect so. There are plenty of lodging houses in Whitley-by-the-Sea. Most of them cater for summer visitors but there are landladies who would be pleased to have a permanent lodger.'

'Permanent? You mean just until you find another job?'

'Of course.'

'And have you thought about that?'

'Don't worry,' Ruth told her stepmother, 'I shall find something; I shan't expect to come home again – ever.'

Ruth regretted her bitter tone the moment the words were out of her mouth but Ada's obvious panic had been hard to bear.

'There's no need to take that tone with me,' Ada bridled. 'I'm only asking these questions because I'm concerned for you and I want you to be happy.'

Ruth stared at her stepmother in astonishment. Then she glanced quickly at her father to see if she could guess what he was thinking, but his expression was masked by wreathing curls of smoke as he drew on his pipe.

'And you, Father?' she asked. 'What do you think?'

'I'm not sure what you mean, Ruth,' he said after a pause. 'But I think you seem to be in a fine fettle with yourself and I'm sorry for that. And, furthermore, I think you should apologize to your stepmother.'

Ruth sat for a moment in silent misery. What had she expected? Had she really believed that her father would break the habit of years and disagree with anything his wife said? That he would go against Ada's obvious wishes and say that his daughter – the daughter of his first marriage – should come home as soon as possible?

Ruth knew then that he was lost to her. She did not believe that he should have stayed single after her mother died. Her father had still been a young man and he'd needed a wife as well as a mother for his small daughter. But what a pity that it was Ada Thirlwell who had come his way. Ada, with no children of her own, and who would probably never have wanted children anyway, because from the moment she'd seen Joseph, there'd been no room in her heart for anyone else at all. Certainly not his motherless child.

Ruth rose from the table. 'I'm sorry if I've spoken out of turn,' she said. This was not exactly the apology that her father had asked for but it was the best she could do. 'And I think I'd better go now.'

Her father looked perplexed. 'No need for that, pet,' he said. 'You can stay for tea.'

'No, I mean, thank you, but I have been invited to Lucy's house for tea. I said I would call for Esther. We are going together.'

The leave-taking was subdued, her father still looking concerned and Ada trying to hide her satisfaction. Ruth guessed that her stepmother knew that it was unlikely that Ruth would ever visit again.

Have I really cut all ties with home? Ruth wondered as she made her way uphill to the Shaws' house. On this late September afternoon warmth lingered and many windows were open. The odours of Sunday cooking drifted out into the dusty town air and were defeated by the smell of the factories and the bone yard. Ruth realized how much she had grown used to the sharper

427

cleaner air at the coast, even if it was colder, and how she would probably have chosen to stay there even if Ada had welcomed her home with open arms.

How different the atmosphere was at Mrs Shaw's house. Esther's brother, Davy, opened the door. Ruth had never seen him look so smart.

'Hawway in,' he said and grinned. 'I'm ready, but Esther's not. I telt her to get a move on but she's still sitting gossiping with Mrs Shaw and Betty.'

'Is Betty here?'

'Aye. She's not supposed to come on a Sunday but she said she'd work an extra day for nothing just to get away from her daughter-in-law.'

Poor Betty, Ruth thought. It must be dreadful to be old and unwanted by your family. Even worse for an old woman than for a child – like the child that Ruth herself had once been. At least the child could grow up and make a life for herself.

When she entered the room three faces looked up with welcoming smiles. 'Ruth!' Esther sprang up from the table. 'I won't be long!' She fled upstairs. Her brother went to sit on the cracket by the hearth and was soon immersed in a newspaper.

'Sit down, Ruth, hinny.' Betty, obviously more friend than servant in this house, indicated the chair Esther had just vacated. 'Do you want a cup of tea? It's no bother.'

'No, thank you. I've just had a meal at ho– at my father's house.'

'And how are your parents?' Mrs Shaw asked politely.

'My father seems very well,' Ruth said. If Daisy Shaw thought it strange that Ruth didn't mention her stepmother she didn't say anything.

'Well, isn't this exciting?' Lucy's mother said. 'You and Esther and Davy off to take tea in Lucy's new house.'

'And why aren't you going with them?' Betty asked.

Mrs Shaw raised her eyebrows and Ruth imagined she controlled a spasm of irritation as she glanced first at Betty and then smiled sweetly at Ruth. 'Oh, you know, I wouldn't want to intrude,' she said.

The old woman looked at Mrs Shaw askance. 'Intrude? And what exactly do you mean by that?'

Ruth thought Mrs Shaw looked vexed but she smiled sweetly again and said, 'Well, you know, the young folk won't want an old woman like me spoiling their fun.'

There was undoubtedly a note of self-pity in Daisy Shaw's voice but Ruth sensed that she wasn't telling the whole truth. And so, obviously, did Betty.

'Now will you stop that nonsense, Mrs Shaw, hinny? We're all friends here and we might as well hev the truth. And that is you hevn't accepted Lucy's man yet, hev you? And that's a pity because he's a good hard-working lad and it's plain to see he thinks the world of her. It's no wonder Lucy is vexed with you.

'And, furthermore, you've no idea how much it grieves me to hev the two people I love better than me own family at loggerheads with each

429

other like this. I feel like knocking yer heads together!'

Daisy Shaw stared straight ahead, tight-lipped and refusing to look at her old friend, who shook her head sadly. Ruth could see how frustrated the old woman was at what she saw to be unreasonable behaviour, but she wasn't sure that Betty had grasped the full extent of the estrangement between mother and daughter. Something had gone wrong between them almost immediately after Lucy's father had been killed so tragically. It was almost as if Lucy was blaming her mother for something. Ruth didn't know what it could be. She wondered if grief could take people that way.

No one spoke until Esther returned; thankfully it hadn't taken her long to get ready. Before they left she went over and kissed Mrs Shaw on the cheek.

'Shall I give your love to Lucy?' she asked.

Betty raised her eyebrows and glared at Mrs Shaw, who nodded and said, 'Mm, of course.'

'And your regards to Arthur?'

Daisy Shaw raised her chin and gave Betty a thin smile before she said, 'I suppose you'd better.'

The old maid laughed and grinned as she said, 'That's right, Esther, hinny. You know what's proper. Now off you gans, the three of yer, off to yer tea party and leave us old wives in peace!'

Chapter Fourteen

'Esther, you look lovely,' Ruth said. 'I feel quite drab beside you.'

Esther was wearing a pale grey skirt and jacket over a white blouse with a frilled neckline. The jacket was in the popular Russian style, with a tightly nipped-in waist and high winged collar. The collar framed her delicate face.

'You don't look drab,' Esther said.

'No?'

'Well, perhaps a little plain.'

'Plain!'

'I don't mean *you* are plain. Far from it. And you look good in blue, you always have. But the cut of that coat is so severe – and your hat ... well, I always think a homburg on a woman looks so businesslike.'

'Not like that daft bit of feathered nonsense you have perched on top of your curls!' Ruth smiled. 'My goodness, Esther, you have become such an expert on fashion. Who would have thought it?'

'Do you mean who would have thought that the dirty, ragged little girl that no one would play with would have the nerve to want to be clean and trim and wear nice clothes?'

'Oh, Esther, did I say the wrong thing? Did I hurt you? I didn't mean to. It's just that in days gone by it was always Lucy who cared about fashion; you and I didn't bother about such things.'

'Well, perhaps you didn't bother, Ruth, but I always wanted something more for myself. A good home for Davy and me, a better way of life as well as decent clothes to wear.'

'Of course you did. I'm sorry.'

'Divven't fret!' Esther grinned as she slipped purposely into her old way of speaking for a moment. 'No offence taken. But it is strange, isn't it? Do you remember the day we went for tea at Lucy's house for the first time? What we looked like? Oh, you were clean and tidy as always.'

'My stepmother had allowed me to wear my new dress; the one I was going to wear to start my employment with Miss Golightly the next day.'

'Yes, you looked smart. But me! Well, I was clean enough – the soaking in the sea the day before had seen to that – but I must have looked like a ragged street urchin. And as for Davy!'

'What about Davy?' Esther's brother asked. He had been trailing along a few paces behind them, but now he caught up and smiled questioningly.

'We're talking about the first day we went to the Shaws' house,' his sister told him. 'And I still remember the look on Ruth's face when we caught up with her on the way there. She was horrified.'

'I wasn't.'

'Yes, you were. Don't fib. I believe you were thinking that Mrs Shaw wouldn't let Davy in the house.'

Ruth felt herself flushing but she just smiled and shook her head.

'Well, she did let him in,' Esther said.

'But Betty took me through to the scullery and

432

made me wash,' Davy reminded them. 'And I wasn't allowed at the table.'

'You had a picnic in the garden,' Esther said. 'Betty thought you would prefer that to sitting and listening to girls' gossip.'

'She was right there!'

'And now look at you,' his sister said. 'You're clean and presentable – a real smart-looking little lad.'

'Not so much of the little. Remember I'm older than I look. But it's all thanks to you,' her brother told her. 'And don't think I'm not grateful.'

'But we owe so much to Mrs Shaw,' Esther said. 'Honestly, Ruth, she's been so good to us. And I don't just mean because she gives me clothes.'

'Her cast-offs,' Ruth said.

'Maybe so. But they're all good quality and she could sell them for a decent price, you know. And until her husband's affairs were settled she could have done with the money,' Esther admonished.

'You're right,' Ruth said. 'I'm sorry.'

'I don't know,' Esther said, and she shook her head. 'Sometimes you seem so ... oh, I don't know what the word is, but you're sometimes so unwilling to believe the best of folk.'

'I know. And I think the word you're looking for is cynical. I can't help it. Perhaps it's something to do with what happened when I was a little girl.'

'You mean your mother dying and your father marrying again?'

'I suppose so. And the way Ada behaved towards me.'

Esther didn't reply, and when Ruth glanced at her she saw that her friend's eyes were glittering.

'What is it?' Ruth asked.

'Think on the way Davy and I used to live,' she said tersely. 'And stop feeling sorry for yourself!'

'Sorry for myself? Oh, no, is that what it sounds like?'

'Yes.'

'I suppose it does,' Ruth said. 'And perhaps I am. And I ought to be ashamed of myself. Oh, Esther, you're so much better than I am. So much nicer. You always have been!'

'Give over,' her friend said; she was smiling again. 'And, anyway, whatever happened in the past, I couldn't be happier now. We're not just like lodgers in that house, you know. We're like family. I'm so grateful to Mrs Shaw.'

'And I hope she's grateful to you.'

'Why should she be?'

'Esther, at the risk of sounding cynical, I'd like to remind you that, until Betty came back to work for her, you were doing all the housework and most of the cooking too.'

'I was pleased to do it. She didn't interfere; she just let me get on with things. It was like having a home of my own. I can't tell you how happy that made me!'

'Well, then,' Davy said, 'if you two are pals again, there's something you ought to know.'

'What is it, Davy?' Esther was smiling but her expression became serious when she saw her brother's anxious eyes.

'Just stop here a minute,' Davy said. 'Pretend you're looking in this shop.'

434

They were walking down Shields Road. Davy took hold of their arms and pulled them towards the shop window. There wasn't much of a display, Ruth thought, and what there was seemed to be a jumble of old clothes and tired-looking shoes. It was a second-hand shop.

'Why on earth would we look in here?' she asked Davy.

'Don't look at the goods. Look at the reflections,' he answered puzzlingly.

'Davy, lad,' his sister said. 'What are you play-ing at?'

'It's no game. Look at the reflections, like I said. Not just at us, look beyond. There's a fellow on the other side of the street staring at you. He's stopped now, but he was following us!'

'Following us!'

'Well, walking down on the Heaton side but looking at us all the time. You were so busy arguing with each other that you didn't notice him. Can you see him, now?'

'Yes, I can,' said Esther. 'And you're right. He does seem to be looking at us. Oh, no! He's coming over!'

Ruth watched the reflections in the window. The tall figure of the man set out across the road and then stopped on the island in the middle where the trampoles stood. Suddenly he was obscured by a passing tram.

'Shall we run for it?' Esther asked.

'No, it's all right,' Ruth said. 'Wait here.'

'What are you doing? Come back!' Esther called as Ruth began to walk away across the pavement.

'It's all right, I know him.' Then she turned to face the man as the tram rumbled away down Shields Road and he hurried forward to meet her. 'Hello, Roland,' she said, and smiled. 'What are you doing here?'

Immediately she sensed that something was wrong. He didn't answer her smile but stood looking at her quizzically.

'Roland?' she murmured.

He looked beyond her towards Esther and Davy, who were still pretending to look in the shop window and then back. 'I live here now. The removal people brought my few bits and pieces up to my new home yesterday. Guinevere is there now cleaning and tidying, but we need some milk for a cup of tea. She's sent me out to find a dairy.'

'Oh, I can help you with that. Go just a little way further on and then turn left – look, the street with the public house on the corner. There's a dairy at the top of the first back lane.'

'Good.'

Still he didn't smile.

'Roland, is something the matter?'

'You didn't seem surprised about my move.'

'Well ... no ... I...'

At last there was a smile, if a very faint one. 'I imagined my dear sister would tell you about it – and my promotion. She's hopeless at keeping secrets. *Did* she tell you, Ruth?'

'Well, yes, she did.'

'And yet you never asked me about it?'

'Guinevere said she thought you must want it to be a surprise. A nice surprise.'

'And is it? I mean, are you pleased for me?'

'Yes, of course I am. Roland, I don't understand this at all. Why are you angry with me?'

'I'm not angry,' he said, although his cold eyes
belied it. 'I'm disappointed.'

'Disappointed? Why?'

'In you. You see, I did want this to be a surprise
for you. I was going to ask you to come out with
Guinevere and me one day soon and bring you to
my new home, tell you about my prospects and
ask you to ... well, ask you to share your life with
me. But fortunately I found out in time what an
unsuitable wife you would make for a man like
me – or any man, come to that.'

'Wife...? Unsuitable?'

Ruth did not know which word surprised and
shocked her most. She had dreamed that one
day, in spite of any doubts she had, Roland might
ask her to marry him, and yet now she had
discovered in one moment that he had
considered the possibility and dismissed it.

'But why? I mean, why unsuitable?'

'I told you. Guinevere is hopeless at keeping
secrets – at hiding things.'

'You found my manuscript?'

'Yes.'

'And you asked her about it?'

Roland shrugged. 'I merely asked her what tosh
she was reading now.'

'And she told you?'

'That's obvious. In fact she told me that your
work was very good indeed and that in her
opinion you would be a most successful novelist.'

Ruth felt both pain and pleasure at his words.
Pleasure that Guinevere had endorsed her work

so warmly, and yet pain because she had disclosed her secret to the very person Ruth had asked her not to.

'Ruth?' Roland was frowning. 'You do see how I could never marry a woman who was taken up with wanting a career of her own, don't you?'

'No, I don't see.'

'There's something wrong with women who want careers. Women are not meant to think like that. It goes against nature. They are meant to be wives and mothers, to look after their husbands, their homes, their children.'

'They can't all be wives and mothers.'

'What do you mean?'

'Your sister, for example. She is neither a wife nor a mother.'

'She has been a mother to me.'

'She works in the library.'

'As soon as I was old enough to understand I begged her not to. She could have sold it and invested the money in a small pension. But she has this stupid devotion to books! Don't you see – if she had behaved more like a proper woman, she might even have been married and leading a more normal existence!'

Ruth felt like telling him that he would have hated that. If Guinevere had married and perhaps had children of her own, she would not have devoted herself so much to her young brother, and he would not have become the spoiled young man he was! But she held her tongue. She knew that it was pointless to argue with him and she was also aware that Esther and Davy were growing restless as they waited for her.

She was about to say a curt goodbye when Roland surprised her by taking her hand. 'It's not too late, is it, Ruth?'

'Too late?'

'I mean you wouldn't consider giving up this silly idea of being a writer and simply being my wife, would you?'

'Writing is silly?'

'No, not all writing. You know I didn't mean that.' He smiled as if she'd made a joke. 'But it's a well-known fact that too much mental labour in a woman can lead to sterility, isn't it?'

'Oh, for goodness' sake!'

Ruth stared at him in despair. For all he had infuriated her, the very touch of his hand had set the nerves singing through her body. Sheer frustration at the choice she was about to make almost overwhelmed her. She pulled her hand away.

'I can't marry you,' she said. She felt the sob that escaped her rather than heard it.

'Are you all right, Ruth?' It was young Davy who stepped forward.

'Of course I am.' She never knew how she managed to smile so cheerfully. 'Davy, Esther,' she said, 'I'm sorry to have kept you waiting. This is Roland Matthews. His sister, Guinevere, runs the Crystal Library. We've been discussing ... discussing some work that Guinevere is helping me with.'

Esther came forward and shook Roland's hand. Ruth saw the moment that Roland looked at Esther for the first time his eyes widened as he took in her beauty and her grace. And she also

439

saw the look in Esther's green eyes as Roland pressed her hand and murmured his greetings.

'Roland has just moved to Heaton,' Ruth said. 'Guinevere has sent him out to buy milk...' she added, and she heard her own voice fade into a whisper. But it didn't matter, for neither Esther nor Roland was listening to her.

Lucy looked with satisfaction at the table she had set in the front parlour of her new home. The embroidered tablecloth, the English china tea service patterned with roses, and the matching bread-and-butter plates and two-tier cake stand.

The sausage rolls, cheese straws, the lemon curd tarts, and the currant cake had all been bought the day before, and now Lucy set them out, then placed a little dish of strawberry jam beside the plate of thinly sliced bread and butter. She stood back to look at everything.

Arthur came into the room. 'Now there's a bonny sight,' he said.

'Do you think so? Do you think they'll mind that it's not homemade?'

'Of course they won't. But I didn't mean the table – I meant you.' Arthur put his arms round her. 'I'm glad you've stopped wearing black. That purple suits you.'

'Arthur! It's not purple!'

'What is it then?'

'It's lilac – although you could call the ribbon trim and the buttons purple, I suppose.'

Arthur grinned and shook his head. 'Aye, well, whatever it is you look pretty. Pretty as a picture.'

Arthur pulled her close and kissed her. Lucy

responded to the kiss but she tried to hold herself away from him. Her body was thickening, she was now visibly pregnant and Arthur did not know how far gone she was. She couldn't be absolutely sure but she reckoned she must have been about two months gone when she had seduced Arthur into making love to her for the first time. Without actually saying so, she had encouraged him to think that she had conceived the first time they had made love in his office at the railway station. She had not yet made up her mind how she was going to explain away a bouncing full-term baby when it arrived 'prematurely'.

'Don't hold me so tightly, Arthur.'

'Why? Don't you like it?'

'You know I do. But we must be careful. You know…'

'Oh, aye! I'm sorry, pet.'

Lucy was filled with guilt when she saw the concern that flooded his face. 'Oh, it's all right,' she said, and she took his face in her hands and drew his head down so that she could kiss his brow, 'I'm not made of bone china – but best not to risk anything.'

She nestled her face against his neck for a moment and savoured the clean smells of shaving soap and his bay rum hair dressing. Then she stepped back.

'You're right.' Arthur put his hands on her shoulders and turned her gently so that she was facing the door. 'Now, hev you got time to come into the kitchen and hev a cup of tea with yer husband afore he gans to work?'

'Yes, I think so.' They made their way into the kitchen, which also served as a cosy living room. 'Arthur, I've been meaning to tell you...' Lucy spooned the tealeaves into the pot as she spoke.

'What is it? Wait – let me do that.' Arthur lifted the kettle from the hob on the range fire and filled the teapot. 'Sit down, pet. I'll get the milk and the sugar. Now what did you want to say?'

Lucy sat at the table and watched as Arthur got cups and saucers from the dresser and brought them to the table. 'You didn't have to go to work just because my friends are coming,' she said.

'I know, but I'd feel out of place sitting there with you lasses in your bonny frocks, and half the time I wouldn't know what you were talking about – especially when you get round to the latest fashions and all that sort of nonsense!'

'But what about Esther's young brother, Davy? He's coming, you know. Are you going to leave him on his own to talk nonsense with us?'

'I've thought about that.' Arthur sat down at the table. 'Do you think the lad would like to come to the station with me for an hour or two? I could show him round – and you could put some extra cakes and things in me bait box and he could share with me in the office.'

'What a good idea. I think Davy might like that.' Lucy smiled at Arthur as he began to pour the tea. 'I had to invite him. Esther won't go anywhere without him, you know, although he would have been safe enough at home with my mother.'

'Aye, but it's not a matter of safe, is it? Esther's overfond of that lad. She's like a mother hen with

442

her chick.'

Arthur pushed Lucy's cup towards her. 'Do you want owt to eat?' he asked.

'No thank you, my friends will be here soon.'

'Are you sure? You've been working hard, cleaning and getting the house ready. You've got to keep your strength up, you know.'

'Arthur, I'm fine. And if I ate as much as you want me to I'd blow up like a balloon!'

'Well, if you're sure...'

'I am.'

'And another thing, Lucy pet, I think you've been doing too much – what with the moving house and buying the new furniture and everything. I wish you'd take it a bit easier.'

'I will now, I promise you. As a matter of fact I've been thinking of taking someone on to help me. A maid-of-all-work. Lucy says that Meg, the little skivvy at Miss Golightly's house, still hasn't found a new position and she thinks she could be trained up nicely. What's the matter? Why are you frowning?'

'Can we afford a maid?'

'Of course we can.'

'I know your da left you provided for, what with the insurance and everything, but there can't be much left now after buying the house, can there?'

'There's enough. We can live quite comfortably, especially as you seem determined to work all the hours God sends – even on a Sunday afternoon! Now tell me again what you are going to do with our little back garden. We're going to have flowers and vegetables, and didn't you say there was even room for an apple tree?'

Lucy had deliberately changed the subject but as Arthur talked about his plans she was only half listening. She had decided almost as soon as Josiah Lawson had left her that day that she was not going to tell Arthur the truth of the situation.

Arthur knew more than anyone else, of course. He'd had to be told that she was illegitimate when they'd arranged the wedding, but he didn't think any less of her and he understood that she wouldn't want her friends to know. She'd made him promise not to tell anyone.

'As if I would,' he'd said, hurt that she'd doubted him.

Lucy had told him it was because her parents weren't married that it had taken so long for her father's affairs to be settled and he'd accepted that. She didn't tell him the truth – that Reginald Lawson, as he really was, had made no provision for the woman and child he was supposed to have loved. That was too painful. Neither did she tell him she'd had a visit from her grandfather who had given her five hundred pounds and settled one hundred pounds a year on her for life. She hadn't told her mother everything either.

Her mother had had to be told about Josiah Lawson's visit, of course, and his instruction that she – that they both – must stay away from the family home. Daisy Shaw was quite happy to do so now that she'd been given the allowance of thirty pounds a year; Lucy had led her to believe that her own allowance was not much more. She'd also told Daisy about the lump sum – she'd had to because how else would she have been able to explain that she could afford to buy a house? But she'd said it was three hundred pounds, not five hundred. Arthur believed it was three hundred too.

So many lies and so many different versions... Lucy knew she would have to be ever vigilant. But she wanted money in the bank; money that no one else knew about; not her mother and not even the man she was married to.

Lucy wasn't sure why she felt the need to protect herself like this. Perhaps it was because the lesson she had learned from life so far was that you can trust no one. Not even the people who are closest to you.

Now, looking across the kitchen table at Arthur, who looked so handsome in his porter's uniform, and who was smiling at her so happily as he talked about the vegetables and the soft fruit he would grow for her, she felt a pang of guilt. For in the very act of marrying him she had betrayed him. But what else could she have done? She could not have told him the truth – and she never could. Arthur must never ever know that he was going to give his name to another man's child.

Suddenly she reached across the table and rested her hand on his. 'Are you happy, Arthur?' she asked.

He looked surprised. 'What's brought this on?'

'Oh, I don't know. Sometimes I feel guilty.'

'Why on earth should you feel guilty?'

'Well, you know, you were walking out with that little nursemaid ... what was her name? Mary? ... and I came along and, well, you know...'

Arthur looked uncomfortable. 'Mary Clark and

I were never sweethearts.'

'No? I'm sure she thought you were.'

'Well, mebbes. But we never … we never did what you and I did.'

Suddenly Lucy couldn't meet his gaze. She squeezed his hand and asked, 'So you've no regrets? You don't ever think of her?'

'Why are you talking like this? Don't you know the way I feel about you?'

'Oh, put it down to the way I am.'

'Aye, I've heard women get funny notions at times like this. But you've nowt to fear. You must know I've loved you since the moment I first clapped eyes on you getting off the train with yer satchel and yer college books.'

'Oh, Arthur.' Lucy smiled at him. 'And are you happy here? The house and the garden and everything?'

'Listen, pet, the house is grand. Having me own garden is more than I could want for. But to tell the truth...'

'What is it?'

Her eyes widened with alarm but he grinned and raised her hand to his mouth and kissed it before he said, 'Surely you know I would be happy anywhere so long as I had you.'

Lucy smiled but she had to fight to keep the tears from spilling over. What had she done to this good man? She'd trapped him with a lie. She hoped that one day she wouldn't have to pay for it.

Ruth wouldn't think me such a nice person if she knew how envious I am of Lucy, Esther thought.

446

She looked round the front parlour of her friend's new home. She has been able to buy anything she wants, even a chiming clock and a china shepherd and shepherdess for the mantelpiece, and pictures of fruit and flowers for the wall. But it's not Lucy's money and material comfort that I envy – it's the fact that she has a home of her own – and a loving husband.

But I don't begrudge her any of it. Lucy is my friend and I want her to be happy – her and Arthur. He's a good man, even if he isn't what Mrs Shaw wanted for her daughter. And he's so obviously head over heels in love with Lucy – and, even though he's much too embarrassed to say so, he's obviously thrilled that they're going to become parents. He'll make a good father.

The moment they'd arrived at the little house at the north end of Whitley-by-the-Sea, Arthur had taken Davy off to show him the garden and the tool shed full of new gardening tools. Esther wasn't sure if Davy was really interested in gardening but he liked Arthur and he'd gone good-naturedly enough.

Lucy had taken Ruth and herself upstairs to show her the room that Arthur was preparing for the baby and then, of course, she hadn't been able to resist showing them the new clothes she'd bought and which were hanging in the wardrobe in her pretty bedroom.

After a quick tour of the kitchen and scullery, with its gleaming new pans and household utensils, Lucy had ushered them into the front parlour and told them to take their places at the table while she made a pot of tea.

Esther glanced across at Ruth, who had been strangely silent during their tour of the house. No, Esther thought, she's been quiet ever since ... ever since we met her friend's brother on Shields Road. He must have said something to upset her, something about the work she and his sister are doing, I suppose. I don't imagine she'll tell me what the matter is. Ruth can be so obstinate at times.

Roland ... what a romantic sounding name that is. And he's so handsome ... I wonder if I'll see him again?

Lucy came back into the room carrying a rose-patterned china teapot with a matching milk jug and sugar basin on a tray. 'Arthur is going to take your brother to the station with him,' she said. 'He's asked him and Davy said he'd like to go.'

'That's right,' Davy said as he followed Lucy into the room. 'Arthur reckons you three will enjoy your gossip better if I'm not here.'

'But how long will you be staying there?' Esther asked.

'Well, there's not much point in Davy coming back here, is there?' Arthur had now joined them, his bulk making the pretty little room look crowded. 'You'll be getting the train home eventually, so you can just collect him from my office. Don't worry, Lucy's packed up plenty for the lad to eat. And if he gets bored following me around there's a pile of newspapers and magazines for him to read.'

'Arthur says that the business gentlemen leave them on the trains,' Davy said.

'Do you like reading?' Ruth asked. It was the

first time she had spoken since they'd finished the tour of the house and she'd done her duty by admiring everything.

'Aye, I do.'

'What sort of books do you like?'

'Well, it's not books so much – although Raymond Fowler lends me his adventure stories sometimes – you know, about explorers and great heroes of the past. But mostly I like to read the newspapers.'

'That's right,' Esther said. 'He buys one every day with his own money.'

'If you worked in the station with me you'd never have to buy one,' Arthur said. And then he smiled. 'Now there's a thought – when you leave school I could get you a job on the railways. You could start off as a lamp boy, like I did, and you're a bright enough lad – who knows where you'd end up!'

'That's kind of you, Arthur,' Esther said. 'But Mr Fowler has already promised Davy a full-time job in the shop.'

'Is that what you want, Davy?' Arthur asked.

Davy shook his head and glanced at his sister hesitantly. 'Not really. I want to be a newspaper reporter.'

Esther was astonished. This was the first time Davy had mentioned such a thing. But then she had never asked him what he wanted to do. She had just assumed that he was happy with his part-time job at Fowler's and pleased that his future was assured.

'Then that's what you must be,' Ruth said. 'Although you'll more than likely have to start by trying to get a job as an office boy at the newspaper. And you'll have to stay at school until you're fourteen instead of leaving as soon as possible and even then, you probably won't earn as much as you would in the shop. Will that matter, Esther?'

'No, of course not! I want Davy to be happy.'

'Well, now that's settled,' Arthur said, 'I'd better gan to work. Hawway, Davy lad. Let's leave the womenfolk in peace.'

Lucy couldn't understand why Esther and Ruth were so quiet. Perhaps they were a little overawed by her new prosperous circumstances, she thought. But they were her friends ... surely they couldn't be jealous? But, whatever it was that was troubling them as they sat sipping their tea, to her vexation, they had barely touched the food.

Esther seemed to be distracted. Perhaps her brother had surprised her by saying he didn't want to work at Fowler's when he left school, but Lucy didn't think it was that that had put the faraway look in her eyes. And Ruth ... what on earth was the matter with Ruth? She looked downright miserable.

Of course her employer had died recently and Lucy knew that Ruth had been really fond of the old lady but she'd had time to get over it by now surely? After all, Miss Golightly wasn't exactly family. If she was, Ruth would have had to go into mourning. No, Ruth must be in one of her moods. But it was very inconsiderate of her.

Suddenly she wondered what Julia, her friend from Miss Jackson's school, would make of her new circumstances. Even Julia Wright would surely be impressed that newlyweds would be able to afford to buy and furnish their own house to such a high standard. But what would she make of Arthur?

Lucy was ashamed to admit that she would be too embarrassed to introduce her husband to Julia. That was why she had decided from the start that she would never invite her here. But, of course, there was another reason. Julia would no doubt talk about her visit at home. Stephen would hear, and then what? Stephen knew that the baby she was expecting was his. Would he cause trouble?

No, of course not. Stephen Wright was about to be married. He would no doubt be overjoyed that she had managed to solve her problems without involving him. The thought left a bitter taste.

Lucy helped herself to another slice of cake; someone would have to eat it.

'Well, then, how is my mother?' she asked at last. Someone would have to say something.

'Oh, she's well,' Esther said. 'I should have told you. And she sends her love – and so does Betty.'

'And is ... and is my mother happy?' Lucy asked.

'As happy as can be expected,' Esther replied. 'She misses your father so.'

'Don't you think I do?'

Esther looked startled. 'Of course ... but you have Arthur ... and the baby to look forward to. It's a pity ... it's a pity that she doesn't come and visit you more often.'

'I have invited her, you know. I wanted her to

451

help me choose things for the house, to come shopping with me like we used to, but she still hasn't forgiven me for what she calls "marrying beneath me".'

'She'll come round,' Esther said. 'I'm sure she will. Once she realizes that you truly love each other.'

Lucy's smile was strained. 'Oh yes, my mother sets great store by love. But, tell me, how does she spend her days? With you and Betty waiting on her hand and foot she must surely be bored.'

'No, I don't think she's bored,' Esther said. 'She reads, she embroiders and ... and she's had an idea – she wants to take some classes.'

'My mother is planning to go to evening class? What does she want to learn?'

'No, she doesn't want to learn; she wants to teach. And not at evening classes but in her own home. Actually,' Esther flushed, 'I suggested it to her.'

Lucy was astonished. And she noticed that Ruth had come back from whatever brown study she had taken up residence in. Both of them stared at Esther as Lucy asked, 'But what exactly is she going to teach?'

'Elocution, of course. She used to be an actress, you know.'

'Of course I know that,' Lucy replied quickly. She wouldn't have liked either of her friends to have guessed that her mother had never mentioned her past life until after her father had died.

'And she speaks so beautifully.'

'Yes, she does,' Ruth said.

'And she's done such a good job of helping me,'

Esther continued, 'that I suggested she should take a few pupils and they should pay for the lessons.'

'Esther, how clever of you,' Ruth said. 'But how is Lucy's mother going to get these pupils?'

'Well, some of the customers in the shop have mentioned now and then that I – that I've changed. Some of them make a joke of it and say I've gone all la-di-da, but one or two of them with children have asked how I managed it. Some parents will pay for things like piano lessons, you know, so I've mentioned that my friend, the lady I lodge with, teaches elocution, and there've been one or two enquiries already.

'And Raymond says we should write out some cards and leave them at the dancing school on Heaton Road. And there's a singing teacher near there too. I was wondering if she would recommend Mrs Shaw.'

'If you mean Mrs Valentine, I'm sure she would.'

Ruth had spoken spontaneously and Lucy saw her flush when she realized that she and Esther were looking at her in surprise.

'Do you mean the singing teacher is Henry's mother?' Esther asked.

'Yes.'

'Well, then, would you ask her to give out some cards?'

'Oh, no, I don't go there. I mean Henry's in London and ... well, no, I couldn't do that. But do go along and ask her yourself. I'm sure she wouldn't turn you away. Lucy, I would love another cup of tea. Shall I go and make it? I don't want to bother you.'

Ruth picked up the teapot and hurried out of the room. Lucy shook her head. 'What happened between her and Henry?' she asked. 'Did she ever tell you?'

'No. Ruth's deep. Sometimes I wonder if she doesn't trust us but I don't think it's that.'

'What is it, then? Pride?'

'Oh, no. The opposite. For all she's so clever I don't think she's very confident. I believe she's frightened of making a fool of herself so she just keeps quiet. She doesn't tell anyone what she hopes for or what she dreams of in case her dreams don't come true and we would laugh at her.'

'But we would never do that!'

'Of course we wouldn't. I hope one day she'll realize that.'

'Do you think she dreams of Henry Valentine?'

Esther shook her head. 'I just don't know.'

'Have you been talking about me?' Ruth asked when she returned with the fresh pot of tea. She was smiling.

'We wouldn't dare!' Lucy said. 'Not when you're obviously in one of your moods,' she said challengingly.

'Look, I'm sorry about that,' Ruth said. 'We met ... we met the brother of a friend of mine on the way here–'

'Roland Matthews,' Esther said, and Lucy noticed Ruth's quick flash of irritation. She thought it was because she didn't like being interrupted.

'Yes, Roland. Well, Roland and I had a silly

argument about some work that Guinevere and I–'

'*Guinevere!*' Lucy exclaimed, and earned a frown.

'–work that Guinevere and I are doing. That's all. It's not important. Would you like more tea?'

Lucy and Esther nodded and Ruth busied herself emptying the dregs into the slop bowl and starting afresh with milk and hot tea.

Why does she look so unhappy? Lucy wondered. Why should it matter if she argues with the brother of a friend? It was almost as if she was trying to convince herself of something just then.

But whatever the truth of the matter, they were all more animated now and, for a while, they talked about more everyday concerns. Lucy told them that she liked her neighbours on one side, a retired sea captain and his wife. Captain Rodgers had worked on the colliers, the coal ships that plied between the River Tyne and London, taking the coal that kept the fires of the capital city burning.

Mrs Rodgers had often sailed with him and would spend a few days in London sightseeing and shopping. They had no children and Mrs Rodgers had already made a pet of Lucy and was looking forward to the birth of the baby.

The neighbour on the other side, Mr Lockwood, was the manager of a variety theatre in North Shields. He was a widower and, since his daughter had married and left home, his unmarried sister had come to keep house for him. She was nice enough, Lucy told her friends, but deaf as a post and Lucy had long ago given up trying to have a conversation with her. She felt sorry for Mr Lockwood, but at least his work took him out at nights.

'And what about you?' Ruth asked. 'Do you mind when Arthur has to work late at the station?'

'I don't much like it,' Lucy said, 'being here on my own, although Mrs Rodgers sometimes comes and sits with me when Captain Rodgers has gone to his club. But soon I shall have Meg to keep me company. You said she wants to live in, so when Arthur has finished preparing the nursery I'll ask him to decorate the little attic room for her.'

'I'm so pleased you're taking Meg,' Ruth said. 'I know she'll work hard and try to please you.'

'And I'm pleased to be able to give up doing all the scrubbing and the cleaning it takes to keep this house clean!' Lucy said. 'I must take after my mother – I want a nice home but I absolutely hate housework!'

Esther shook her head and smiled gently. 'I know you do, but I can't imagine why.'

Lucy was astonished. 'Can't you? Can't you really? Esther, what a strange person you are.'

'But don't you see that's part of the joy of having your own home – to be able to keep it just the way you want it,' Esther said. She looked from Ruth to Lucy and smiled. 'But I can see I'll never be able to convince either of you of that.'

'No, you won't,' Ruth said. 'I don't mind doing housework as much as Lucy does, but I can't say that I enjoy it. I would do it because I like order, not because I would enjoy it.'

'We're very different, aren't we?' Lucy said.

'But I'm so glad we're friends. I've really enjoyed myself today and I hope you'll come and visit me as often as you can. And perhaps next time, Esther, you would persuade my mother to come.'

'I will.'

Lucy suddenly shivered.

'Are you cold?' Ruth asked. 'I'll start the fire going, shall I?'

'No, I'm not cold. It's just I had one of those strange moments, you know – they say someone has walked over your grave. But, in any case, it's time to light the fire. There's a box of matches behind the china dog on the sideboard.'

The fire in the hearth of the front room had been laid ready. Ruth found the matches and then kneeled down and, striking a match, she held it to the rolled-up newspaper that protruded in several places through the bars of the grate. The paper burned quickly and soon the sticks that lay under the coal were crackling. After a minute or two curls of smoke drifted up through the glowing coals. Ruth sat back on her heels.

'That was a well-laid fire,' Esther said.

'Arthur did it. I don't even know how to clean the grate out properly!'

Ruth resumed her place at the table and the three of them sat quietly for a moment, enjoying the companionship and the comfort of the room.

Outside the shadows were lengthening and, eventually, Lucy rose from the table, took a spill from the jar near the hearth and lit the gaslamps that were fitted to the wall at each side of the fireplace. She nipped out the spill, returned it to the jar and then went to the window to draw the curtains. Before she did she paused and rubbed the small of her back with one hand.

'Are you all right?' Esther asked.

'Yes, I'm fine,' Lucy said. 'Just a little weary.' She reached for the curtains again and then a movement outside caught her eye. Someone had opened the garden gate and was coming up the path. She moved the window nets aside. 'Why, there's Davy,' she said. 'I thought he was going to wait at the station.'

'Perhaps he got tired of waiting,' Esther said. 'We've stayed longer than expected. No, you sit down. I'll go to the door.'

'I suppose we'd better go now,' Ruth said when Esther had left the room. 'But we'll clear the table and wash the dishes for you first.'

'Mm? Oh, yes, thank you.'

But Lucy wasn't really listening to Ruth. She was concentrating on what was happening in the hallway. When she'd looked out of the window and seen Davy there'd been something about his movements that had alerted her. He had paused at the gate and hung on for a moment as if he'd been out of breath. She hadn't been able to make out his expression but she'd seen his body move as if he was panting to get his breath back. He'd been running.

And then he'd opened the gate and he'd paused again. Had he looked up and seen her watching through the window? She thought he had. But he'd avoided her glance as he made for the door.

'What is it, Lucy?' Ruth asked. 'Why are you frowning?'

'Hush ... listen.'

Esther must have opened the door. 'Come in, Davy,' Lucy heard her say.

'No, wait a moment,' he replied.

He began to say something but he spoke so quietly that Lucy couldn't make out what he was saying.

Then Esther said quite clearly, 'What did you say? Oh, no, Davy, no!'

Lucy rose to her feet slowly. She could feel her heart thudding. By now Ruth, equally alarmed, had come to stand beside her. Esther came back into the room. Her face was drained of colour.

'What is it?' Lucy whispered, and she felt Ruth's arm go round her waist.

'There's been an accident,' Esther said, 'at the station.'

'Arthur?'

Esther nodded.

'Is he ... is he...?'

'He's at the infirmary,' Esther said. 'But it's bad, Lucy. Very bad.'

Chapter Fifteen

'Why won't you let me see him?'

Before Ruth could stop her Lucy rose from the bench seat in the draughty entrance hall of the infirmary and accosted the tall, vinegar-faced woman in the starched cap and apron, who had just emerged from the door leading to the wards.

'How many times do I have to tell you, Mrs Purvis? Your husband's condition is critical.'

'All the more reason why I should be with him. Don't you know how cruel this is? Keeping man and wife apart like this?'

'Mrs Purvis,' the woman's face registered no emotion, 'there are rules. We couldn't run this infirmary without them. Visitors are restricted to particular days and times.'

'Why?'

The woman drew in her breath and spoke as if she were exercising great patience. 'I don't have to explain the rules to you,' she said.

'It would be kind if you did.' Ruth spoke for the first time.

She had been standing just behind Lucy but now she stepped forward and took her arm. When Lucy glanced round at her, Ruth raised her eyebrows and shook her head very slightly as if saying, 'Leave this to me.'

'I beg your pardon. Are you questioning my authority?'

'Certainly not. But I'm a friend of Mrs Purvis and I'd like to apologize for her seeming rudeness. I assure you, she means no disrespect.' Lucy moved impatiently and Ruth grasped her arm and held it tightly. 'Mrs Purvis has had no sleep—'

The woman's eyes flashed. 'I told you last night to take her home.'

'And that was kind of you to be concerned for her welfare and, I agree, in her condition, she should have tried to rest.'

'Condition?'

'Oh, I thought you knew, she's expecting a baby.'

Miraculously, the woman's harsh features softened a little. 'I didn't know. That coat she's wearing conceals her figure.'

'Perhaps I should have told you,' Ruth said.

The woman sighed. 'It would have made no difference. We can't have relatives upsetting the routine on the wards.'

'But if ... if Mr Purvis's condition was to deteriorate...' Ruth began. She heard Lucy gasp and put her arm round her as she began to slump.

'I should see to it that they had some moments together.'

Lucy groaned and, turning towards her, Ruth saw that she had gone deathly pale.

'Bring her to my office,' the woman said. 'Follow me. Nurse Brown,' she called to a startled younger woman who had just arrived and was still wearing her cloak and bonnet, 'see about a cup of tea for Mrs Purvis.'

Once settled in the matron's office, for that was who the woman was, they were left on their own. Then Lucy's eyes had closed and her head flopped sideways. Ruth kneeled before her, grasped her hands and said helplessly, 'Please open your eyes, Lucy. I have no idea what to do.'

'For a start you can loosen her clothes and give her some air.' The nurse had appeared bearing a tray with two cups of tea. 'Here, let me see to her.'

Ruth watched as the nurse placed the tray on the matron's desk, then undid the buttons of Lucy's coat, loosened her collar, placed a hand on the back of her head and gently pushed it down.

'Open that little cupboard on the wall,' she said over her shoulder, 'and pass the smelling salts.'

Ruth did so and a moment later Lucy was spluttering indignantly as the smell of ammonia drifted across the room.

'For goodness' sake, what's in that?' Lucy asked.

'Matron's own,' the nurse replied. 'And you shouldn't complain. It's good stuff; ammonia mixed with lavender and peppermint and all kinds of nice things. Here,' she said as she put the cork back in the bottle, 'put it back in the cupboard, will you? And see if you can find a stone bottle at the back of the top shelf. There's no label on it.'

'Is this it?' Ruth asked.

'That's it. Give it here.'

'What is it?' Lucy asked suspiciously.

'Matron's little secret.' Nurse Brown smiled.

'Now that you've recovered a little you need a drop or two of this in your tea to pull you round.'

Ruth watched as the nurse measured two teaspoons into one of the cups of tea, then added two spoons of sugar and handed it to Lucy. 'Sip this slowly,' she said. 'It's brandy.'

Nurse Brown put the bottle back in the cupboard herself and, closing it, she turned to face Ruth. 'Go on, drink your tea,' she said. 'You look as if you need it almost as much as Mrs Purvis does.'

Lucy was sipping her tea as she'd been told and already there was a better colour in her cheeks.

'Matron says I have to stay with you,' the nurse told them. 'She's worried about Mrs Purvis.'

'I suppose she doesn't want her causing a fuss and upsetting the routine,' Ruth said caustically.

'Now, now, Matron isn't as bad as that. She has to answer to the governors, you know, and they are very strict. They have to be. You wouldn't believe the trouble some people cause. They're not at all grateful for the free treatment they receive.'

Lucy bridled at this. 'My Arthur doesn't expect free treatment. His weekly subscription is fully paid up. He's not a charity case.'

'I didn't say he was, Mrs Purvis.'

Lucy wasn't listening. 'And any extra medicine he needs – anything at all – I'm quite prepared to pay for.'

'There, there, dear. I'm sure you are. Please don't upset yourself. If you get into a state Aunt Grace will be very cross with me.'

'Aunt Grace?' Ruth said. 'The matron is your aunt?'

Nurse Brown smiled. 'Mm, how else do you think I know of her little secret?' Ruth couldn't help smiling. 'Oh, don't worry, my aunt is not a tippler. It's just that she believes in the medicinal properties of strong spirits – when taken in moderation, of course. Oh, my dear...' She broke off and looked at Lucy in dismay. 'Don't cry.'

'What do you expect me to do?' Lucy sobbed. 'My husband suffers a dreadful accident, he is brought to the infirmary and taken straight to the operating theatre and then whisked away to some ward and I am not allowed to see him. I have been sitting in that draughty hall all night, no one has told me anything and now I must sit in that fierce woman's office while you two prattle on and all I want to do is go to Arthur.'

'You'll see him soon,' the nurse said. 'That's where Matron has gone – to ask the surgeon's permission. The doctors here are like gods on high, you know, and only someone as senior as my aunt is allowed to approach them. But don't worry, even some of the doctors are in awe of her. I'm sure you will be allowed to go to your husband's bedside soon.'

'Will I?' Lucy stopped crying and began to feel in her pockets for her handkerchief. She didn't find one and reached out blindly when Ruth offered hers. Then she began dabbing at her eyes. 'Have you seen Arthur?' she asked at last. 'Can you tell me how he is?'

'I haven't seen him this morning,' Nurse Brown replied, 'but you must believe me, the very fact that he is still alive is a tribute to the surgeon's skill. And Mr Purvis is young and healthy. I'm sure he will pull through.'

'That's not what that odious man said last night,' Lucy muttered.

'Which man?'

'The one who questioned us when we arrived. He took our details, names, addresses, you know.'

'Ah, Mr Hunter. He's not the soul of tact.'

'Absolutely not!' Lucy said.

'But he tries to be kind.'

'Kind? Do you know when I told him that Arthur's employer was the railway company he said that as the accident happened at work I could be sure they would provide a very handsome coffin!'

'Oh dear. But Mr Hunter is not a doctor. He's a clerk, and many widows are worried about the cost of the funeral. He was, as I say, trying to be kind.'

Lucy was lost for words. She simply opened her eyes wide and glared at poor Nurse Brown.

'Mrs Purvis, I saw your husband when he was brought in last night. He was in a bad way. We didn't think he was going to live.'

Lucy started crying again and Ruth hurried to her side.

'But perhaps it looked worse than it really was. I didn't think he would still be with us when I came on duty this morning. But he is. So dry your tears and make yourself presentable. He won't want to see you in that state.'

Ruth thought that the nurse had been rather severe but it had the desired effect on Lucy.

'Is there somewhere I can wash?' she asked quietly.

465

'Of course, dear. You and your friend may use the nurses' bathroom, it's just along the corridor.'

When Ruth and Lucy returned to the office the matron was waiting for them. She was smiling encouragingly but her manner was grave.

'You may see your husband now, Mrs Purvis,' she said. 'I will take you. But you must prepare yourself.'

'Prepare myself?' Lucy's voice shook slightly.

'The surgeon has performed miracles. He has saved Mr Purvis's life, but he could not save his leg.'

'Take me to him.'

Nurse Brown caught Ruth's arm and prevented her from following Lucy. 'Not allowed,' she whispered.

But, in any case, Lucy had made a small gesture with her hands as if pushing Ruth away. Ruth understood that her friend wanted to be alone with her husband.

'You can't wait here,' Nurse Brown told her. 'Matron will be holding the morning meeting soon. You could go to the waiting room, I suppose, although I don't recommend it.'

'Why not?'

'It's already half full of poor people who can't afford to go to a doctor, so they come here for free treatment. They're coughing and sneezing, which is bad enough, but some of them are verminous and some can be quite violent.'

'Where shall I wait, then?'

'I recommend the entrance hall, draughty though it is.'

Soon Ruth was sitting once more on the

uncomfortable bench where she and Lucy had waited all night. Mr Hunter was behind his desk once more, questioning people who came in, filling out forms and directing them either to the waiting room or the examination rooms if they had appointments.

Ruth was desperately tired. She closed her eyes and leaned back against the wall. She realized her head was aching. The sound of many footsteps on the stone-tiled floor seemed to echo round her head. One set of footsteps came hurrying across the floor and then stopped. 'Ruth?' a soft voice said. 'Where's Lucy?'

She opened her eyes to see Mrs Shaw standing before her. Before Ruth had gathered her wits sufficiently to answer, Lucy's mother asked, 'How's Arthur? He's not...?' She broke off and bit her lip.

'Lucy is with Arthur,' Ruth said as she shook her head to clear it, and sat forward. 'He ... he survived the night. But ... but they've had to amputate one leg.'

'Oh, no. Poor Lucy.' Mrs Shaw sat down beside her.

'And poor Arthur,' Ruth said softly.

'Of course. But you can't blame me for thinking of my daughter. She will have to cope with...'

'A cripple?'

'Don't be cruel, Ruth. I know what you're thinking. Of course I feel sorry for Arthur but it's Lucy who will have to bear the burden of a child and a husband who will not be able to work for a living.'

'But she's not poor, is she? I mean her father

467

left her provided for, didn't he?'

'Provided for?' Mrs Shaw sighed. 'I don't know what was left to Lucy. The solicitor dealt with us separately.'

Ruth thought it strange that the mother and daughter had not confided in each other, but ever since Mr Shaw's death in the railway accident the atmosphere between them had been strained. Esther had told her that she thought there was something of a mystery, and Ruth was inclined to agree.

But both of them had come to realize that Lucy could be quite secretive and they'd accepted that they might never know the full story. And now, in the hospital in the early morning, it would certainly be improper to question Mrs Shaw any further.

Ruth changed the subject. 'Did Esther tell you what happened at the station?'

They had decided the night before that Esther and Davy should go home to Mrs Shaw's. Esther had to go to work in the shop the next day and Davy to school. On the way to the station they would take a note to Mrs Fairbridge, telling her what had happened and that Ruth would be staying with Lucy.

'Yes,' Daisy Shaw said. 'Or rather Davy did. He saw it happen, you know. He said Arthur was standing near the edge of the platform when a train drew in. Someone opened a carriage door before the train had stopped properly and it flew back, catching Arthur and knocking him off his feet. He ... he fell between the train and the platform ... he was dragged along. Davy said he heard him screaming ... it must have been terrible.'

'Davy stayed there until they had managed to free Arthur from the wheels of the train,' Ruth told her. 'Once he knew where they were taking him he came back to Lucy's house.'

'And you and Lucy?'

'We caught a cab to the infirmary here.'

'And you've been here with her all night?'

'Yes.'

'What are you doing here?'

Intent on their conversation, neither of them had heard Lucy approach and now they turned to find her staring at them; her eyes huge and haunted in her pale face.

Daisy Shaw moved towards her daughter but stopped when Lucy flinched visibly and drew back. 'Lucy ... I came to see if I could help you.'

'Why?'

'How can you ask that? I love you. I want to be with you now ... now...'

'Now that I'm a widow.'

Only Ruth caught the dangerous gleam in her friend's eyes and she held her breath as Mrs Shaw blanched and whispered, 'Widow...? Arthur has passed away?'

'Is that what you're hoping? That poor unsuitable Arthur has died?'

'Hoping? Unsuitable? Lucy, what are you talking about?'

'You didn't want me to marry him, did you? You wanted someone better than a railway porter for your daughter. Well, at least he married me, didn't he?'

Ruth was aware of an undercurrent of meaning that she couldn't quite grasp, but even so, she knew that her friend was being cruel. Was it cruelty brought on by grief? Had Arthur really died?

'Lucy,' her mother said, 'don't talk like this. Of course I don't wish your husband dead. Please tell me that he isn't.'

Lucy stared at her mother as if searching her face for reassurance and then said quietly, 'He's fine. He's very weak, but with careful nursing he's going to survive.'

'Thank God,' her mother whispered. 'I'm truly happy.'

'Do you mean that?'

'Of course I do. I'm sorry I ever opposed your marriage. He's a good man and you love him. I would never want you to suffer the misery I've been through.' She paused and suddenly sounded weary. 'Oh, I know you've had little sympathy for me—'

'That's not true.'

'Well, that's how it seemed. All you could think about was your own anger at the situation we found ourselves in.'

Again Ruth sensed that something was being hinted at, some problem that she had already guessed existed, but she also knew that what it was would forever remain a secret between mother and daughter.

'Mother—'

'You blamed me,' Mrs Shaw said. 'We should have comforted each other when your father was killed, instead ... instead of drifting apart the way we have.'

There was a silence, during which Ruth could hear footsteps echoing along hospital corridors and the low murmur of voices from a nearby ward. Then Lucy said, 'I know.' She took a step towards her mother. 'And I don't blame you ... I know it wasn't your fault.'

Ruth couldn't fathom the look that passed between them but she knew that something very important – some old ghost – had been laid to rest. Daisy Shaw enfolded her daughter in her arms.

Ruth thought they had forgotten about her and she waited awkwardly, not knowing what to do, but, after a moment, Lucy drew back from her mother and turned and smiled.

'Ruth,' she said, 'I was going to ask you to go to my house and bring my soap bag and some toiletries. I must look like an old witch and I want to freshen myself up for Arthur.'

'No, that's all right,' Lucy's mother said. She drew back a little but kept one arm round her daughter. 'Ruth, thank you for everything you've done but now you must go home and rest. I'll get anything Lucy wants and then I'll come back and stay with her for as long as she needs me.'

Ruth didn't go straight home to the house in Catherine Terrace. Tired as she was there was something she had to do first. The infirmary was not too far from Tynemouth station and she could have got the train but she decided to get a cab back and travel from door to door in relative comfort.

She was weary and she wanted to save all her strength for the confrontation to come. The cab was old and the horse was tired. Ruth imagined she could have walked more quickly, but at least the journey gave her time to prepare herself, although the creaking motion – like a ship at sea, she thought – would have sent her to sleep if she hadn't been so cold.

It had been raining overnight and the sky was overcast. The streetlamps were still lit and, as the cab passed Christchurch, Ruth could see the light reflecting on the glistening tombstones. The sight made her shiver.

Here, not far from the mouth of the River Tyne, a dank mist had crept up through the old cobbled streets, and she could hear the mournful clanging of the bell on the warning buoy anchored above the Black Middens; rocks that had been the cause of many shipwrecks over the centuries. By the time she reached her journey's end a mere twenty-five minutes later, she was utterly depressed and chilled to the bone.

The library was not yet open but Guinevere must have heard the cab stop and looked out of the window of the upstairs flat. By the time Ruth had paid her fare, Guinevere was standing at her front door.

'I heard what happened to your friend's husband,' she said. 'Is he...? Has he...?'

'Arthur has survived but he's lost a leg.'

'Poor man – and your poor friend. Lucy, isn't it?'

'Yes. But how did you hear about it?'

'This is a small town. News of the accident got round. But come in, you look exhausted. Have you been to the infirmary?'

'Yes.'

Ruth knew her manner was cold and she wasn't surprised when Guinevere blinked nervously. 'But don't stand here in the cold and the damp. Are you coming in?'

'No ... er...'

'I can make you a cup of tea ... make you some breakfast.' Guinevere stepped back and turned to go upstairs, giving Ruth no choice. 'Close the door behind you,' she said.

'I'll come upstairs, but just to collect my manuscript. I won't stay. Don't bother to make tea.'

But it was too late. By the time Ruth had ascended the stairs Guinevere was in the small kitchen and Ruth could hear her filling the kettle and striking a match for the gas stove. A moment later she appeared in the neat living room with cups on a tray.

'Sit down,' she said. 'The tea won't be long.'

'No, really, I just want to collect my manuscript and go.'

Guinevere placed the tray on the table, looked down for a moment and then turned to face Ruth. 'You're angry with me.'

'Why did you tell him?'

'Roland found the manuscript when he was packing up his papers.'

Ruth raised her eyebrows sceptically but didn't say anything.

'No ... really. I had been reading it at the table and I left it there when he called me to help him fold his shirts. While I was occupied in his bedroom he came in here and ... and found it.'

473

'And he asked you what "tosh" you were reading now.'

Blotches of ugly colour stained Guinevere's faded cheeks. 'Yes, that's what he said.'

'You needn't have told him.'

'I beg your pardon?'

'You needn't have told him that it was my work. Surely it would have been easy enough to lead him to believe that it was another novel by Miss Golightly.'

'I'm not quick-thinking, nor am I a good liar.'

'Oh, really! It needn't have been an outright lie.'

Guinevere sighed. 'You're right, of course. But the truth is I wanted him to know.'

Ruth stared at Roland's sister. She could hardly believe what she had just heard. 'You *wanted* him to know?'

Miss Matthews nodded unhappily.

'But why? I asked you not to. You know what Roland thinks of books and reading. You must have known that it would cause trouble between us.'

'I did.' Guinevere clasped her hands. 'But I had to tell him. I hope you'll understand.'

Ruth shook her head. 'How can I? I thought we were friends and you've betrayed my confidence.'

'Ruth, the kettle will be boiling – sit down. I'll make the tea.'

Guinevere left her to hurry back into the kitchen and Ruth sat in the armchair by the hearth where a small fire was burning. Roland's chair, she realized suddenly and, leaning back, she began to weep silently.

'Please don't cry.'

Ruth opened her eyes to find Guinevere kneeling beside her. She was holding out a clean white handkerchief and Ruth took it and dabbed at her eyes. While she was doing so Roland's sister drew up a small table and placed a cup of tea on it.

'I've put sugar in,' she said. 'I think you need it.'

Ruth sipped her tea. Guinevere took her place at the other side of the fireplace but left her own tea to grow cold on the table.

'I love my brother very much,' she said at last.

Ruth looked up and studied Guinevere's face, a hurtful suspicion growing inside her. 'You guessed he was going to ask me to marry him?'

'Yes.'

'And you didn't want him to. Is that it?'

Guinevere nodded. Ruth saw that there were tears glistening in her eyes.

'But I thought you were my friend!'

'I am.'

'You haven't acted like a friend! I'm not good enough, is that it? I'm not good enough to marry your precious brother!'

'No, Ruth, no! That's not it at all. I'm fond of you – more than that – you are the closest friend I've ever had. I love you as I would have loved a sister. That's why I couldn't let you marry Roland. Don't you see?'

'No, I don't. I don't see at all. You say you love me and yet you don't want me to be part of your family.'

'You would never have been happy as Roland's wife!'

475

'How can you say that?'

'Oh, I know there is – there was – an attraction between you, a physical attraction, that was obvious from the start, but it was also obvious that you were completely unsuited for one another.'

'In what way?'

'Don't pretend you don't know. You like reading, you have an active mind – you are very intelligent.'

'So is Roland.'

Guinevere tutted in exasperation. 'Yes, he's clever. He will do well in his chosen profession, but his mind is closed to anything other than facts and figures and a healthy profit margin for his company.'

'Selling insurance policies is not a bad thing, surely?'

'I'm not saying it is, and Roland would always do the best for his customers, but there's a world beyond profit and loss – the world of the arts – and Roland would never want to go there.'

Ruth knew that what Guinevere was saying was true. She had lain awake on many a night thinking how different she and Roland were. 'But surely a husband and wife can have different likes and dislikes?' she said.

'You have been fooling yourself if you've imagined it's a matter of likes and dislikes,' Guinevere said. 'Roland would not allow his wife to be different.'

'Allow?'

'Oh, yes. As I said, I love my brother but I know his faults. He's very authoritarian – not to say arrogant. Roland wants a wife who will provide him with a clean, comfortable home, who will cook and clean and see to his creature comforts, just as I have done for all these years, and who will accept that he is the master.'

'Master?'

'He simply could not bear to have a wife who would want to think for herself, who might be just as important, if not more important, than he is and who would not spend every waking moment putting him first. And you could never be such a wife, Ruth, and, what is more, I love you too much to allow you to attempt it.'

'Attempt it?'

'I'm pretty sure Roland will try to persuade you to give up the idea of being a writer.'

'Oh...'

'What is it? Oh, I see, he already has, hasn't he?'

Ruth nodded.

'And what did you say? Oh, Ruth, you haven't agreed, have you?'

'No, I didn't – at least I didn't answer him.' Ruth wondered if Roland had told Guinevere that he had met her yesterday – was it only yesterday? – but if he had, he obviously hadn't told her what they'd said to each other.

'He'll ask you again. Roland likes his own way.'

'No, I don't think he'll ask again.'

'What makes you say that?'

'Because he ... because ... I just don't.'

What could she say? It sounded too far-fetched to tell Guinevere that her brother had fallen in love with someone else. Someone he had only just met. But when Ruth remembered the way Roland and Esther had looked at each other yesterday she was sure that's what had happened. In any case, he had not uttered another word to her.

He had said goodbye and told Esther that he hoped they would meet again and then raised his hat and hurried away down Shields Road. But he had turned round once and waved and smiled – at Esther, not at her.

'Then, if you're sure it's over...'

'It's over.'

'Then I must say, sad though it is, it's just as well. I would not have spoken like this if you had agreed to marry him, but I have watched you change from the wary little creature that first came into the library to a young woman growing in confidence in her own ability. You might have found yourself opposing Roland's wishes, and he can be ... he can be angry when he's thwarted.'

'Don't worry, I am not going to be given the chance to oppose or thwart your brother!'

Only too clearly Ruth remembered Roland's words. He had told her she would not make a suitable wife for him or for any man. And he had lost interest in even trying to persuade her to mend her ways once he had been introduced to Esther. Esther, who, as well as being breathtakingly beautiful, would make a perfect housewife.

'I must go now,' Ruth said, and she rose wearily. 'May I have my manuscript?'

'Of course. I've finished reading it and I've made some notes. I was hoping to discuss them with you.'

'I'll come and ask you if there's anything I don't

478

understand,' Ruth said, but she knew she wouldn't.

'And I've made a list of publishers I think you should submit it to. Ruth, I don't think any of them would reject your novel. It's marvellous.'

'Thank you.'

Ruth should have been elated but she felt strangely distant. Too much had happened too quickly and she just wanted to go home to bed. Home... The house in Catherine Terrace had become her home. She had been happier there than she had expected to be, and now she must find somewhere else to live.

'Goodbye, Ruth, dear,' Miss Matthews said as she came with her down the stairs and showed her to the door. 'I hope we can still be friends?'

It was hardly raining but there was a light drizzle and two women huddled under an umbrella at the library door. Each had a basketful of books to return and they looked cross.

'You're late in opening up, Miss Matthews,' one of them said peevishly.

'I'm so sorry.' Distracted, Guinevere shut the house door behind her and reached in her pocket for the keys to the library.

'And about time too,' the other woman said.

Caught up in a fluster of their grumbles and her own apologies Guinevere Matthews did not notice that Ruth had hurried away without replying.

Esther weighed out half a pound of broken biscuits for the grubby child whose tangled curls she could hardly see above the counter. 'It's for wor tea,' the little girl told her. 'A treat.'

Esther smiled and, when Raymond gave her the nod, she added a handful of Garibaldi's, knowing that the biscuits full of squashed currants were a favourite with most of the children. 'Flies' graveyards', they called them.

Esther had long ago realized that customers like this one seemed to come to the shop in the afternoon when they knew Mr Fowler would be absent. Raymond was in charge when his uncle and aunt went up for their afternoon break and, although he was a keen businessman, he also had a soft heart.

'Now, carry that carefully,' Esther said as she came round the counter to place the bag of biscuits in the child's hands. 'You don't want to crush them.'

'I know,' the child replied and nodded wisely. 'If I do I'll get a clout around me lughole.'

Esther waited until the door had closed before turning to Raymond and shaking her head. 'Poor bairn,' she said.

Raymond smiled. 'Divven't fret. Bairns like that are used to it.'

'Well, they shouldn't have to be. I would never hit a child of mine.'

'I know you wouldn't. Davy is lucky to have you to look after him.'

'Well, he wasn't always lucky. My father thought the best way to discipline a child was to take his belt to him.'

'You did well to get out of that house,' Raymond said. 'And that reminds me, a poor-looking

480

woman came asking for you on Saturday night – you'd already gone home and I was helping me uncle lock up.'

'Did ... did she come into the shop?'

'No. She was hanging around outside. I asked her if she wanted anything and she just shook her head. Me uncle said if she didn't skedaddle he'd call the polis. That seemed to terrify her. She said she just wanted to talk to you. But I don't think me uncle believed her. He told her he didn't want to see her hanging around here again.'

'What did she look like?'

Raymond shrugged. 'Like many another poor wife around here. Thin, hard-bitten; looked old beyond her years.'

Esther felt her heart begin to race; she clutched at the counter. 'Did she say who she was?'

'No, she cleared off pretty quickly once the polis had been mentioned. Are you all right, Esther? You look femmur suddenly.'

'No ... I'm fine. Just tired. I got back late last night from Lucy's and then I had to break the news about Arthur to Mrs Shaw. We didn't have much sleep.'

'I don't suppose you did. And I noticed you barely touched your sandwich at lunch time. Look, go in the back shop and sit down. I'll make you a cup of tea. We'll hear the bell if anyone comes into the shop.'

Esther was pleased to do as she was told. Could the woman who had called at the shop have been her mother? She couldn't think of anyone else who would come looking for her like that.

Raymond could see that she was tired and he

left her with her tea while he started to make up the orders that Davy would take out when he came to the shop after school. This meant going up and down the stairs from the cellar storeroom but, every time the bell above the shop door tinkled he insisted on going through himself.

Then, just as Esther had decided she must get back to work, the shop door opened again and, after a murmur of voices, Raymond came through and said, 'It's someone for you, Esther.'

She stood up too quickly and she felt her head spin but Raymond's next words quelled her hopes. 'It's Mrs Shaw's maid, Betty. She just wants a quick word with you. If you like I'll send her through.'

Esther smiled her thanks and sat down again.

'I'm going to stay at the house – sleep there – with you and Davy until Mrs Shaw gets back,' Betty began as she took her place at the little table.

'Gets back?'

'Oh, aye, I forgot, she didn't decide until after you'd left for work this morning. She's going to stay at Lucy's place for as long as the lass needs her.'

'Did Lucy ask her ... I mean...'

'I know what you mean. And no, she didn't. Lucy didn't even know her mam was going to the infirmary, but Mrs Shaw said that Lucy needed her and she wouldn't take no for an answer. I don't think she'll come back to Byker tonight, do you?'

'No, perhaps not,' Esther said. 'And perhaps those two will be friends again now. I hope so.

But how sad that it's taken such a terrible accident to mend things between them.'

'Aye, it's an ill wind. But, anyways, I'm stopping at the house so's I'll be handy for any washing she brings up or any extra cooking she wants – you know, broths and things for the invalid. I can make them and Mrs Shaw said she hoped you or Davy would take them down to Lucy's house.'

'Of course we will. But Arthur is still in hospital and I don't know when they'll let him go home.'

'But he's not the only one to think of, is he?'

'What you mean?'

'Lucy and the bairn she's expecting. Let's pray to God that this shock doesn't bring something on.'

'Oh, no, I never thought of that.'

'Well, Mrs Shaw did. And I can tell you, Esther, no matter what she thought about this marriage in the first place, she doesn't want to lose her grandchild now.'

The two women looked at each other solemnly for a moment and then Betty rose from the table. 'I'd better gan back,' she said. 'Your Davy will be calling in to leave his schoolbooks and I want to make sure he swallows a bit broth before he comes here to the shop to work.'

'Thank you, Betty, that's good of you. And I'm sure Mrs Shaw will be grateful that you've agreed to stay.'

Betty smiled. 'Not half as grateful as I am. You've no idea how pleased I am to get away from that daughter-in-law of mine for a spell. I divven't know why our Clive married her. He's as soft as clarts but that bad-tempered bitch of a wife of his has got a heart of stone.'

The walls were bare of pictures, the carpets and rugs had been rolled up and there were packing cases in every room and even on the landings. Even since Ruth had left the day before, the work had progressed to such a point that the house no longer looked like a home. One packing case had been set aside for Flora.

Mrs Fairbridge had asked Mr Golightly if, in view of the fact that the chambermaid was to be married soon, she could give her one or two useful household objects such as incomplete sets of napkins, darned tablecloths and bath towels and the odd pot or pan that surely no one would want again. Mr Golightly had agreed and left it to Mrs Fairbridge's discretion.

'I'll put one or two things aside for you too, Ruth,' the kindly housekeeper had said. 'If you're going to take a bedsitting room you'll need some things of your own.'

When Ruth had returned to the house after leaving the Crystal Library Mrs Fairbridge had taken one look at her, sat her down to a substantial breakfast and then sent her up to bed.

But an hour or two later, even though she was physically exhausted, she was still wide awake. Her head was full of scenes that played over and over again in her mind's eye like the stories in a magic lantern show.

She remembered the moment when Esther had told Lucy about Arthur's accident. Her friend's expression had not simply been one of shock and grief. There had been something else there. Ruth could have sworn that it was guilt. But that was crazy. Why should Lucy feel guilty?

And then, while she was sobbing and choking on her grief, Lucy had murmured something about knowing she would have to pay for it. Pay for what? For being so happy? Perhaps, but Ruth thought it was deeper than that.

Next to present itself was a scene from her own drama. The scene she was most reluctant to return to. Meeting Roland on Shields Road yesterday. She had been so pleased to see him – and he had been so cold, so angry. So dismissive of her ambition to be a writer. There had been a moment of hope – the moment when he had taken her hand and asked her if it was not too late.

She had looked at his face then and seen all that had first attracted her to him. His handsome, clean-cut features, his clear blue eyes. But it was the expression in those eyes, of course, that had warned her. There was no pleading there, only an imperious certainty that he was going to get his own way. That was what had made her hesitate. And so she had lost him. But wasn't that just as well?

She ought to have realized from the start that Roland, like the majority of men, preferred housewifely women with pretty faces and empty heads. The sort of woman she could never be. She had allowed the undeniably powerful call of her senses to dull the workings of her mind.

And the final act played out in Guinevere's flat above the library. Ruth wondered now if she had noticed before how severely neat the place was? How Guinevere would start up nervously when she heard Roland open the front door and tidy away anything that was out of place such as a newspaper; or straighten the antimacassars on the backs and arms of the chairs. Was that to please herself or to please Roland? And had Guinevere always been a little too anxious to make sure everything was just as he liked it?

Ruth pushed aside the bedclothes and got up. It was no use, she couldn't sleep. She had taken off her skirt and blouse and lain down in her underclothes. Now she simply pulled on her robe and, arranging the bedside table like a desk, she opened up the manuscript of her detective story. Pushing all other thoughts out of her mind she began to prepare her work for submission to a publisher.

'Go home now, Esther,' Mr Fowler told her. 'I'll be locking up in a minute or two.'

'I thought I would wait for Davy. He's out on his last delivery, he should be back soon.'

'There's no need,' Raymond said. 'I'll walk home with him, if you like, see he doesn't tarry.'

'No, it's not that. Davy's old enough to come home on his own. I just like to keep him company.'

'Have you ever thought he might not like being seen everywhere with his big sister?' Raymond asked her.

'Whyever not?'

Raymond grinned. 'Hawway, man, Esther! Use yer imagination. He's a big lad, now. He doesn't want his pals to think he's a sissy.'

Esther smiled. 'You're right. I sometimes forget. I'll go home. But don't trouble yourself, Raymond; he can come home on his own.'

'I know he can. But he forgot to bring one of my books back; I'll come and get it.'

Esther could have said that surely tomorrow would do for the book, but she didn't want to argue with Raymond; he was kind to Davy and the lad looked up to him. But she knew the real reason why Raymond wanted to walk home with her brother. He had done so before, and he would be hoping to be invited in, perhaps offered a bite to eat, and therefore have an excuse to spend some time with Esther.

So be it, she thought. Davy needs an older lad to look up to. Raymond has been like a big brother and for that I should be grateful. If only I could be sure that Raymond will not take this as an encouragement to get closer to me.

It didn't seem right, somehow, young Raymond making up to her the way he did. It made her uncomfortable when he looked at her with an expression that should only be seen in the eyes of a grown man. The look unsettled her; she was ashamed to admit that she found herself wanting to respond to it. She had to remind herself that, clever as he was, he was only a big bairn ... wasn't he? It wouldn't be right to encourage him.

'Off you go, lass,' Raymond's uncle said. 'You're stopping this big booby from cashing up and I want to get to the night safe and back afore Mrs Fowler has me dinner on the table.'

It was drizzling rather than raining but it was

wet enough to make folk want to get home quickly. People hurried by in both directions but Esther noticed one or two of them glancing suspiciously at the huddled figure of a woman in a shawl. The woman was standing half in and half out of a wide archway that led to the courtyard of an old inn.

As Esther walked up the street she noticed that she would move out and stand with her head slightly cocked as if she were studying the faces of the people passing by her for a moment and then move back again.

Two young women coming towards Esther walked past the beshawled figure and one of them exclaimed, 'Begging in a decent street like this! Shameful!'

'I don't think she was begging, Ivy. She didn't hold her hand out or anything.'

'That's because I glared at her. She didn't dare.'

Esther had turned her head to listen as they passed and, when she looked the way she was going again, she stopped in her tracks, her heart thudding. The woman stood right in front of her.

'Mam,' Esther said. 'At last.'

'Whisht,' her mother said. 'Not so loud.' And she took Esther's arm and drew her into the shadows of the archway.

Esther was shaking and for a moment she couldn't speak. Her mother looked her up and down. 'You look real bonny, lass. And you've done well for yerself – and Davy too, I hear.'

'He isn't dead,' Esther said at last.

'What are you talking about?'

'Me da. You didn't kill him.'

Her mother flinched and turned away. She pulled the shawl more tightly round herself and her head dropped before she murmured, 'I ken that. More's the pity.'

Esther was shocked by the amount of venom in those last words. 'I've been looking for you,' she said, 'ever since you ran off that night. I wanted to tell you that it was all right. That you weren't a murderer.'

'Is that what it was, then?'

'What do you mean?'

'Morder? If I had killed the brute – the man who tried to beat the life out of me – would it have been morder?'

'Well … no. But that's what they would have said, isn't it? If he had died they would have hanged you.'

'Aye, there's no justice. Not for women.'

'But he didn't die that night. You're not a murderer. You could have come back.'

'Are you totally witless, Esther? Come back! Back to him? If the justice didn't hang us, do you think yer da would hev let us live after what I'd done? And who would hev blamed him for settling things with a wife who'd half mordered him?'

They stared at each other in the half-light. Ribbons of mist curled up from the damp cobblestones. There was a burst of conversation as the inn door round the corner opened and then silence when it closed again.

'No,' Esther sighed. 'Even then I knew you could never come back to live with us. But I thought you might have let Davy and me know that you were all right.'

'And risk you letting on to yer da?'

'I would never have done that!'

'Perhaps not.'

'Definitely not. And neither would Davy.'

'I couldn't be sure. You were only bairns. Especially Davy. Who's to say he wouldn't hev let something slip and then it would only hev taken yer da to take his belt to him fer me secret to be out.'

'But you're telling me now?'

'Aye. I had to stop you looking fer me. Esther, hinny, every time yer gans into town and asks questions word gets round. I can't risk anything getting back to yer da. Not now.'

'Why not now?'

'Because I've found a safe haven and I divven't want to move on again.' Her mother shook her head. 'You can hev no idea what me life's been like these past years. What I've been reduced to just to keep meself alive.'

'Tell me.'

'No. That's my story and I'm telling it to no one. Not ever. But things hev changed. I've got a job of sorts, and I'm fed and clothed.' Esther's mother looked down at the skirt and shawl she was wearing and a rare smile crossed her face. 'All second-hand, mind, but clean and mended and lop free.'

'Where are you working?'

Her mother shook her head. 'There's no need fer you to know.'

'No need? Do you not care that I've been worried sick about you all this time?'

'Hev you?' Her mother looked at her wonderingly. 'Poor bairn, I think you hev. But I can't imagine why.'

'You're my mother!'

'But not a very good one.' They stared at each other and, try as she might, Esther could not deny the truth of her mother's words. Eventually Agnes Robinson said, 'Esther, pet, you're a better person than I am. Davy was lucky to hev you.'

'Tell me, what would you have done if Davy hadn't had me? Would you just have abandoned him? Left him with my father?'

Her mother stared at her bleakly. 'What else could I hev done?'

'I'm not going to see you again, am I?' Esther asked.

'No.'

'Can I at least tell Davy that you're alive and well?'

Her mother frowned. 'I'll hev to trust you on that one. When he's grown perhaps. You be the judge. But tell him that I'm working a long way away from here.'

'And is that true?'

'It's far enough.'

'And what exactly do you do?'

'Work in a big kitchen.' She laughed softly and shook her head as if she couldn't believe in the turn of events. 'I was never much of a cook, was I? And now I'm scrubbing tatties and chopping carrots and onions and all kinds of vegetables for the broth.'

'You work in a soup kitchen?'

'No, but it was in a place like that that the

woman rescued me. Esther, hinny, I'm not going to tell you much more – but the good wife who saved me runs a home for badly treated bairns. She takes them off the streets and feeds them and clothes them and schools them so that when they're grown they'll find good jobs. And all the people who work for her have been taken off the streets too.

'And now I've got to gan back. She gave us a couple of days off to find yer and tell yer not to come looking fer us no more. She likes us to cut the ties with wor past lives. Think on what it would be like if yer da turned up on the doorstep and created morder!'

Agnes Robinson started to draw away and Esther made no move to stop her. She leaned back against the damp bricks of the wall of the inn and closed her eyes briefly. When she opened them her mother had gone. Esther stepped out of the archway on to the pavement and looked up and down the street. The thin figure of the woman in the shawl hurried away through the swirling mist.

She hadn't said goodbye. Esther's cheeks were damp but it was with raindrops, not with tears. She found herself totally dry-eyed as she watched the woman who had so cruelly neglected her own bairns hurry back to her job of helping to care for other children.

And not once while they had been speaking had Agnes Robinson made a move towards her daughter. She had not taken her in her arms, nor kissed her on the cheek. She had not even taken her hand and wished her well for the future. Well, that's over then, Esther thought. I need never search the streets again for her – nor even think of her. Why should I? I doubt if she ever thinks of Davy and me.

And yet, although she tried to harden her heart towards the woman who had failed in every way as a mother, she could not forget how badly Agnes Robinson had been treated as a wife. Who knows what our lives would have been like if my father had been a decent sort of man, Esther thought. And I thank God I have a better life now for if I do not have good parents, I know how blessed I am to have good friends.

It was Davy's last delivery and he was cycling along a neat row of terraced flats near Heaton station. He'd worn his waterproof cape to please Esther and this made pedalling awkward. Furthermore, the sou'wester might be keeping his hair dry but it impeded his vision and he had to keep his head up at an uncomfortable angle and peer through the raindrops that dripped off the brim.

He was tired. They'd been late home last night from Lucy's place and then they'd sat up for hours and talked to Mrs Shaw about the accident and what they were going to do to help Lucy. When he'd got to bed he hadn't been able to sleep properly. He kept thinking about poor old Arthur and how friendly he was, and how proud he was to be head porter – assistant station-master, really – and soon to be promoted officially, he'd told Davy.

And he wasn't going to stop there. Oh, no, he

fully intended to be stationmaster one day, and when he was he'd be provided with a nice little house.

'But you've already got a house,' Davy had said.

'That's Lucy's. Her and me hev talked about it. When I'm stationmaster, Lucy will find tenants for the house. She'll be able to save the rent she collects and it will be a nice little investment for us. A nest egg for our old age.'

Now all those hopes and dreams had come to nothing. Arthur's career with the railway company was over and, from what Davy had heard when listening to the other porters talking after the accident, the future was bleak. If Arthur died, the widow would get a nice coffin; if he survived, the company was supposed to pay some sort of compensation, but they'd try to get out of it by arguing that it was Arthur's own fault. That's what the other lads had said while Arthur was lifted on a stretcher into a rubber-tyred one-horse cart they called an ambulance.

Davy had watched the ambulance set off for the infirmary and then he'd run back to Lucy's house to break the news. She'd taken it very bad, very bad indeed. 'Arthur, oh no, not Arthur,' she'd kept saying. And then something puzzling. 'What have I done to him?'

Well, Davy couldn't see that Lucy had done anything wrong. She hadn't been the cause of the accident. She hadn't even been there. But Esther had told him that grief did funny things to people. That must be it. The poor woman had been crazed with grief. It was a good job Esther and Lucy had been there. They were her best

494

friends – and they'd certainly been needed last night.

Lost in gloomy thoughts, Davy hadn't been concentrating and when a horse and cart clattered by sending up sprays of dirty water, he got drenched. Some of it landed on his face and in his eyes. He blinked, lost control momentarily and swerved towards the kerb, bumping into a chap who had just stepped into the road.

'For goodness' sake, lad!' the chap shouted, and began to brush down his smart coat as if Davy had soiled it. Which he hadn't.

'I'm sorry, sir,' Davy said, and seeing that no harm was done, he was about to ride off.

'Wait a moment. Don't you know you shouldn't ride dangerously like that? Who do you work for?'

'I wasn't riding dangerously. That horse and cart – that was dangerous – going at such a clip with the roads wet. It took me by surprise,' Davy said.

But the chap wasn't listening. He was peering at the metal plate just below the crossbar. 'Fowler's,' he said. 'You work at Fowler's. Your employer ought to be told ... wait a minute ... let me look at you.'

Puzzled, Davy stood astride the bike and held on to the handlebars with one hand, as he pushed back the brim of his sou'wester with the other. He looked into the man's face and saw recognition leap in his eyes just as he also recognized his tormentor.

It was the man who had upset Ruth yesterday. Ruth had sworn everything was fine, but she'd been very quiet on the train on the way down to the coast. And Esther, who should have been concerned about her friend, hadn't even seemed to notice. His sister had been in a strange dreamy sort of mood; staring out of the window without really seeing anything. Lasses, Davy had thought, he'd never understand them.

'You're Ruth's friend's brother, aren't you? Davy, isn't it?' the chap said.

'Yes.'

'And do you live near here?'

'Not far.'

'With your parents?'

'No, with me sister. She ... she looks after me.'

Davy saw the man – Roland Matthews, Ruth had called him – frown slightly, but then he asked, 'And you work at Fowler's?'

'After school and at weekends.'

'You're a little lad to work so many hours,' Roland Matthews said with an air of false jollity. Davy knew it was false because the man's smile didn't reach his eyes.

'I'm older than I look and, besides, Esther looks out for me.'

'Does your sister work there too?'

'Yes. And she's very well thought of.'

'I'm sure she is. And do you know what I've decided?'

'No.'

'I've decided I'm not going to complain to your employer about your carelessness. It would only upset your sister and we don't want to do that, do we?'

Davy shook his head.

'Now here's a penny and off you go.'

'What's the penny for?'

'Don't your customers give you a penny or two sometimes when you bring the groceries?'

'Yes, but I haven't brought you any groceries.'

'Not yet, I know. But you're going to. I've heard that Fowler's is an excellent provision store so I've decided to give them my weekly order.'

'Do you want me to call and collect the list? If you give me your address I could call after I've delivered these.'

'No, it's late and I've kept you long enough. Your sister will be getting worried about you. I shall bring the list to the shop myself, in the morning before I go to the office.'

Well, at least he's not going to complain about me, Davy thought as he got on his way. But although he should have been relieved he remained uneasy. Because his instinct told him Roland Matthews wasn't going to the shop to order his groceries. That was only an excuse. He was going there to see Esther. And Davy didn't like that at all.

Chapter Sixteen

January 1895

'I still can't believe you're a married woman, Esther. It all seems to have happened so quickly. I mean, we had no idea that you were walking out with anyone, let alone courting seriously.'

Esther smiled. 'Listen who's talking! Your wedding was just as much a surprise, wasn't it?'

Lucy sighed and settled her bulk as comfortably as she could in the armchair near the range. 'You're right. It's the pot calling the kettle black, isn't it? And are you happy?'

'Happy?'

'What a silly question. Of course you are happy. You have a clever, handsome husband and a perfect little home. And, I must say, Esther, you keep it spick and span. I've never seen anywhere so sparklingly clean and tidy. And the smells of baking coming from the back kitchen are just delicious. In fact, all this makes me very reluctant to go back to the madhouse!'

'Madhouse? Aren't you pleased to have Arthur home with you after all those weeks in the convalescent home?'

'Of course I am. Pleased and delighted. It's just that everyone else is pleased and delighted too, and they come to see him all the time. We've put a bed up in the front parlour but he won't stay in it. He doesn't want his visitors to see him as an invalid.'

'I can understand that.'

'And I never knew he was so popular at work. It seems everybody has been to visit: the lamp boy, the porters, the ticket clerks, the old woman who cleans the waiting rooms and even the stationmaster.

'Honestly, Esther, you should have seen Arthur the day the stationmaster came to call. You would have thought we were entertaining royalty!'

'And how is Arthur?' Before Esther sat down she kneeled to put more coals on the fire and then sweep an already spotless hearth.

'Arthur is fine. I'm the one that's suffering.' Lucy realized she'd sounded peevish when Esther looked up questioningly. 'Oh dear, I didn't mean to sound so cross,' Lucy said. And then: 'Oh, for goodness' sake, stop fiddling with that brush. The hearth is clean enough to eat your dinner off!'

Esther's eyes widened. She stood up, brushed down her dress and sat opposite Lucy. She looked hurt.

Lucy sighed. 'I'm sorry, I'm sorry, I'm sorry. It's just the way I am. I hate being as big as this – so clumsy. Arthur says I am as beautiful as ever but he's just being kind.'

'No, Lucy. You don't have to apologize. We're friends. I saw how my mother suffered through so many pregnancies; I know it isn't easy. But you are young and strong and healthy and, furthermore, Arthur is right. You are beautiful. Never more so. But...'

'But what?'

'Perhaps you're overdoing things and that's what's making you irritable.'

'Oh, no, I'm lucky. I have Meg, remember, my little maid-of-all-work, and, as well as that, everyone wants to help. My mother just about lives at our house – although of late I've suspected an added attraction is our neighbour, Mr Lockwood.'

'The theatre manager?'

'The very man. He's given her complimentary theatre tickets once or twice and they've even been out for a little supper *à deux* after the show.

'And then there's Betty – now that you and Davy have left my mother's house, Betty has no one to cook for most of the time and she's forever turning up with bags of vegetables and pounds of meat and making nourishing broths and stews in my kitchen.'

'But that's wonderful.'

'Yes, it is. And I'm grateful. But for two things...'

'Tell me.'

'Strange as it may seem I would like to have more time alone with my husband.'

'Of course you would. And the other thing?'

'Well ... I'm not sure how to put this...' Lucy paused. Then she could not quite meet Esther's eye as she continued, 'Remember Mrs Rodgers?'

'The captain's wife?'

'Yes, my other neighbour. Well, she said ... she said that I should take care in case all the extra work and worry brings something on ... you know...'

'No – oh, of course I do. Mrs Rodgers thinks the baby might come before its time.'

'Mm. Do you think that's possible, Esther?'

'I suppose it is. And you must try to rest whenever you can. Tell your mother that you're worried. I'm sure she'll do her very best to look after you.'

'Right. I will.'

Lucy was pleased. Esther had said exactly what she'd wanted to hear. And so had Mrs Rodgers – for, if the truth were known, her kindly neighbour had had to be prompted to say what she had. Lucy had been visiting one day when she'd suddenly clutched at her throat, pretended to feel faint, then clutched her 'bump' and said she had a pain.

She had no idea whether any of this meant anything medically, but she decided that she must take after her mother as far as acting ability was concerned, because her poor neighbour made her promise to look after herself better or the little one might come into the world too soon.

Lucy, of course, was preparing the way for everyone to think this had happened. When her baby was born, which if her chaotic calculations were anywhere near correct, might be quite soon, they would have to believe it was premature. Especially Arthur. He would be the one who would need convincing, otherwise he would discover that he had been tricked into marrying her. And she wouldn't be able to bear it if that happened.

Not because she feared Arthur would leave her. He was hardly in a position to do that. But because she didn't want him to think badly of her and, more than that, they had been told that there might not be any more children. This baby would be their only child. And because she had grown to love Arthur so very much, Lucy wanted him to believe that the child was his. That much she could give him.

'You haven't told me how Arthur is managing,' Esther said.

Lucy smiled. 'He's managing very well. I bought him a Bath chair, but he prefers to get around with his crutches. He's very determined, you know – and he gets so bored doing nothing. I decided to get him out into the garden so that he can get on with the work he planned. Even though it's winter there are things to do, apparently.'

'But how can Arthur manage to work in the garden?'

'I pay a lad to come and help him. Arthur gives him instructions. And I've had a greenhouse built. He sits in there for hours doing whatever you have to do to make seeds grow into flowers! Apparently there was a man who taught such things in the gardens of the convalescent home. Some of the men who live nearby have started coming and asking Arthur's advice. It's a regular little gentlemen's club that meets in his garden shed.'

'That's wonderful.'

'Yes, it is, isn't it?'

'Roland and I just had a small wedding, you know,' Esther said.

Lucy was startled by the abrupt change of

subject but, when she glanced at her friend more keenly, she realized that she must have been worrying over the matter ever since she had arrived. Was that why she had been so distant? Had she imagined that Lucy had come to berate her for having been kept in the dark about Esther and Roland's courtship and about their wedding?

'Well, Arthur and I hardly had a grand affair.'

'But you did at least invite your friends. And you had such a nice wedding breakfast at your mother's house.'

'Yes, we did, didn't we? I was surprised.'

'Surprised? Why?'

'My dear mama was so disgruntled by my choice of husband that I thought she would want nothing to do with it.'

'That's not fair. She loves you. And if you had given her longer to get used to the idea, time to know Arthur better, it would have been a much happier occasion.'

For once Lucy was stumped for words. She wanted to say that Esther must know very well why she and Arthur had to get married in such a hurry and yet she couldn't risk Arthur ever finding out that her friends and family believed her to have been already pregnant. Oh, what a muddle, she thought.

My mother and my friends believe that I was already pregnant when I got married – as I was – but that the father of the baby is Arthur. Which he isn't. I'm always going to have to watch my words, always be on my guard. Still, that's a small price to pay, I suppose…

She sighed. 'You're right, of course. And my

503

mother did lay on a grand little feast – even if, as I suspect, it was to overawe poor Arthur and impress on him that he was marrying above his station!'

'But they get on well now, don't they?'

'Indeed they do. My mother is impressed by Arthur's courage and she can't help but notice how well he gets on with people, no matter what their station in life.'

'They're very alike in that, aren't they? Arthur and your mother?'

'Mother and Arthur alike! What do you mean by that?'

'Because they have the ability to talk to people they like no matter what their position in life. And people like them.'

'That's true.'

'Your mother is such a lady and yet she treats Betty more like a friend than a servant and just look at the way she took me under her wing. And how kind she has been to Davy.'

'Yes. I believe she truly loves you. And that makes it all the more strange that you didn't invite her to your wedding. Or us,' Lucy added. 'I mean Ruth and me. We're supposed to be your friends, aren't we?'

'Well, you see ... oh,' Esther glanced up at the clock on the mantelpiece. 'Wait a moment, I have to get the cake out of the oven.'

'Very well. But I would like an answer to my question.'

Lucy watched as Esther, apparently unflustered, rose and, taking up a cloth, opened the door of the range oven and took out her baking. She hurried through to the small scullery, leaving the door open. Lucy saw her tap the tin before easing the cake out on to a wire stand resting on the wooden bench near the stone sink.

'Would you like one of these currant scones I made earlier?' she called. 'They're just about cool enough.'

Lucy would have loved a scone. She could imagine it dripping with butter and covered with jam, but she willed herself to refuse. 'No, thank you. In spite of what Betty tells me, I have no intention of eating for two. The midwife says that's just an old wives' tale and, if I were to take any notice of it, I should end up looking like a beached whale.'

'A cup of tea, then?'

'Mm. I could manage a cup of tea.'

Neither of them spoke while Esther made the tea and Lucy thought she would have to remind her friend that she still hadn't answered her question. But when she had settled by the fire again she said, 'Roland wanted a quiet wedding. No fuss.'

'Why?'

'Well, he has no family except his sister and I have no one ... I mean, no family, that I would want to come to my wedding. Except Davy, of course.'

'Do we not count as your family? My mother and Ruth and I?'

'Yes, you do, but it wouldn't have been fair to Roland, would it? I mean, when all he has is Guinevere.'

'I really don't see why not, Esther. But fancy

getting married with only a couple of witnesses present. Who were they, by the way? His sister and your brother, I suppose.'

'Guinevere, yes, but Davy is too young, of course. Roland asked a colleague from his office.'

'Someone you don't even know! And I imagine you didn't even have flowers to cheer the occasion, did you?'

'Yes, I did. Guinevere gave me a posy of silk flowers to carry – look, there it is in that vase on the sideboard. Roses and lilies of the valley.'

Lucy glanced at the flowers. 'Um, it's very nice. What's she like, by the way, Roland's sister?'

'I like her very much – and I feel so sorry for her.'

'Sorry for her? Why?'

'Well, she brought Roland up, just about. Their mother died when he was still quite small. She's always doted on him – and now she misses him dreadfully.'

'But don't you go to see her? Doesn't she come here to visit?'

'Roland doesn't encourage it.'

'Whyever not?'

'He said it's for my sake. That she might interfere and tell me how to run the house.'

'You sound as though you don't believe that.'

'Oh, I do. I mean, I believe Roland has the best intentions ... but I don't believe that Guinevere would interfere. She's too nice.'

'Poor old Guinevere. She must be lonely. Especially now that Ruth seems to have fallen out with her.'

'Has she? Why?'

'I have no idea. But they became friends when Ruth started visiting the library for her employer. Apparently she doesn't go there any more. She told Arthur that she has become a member of a subscription library in Newcastle. The Literary and Philosophical Society! Doesn't that sound grand? And just like Ruth!'

'She told Arthur, did you say?'

'Oh, don't be surprised at that. Ruth seems to like talking to my husband – as does everybody else.' Lucy smiled. 'I'm grateful for it, really. He's so interested in everything that's going on, it would be dreadful if our friends ignored him or thought less of him because he's ... well, because he's crippled, wouldn't it?'

Esther didn't answer and when Lucy looked at her she found her staring into the fire pensively. 'I haven't seen Ruth for ages, you know.'

'Well, you haven't seen much of me either, have you?'

'Not since I've been married just before Christmas, no. But even before that Ruth seemed to be avoiding me.'

'Are you sure?'

'Mm. I know I was working but she used to call into Mrs Shaw's sometimes or pop into Fowler's but she stopped doing that, oh ... I'm not sure exactly when. I think it was not long after Arthur's accident.'

'Ruth moved just about then – to her little room overlooking the sea,' Lucy said.

'Have you been there?'

'Once. She invited me along to inspect the place and we toasted teacakes by the fire and she

507

warmed some milk for cocoa on a tiny gas ring on the landing. We sat in the bay window – she's at the top of an old house – and looked out over the sea. It was a blustery day and the wind was troubling the sea – those were Ruth's words, by the way. I told her she was like a princess in a fairy tale – you know, all alone in her little room in a tower being buffeted by the elements. Ruth told me she loves it there.'

'She hasn't invited me to visit.' Esther looked troubled.

'Hasn't she? Well, perhaps she thinks you've been too busy setting up home.'

'Perhaps.'

'Look, Esther. I'm sure there's a reasonable explanation. I only went the once, you know. I told her that although I'd enjoyed myself, I couldn't face the climb to the top floor again – not until after the baby is born. And she said that was all right because she's very busy.'

'I see ... no, I don't. What exactly is she doing?'

'Some sort of paperwork for the Golightly family. She changed the subject when I asked about it so I suppose it's confidential. I'm used to that sort of thing from my days working at the solicitor's office, you know.' Lucy sighed. 'Strange, isn't it? We are supposed to want nothing more in life than to find a husband, have children and look after the home, and yet I sometimes yearn for the days when I was an independent young working woman with no one to think of but myself.'

'You regret marrying Arthur?'

'No, of course not. I should never want to be an

508

old maid – which Ruth seems set to be. But what about you? Silly question! Why on earth would you miss working in Fowler's when you have Roland and this cosy little home!'

Lucy smiled at Esther but got no smile in return.

'Well now, I must be leaving,' Lucy said as she heaved herself to her feet. 'I can see you looking at the clock.'

'No, really, I ... er...' Esther flushed.

'Don't deny it. You're thinking I've stayed long enough and it's time you got your husband's evening meal ready, aren't you?'

'Well...'

'And Davy, too. Is he still working at the shop after school?'

'Yes, he is.'

Lucy noticed how distracted Esther had become and she kept up her inconsequential chatter while she put on her coat and hat and made her way clumsily down the stairs to the front door. In fact the door that opened into the back lane would have been handier for the station, but the steep stone stairs that led down from the scullery into the back yard were not only chipped in places but they were covered in frost. Esther did not advise her to go that way in her condition.

The train journey home took about half an hour. The carriage was warm and, thankfully, Lucy had it to herself. The previous two trains would have been full of school children; the trains that came later full of men and women who worked in Newcastle and lived at the coast.

Lucy had time to think about her visit to

Esther. It hadn't been planned. But Arthur had been persuaded to go to bed and rest after lunch, and her mother was instructing an enchanted Meg how to set up the table properly for a dinner party. Lucy had decided to leave them happily occupied and get out for a while.

Esther had been surprised to see her, Lucy thought. No, not merely surprised. She had been disconcerted. For a moment, on the doorstep, Lucy had imagined that she was not even going to invite her in. But Esther had soon recovered and, indeed, she had seemed pleased to see her.

It was as if she had been sitting worrying about something, Lucy thought. And, heaven knew, she knew what it was like to have private worries. And, after the first few moments, Esther had relaxed and they had chatted just like in the old days. Or had they?

Lucy had sensed a certain reserve. Perhaps she was embarrassed, Lucy thought. And so she should be. After all, since meeting Roland it was almost as if she had forgotten her old friends entirely. Was she so happy in her new life that she didn't need her friends any more?

Happy... Lucy suddenly remembered that Esther hadn't answered when she'd asked her if she was happy. But then she hadn't given her the chance...

Well, happy or not, she certainly hadn't invited Lucy to come and visit her again – nor had she said she'd call and see how Arthur was. Well, I don't know what to make of it, Lucy thought. I must ask Ruth what she thinks. Although she hardly seems to want to mention Esther's name these days.

And Ruth is up to something although I don't know what it is. She spends hours in that room of hers all on her own. She doesn't seem to need anyone. Is our friendship over, I wonder? After all these years are the three of us drifting apart?

Perhaps it's inevitable now that two of us are married. Lucy smiled sadly and leaned back and closed her eyes. So be it, she thought. I have Arthur and my mother and soon I'll have my baby ... that's all I need...

'I'm sorry you'll be leaving us, Davy,' Raymond said. 'I know me uncle had planned to take you on full time when you leave school.'

The lad didn't look up. Esther's brother was squatting beside the delivery bicycle in the back yard of the shop, cleaning the wheels with a piece of oiled rag. Raymond stood in the open doorway and watched. The only light was that spilling out from the barred window of the back shop and Davy's face was in shadow as he concentrated on polishing each spoke.

He'd taken off his jacket and rolled up his shirtsleeves. Raymond could see streaks of oil on the lad's forearms. He'd remind him to have a good wash before he went home.

'That's kind of Mr Fowler,' Davy said without turning to look at Raymond. 'But I had other plans anyway.'

'Aye, I know. To work for the newspaper. And what's become of that dream?'

Davy shook his head. He picked up the oilcan and oiled the chain slowly and carefully. Raymond noticed that he had spread old newspapers out on the yard before starting.

'I still intend to be a reporter,' Davy said. 'But I'll go along with Mr Matthews' arrangement for the moment. It'll be easier for Esther if I do.'

'And what exactly is that arrangement?'

'Mr Matthews knows of a position going in a big house in the country. They're looking for a hall boy.'

'You're going into domestic service?'

'Aye. Looks like it. It's not much money but it's all found and, as it's a proper job I'll be allowed to leave school.'

'He's got it all planned.'

'He says it'll be easier for Esther. She won't hev to spend her time washing and cooking for me any longer.'

'And he'll hev her all to hisself,' Raymond said.

Davy stood up, took a clean rag from his pocket, and wiped his hands. 'I'll clear up now and then I'd better gan yem. He doesn't like it if I keep him waiting when his meal's on the table.'

Davy locked the bike in the outhouse, tidied the yard, and reached for his jacket, which was hanging over the latch on the coalhouse door.

'You'd better come in and hev a wash,' Raymond said. 'Divven't give him anything to find fault with.'

Esther's brother glanced at him and then his eyes swivelled away. He'd never actually complained about his sister's husband but there'd been plenty of hints – if you were sharp enough to pick them up, that was. Also, Raymond had seen the lad's character change. Once bright and cheerful, Davy now went about his duties as efficiently as ever but he hardly spoke beyond asking for the grocery lists and acknowledging instructions.

Mebbes he just didn't like the man that his sister had married. Could be that he was jealous. That would be understandable, considering he'd had Esther to himself all these years. But Raymond had thought it was more than that. He'd taken against Roland Matthews himself the minute he'd set eyes on him when he'd come into the shop for the first time a few months ago.

Raymond had tried to be fair – and failed miserably. He was honest enough to admit that he'd never felt so jealous as when he'd seen Esther's beautiful eyes light up at the sight of the man. Roland Matthews had swept the lass off her feet. Right from the start he'd never left her alone. And he'd done all the things that lasses seemed to appreciate. Flowers and chocolates and little notes sent by some messenger when he was going to be working late and couldn't call to see her that night.

Raymond had seen one of the notes once. Esther thought she'd slipped it into her pinafore pocket but it had fallen on to the floor behind the counter and, when she wasn't looking, Raymond had picked it up and put it in his own pocket.

Later that night he'd read it and burned with jealous rage.

My dearest Esther, *the letter said*
I can't tell you how much I am looking forward to marrying you and taking you away from that

513

shop. How wonderful it will be to come home from work each evening and find my wife waiting for me. Not much longer, my dear, and thank you for going along with my instructions to keep all arrangements to ourselves and my wish to have a small wedding. You and I need nobody but each other.

Yours with love,
Roland

So even then he must have been thinking of getting rid of Davy, somehow, Raymond thought. I'm just amazed that Esther has agreed to this plan.

Raymond stood aside so that Davy could enter the little room at the back of the shop and wash himself. Still remembering the letter, Raymond said, 'What does your sister think of this job he's found for you?'

'She's happy, if I'm happy.'

'And are you happy?'

'That's what I've telt her.'

'Why, Davy, man? I divven't believe you want to gan and live in the country!'

'I do. Get away from town – the stink – the noise.'

'Hawway, man! What are yer on about? I know fine well yer love the town as much as I do!'

All this time Davy had been standing with his back to Raymond as he rested his hands on the rim of the stone sink. 'Mebbes,' he said quietly. 'But divven't you gan saying owt to Esther. It's best for her if they can be alone together.'

Bitterness lodged like a stone in Raymond's

514

gut. He didn't say anything for the moment but lifted the kettle from the hob on the small range and took it over to the sink. Davy had already half filled the enamel bowl with cold water and now Raymond carefully added hot water from the kettle. The steam swirled between them, obscuring Raymond's vision. Just before he turned away he saw Davy pick up the bar of soap and plunge his hands into the bowl.

'Like lovebirds are they, then?' he said at last.

'Aye, that's right.'

'But I still can't believe Esther would want rid of her brother like this.'

'I've telt yer. It's fer the best.'

Something about Davy's voice – a suppressed hint of desperation – made Raymond look at him keenly. The lad's head was down as he washed his hands, turning the soap over and over in the water. Raymond walked nearer and looked more closely.

'What about yer arms?' he asked. 'Aren't yer going to wash them?'

The lad's reaction was startling. He dropped the soap quickly and reached for the towel that was on the bench. Raymond was just as quick. One arm shot out and he grabbed one of Davy's arms, pulling it towards him. As the steam cleared he stared down at the marks on Davy's forearm.

'It's not muck,' he said. 'Here, give us yer other arm. These are bruises, aren't they? How did yer get them? Or do I need to ask?'

Davy shook his head.

'Does Esther know?'

'Of course not. It's just me – I anger him. He's guessed I divven't like him, I suppose.'

Davy dried his hands on the towel, pulled down his shirtsleeves and put on his jacket. Raymond didn't know what to say. He could have told the lad it was probably jealousy, that he'd had his big sister to himself for so long that he couldn't stand another man being important to her. That would be natural. But he knew it was more than that. There was something about Roland Matthews that made his nerves jangle.

'Listen, Davy ... I divven't know how to put this ... he doesn't ... I mean he wouldn't harm Esther, would he?'

'No. He treats her like china. And she can hev anything she wants as long as she pleases him.'

'Pleases him?' Raymond's voice faltered at the images that leaped into his mind. He suppressed them; he knew that Davy was too young to know what his words could have meant.

'You know ... keeps the house nice – and she's good at that. Has his meals ready – she's in her element in the kitchen – and doesn't want to talk about anything but him and her and their life together.'

Raymond sensed the misery behind Davy's words and he could have wept for the lad.

'So she's happy?' he said.

'Oh, aye. And that's why it's best if I skedaddle. Leave them in peace. It was easy enough to convince her that I would be happy living in the country – especially after Roland went on about how small I was for my age and how I would thrive in good, clean country air. He's got her

516

worried that I might get consumption if I stay here.

'But, divven't worry.' Davy suddenly grinned. 'As soon as I'm old enough and hev a bit saved, I'll do what I like. And now I'd better gan yem. Our Esther'll hev the dinner ready.'

Lucy was tired but she didn't go straight home. She'd upset herself thinking about the three of them growing apart and she wanted – no, needed – to go to see Ruth and talk about it.

She realized that once they married they would grow apart a little. They had always been different from each other. They came from different backgrounds and had different interests. And yet, the one thing they had in common was that they'd never really been part of any other group of girls, either at school or in the workplace once they'd left schooldays behind.

And now Esther is so taken up with Roland that she hardly has time for us, and Ruth never talks about what she's doing any more. I love Arthur – although at first I thought my feelings were just gratitude and relief. But now I know that I truly love him. When it seemed he might die I thought my heart would break.

But no matter how much he means to me, my friends are still important. And so they should be. I can only hope that, once the newness of her situation has worn off, Esther will come back to us. And as for Ruth ... it's time I found out what it is that is keeping her so occupied.

The wind was cold and the tall houses on the promontory rose like cliffs against the darkening sky. Lights shone in some of the windows and smoke rose from the chimneys. It was time to close the curtains and shut out the world and sit with your family by the fire. Lucy half-wished she hadn't decided to come here. She glanced up to Ruth's window at the top of the house. It was dark; completely dark, with not even the glow from a fire reflecting on the panes.

Frost sparkled on the path leading to the front door and Lucy trod carefully. She rang the doorbell and it seemed to take ages before she heard footsteps echoing in the passage. The door was answered by Mrs Elliot, Ruth's landlady. She recognized Lucy and frowned.

'Didn't Miss Lorrimer tell you?' she asked. 'She's gone away for a few days.'

'Away?'

'Aye. She's gone to London.'

'London! But why?'

'I couldn't say, I'm sure. And if she'd wanted you to know, she would have told you. Now if you don't mind, madam, I'd like to get back to my fireside.'

Without even waiting for Lucy to step back off the doorstep Mrs Elliot closed the door.

Lucy was both angry and mystified. Angry that Ruth, by not confiding in her, had exposed her to this snub, and puzzled that she should have taken such a trip. London! The rising wind buffeted her as she walked northwards along the promenade, and it was so sharp that it seemed to cut through her clothes. Suddenly, from nowhere it seemed, a gentleman's hat came bowling along towards her; a bowler hat, she observed, and laughed.

The wind snatched her laughter away and the hat suddenly veered towards her, causing her to stumble. But she righted herself quickly and made a grab for the hat.

'Well done!' A man's voice called and, a moment later, he was standing beside her. 'Thank you,' he said as she handed him his hat. 'Wild, isn't it? Just look at those breakers!'

Together they paused and held on to the iron railings as they looked out to sea. 'Heaven help the sailors on a night like this! That's what they say, isn't it?' the young man said. 'Well, thanks again. Best be on my way.'

He hurried away along the promenade leaving Lucy wondering at the whole episode. That would have amused Ruth, she thought. And then stopped smiling when she remembered that she was vexed with her old friend.

She turned to go and a dull pain tugged at her insides. Oh no, I've wrenched something dodging after that wretched hat, she thought. She clung on to the railings, wondering how she was going to go on, but soon, the pain went away.

By the time she arrived home she was breathless with walking into the wind and she was grateful that the scene there was relatively peaceful.

'Yer ma's gone out,' Meg said. 'To the theatre in Shields again. And, ee, Mr Purvis hasn't half missed yer.'

Lucy gave the little maid her outdoor clothes to put away, before going into the cosy living room at the back of the house. Arthur was sitting reading the newspaper by the fire, his crutches propped up against the wall, but within easy reach. He looked up and smiled.

'I thought you'd run away and left us,' he said.

'As if I would.' She went over to him and stooped to kiss his brow. The pain tugged at her insides again and made her gasp.

'What is it?' Arthur asked.

'Nothing. Well, I nearly fell down on the way home. I think I've torn a muscle because it's been nagging on and off ever since.'

'Do you need the doctor?'

'No, I don't think so.'

'But what exactly happened?'

'I'll tell you about it in a moment, but first I'm going to ask Meg to bring me something to eat. I'm starving!'

While she waited for Meg to warm up some chicken broth she entertained Arthur with the tale of the bowler hat. They both wondered about the cheerful young man and where he could be going. And they laughed when Lucy stood and mimed how she'd hung on to the railings to save herself being blown away just like the hat. Then Lucy suddenly felt a sort of tear somewhere inside her and a hot gush of water.

'Oh!' she gasped.

'What is it?' Arthur was up and reaching for his crutches. 'Is it ... is it the baby?'

'Yes, Arthur, I think it is.'

'But it's too soon, isn't it?' His face was creased with worry. 'You've been doing too much – and the fall tonight... Can the bairn survive if it comes now? God in heaven, Lucy, what are we going to do?'

'We're going to send Meg next door for Mrs Rodgers,' she said, 'and then tell her to run for the midwife.'

Her husband was already hobbling across the room on his crutches and Lucy was wrung with guilt at the worry she must put him through. But there was no way she could tell him that the birth was not going to be premature. She would just have to hope that her labour would not be too long – and that the baby would be healthy.

'Arthur,' she panted. He looked over his shoulder, his expression anguished. 'It's going to be all right,' she said. 'Our baby is going to be all right.'

'I pray that will be so,' he muttered. 'And you as well. If anything happened to you I'd lose everything I hold most dear.'

I can't believe this is happening, Ruth thought. I can't believe I am here in London. After leaving her publisher's office she had wandered about the West End, staring with delight at the displays in the shop windows. She had observed the endless crowds of people, listened to the constant rattle and rumble of the cabs and the horse buses, the cries of the street traders and the hiss and flare of the lamps hanging above the stalls set up on corners or in little alleyways.

She paused to buy a bag of roast chestnuts – and then wondered if she would even like them. After peeling one and nibbling it cautiously she decided that she didn't and thrust the bag into the hands of a ragged urchin who scuttled off with it quickly before she could change her mind.

Then she realized that she didn't know where she was. A girl who worked in the office at her publisher's – her publisher's! – had drawn her a map and told her that the theatre wasn't far. But Ruth had had nearly three hours to kill and she'd wandered about like a typical provincial, taking in the sights and sounds of the capital city, and loving every minute.

She approached a respectable-looking middle-aged couple and asked them for directions. She showed them the map, and also asked them the time. The woman smiled at her and told her that the theatre was just around the corner – and also that there was a very nice little tearoom in the department store over the road. Quite respectable and safe for young ladies on their own, she said.

The woman seemed kind and it was obvious that she was curious about the slim young woman in smart new clothes who didn't know her way around London, and who was going to the theatre. She's probably speculating right now whether I'm going to meet someone – or even what I'm doing here in the first place, Ruth thought.

She had to fight down the urge to say, 'Thank you so much. I'm here on business, you know. I've just been to see my publisher and now I'm off to meet an old friend, a musician. He's playing in the orchestra at the theatre.'

But instead, she simply thanked the couple and went into the store to find the tearoom.

The place was busy. Most of the tables were occupied by women with shopping bags, who were talking so volubly that they almost drowned out the sound of the little string orchestra. As Ruth joined the queue for tables, waiting in a sort of wooden pen, she was able to peer through the leaves of the tall potted plants at the musicians. To her surprise and delight they were dressed like gypsies and the music they were playing, dominated by the violins, sounded soulful and romantic.

She wondered if Henry had to dress up for any of his engagements and the thought amused her. She realized that she must have laughed out loud when the young woman standing next to her in the queue raised her eyebrows, grasped the hand of her little girl and moved ostentatiously away.

After that reaction Ruth was all the more pleased when the waitress came and opened the little gate and beckoned to her first. There was a tiny table for one squeezed up between an ornamental pillar and the service table. 'Would that do?'

'Very nicely,' Ruth said, and smiled sweetly at the snooty young matron as she was led away.

She ordered a pot of tea and toasted teacakes and it wasn't too long before they arrived.

'Don't worry, love, you can take your time,' the waitress said. 'There's not much call for this table.'

The chatter from the tables round about, combined with the music, seemed to create a wall of sound that both shut her out and yet cocooned her in a world of her own. As she sipped her tea she allowed herself to relive the excitement of the last two weeks.

The letter had come just after Christmas. Not only had her novel been accepted for publication, but the publisher wanted to meet her and discuss the possibility of a whole series of books based on her woman detective. This was exactly what Ruth had been hoping for.

She had known instinctively that her heroine could engage in further adventures of detection but she had not suggested that in her polite, almost deferential, letter of submission. At that stage, her hopes and dreams had gone no further than wanting to see this one book in print.

After reading the letter at least twice while sitting by the hissing and popping gas fire in her little room overlooking the sea, she had wanted to run out and share the wonderful news – and she had realized that she had nobody to share it with.

She never went home any more. She had not even gone at Christmas. Instead she had accepted Mrs Fairbridge's invitation to spend a few days at the cook-housekeeper's new home, her brother's farm in Shiremoor.

And what would be the use of going now to tell her father and stepmother that she was going to be a published author? Her father would be proud of her – surely he would – but Ada would be sure to find a way of spoiling things. And in the long run, if she were successful, Ada would only be concerned with how much money she would earn.

And what of her friends? She had never told them she was writing a novel and suddenly she realized she was shy of doing so now. Besides, it was probably the wrong time. Lucy was taken up with looking after Arthur and preparing for the baby, and Esther...

Esther had married Roland and, although her friend could have had no idea that Ruth had once dreamed of being his wife, Ruth felt awkward about facing her. After all, handsome as he no doubt was, and charming as he could be, Ruth had had time to reflect on his personality. She would never be able to tell Esther that she actually felt sorry for her being married to such a shallow and self-centred man.

Ruth had not felt able to go to visit her in their married home and, since meeting Roland, Esther herself had made no move to visit her old friends.

But, at the same time as dismissing the idea of telling her friends the good news now, Ruth knew that she would tell them one day. Once the book was published she would show it to them. She smiled as she imagined their reactions. She knew that, whatever their circumstances, they would be pleased for her.

And Guinevere Matthews? Ruth sighed. She had not seen Guinevere since the morning after Arthur's accident. Since Ruth now realized how foolishly she had behaved over Roland she was far too embarrassed to face his sister.

But her own diffidence in this matter distressed her. Guinevere had been so kind, so helpful, and she had believed totally in Ruth's talent to write. Perhaps I'll send her a copy of the book when it's published, Ruth thought. And maybe by then I'll be ready to face her again. Who knows?

Ruth found that her cheeks were wet with tears. Am I feeling sorry for myself? she wondered. My dreams have come true and all I can do is sit here and weep because I have no one I can run to. No one who would understand what this means to me except Guinevere, and that friendship has been tarnished.

Ruth went out on to the top landing where there was a tiny kitchen area. She filled the kettle and put it on the gas ring. A little later, as she sipped her tea and toasted some bread at the fire, she remembered that there had been someone who would have understood, and who would have been as thrilled for her as she was for herself. What had he said?

'...*we are the same kind of people ... and one day I hope you'll realize that...*'

Henry Valentine...

What had he said in his letter?

'...*when you wish to contact me, you can always get the address from my mother...*'

It had taken courage but she went to visit Henry's mother. To her dismay her reception had been cool. Cordelia Valentine seemed unwilling to tell her where her son was living. But after a frosty few moments she had written the address on a piece of paper. Then holding it tightly against her breast, she said, 'I hope you won't toy with my son's affections, Ruth. He is a fine young man and he doesn't deserve it.'

Ruth almost fled without the address, but Mrs Valentine thrust it towards her and relented sufficiently to give her a swift hug.

Once home she'd spent a sleepless night with much heart-searching. But before dawn the next morning, with the wind hurling rain against the windows of her eyrie, and the waves crashing against the cliffs below, she rose, lit the candle on her bedside table and wrote a letter to Henry. She pulled on her warmest clothes and hurried out before breakfast to post it before she could change her mind.

She had been honest. She'd told him that she was coming to London because of a book she'd written. She couldn't have him believing that the sole purpose was to see him, although she hoped that he would realize that if she hadn't wanted to see him she needn't have told him she was coming.

He had replied by return of post. But he hadn't suggested that he would meet her at the station as she'd hoped he would. Instead he had sent her a ticket for the theatre where he was working at the moment. 'A Seasonal Entertainment,' he called it, and said that he would meet her after the show. She didn't know whether she should be disappointed but decided, in view of the way she had behaved, Henry had every right to be as cool as his mother had been.

And very soon now she would be seeing him again. She saw that her hand was shaking and she put her cup down; it rattled in the saucer.

'All right, love?'

Ruth looked up to see the same cheerful waitress looking at her with concern.

'Mm.'

'You don't look all right, if you don't mind my saying. Are you feeling poorly?'

'No ... it's just ... I – I'm about to meet some-one that I haven't seen for a while.'

527

Ruth didn't know why she suddenly found herself confiding in this stranger – unless it was because the woman looked genuinely concerned.

'A man?'

'Well ... yes.'

'Did he treat you badly?'

'Oh, no! It was the other way around. I ... I didn't realize ... I mean...'

Ruth was amused that she should be lost for words. She was supposed to be a writer, wasn't she? But no matter how convincingly she could write about the motives and emotions of characters in her stories, she had always had difficulty in expressing her own feelings. She smiled ruefully.

'That's better,' the waitress said.

'Better?'

'You're smiling. Just a little smile, mind you, but a smile nevertheless. So, you let a good man slip through your fingers, did you, and now you're going to try and put things right?'

Ruth stared at the waitress in astonishment. 'Well, not quite ... but, yes, I suppose that's near enough. But how did you know?'

The woman laughed. 'It's working here that does it. I can tell by just looking at a girl whether she's waiting for her sweetheart – that's an easy one – or waiting for someone else – someone she didn't ought to be seeing. And then there's the ones with all the cares and worries of the world on their shoulders – ones you can tell just don't want to go home – wherever that is. Sometimes they tell you about it – makes your heart bleed for them, it does.' She shook her head. 'You

528

wouldn't believe some of the stories they come out with. Sometimes I think I could write a book.'

'You should!'

'What? Me? Don't be daft!'

'I don't see why not. I've written a book – that's why I'm here in London, to visit my publisher.'

'Oh, yes.' The waitress's smile faded and she glanced uneasily away. 'Well, it's been nice talking to you, I'm sure, but I'd best get on.'

She hurried off through the busy tearoom. She doesn't believe me, Ruth thought. She thinks I've made it up – that I'm just telling a story like some of her other customers. How embarrassing.

Ruth slipped a coin under her plate for a tip, paid the bill at the counter near the door, and hurried out into the city streets again. It was time to head for the theatre.

The show was a sort of pantomime with fairy-tale characters dancing and singing in a winter wonderland of painted forests, lakes, castles and pretty little cottages where roses bloomed round the door even in the middle of winter.

Ruth didn't recognize the story, but in the end the princess in the castle found true love with the cowherd in the cottage who, once she had sworn to love him for ever and a day, revealed himself to be a prince in disguise. So everybody was happy – including the band of pretty ballerinas, who kept interrupting the story in order to perform miracles of acrobatic dancing.

Ruth loved the atmosphere of the theatre; the red plush seats, the gold tassels on the curtains. Her seat was in the front row of the dress circle so she had a wonderful view of the stage and the orchestra pit, although she could see very little of Henry as he sat behind the piano. She could also look down on the audience in the stalls. Inevitably there were a lot of children with their parents and nannies but, judging from their clothes, these were privileged little boys and girls who, no doubt, would return home to substantial houses in places like Kensington.

Ruth had studied a map of London before she left Newcastle; not just in order to find the small hotel near King's Cross Station recommended by her publisher, and where she had booked herself in for four nights, but also to mark out the places of interest like the Tower and Buckingham Palace. She'd decided to give herself a small holiday and visit as many of these places as she could.

Henry was lodging with some fellow musicians in a place called Chelsea. She had seen on the map that this was close to the river, the Thames. But she didn't imagine the street where Henry lived would be anything like the steep cobbled streets where she had grown up on the banks of the River Tyne.

During one of the intervals a programme seller came to her seat and told her that Mr Valentine had arranged for a cup of coffee to be served to her in the circle lounge after the show, and would she please wait there for him.

So she made her way there as the audience left at the end of the performance. There was much talk and laughter and the buoyant mood added to her own excitement. What a day this had been,

Ruth thought as she sat and drank her coffee.

The office she'd had to report to had been at the top of several flights of stairs, and the elderly gentleman who had greeted her had looked like someone from a previous age in his faded formal clothes.

Perhaps he had been taken aback by her youth but he hadn't mentioned it. He had got straight down to business, talking about the way he wanted her novels to develop and what her payments would be. By the time she'd left, her mind was whirling.

She had been grateful to the young woman in the outer office, who had whispered, 'Don't worry, you'll get a letter explaining everything in black and white.' She'd made her a cup of tea and drawn the map of how to get to the theatre.

Ruth hoped she had retained enough of the meeting to tell it all to Henry. After all, hadn't she decided that he was the only other person who would understand?

From where she was sitting now at the back of the grand circle she could look down on the rows of empty seats. The theatre staff started cleaning straight away: tipping up the seats, gathering up empty confectionery boxes and dropped programmes. Work stopped for a moment when one of the girls found a wallet. The others gathered round, and one of them, an older woman, took the wallet and looked inside.

'There's a name,' she said as she took out a piece of card, probably a calling card. Ruth thought the girl's shoulders sagged. 'But from the looks of this address,' the woman continued, 'you should get a nice little reward.'

Ruth began to weave a story in her head. She imagined the girl taking the wallet to the house of its owner, climbing the steps that led to the front door – there would be sure to be a set of grand steps – and nervously ringing the bell. Then, if it was a love story, the owner of the wallet would prove to be the rich handsome son of the house. He would take one look at the girl and fall in love with her!

But I wouldn't write that kind of story, Ruth mused. No, what if the owners of the house deny all knowledge of the wallet? In spite of the name and address printed boldly on the calling cards inside, they say that they have never heard of such a person. And, even though there is a considerable amount of money inside, they tell the girl to keep the wallet. And then, on the way home through the fog – there has to be a fog – she hears footsteps... She is being followed...

'Goodness, Ruth, you're miles way!'

Ruth looked up to see Henry smiling down at her. She rose to her feet, knocking the table; her cup and saucer slid towards the edge. Smilingly Henry steadied the table and rescued the crockery before it fell. 'I'm sorry,' he said as he straightened up and smiled at her. 'I frightened you.'

'No ... I mean, yes, you startled me but that's all right.'

'All right?' His eyebrows rose quizzically. And then his expression changed. She saw that look in his eyes – the look that used to worry her because it was so intense.

But now she knew there was nothing to fear. She was ready to face what being close to Henry – what loving him – would mean. She was ready to let down the barriers and allow him to know her innermost thoughts, her feelings. What moved her, what made her afraid, what filled her with hope. At last she felt confident enough to cope with a man such as Henry.

Far from making her a prisoner, as her stepmother's love had of her father, Henry's love would at the same time enfold her and yet set her free. It would give her the strength to realize her dreams.

'You're trembling,' he said softly.

Ruth was indeed trembling. More than that, her heart was thudding so violently against her ribs that she was sure that Henry would hear it. She looked into his dear familiar face and acknowledged something she should have realized long ago.

How could I have been so bedazzled by Roland Matthews, she wondered, when Henry Valentine is so exactly the sort of man I want? The sort of man I need.

'What is it, Ruth? Surely the mere sight of me hasn't made you cry?'

She raised a hand to brush the tears from her cheeks. She hoped and prayed that she hadn't left it too late. 'Oh, Henry,' she said. 'I'm so very pleased to see you.'

Chapter Seventeen

April

'You should cover your mouth when you cough, Davy,' Roland said.

Esther glanced anxiously at her brother. Davy had barely touched his porridge and, to her dismay, his latest coughing fit had resulted in lumps of it being deposited on the tablecloth.

'I'm sorry, Esther,' he said, 'I tried but I wasn't quick enough.'

'That's all right, pet,' she replied. She saw Roland frown.

'It's not all right,' her husband said. 'The boy must learn decent manners. Now clean that up yourself, Davy, and let your sister sit down and have her breakfast in peace.'

Davy got up obediently, spooned the lumps of porridge off the cloth and then took his bowl through to the kitchen where Esther heard the coughing begin again. She half rose but Roland caught her hand. 'Stay here,' he said. 'You've hardly touched your breakfast. Eat it up before it gets cold.'

Miserably she attempted to eat her own porridge then, after a few mouthfuls, she was surprised when Roland took her hand. He smiled kindly at her and, as she looked into his eyes, she could see that he was sorry that he had spoken sharply before.

'All right, my love. Leave it if you want to,' he said. 'I can tell you're worried about your brother. He's had this cough for a day or two now, hasn't he?'

She glanced up at him gratefully. 'Yes, he said most of his class at school are coughing and spluttering. I'm sure it's only a feverish cold, but I'm so frightened it will turn into something worse.'

'Of course you are. And the sooner Davy is living in the fresh air in the countryside, the better. But, meanwhile, would you be happier if Davy stayed at home today and didn't go to school?'

'Oh, yes, much happier.'

Davy came through from the scullery, looking subdued and pale. Esther rose and went to give him a hug. She was surprised when he winced and pulled away slightly but she thought he probably didn't want to be babied in front of Roland.

'Roland says you can stay at home today, Davy. Now sit by the fire here and I'll make you some toast.'

'I hardly think toast's the thing if he's got a sore throat,' Roland said.

'Well, no,' Esther replied, 'but he could dip it in his tea. Or I could make him some boily. That's it – bread and sugar with hot milk poured on it. He'll be able to manage that.'

'I'm sure he will. But at least drink your tea before you start fussing. If Davy is poorly enough to stay at home then he should be in bed. You can take him a tray after I've gone to the office.'

Roland sounded cool again, so Esther was grateful that Davy simply smiled wanly at her and left the room. She couldn't help noticing how much happier Roland looked once the door had closed.

'Here,' he said, 'let me spoil you a little. I'll warm up your tea and toast you a slice of bread.'

Esther didn't protest. She had learned that it was better to let Roland have his own way. And, besides, he was only behaving like this because he loved her and wanted to look after her. She could never have imagined her father kneeling by the fire to make toast for her mother – or even pour her a cup of tea.

If only Roland and Davy got on better, she thought. But Davy crept about the place with hardly a word these days and, instead of being happy for her, he seemed to resent Roland. Of course, since leaving home, her brother had never had a man to tell him what's what, and she acknowledged that she had probably spoiled him. She supposed Davy resented it when Roland told him what to do.

She had never been apart from her young brother and she knew that she was going to miss him dreadfully when he left to go to work in the country. But she had accepted it was for the best. Especially as she had begun to worry about his health.

Roland controlled his irritation as he observed Esther's expression. She might at least try to smile for me, he thought. She spends far too much time worrying over that brat of a brother of

536

hers. And as for this coughing business, I don't believe there's anything wrong with him. He's just doing it to annoy me – to make sure that I don't enjoy a peaceful meal at my own table.

But it suits me to let her think he's ill. Let her play the nursemaid today and coddle him. Not only will she be grateful to me for suggesting it, but it will be even easier to convince her that we're doing the right thing by sending him away from the town and into the healthy air of the countryside.

Ruth waited until the elderly gentleman had taken his books to the counter to be stamped and then stepped forward. Guinevere did not look up. Her hair was more straggly than ever and her complexion pale. Ruth looked at her hands in their fingerless mitts and saw how thin her fingers had become. Still without glancing up, the librarian reached for the book that Ruth had placed on the counter and opened it.

Ruth knew she would savour this next moment for ever. Her old friend paused as she realized that this was not a library book, and then turned the page to look at the title. Ruth saw a delicate flush creep up Guinevere's painfully thin neck and suffuse her face. A slight sob escaped her and, at last, she looked up at the young woman standing at the other side of the counter.

Ruth drew back a little, aware that she had been holding her breath. She was glad of the half veil on her hat that came down past her eyes and hid the fact that they were glistening with tears.

'Ruth?' Guinevere said hesitantly.

'Yes.'

'You look ... so grown up. So fashionable.'

Guinevere Matthews, the least vain of women, glanced down at her own clean but dowdy attire and looked up again. She seemed disconcerted. In that moment Ruth wished she hadn't dressed in the new maroon skirt and jacket she had bought in London. What if Guinevere thought she was showing off?

'And this...' Guinevere looked at the book in her hands. 'Your book, *The Mystery of the Missing Page* by Ruth Lorrimer! And you've signed it... "To my dear friend Guinevere Matthews." Thank you, Ruth. I can't tell you what this means to me.'

'Good. Well ... I suppose I'd better be going.' Ruth began to back away.

'No, you can't run away this time. Please stay! I'm just about to lock up and go upstairs for my lunch – come with me.'

'Well...' Ruth hesitated. She wanted to talk to Guinevere and yet she wasn't sure if she was ready to cope with going up to the flat above the library with all its memories of how foolish she'd been.

Guinevere must have read her mind. 'There's no trace of him there, Ruth. I live to suit myself now.'

Ruth didn't deny that that was what had been worrying her. 'All right then.'

The appearance of the apartment had indeed changed. Still clean and reasonably tidy, it had a more lived-in appearance. A couple of *Ladies' Journals* lay on the hearth rug, and a tray with the remains of a light breakfast was on a little table near the armchair. In former days Guinevere would not have dreamed of going down to open the library without washing her breakfast dishes first – and neither would she have eaten her breakfast from a tray near the fire.

She flushed slightly and picked up the tray. 'Am I turning into a slovenly old woman?' she asked.

Ruth smiled. 'I don't think so. Sometimes you simply have to relax a little. I know when I'm writing I often neglect to keep my room as tidy as it should be.'

'Are you writing another book?' Guinevere asked. 'Wait a moment – I'll boil the kettle for tea and while I make us some sandwiches why don't you come with me into the kitchen and tell me all about it?'

A little later, as they sat at the table with their meal, Ruth answered all Guinevere's questions about her book and the books that were to follow. Then, hesitantly at first, but with growing confidence, she told her about Henry. She hadn't known what to expect and she was moved when she saw the genuine pleasure in her old friend's eyes.

'I'm happy for you, Ruth,' Guinevere said. 'I know the young man in question. I've heard him play at the concerts at the hotel and in church. He's very talented as well as good-looking, isn't he?'

'Henry? Good-looking? Do you think so?'

'But of course.' Guinevere smiled as she admonished her playfully. 'Don't pretend you don't think so.'

'Well ... yes, I suppose he is. But that's not the

reason. I mean – looks aren't the most important thing, are they?'

Guinevere was silent and Ruth wondered if she had strayed into dangerous territory – if she had been tactless. But then her friend smiled and said, 'I'm glad you've realized that.' After that Ruth was relieved when Guinevere changed the subject. 'And what about Miss Golightly's poor *Angel?*' she asked. 'What have you done about your late employer's novel?'

'Wonderful news!' Ruth said. 'I took your advice and rewrote it. And, you know, it didn't take as long as I thought it would. After all, I had been working on it for so long I seemed to know just what was wanted.'

'And you've found a publisher?'

'I have. And then I had such a surprise. Miss Golightly's solicitor informed me that her will stated that should she die before her novel was published, any advance paid and all royalties were to come to me. I had no idea that she had been so generous.'

'But how appropriate,' Guinevere said, 'and no more than you deserve. But what about Miss Golightly's short stories and poems?'

'I've done my best with them and Miss Golightly's nephew is going to have a limited edition published at his own expense. The book's to be given to family and friends. I'm sure he will be giving one to you.'

'I shall treasure it. I mean that. That's that, then. And now you have a happy and exciting future to look forward to.'

'Yes. But there's something more I must do.'

540

'What's that?'

'I must settle this awkwardness between Esther and me. I haven't been to see her because I'm a coward – embarrassment, you know. So I've decided to write to her and ask her to meet me in town. We could go to Tilley's for lunch together.'

'That might be difficult.'

'Why?'

'Well, I suppose it's because they're newlyweds but she hardly goes anywhere. They don't come to visit me here, and I'm not encouraged to visit them. My brother is very possessive, you know.'

Ruth didn't say anything but she remembered that this was true. Roland used to get upset with her any time she had wanted to visit her friends or even her father.

'Did you know that Roland has found employment for Davy in a large house in the country?' Guinevere asked.

'No, I didn't. Davy had different plans entirely. Why is Esther allowing this?'

'It seems that Roland has persuaded her that it's better for the lad's health. He's convinced her that he's weakly.'

'But that's nonsense. Davy is small for his age but far from weakly. Esther has looked after him too well for that.'

Guinevere shrugged. 'Well, perhaps it's for the best. Davy can't be happy knowing that his sister's husband doesn't want him there.'

'Poor Davy,' Ruth said. 'And foolish, foolish Esther. Forgive me for saying this, Guinevere, but it might have been better if she had never met your brother.'

'Are you sure it's all right, Esther? He said I was to stay in my room.'

'I know, Davy, but it's cold in there. You sit here by the fire and drink this mug of milk and honey.'

Esther smiled. Davy, in his nightshirt, looked more like a child than ever. She arranged a rug round his shoulders and another over his knees before kneeling to make up the fire. She straightened up to find him grinning at her over his mug of milk.

'Take care,' she said. 'Don't spill that on the hearth rug.'

Obediently Davy steadied the mug. 'I must look like an old woman in a shawl,' Davy said. 'Or a baby. I wish you wouldn't baby me, our Esther. It's only a bit cough I've got.'

Esther was relieved to see that his mood had lifted and she smiled. 'I know, and now I'm going to go along to Shields Road to the chemist's to get you some pastilles to suck for your throat, and a cough bottle. And while I'm out I'd better call in at Fowler's to tell Raymond that you won't be working tonight.'

'You won't be too long, will you?' Davy asked.

Esther saw the anxiety in his eyes and bit her lip. 'I'll be as quick as I can. But in any case, I'll use the back door. If you hear the front door opening, just nip into bed and take those blankets with you. There's no point in annoying Roland when he's been good enough to let you have a day off school.'

'Divven't fret. I know what's what.'

Davy's grin reassured her and, in spite of his

protestations, she stooped to kiss the top of his head before leaving him by the fire.

'Ruth! You look wonderful! You're so slim, and that three-quarter-length coat and matching skirt is so fashionable. And, for once, you're not wearing blue,' Lucy said.

'You like it? I was a little doubtful about buying red.'

'I certainly do. And, anyway, it's more maroon than red – and with your dark hair it's so ... so dramatic!'

Ruth took off her coat and handed it to Meg, who was looking at her with wide eyes. 'Ee, you do look a proper mazer, Ruth,' she said. 'Are you going to give us yer hat, an' all?'

'No, I don't think so. It took me ages to arrange it like this at just the right angle and I had to use three hatpins to secure it.'

'Meg, I know you used to work with Ruth,' Lucy said, 'but she's my guest and you must call her Miss Lorrimer.'

'Oh that's all...' Ruth began when she saw the little maid's face fall, but she stopped herself in time. It wasn't her place to interfere. Meg worked for Lucy and her friend was entitled to order her own household.

'Meg, when you've hung Miss Lorrimer's coat up in the hall please go out into the garden and tell Mr Purvis that Miss Lorrimer is here.'

'Yes, missus.'

'Meg! Don't say "missus" say– Oh, never mind. Off you go.'

Lucy turned to Ruth smilingly. 'My mother is

supposed to be training her; I haven't got the patience. But do sit down. And, tell me, do you notice anything?'

Ruth sat down and looked all round the pretty front parlour. 'The daffodils in the vase – are they from your garden?'

'Yes they are, but that's not it.'

'The room's tidier than usual?'

Lucy tutted with exasperation. 'Yes it is and for a very good reason. For goodness' sake, it should be obvious. I thought writers were supposed to be observant.'

'The bed's gone.'

'That's right. Arthur is sleeping upstairs again. With ... with me.' Lucy flushed slightly.

'But how ... I mean...'

'Arthur has had an artificial leg fitted. And, Ruth, he's been so brave. I mean it hurts him so – and it will until he gets used to it but he's determined to master it. My mother thinks he's wonderful – almost as wonderful as her grandson, in fact.'

At her words Ruth looked round in surprise. 'Where is Tom?'

'Have you just realized he's missing? It's plain to see you're not a mother,' Lucy said, rather smugly Ruth thought. 'Thomas Reginald Purvis is sleeping, I hope. He's in his perambulator in the back garden. Arthur likes to have him nearby all the time. He absolutely dotes on him.

'But before Arthur comes in do tell me – are you really going to marry Henry Valentine?'

'It seems so.'

'When?'

'I'm not sure. When he returns from London, I suppose.'

'Oh for goodness' sake, Ruth! Can't you seem more eager – more enthusiastic?'

'No, I can't.'

Lucy looked shocked. 'Don't you love him?'

'With all my heart.'

Her friend frowned and shook her head. 'I don't understand you. I ask you about the man you love and you sound as cold and as matter-of-fact as if … as if he were part of your shopping list. "Tomorrow must remember to buy a pair of gloves, half a pound of digestive biscuits and – oh, yes – marry Henry."'

Ruth laughed. 'Is it as bad as that?'

'Yes, it is. For someone who is a published author you are very bad at expressing yourself in conversation.'

'I know I am. It's as if my feelings, my emotions, are locked up somewhere and I can only find the key when I take up my pen. And even then it's the characters in my stories who benefit. They can say the things I'm too frightened to say in real life.'

'But why should you be frightened?'

'Perhaps I've always been afraid to make a fool of myself.'

'That's pride.'

Ruth was startled. 'Is it? Surely not.'

'Yes, it's a sort of pride. You don't want people to think less of you. You're frightened of being mocked. Well, let me tell you that friends should be able to say what they like to each other so, however you behave with strangers, I'll thank you to be a bit more forthcoming with me in future!'

Ruth saw that, in spite of her firm tone, Lucy was smiling. 'I'll try,' she said. 'Now is the lecture over?'

'Yes, because now I'm going to tell you of another wedding. Apart from Arthur and me, you'll be the first to know. My mother is going to marry Mr Lockwood.'

'Your neighbour?'

'Yes, the theatre manager. Isn't that marvellous?'

'Well, yes, it is – if you think she'll be happy.'

'They're perfect for each other.'

'And will she give up the house in Byker? Is she going to live next door?'

'Yes to the first question, no to the second. At first I thought she would be moving in next door and I had mixed feelings about that. I mean, she and Arthur get on well these days, and she's been a wonderful help to me. But sometimes I just long for her to go home and leave us on our own.'

'I can understand that. Henry and I are going to have to live with his parents at first and, although I love them dearly, we plan to find a place of our own as soon as possible.'

'Well, anyway,' Lucy said, 'Mr Lockwood has just secured a new position. He's to be manager of the Tyne Theatre in Newcastle so he's decided to move to town – and he will be able to afford to do so. My mother is in her element. She has always wanted to live somewhere more fashionable than Byker and now she spends her days looking at properties in Jesmond.'

'But what will happen to Betty?'

'She's going with them. She'll be able to live in – and so will Mr Lockwood's funny old sister – who is already panicking at the top of her voice about being usurped. I feel sorry for the poor man, but Arthur says my mother will be quite capable of making the house run smoothly.'

'Of course she will. I'm so happy for her.'

'I wonder where Arthur has got to?' Lucy said suddenly. 'I should have told Meg to ask him to come in. Shall we go and find him?'

They found Arthur sitting by the fire in the cosy back parlour cradling the baby, who was fast asleep. Ruth tried not to look at Arthur's legs. But, of course, there was nothing to see. Sitting there like that, with his legs stretched out slightly there was no way of telling that he was in any way different from any other man.

'Why didn't you come through to the front parlour?' his wife asked.

Arthur looked up and smiled. 'I thought I'd leave you two to gossip for a while. I thought Tom and me might spoil your style.'

The baby whimpered and Arthur immediately looked down into his face anxiously. 'Nearly time for his next feed,' Arthur said. But Tom kept his eyes closed, although he moved his mouth as though he were sucking. 'Look, he's dreaming of his next meal,' Arthur said, and he smiled at the child tenderly.

Ruth found the sight of the big man cradling the child moving and she glanced at Lucy smilingly. She was disconcerted to find that there were tears in her friend's eyes. Ruth raised her eyebrows questioningly but Lucy shook her head and, biting her lips, she tried to smile.

For a moment an old suspicion flared to life but Ruth suppressed it. She persuaded herself that Lucy had probably been overcome with emotion; for the next moment she swept across the room and leaned down to kiss her husband on his brow.

'You're a big softy, Arthur Purvis,' she murmured. 'And I don't know what I'd do without you.'

Esther heard the scream when she was halfway up the stone stairs in the back yard. She stopped and gripped the wooden hand rail. She turned and looked out over the neighbouring yards divided by high brick walls. She couldn't see anyone. She looked beyond. The only movement came from the flapping of the washing pegged to the lines slung across the back lane.

She heard another scream and turned and stared at her own back door in horror as she realized the sound came from within. She gripped the rail more tightly as the years drained away and the sound of her mother's screams of terror echoed in her memory. But that wasn't her mother screaming … it was Davy!

Could her father be inside her house? Could he be thrashing Davy? Had he discovered that his wife was still alive and had come to wreak his revenge because Esther hadn't told him?

She rushed up the rest of the way, not even stopping when she turned her ankle on the broken step. She opened the door, leaving it to clash against the wall, and hurried into the

548

scullery. The door into the living room was open and what she saw being enacted in there was terrifying.

He was standing with his back to her and he had hold of Davy's shoulder with one hand; the other hand was raised ready to strike. Esther's heart began to pound and her breath stopped in her throat. Something tight was winding itself round her head and squeezing until her eyes began to hurt.

She remembered all those times she had placed her own body between her father and her mother or her father and Davy. She thought she had left those days behind her.

But then there had been that last near-fatal time when she hadn't been there to help, and her mother had defended herself...

Davy screamed again as her father's arm descended. She felt herself sway as the scene before her blurred. The shopping basket, which she hadn't realized she was still carrying, dropped to the floor. But she willed herself not to faint... She reached for the cast-iron pan draining on the bench and hurled herself forward.

Before he could strike again Esther had burst into the room. As she raised her arm, Davy caught sight of her and the movement of his eyes gave her away. Her father turned his head at the very moment that she swung the pan against the back of his neck and Esther recoiled in horror. But it was too late to stop the blow.

It wasn't her father; it was her husband who sank down on to the floor at her feet.

Ruth was upstairs with Lucy. They had just placed the baby in his crib when Meg came to the door and beckoned them. They left the nursery quietly and then Meg whispered, 'Davy is at the door. He won't come in.'

'How strange,' Lucy murmured. 'You stay here, Meg, until Tom settles. We'll go down and see what he wants.'

Davy stood on the doorstep. Outside the shadows were lengthening across the garden. A light mist was rolling in from the sea and creeping up the tidy streets of the suburbs, deadening all sound. Ruth stood slightly behind Lucy as she tried to urge Esther's brother to come in rather than stand in the chill air; but he shook his head repeatedly and all he would say was, 'You've got to come. Esther needs you.'

'But what is it, Davy? What's the matter? Is Esther poorly?' Lucy asked.

'Just come – please – both of you.'

Lucy turned to Ruth and asked, 'What shall we do?'

'I'll go with him,' Ruth said, although she would have given anything not to. 'You must stay with Arthur and the baby.'

'No!' Davy said. 'She needs you both. "Fetch Ruth and Lucy." Those are the only words she's said since ... since...'

'Since what, Davy?' Ruth stepped forward.

But Davy's brother shook his head. 'You've got to come. Both of you. Esther needs you. And please hurry – I've left her on her own.'

'Very well.' Lucy suddenly sounded decisive. 'We will. Now are you going to stand out here in the cold or will you come in while Ruth and I get our coats on?'

'I'll wait here.'

Lucy looked at Ruth and raised her eyebrows. 'I don't like this,' she said, 'but it's clear we have no choice.'

Ruth followed her into the living room where she told Arthur what was happening. 'Esther is all alone,' she said, 'and I think she must be ill. She's asked for both of us.'

'Then you must go,' Arthur said. 'If you're not back when the bairn wakes, Meg can bring him down and I'll give him a bottle. You don't need to worry about that.'

Lucy leaned over and kissed him and then she hurried upstairs to give instructions to Meg. A short while later Ruth, Lucy and Davy set off for the station and, although they tried their best to get Davy to tell them why they were needed so urgently, he refused to say anything. On the train he sat staring out of the window at the darkening countryside rather than meet their eyes.

'I don't understand this at all,' Lucy said to Ruth. 'Why is Esther on her own at this time? It's getting late.' She turned to Davy. 'Where's Roland?'

Ruth had been watching Davy. The lamps were lit inside the carriage and she could see his reflection in the window. At Lucy's question his eyes widened for a moment but all he said was, 'She's on her own. There's no one to help her but you and Ruth.'

After that no one spoke again.

When they arrived at Heaton, Davy set off

551

ahead of them and he seemed to walk quicker and quicker. Ruth could hear Lucy panting slightly as they hurried along a back lane and followed Davy into the yard. Halfway up the steps he paused and turned to face them.

'Be careful,' he said. 'Keep hold of the rail. One of these steps is broken.'

Ruth wasn't sure what she was expecting when they stepped inside. She and Lucy followed Davy hesitantly through the scullery and into the living room. Then they drew back and clutched at each other's arms in shock.

The body of a man lay on the floor. Someone had thrown a rug over him but they could see the awkward angle of his head as it lay across the fender. As if he'd been placed on the executioner's block, Ruth thought.

Ruth was aware of her pulse racing as she glanced around the room quickly. There was no sign of Esther but she noticed a light-coloured stain on the flowered hearth rug spreading out from a fallen pottery mug. There was another stain, darker, more sinister, in the hearth under the man's head.

'My God, what has happened here?' she heard Lucy say. 'Did some villain break in and attack your sister?'

Davy didn't answer. Ruth frowned as she saw him crouch down beside the table and lift the tassels of the green chenille cloth. He peered into the shadowy space and said quietly, 'Esther ... they're here. I've brought them ... Ruth and Lucy. Will you come out now?'

Then he half vanished himself as he crawled

beneath the cloth. They heard a soft murmur of voices and watched as he backed out again, pulling Esther with him. Still on her knees she blinked and looked up at them. Ruth thought she looked like a frightened wild creature.

'I've killed him,' she gasped and her voice was hoarse as if she'd been crying for a long time. 'He was beating Davy ... I thought it was my father...' She began to sob. Great wracking sobs that shook her body.

Lucy hurried forward and, with Davy's help, she got Esther into the armchair.

Ruth stayed where she was. 'Who is it? she asked. 'Who is it if it's not your father?'

Esther sobbed all the more and Davy shot Ruth a helpless look. She felt as though her feet were made of lead as she moved towards the body. She kneeled down and lifted the rug back from the man's face. It was Roland.

She was unaware that she had begun to shake until Lucy moved forward swiftly and gripped her arms.

'No time for that!' she said. 'Cover him up and make a pot of tea. We need to know what happened and what we're going to do about it.'

As Ruth caught her breath she saw that Esther had stopped crying and was looking up at Lucy gratefully. Davy kneeled down to cover the body, then stood up and took Ruth's hand.

'She was trying to save me,' he said. 'She thought it was me da. I divven't think she would have hit him so hard if she'd known it was Roland.'

Ruth pulled herself together and lit the lamps

and drew the curtains. It was Davy who made the tea and pulled the table back so that they could all sit round it without any one of them being too near the dreadful object on the hearth rug.

First Lucy questioned Davy and they learned that he'd fallen asleep in front of the fire while he was drinking his milk, unknowingly dropping the mug and staining the hearth rug. The next thing he'd known was that he was being roused violently by Roland who had come home unexpectedly early.

'I was supposed to listen out for him,' he said, 'and nip back to bed if I heard his key in the lock.' He glanced at his sister. 'I'm sorry, Esther.'

Esther began to weep again, this time silently, the tears streaming down her cheeks.

'And he beat you?' Lucy asked.

'He was angry because he'd telt me to stay in bed. I'd disobeyed him.'

'And he thought beating you a fitting punishment?'

Davy nodded, tight-lipped, and Esther groaned.

It was Ruth who asked, 'Had he beaten you before?'

Esther's brother stared at her aghast. It was obvious he didn't want to answer the question. He glanced nervously at his sister.

'Tell me the truth, Davy. Had Roland beaten you before?' Ruth said.

Davy nodded silently.

'Often?'

'Yes,' he whispered.

'Why didn't you tell your sister?'

'She loved him so ... she seemed so happy – and he was good to her. He never lifted a finger to her. And she could hev anything she wanted. I didn't want to spoil things for her. Not after the way she's looked after me all these years. I wanted her to hev what she wanted. I thought it best if I just kept quiet and left home as soon as possible. Then everything would be all right.'

Esther suddenly cried out, 'I didn't know! You do believe me, don't you? I had no idea!'

'Of course we believe you,' Lucy said, 'and now we've got to decide what we're going to do.'

'What can we do?' Esther asked. 'We must send for the police.'

'And tell them what, exactly?' Lucy said. 'That you've killed your husband? They'll hang you.'

Esther and Davy looked terrified and even Ruth was chilled by Lucy's tone.

'But I didn't mean to kill him,' Esther said. 'It was an accident.'

'You mean you accidentally hit him over the head with a cast-iron pan. A likely story.'

Esther gasped and Ruth said, 'Lucy, what do you think you're doing, talking like this?'

'I'm trying to save Esther's life.'

'Then you're going a funny way about it.'

'No I'm not. For goodness' sake, Ruth. What does this look like? A man lies dead in his own home. His wife says it was an accident. How accidental can it be to hit someone with a heavy pan?'

'But he was beating her brother,' Ruth said.

'All the more reason to kill him.' Lucy reached out across the table and took Esther's hand. 'Tell me, Esther, what exactly was going through your mind when you picked up the pan?'

Esther frowned as though she was trying to recall what had happened. 'I thought it was my father,' she began. 'I could see him hitting Davy again and again. Davy was screaming. I knew I had to stop him.'

'By hitting him?'

'Yes. I knew I wouldn't be strong enough to pull him away. I had to stop him. The only way was to distract him ... to hurt him.'

'Did you mean to kill him?' Lucy asked.

Esther remained silent for a long time and then she said. 'I was angry ... angry because he was hurting Davy, who had never done him any harm. Angry because of all our childhood years when he beat my mother and made all our lives a living hell. But as for killing him ... I just don't know.'

Ruth suddenly got up and went over to where Roland's body lay before the fire. The fire was burning low. No one had had the will to see to it. She kneeled down and pulled back the rug.

'What are you doing?' Lucy asked.

'Wait a moment.' She forced herself to look at Roland's head and then, gingerly put a hand out to move it slightly. She heard the others gasp. A moment later she pulled the blanket up again and took her place at the table.

'I think it really was an accident, Esther,' she said. 'I don't think you have the strength to deliver a fatal blow with the pan. Roland hit his head on the brass ornament on the corner of the fender when he fell. I think that's what killed him.'

'But they'll still blame Esther,' Lucy said. 'He

wouldn't have fallen if she hadn't hit him.'

Ruth remained quiet. It had taken every ounce of courage to touch Roland like that. She had been expecting him to be cold; but because he was lying near the fire, probably, his skin was warm to the touch like living skin. It was as if his beautiful features were composed in sleep rather than death. She closed her eyes and tried to calm herself.

When she opened her eyes again the others were sitting in glum silence. Lucy drummed the table with her fingers as she frowned in concentration. 'They mustn't find him here,' she said at last.

'What do you suggest we do? Throw his body in the river?' Ruth asked.

Esther seemed to shrink inside herself and Lucy shot Ruth a furious glance. 'That was both stupid and unfeeling.'

'I'm sorry. Truly I am. But what exactly do you mean?'

'I mean they mustn't find him in the house. Esther, do you have any drink in the house? Any spirits?'

Esther looked puzzled. 'There's a bottle of whisky in the sideboard. Roland would take a drink occasionally.'

'Get it.'

Esther remained staring helplessly, but Davy, responding to Lucy's tone of command, got up and went to the sideboard. A moment later he put the bottle on the table before Lucy. She left it there and, getting up, went over to the body. She kneeled down and drew back the blanket.

'Good, he's still wearing his overcoat. Is it dark outside?'

Davy looked puzzled but he crossed to the window and drew back the curtain. 'Aye, pitch-black. There's neither moon nor stars.'

'Just what we need. Now get me a small glass.'

'What are you going to do?' Ruth asked.

'We all accept that this was an accident, don't we?' No one answered. 'Well, don't we?'

Everyone nodded except Esther, who buried her face in her hands.

'Well, we're going to make sure that everyone else believes there's been an accident,' Lucy continued. 'Does – did – Roland ever work late?'

'Aye,' Davy said. 'Many a night he would visit clients after office hours. Sometimes he would come home first for a meal. Sometimes he wouldn't.'

'Well, tonight he didn't. Esther had his meal ready and got more worried the later it got. You sat up with her to keep her company, and it was only when you went down to the lavatory in the back yard that you found him lying at the bottom of the steps. It'll have to be you that finds him, Davy, because I don't trust Esther not to give the game away. All I want her to do is weep.'

Davy's eyes had grown wide. 'But how did he fall?' he asked.

'The poor man had taken a drink to keep the chill out,' Lucy said. 'Maybe more than one. You'll be able to tell the policeman how he liked his whisky a little too much.'

'But he didn't–' Davy began and stopped when he saw Lucy's glare. 'Oh, aye,' he said. 'I understand.'

'So, with his judgement clouded, he must have

stumbled on the broken step. The poor man fell all the way to the bottom and hit his head. And you and Esther have no idea how long he had been lying there before you found him.'

'Wait a moment,' Ruth said. 'What if the police ask your neighbours? They would be able to tell them that Roland didn't drink too much.'

'No they wouldn't,' Esther said quietly. 'We hardly know our neighbours. Roland discouraged me from getting to know them. We kept ourselves to ourselves.'

'That's right,' Davy said.

'Good. Then let's get on with this. Give me that glass, Davy.'

Lucy filled the glass with whisky. 'What are you going to do?' Ruth asked.

'He has to smell of drink.'

They watched in horror as Lucy pulled back the blanket again and attempted to turn Roland's head into a better position. 'It's no good, you'll have to help me, Ruth,' she said.

'I can't.'

'You must. I've got to open his mouth somehow and get some of this inside.'

'No!' Esther said. 'Please don't. It's ... it's not right.'

Lucy glanced up at her and sighed. 'Very well,' she said. And then she leaned over and dribbled the whisky on to Roland's clothes instead. 'That will have to do. Now, I can't do this myself. I'm sorry, Esther, but we've got to throw him down the steps.'

What followed was a nightmare. They knew they couldn't expect Esther to help, so Lucy and

Ruth between them dragged Roland's body to the back door. Then they put out all the lights before Davy opened the door for them. They waited for a moment until their eyes had adjusted to the darkness and looked down into the yard. And then the plan almost faltered. They knew immediately they didn't have the strength to throw him down the steps.

'What are we going to do?' Ruth whispered. 'Sit him on the top step and give him a push?' She felt sick.

'No,' Lucy said. 'He might not go all the way down. Here, help me turn him round. Get him on his back, that's right. You and I are going to drag him down backwards. That way it will look as if he's fallen.'

So, one at each shoulder, they eased Roland down the steep stone stairs into the back yard with Davy guiding his feet.

When it was done, Lucy clutched Davy's arm and spoke quietly. 'We'll go back in now,' she said, 'and then Ruth and I must go. I don't think anyone saw us arrive and, even if they did, we can just say we were visiting and that Roland hadn't come home by the time we left.

'It's up to you, Davy. You must be the judge of when to go for the police. But, before you do, you must clean that ... that stain from the hearth.' She hurried on, 'And be sure to tell Esther that she's got to do everything to save herself. Just say that if they were to hang her, you wouldn't be able to manage without her. She's looked after you all these years and you don't want to lose her now.'

It was only when they were back inside and Davy had lit the lamps once more that Lucy noticed the whisky bottle.

'We should have put that in his pocket,' she said.

'Why?' Ruth asked.

'Because the smell of whisky on his clothes might fade by the time the police get here.'

Lucy sighed and sat down wearily, and Ruth suddenly realized how much this had cost her. She had a busy life with her crippled husband and her baby; she was probably still recovering from the birth. Ruth remembered how out of breath she'd been when they had been trying to keep up with Davy earlier.

'I'll take it down,' Ruth said.

She closed the living-room door after her and went silently through the darkened scullery. At the bottom of the steps she crouched and felt for Roland's coat pocket. After easing the bottle inside she was just about to stand up when she heard a groan. Her heart almost stopped with fright.

She stared down at Roland. Was he alive after all? Had he simply been stunned before, and had the cool air revived him? She remembered something Meg had said the day Miss Golightly had died. Mrs Fairbridge had held a mirror to the old lady's lips to see if she was still breathing.

Should they have done that before dragging Roland down here? Should she do that now?

But what if he was alive? Involuntarily she glanced over her shoulder in the direction of the house. Would Esther go to prison for attacking her husband? She would rot in gaol for years, and what would happen to Davy if he was left in Roland's charge? Roland might even see to it that Davy went to prison too.

Roland had been warm when she'd touched him before. That should have told her – although she'd thought it was because he'd been lying near the fire. So what if he was still alive? No matter what the consequences were, she couldn't leave him here in the cold yard where he would certainly perish before the morning.

Ruth steeled herself and crouched down further so that she could see his face. Roland's eyes were open. They had been closed before. She drew back but then realized that his stare was unfocused, his gaze unseeing. Still uncertain, Ruth opened Roland's coat and put her head on his chest. She lay there until she was certain that she could hear no heartbeat.

Roland was dead. But she was almost sure that he had not been dead when they had dragged him down here. The cold air must have brought him round and perhaps he had lain here wondering what had happened and why he was alone in the darkness. Ruth stifled a sob when she realized that the groan she had heard a minute or so ago must have been his dying breath.

Ruth buttoned up Roland's coat and gently closed his unseeing eyes before she dragged herself back up to the flat where her friends were waiting, and no doubt wondering why she was taking so long.

She wouldn't tell them what had happened. It

was too harrowing. How could she place such a burden on Davy's young back, and make Esther feel even more guilty than she was feeling already? It would destroy them.

And as for Lucy; Lucy who had been the first to realize the consequences and had taken charge of the situation, determined to save Esther from the gallows while she, Ruth, had, just for a moment, allowed her own feelings to come before her friend's welfare.

Thank goodness Lucy had been more clear-sighted and more resolute. But what would it do to kind, brave Lucy if she learned that the man she had dragged down the steps into the cold yard had not been dead after all and that her actions had been his death sentence?

No, she could never tell them. This was something she would have to keep to herself and live with for the rest of her life. She owed them that – in the name of friendship.

Epilogue

July 1900

The children were making a sandcastle helped by their fathers. It was a large affair with turrets and moats, and it would have been even grander if the smallest of the children, a sturdy red-haired toddler, had not kept breaching the walls by the simple expedient of plonking himself on top of them.

'Stop it, Jack!' the other children kept shouting. And his father would lift him high in the air and hold him there while he laughed up at him.

The eldest child in the little group, Tom, golden-haired and solemn, was giving orders to Max and Clara, enchanting dark-haired twins, who obeyed him slavishly, Clara particularly hanging on his every word. The twins' father, in his shirtsleeves like the other men, kept up the pretence that Tom was the foreman and would touch an imaginary cap every time the little tyrant gave an order.

The third father sat a little apart, his legs stretched out across the sand as he helped his daughter, Susan, Tom's little sister, make sand pies. He would fill the bucket and turn it over on the sand, and then she would bang on it gleefully with her wooden spade. Each time her father lifted the bucket carefully to reveal the 'pie', her eyes would widen with wonder.

Lucy, sitting further up the beach with Ruth and Esther, kept glancing at them and smiling indulgently. No one will ever know how grateful I am that we have Susan, she thought. Arthur's own child. And he loves his daughter just as much as he loves Tom, whom he believes to be his son.

Her smile wavered for a moment and that familiar ache lodged in her throat. Was it so wrong of her to have let Arthur believe that Tom was his? The time for confession, if there ever had been such a time, was long gone. If Arthur learned the truth now it would break his heart. He'd spoiled him, of course. Just as he was spoiling Susan. Arthur, who had grown up in an orphanage, was the most indulgent of fathers, and young Tom was becoming too used to getting his own way. It was just as well that his grandmother had proved to be the most surprising of disciplinarians.

When Grandmother Daisy came to call, Tom and Susan had to mind their manners and learn to behave as the children of gentlefolk should. Lucy thought the combination of her husband and her mother was probably confusing for the children, but might work out quite well.

It had been Lucy's idea to come to Cullercoats Bay for the picnic to celebrate Susan's third birthday. It was also ten years, almost to the day, since Ruth and Esther had pulled her out of the sea. She'd had to choose a Sunday, of course, because she'd wanted their husbands to come too.

Incredibly, Arthur had managed to go back to work for the railway company. Not as a porter, of course, and he'd had to give up his dream of becoming a stationmaster, but he was happy with his position as a ticket clerk. He loved the bustle and the life of the station and he would have been perfectly miserable sitting at home and having to be dependent on his wife.

She still hadn't told him, and might never do so, that there was absolutely no need to worry about money. He valued his role as provider.

She admired him all the more for his decision, and constantly blessed whichever guardian angel had made sure that Stephen Wright had refused to marry her. Thinking of Stephen she allowed herself a wry smile.

Now and then she would meet his sister Julia out shopping. Julia would stop and make such a fuss of Tom and Susan. Poor Julia, unmarried herself, and not even a niece or nephew to indulge, as her brother and his wife had not yet managed to produce an heir to the undertaking business.

Julia was lonely and it was easy enough to encourage her to gossip. All it needed was a sympathetic smile and a kind word or two. Lucy learned that Stephen's wife, Celia, had two married sisters who both had children. She was devastated not to have babies of her own and, in her shriller moments, impugned Stephen's manhood.

This infuriated Stephen – well, that was natural wasn't it? – and he would accuse Celia of being barren. Furthermore Stephen was increasingly reluctant to face his shrewish wife and he had taken to staying out all hours – sometimes all night.

Julia's voice would fall to a whisper at this point. She certainly didn't know where it was he went – although by the way her face flushed Lucy suspected that she guessed – but it wasn't doing his health any good. Something seemed to be wrong with him, worryingly wrong. He had become a frequent visitor to the doctor's surgery.

No, his marriage didn't seem to have brought him any joy.

I wonder what Lucy is looking so smug about, Ruth thought. Is it because this idea of hers has proved to be so successful? We all have such busy lives, and now that we have children it is getting more difficult to keep in touch. But we should. Lucy is right. We should renew our friendship – which started here – as often as we can.

But how imperious young Tom is. Not a bit like his easy-going father, Arthur. For Arthur was his father, as far as Ruth was concerned. She had decided never to confront Lucy with her suspicions. Why on earth should she? Whatever her friend might have done it was obvious that she loved her husband deeply. And as for Arthur... Not only did he adore Lucy but Ruth considered that he was lucky to have such a woman for his wife.

It's just as well the child has charm, she thought, perhaps inherited from his grandmother. And my two scallywags are certainly impressed by him. I think poor Clara's four-year-old heart has been stolen away, and her brother, it seems, has met his master at last.

Ruth closed her eyes for a moment and gave herself up to the luxury of the sun warming her skin. She didn't get out enough. Henry had told her so, and she knew it to be true. She was enjoying success as a writer of detective stories, and she didn't begrudge the hours spent shut away in her study; but she realized that she must try to bring a little more balance into her life.

Henry was marvellous with the twins. They employed a nursemaid, of course, but neither of them wanted to be the sort of parents who handed their children over to a nanny and only saw them once or twice a day. Henry was still teaching and giving recitals and he was able to arrange to have even more time with the children than she could.

Sometimes, when she was frantically working towards a deadline, Henry would take the twins to his parents' house, where Walter played the piano and sang along with them and Cordelia overfed them as a sign of her love. Henry's parents had been wonderful. They had been overjoyed when Henry had announced their engagement and, when it became obvious that Ada wanted nothing to do with the wedding, Cordelia had taken over.

'No, please, don't be upset about it,' she had told Ruth. 'I couldn't be happier. Don't you see? I haven't got a daughter of my own – only Henry. This will be my only chance to arrange a wedding. How marvellous!'

And what an occasion the wedding had been. Henry and Ruth still talked about it in their quiet moments together. The celebrations had started as soon as they had left the flower-decked church. The wedding party had walked the short distance to the Valentines' house on Heaton Road and, all the way, Ruth and Henry had been showered with flower petals and rice.

When they arrived Ruth was startled to see a house magically transformed. Ribboned garlands of flowers were draped on the banister rails and great vases of exotic blooms stood in every niche. A string quartet played soft music and the wedding breakfast had been laid out buffet-style in the dining room on the first floor.

Ruth's friends mingled happily with Cordelia's extravagantly theatrical friends, and Ruth didn't think that she and Henry had stopped smiling for one moment – or refrained from clinging on to each other's hands, even when they managed a bite of wedding cake or sipped their champagne.

She had been so happy that she had even managed to ignore Ada's resolutely unsmiling face – although she had been glad when her father had taken his wife home.

Her father...

Ruth's father had seen his grandchildren only once. Ruth had not been to her father's house since the wedding and Henry had insisted that they should take the twins for a visit. But the occasion had not been a happy one. Ada had seemed resentful of Ruth's success and had shown not a jot of interest in the babies. And Joseph Lorrimer... Ruth could still summon tears when she remembered how puzzled and unhappy he'd been.

Puzzled because it seemed he genuinely couldn't understand why Ruth had stayed away so long, and unhappy as it gradually dawned on him that it might be Ada's fault. Ruth had seen him watching his wife with a new light in his eyes and she couldn't bear it. She couldn't bear that her father should be unhappy because of her, and she'd told Henry that it was unfair to divide his loyalties like this.

Joseph Lorrimer should have realized what was happening years ago. But he hadn't. And now it was too late. 'Besides I have you, my darling,' Ruth had told Henry. 'And who could wish for more?'

So they'd stayed away, only sending Christmas cards and the occasional letter outlining the twins' progress.

Somebody else Ruth never saw was Guinevere Matthews. The promises she'd made when she'd presented her with a copy of her first published book were impossible to keep after that dreadful night when Roland died.

The police had accepted that his death had been accidental and, even though that was what they'd been hoping for, neither Esther nor Ruth could face his poor sister with the lie of his drunkenness lying between them.

Whether Guinevere suspected anything they never knew. And probably would never know, for not long afterwards, she'd sold the Crystal Library and retired to the Lake District. She did not exchange addresses with either of them.

Ruth opened her eyes when she heard all the children shout at once and laughed when she saw what had happened. Jack Fowler had not only breached the walls of the sandcastle, he had managed to sneak past the defences and sit himself on top. It began crumbling beneath him.

The other children were beside themselves but, shamefully, Jack's father seemed not at all angry. 'He's the king of the castle!' he shouted and picked him up and rewarded the miscreant with a smacking kiss.

As her own darling Henry immediately set about directing the children to repair the damage, Ruth sneaked a sideways glance at Jack's mother. Esther had remained silent. She saw Ruth looking at her and smiled. But the smile didn't reach her eyes.

'It's all right to be happy, you know,' Ruth said.

'Is it?'

'Of course it is. You have a good husband and a darling baby. Why shouldn't you be happy?'

'Because I don't deserve to be.'

'Oh, Esther, not today.'

Ruth recalled all the times over the years that she and Lucy had comforted Esther. All the hours, and all the tears, and all the conversations lasting long into the night when she had come to stay at either of their houses.

In the end Lucy had pointed out quite sharply that she was ruining young Davy's life, and she owed it to him to pull herself together and get on with things and perhaps get a job to occupy herself. Not knowing what else to do Esther had gone back to Fowler's. And Raymond, over the moon to have her there again, had simply not given up until she'd taken him seriously and agreed to marry him. And it was probably his friendship with Davy that had won her over.

Ruth had sometimes wondered if there was method in his madness, that he was helping the brother in order to court the sister. But, eventually, she'd decided that Raymond's interest in Davy was genuine, and he had seemed as pleased and impressed as Esther was when Davy progressed from errand boy to office boy and lately to junior (very junior) reporter at the local paper.

'Esther,' Ruth said suddenly. 'You love Raymond, don't you?'

Esther's eyes widened. 'Yes, I do,' she said. And then she smiled softly as if she was mocking herself. 'Although it took me a while to realize he was a grown man and not just a bairn.'

'And you both love Jack.' It wasn't a question.

'Of course.'

'Then, my friend, it's time to move on.'

'What do you mean?'

'Lucy brought us here today because it was the place our friendship began ten years ago. Something started that day ... something we've all benefited from. So make today a new beginning as well. Try to put what happened behind you.'

Esther smiled wanly and got up. She wandered off towards the shoreline. Ruth let her go.

The tide was coming in and Esther noticed that Henry had begun to direct the children to move further up the beach. They had chosen the northern part of the bay for their picnic and now Esther wandered along to the southern end. It would be a while yet before the incoming tide reached the cliffs and cut the bay in two.

There was a queue at the refreshment stall and Esther remembered Jane McKenzie, who had started it all by persuading Lucy to buy her an ice-cream. I wonder what has become of Jane, she thought. She's probably married with children, as we all are, and, for her husband's sake, I hope she's learned to control that sharp tongue of hers.

Esther laughed – and then realized she was laughing and her spirits lifted a little. Ruth was right. There was absolutely nothing she could do to alter what had happened, and life was wonderful whether she deserved it or not. She had Raymond, Jack and Ruth and Lucy.

How different Ruth, Lucy and she were and what different paths their lives had taken. But the memories they shared would always unite them. Their friendship would always be a source of strength. Esther turned and walked back to rejoin her family and friends.

The publishers hope that this book has given you enjoyable reading. Large Print Books are especially designed to be as easy to see and hold as possible. If you wish a complete list of our books please ask at your local library or write directly to:

Magna Large Print Books
Magna House, Long Preston,
Skipton, North Yorkshire.
BD23 4ND

This Large Print Book for the partially sighted, who cannot read normal print, is published under the auspices of

THE ULVERSCROFT FOUNDATION